VOYAGE OF DECEPTION

A JAKE OLIVER MYSTERY AND ADVENTURE

STANTON JACOBS

This book is a work of fiction. Places, events, and situations in this story are purely fictional. Any resemblance to actual persons, living or dead, is coincidental.

ISBN: 1-4107-8425-8 (e-book)
ISBN: 1-4107-8424-X (Paperback)
ISBN: 1-4107-8423-1 (Dust Jacket)

Library of Congress Control Number: 2003099360

This book is printed on acid free paper.

Printed in the United States of America
Bloomington, IN

1stBooks - rev.12/12/03

To Marilyn:
Your continued support and confidence in my abilities has always been appreciated. We have shared much happiness with many more years to come with our special daughters,
Anna and Lauren

To Jane:
You have stood beside me my entire life and I have always been proud to be your son.

To Gary:
My best editor, critic and mentor in the hospitality industry.

To my many friends and business associates:
Your support and hard work provided the inspiration I needed for many of the characters depicted in this work.

Prologue

(September 30, 1930, Hong Kong)

The night was warm and humid with what appeared to be a thick haze that hung over the harbor. The workers, carrying large wooden crates up the gang plank into the ship, found the ramp slippery from the dampness in the air and from their own sweat. Over the past two hours they had loaded roughly 20 wooden crates of various sizes, all of which were heavy and awkward to handle, especially on such a hot and muggy night. All were dressed in similar black uniforms and were small in stature in contrast to the much larger foreman that yelled orders to the men harshly in a dialect of Chinese the workers appeared to understand and fear.

When the last of the cargo was loaded, the workers scurried aboard as the ships foreman, Lee Wai Han, walked over to the long dark Rolls Royce parked nearby. In the darkness, it was impossible to see into the backseat and view the occupant or occupants inside. As Han walked toward the vehicle a cold sweat formed on the back of his neck. Strange, he thought, that he should feel chilled on such a warm night but he knew that this feeling was not due to the weather but to his own anxiety. He knew how easily his employer could be angered.

Han approached the vehicle tentatively. Just as he was about to speak the voice he feared most spoke to him. "All is loaded?"

"Yes sir. All is set and the men are on board and ready to leave port."

"Good. You know what to do when you arrive?"

"Yes sir. I have been told the space is being readied as we speak and it should be complete upon our arrival." Han shifted nervously as he spoke.

He peered in the dark and could see the glow of a cigarette from the occupant in the back seat. The blue smoke drifted out the window into the night. After a second drag on his cigarette, the man again spoke. "You realize the importance of the cargo and what will happen if word of this is spoken to anyone?" Han nodded quickly and stepped back slightly as he did so.

"Good, see that all goes as planned. You will be contacted when you arrive."

"Yes sir."

"Then make haste and, Mr. Han…no mistakes." The finality of these last words caused the cold sweat Han felt earlier to run freely down his back under an already drenched uniform.

Han returned to the ship and directed the captain to depart immediately. Although it was not uncommon for cargo ships to depart in the middle of the night, many of the crew noted with great curiosity that no one from customs or the local port authority had been present to inspect what was being loaded. Other more observant workers saw that the ship was departing without using the assistance of a pilot boat, which was standard procedure for a large freighter of that size. Someone had gone to a lot of trouble to conceal the cargo and departure of the *Golden Star*.

……………………………………

The freighter entered in San Francisco Bay at 1:00 a.m. to similar weather conditions as when it had departed from Hong Kong two weeks earlier. The dock area was almost entirely deserted at that time of night and felt unseasonably warm for this traditionally cold city. A key difference, however, was that the haze they had left behind in Hong Kong was replaced with a dense fog that limited visibility to less than ¼ mile at times. This had delayed the arrival of the ship by two hours from its scheduled time.

On the dock two men waited impatiently. Their images were silhouetted by the glow from one of the dock lamps they stood under.

"Where is the ship?" Stated the one man as he paced around and nervously threw his cigarette into the water. He was Asian, in his mid 20's, tall and lean with short cropped jet black hair. He was dressed in a dark suit and gray full-length topcoat and hat.

"Patience, my young friend. Have you learned nothing during the time we have worked together." The other man was also Asian, shorter in height and far stockier in appearance. He was easily 30 years the other man's senior. His motions and gestures were slow and deliberate.

"But Mr. Soon will want to know what is going on. We must report within the next hour." Before, the older man could respond, the image of the ship materialized out of the blanket of fog and both were momentarily stunned that such a large vessel could have gotten so close to them without sensing its presence. The ship was docked and secured thirty minutes later and the gangplank was extended to the dock. A large heavyset man was the first to exit the ship and approached them tentatively not sure if they were his designated contacts when the older of the two men spoke.

"You must be Mr. Han?" The big man simply nodded. "We were growing concerned. All is prepared but we must hurry. Please select a limited number of men to unload the cargo immediately."

"Of course, sir, right away. But the American authorities, they___"

"That has been taken care of. Now please proceed."

Han returned to the ship and assembled his men for the unloading of his employer's precious cargo. The twenty crates were quickly loaded on to two trucks parked and waiting on the dock. Two trucks were necessary to accommodate, not only the crates, but the 10 workers that would travel with the cargo to its final destination and assist with its unloading. One such worker was Jun Sing Tsang, a 30 year old dock worker that had signed on for the voyage because he needed the money for his wife and newborn son. He also looked forward to seeing America for the first time.

Jun Sing was excited and wanted to see San Francisco but the trucks used unfortunately had heavy canvas sides that were completely secured to assure privacy. In turn, Jun Sing was only able to gather brief glimpses of the tall buildings as the trucks drove by.

The two trucks drove for what appeared to be several miles within the city until they pulled down a narrow alley and stopped.

As the workers exited from the truck, Jun Sing looked up at a 12-story white building in front of him. He turned to one of his fellow workers and asked, "What is this place?"

Another worker grabbed his shoulder and whispered. "Quiet, Jun, we were told not to ask any questions and not talk about our actions to anyone."

"Well that should be easy since I don't know where we are or what is in these crates."

"Silence," shouted Mr. Han who had walked up behind them, "get to work and no talking!"

The workers quickly began unloading the crates mindful of Mr. Han's nearby presence. The men were directed to take the crates in through what appeared to be the rear entrance or delivery entrance of the large white building. They then proceeded down to a lower basement level with a concrete floor. The entire basement of the building appeared void of people as expected at that time of the night, or in reality early morning, and was dimly lit due to a limited number of overhead lights. They were directed down a corridor to what appeared to be a section blocked off to the building's occupants. A temporary construction partition was moved to one side to allow the workers to deliver the crates. When Jun Sing and his partner carried the first crate into this area, Jun Sing looked around in awe at the large hole, or rather tunneled out room that had been created in the side wall of the basement. This room, or rather underground vault, appeared to be 30 ft. by 20 ft. with a 10 ft. ceiling. All four walls and the floor of this room were concrete and appeared to Jun Sing to be very thick. The crates were placed on pallets to keep them off the floor and stacked as high as possible before starting another row.

It was apparent to Jun Sing that much effort and expense had gone in to shipping this cargo to a destination on the other side of the world. But what puzzled Jun Sing was why someone would go to all of this trouble just to place the contents of these crates in an underground vault for no one to see.

By the time the last of the crates were placed in the tunneled out room, there was little space for anything else, let alone create an environment for the viewing of the items inside. Although Jun Sing had not personally looked inside any of the crates, he had heard rumors that they contained very ancient Chinese artifacts. If this was true then perhaps the owner of this cargo had reasons for not wanting to announce that he possessed such treasures, especially since the items were being taken out of the his country. If this was the case then all Jun Sing was concerned about was getting paid and returning home as soon as possible. He wanted no trouble, just to get back home safe.

The workers were herded out of the vault area quickly. Jun Sing was one of the last to leave and as his eyes adjusted to the darkness he noted for the first time that other Chinese workers were standing by in the shadows. Perhaps they had been the individuals that had created the vault in the first place. Lee Wai Han noticed Jun Sing looking in the worker's direction and grabbed him roughly by the arm and shoved him toward the other crewmembers that were heading back to the trucks.

Once the workers were back in the trucks, the canvas was again strapped down making it difficult for the workers inside to see out. The trucks proceeded out of the alley from behind the white building and turned on to what appeared to be a major street. At 4 a.m. in the morning the streets were almost completely deserted. Jun Sing tried to look out as they drove by but could not quite make out the name on the sign attached to the front of the building. What startled all of the workers, however, was the sudden clanging of a bell nearby. One worker looked out from a small tear in the canvas and laughed explaining to the others that the bell was on a funny looking train that was passing.

When they returned to the ship, Jun Sing noticed his foreman, Lee Wai Han, talking to the two men that had been on the dock when they were unloading the crates. Something concerned Jun Sing but he could not place what exactly it was. It was a feeling that something terrible was going to happen. This feeling became stronger when the two men from the dock boarded the ship with Mr. Han. They were apparently returning to Hong Kong with them.

Jun Sing and the other workers were kept below in their bunks the remainder of the night and the ship departed the following morning. During the two-week cruise back to Hong Kong, the feelings that he had experienced when returning to the ship persisted. Perhaps it was the gift his father had said he had in which he could sense what the future had to offer. Jun Sing had had such feelings before and true enough most of his premonitions did eventually come true. If his current feelings were correct, then he was in great danger.

Jun Sing decided to take some precautions in the event of the inevitable. That first night after the other workers were asleep, he wrote down a chronological summary of what had occurred and hid the document hoping that his actions would simply be a waste of effort. As ill fortune would have it, however, Jun Sing's premonitions would become reality very shortly.

The night before the ship's arrival in the port of Hong Kong, the workers were awakened by a gunshot from the adjacent cabin where Mr. Han had been sleeping. No one realized that Mr. Han would not be yelling at them again. The two men that had boarded in San Francisco quickly entered the room where Jun Sing and his fellow crewmembers had been sleeping. Each had hand guns and they directed the workers who had delivered the crates to proceed topside and to not speak. Once on deck, each crewmember was told to walk to the port side bow. Jun Sing reviewed his surroundings quickly to determine what options he had left. Each member was directed to stand next to the railing. Jun Sing surmised that one by one they were going to be shot and thrown overboard.

The younger of the two men pushed an older worker standing in front of Jun Sing harshly. "Keep walking and keep your eyes straight ahead!"

"Settle down Mr. Lee, there is no reason for that," said the older man.

"I will do as I please, Mr. Ma," replied the younger man.

Jun Sing began to follow his co-workers as his mind raced. Lee and Ma? The names meant nothing to him and both were such common names. He considered running and jumping overboard, taking his chances with the sea. Being an experienced seaman, however, he knew that to survive such a jump required that he get far enough away from the ship when hitting the water or be pulled under by the draft of the ship as it powered through the sea. If this were to occur, his only wish would be to drown quickly before his body encountered the ship's propellers, a most agonizing way to die. His next concern was that if he survived the jump, he had to remain below the surface long enough for the men on the ship to assume he had drowned. This concern was feasible to Jun Sing who was an excellent swimmer and could hold his breath for almost 3 minutes if he had to. The final concern was how he could survive in the open sea. His only option would have to be that he hold on long enough until another ship passed and rescued him.

Given these three key concerns, Jun Sing viewed his chances of survival as minimal but certainly better then a sure and fatal death from a bullet in the head, Jun Sing Tsang fell in line behind the other workers until he neared the railing. He then broke into a sprint to gain momentum for his jump over the rail into the sea. His actions apparently caught Mr. Ma and Mr. Lee by surprise and before either could get a shot off, Jun Sing sailed over the railing and vanished into the darkness below.

....

The *Golden Star* arrived in Hong Kong the following morning. The story was told to the families of the missing workers that they had contracted some type of illness and all had died at sea. To preserve the health of the rest of the crew they were buried at sea. The owner of the shipping company that employed the workers proved to be extremely generous. Each of the worker's families were well compensated for the loss of their loved one and soon the matter was forgotten or rather intentionally overlooked by the Hong Kong authorities.

One family, however, did not forget what happened. Two days after the *Golden Star* docked, a small cargo vessel, the *Lotus Stem,* was following the regular shipping channels when a lookout noticed a man floating in the water. A lifeboat was launched and soon returned with a man who clearly suffered from exposure and extreme dehydration but glad to be alive. When asked what he was doing out at sea with no other ship in sight, Jun Sing Tsang responded that he had fallen overboard and his shipmates must have assumed he was dead. When asked what ship he had been on, Jun Sing feigned ignorance stating that he had just signed on the voyage and had not paid attention when boarding. Both explanations appeared weak and questionable but they were eventually accepted.

Once the *Lotus Stem* docked in Hong Kong, Jun Sing gathered his wife and son and they departed the city immediately. Jun Sing knew that, if word got out he had survived, then the men that had killed his co-workers would try again. They found a place in the countryside and Jun Sing Tsang put the matter behind him, thankful to be alive.

....

Fifty years later Jun Sing lay on his death bed with his wife and daughter seated on one side of the bed and his son, Benjamin, standing on the other side. Jun Sing, now 80 years old was weak and drifted in and out of consciousness. During these episodes, he would ramble and tell stories. His family questioned if they were truth or fantasy. One such story recalled the theft of priceless artifacts from a museum in Hong Kong some fifty years earlier. His family never understood what his fascination had been with this particular event in history and what the connection was to his subsequent story of his extraordinary adventure to the United States. At first Benjamin Tsang paid little attention to the ramblings of his dying father. Benjamin was an up and coming business executive for one of Hong Kong's most powerful organizations and he had no time for such trivial tales from an old man, even if it was his father. He assumed that delirium was setting in and it was simply a matter of time before his father's body began to shut down for eternity. But the stories persisted with tales of crates delivered to a special underground vault in the great city of San Francisco. Benjamin decided to humor his old man by asking where this underground vault was. Jun Sing shook his head back and forth stating he did not know. He said that it appeared to be a public building or possibly a hotel, but he was sure it was one of great stature from what little he saw. He was sure of it. Jun Sing then gestured toward a clay pot located on a table next to the bed. Inside the pot was a piece of paper that was very old and brittle. It had obviously been wet at one time, given its wrinkled appearance. Jun Sing handed it to his son.

Before Benjamin could open and read the folded up document, the old man grew quiet and shook his head in disgust. Noticing this change in behavior, Benjamin leaned toward his father to hear better what was troubling him.

"What is it, father?"

Jun Sing paused to gather his thoughts and then indicated for his son to come closer. Benjamin did as he was told. "The old man took it all and no one ever knew! He stole from his own people and the world must know what he did." Jun Sing then gave a slight chuckle, which led to a coughing attack that lasted several minutes. Benjamin continued to console his father until he was ready. to continue. "The funny thing is, he never got the chance to benefit from his voyage of deception. He failed to recognize the envy and ambition of those close to him. And for this he paid the ultimate price."

Benjamin backed away and tried to decipher what and whom his father was speaking about. He opened the document given to him and stated to read it when Jun Sing Tsang grabbed his arm and pulled him close. As he exhaled his last breath, he whispered the man's name and Benjamin stared at disbelief as his father closed his eyes for the last time.

CHAPTER ONE

(August 30, 2000, San Francisco)

The fog was beginning to roll in over the South San Francisco foothills as the day came to a close, a daily event that most residents simply took for granted. For the four individuals driving north on Interstate 101 since early that morning, however, the sight captured their interest as both beautiful and mysterious. For the younger occupants of the car, the fog resembled whipped foam being poured over the hills engulfing all trees and homes in its path. To the adult passengers, the fog suggested that the city by the bay had a dark and mysterious side that was not to be underestimated. To the east, the jets were lined up two by two on their final approach into San Francisco International skimming across the mild waves of the South San Francisco Bay now a shimmering gold as the setting sun to the west filtered through the approaching fog. The air was crisp and cool, a sign that fall was just around the corner and summer was about to end.

For Sarah, 7 and Briana, 5, it meant starting school again but this time in a new city away from the friends they had left behind. For Marilyn, their mother, she was excited about their move to San Francisco. A loving wife and caring mother, she had always supported her husband, Jake Oliver and his career through the good times and the bad. She viewed this move as an opportunity for her husband to leave behind the pressures of his previous job and the unfortunate incident they were all trying to forget. Starting over in San Francisco was what both Marilyn and Jake desired to bring happiness and stability back to their family.

Jake Oliver had just turned 39, but his prematurely gray hair made him look older. He had hazel eyes and a weathered tanned face from his years of weekend boat excursions along the California Coast. Jake was just shy of six feet tall who was constantly fighting to control his weight through exercise and his wife's persistence that he eat right. His joy for good food, wine and an occasional good cigar, however, did not coincide with Marilyn's health conscious plans. A man that actually thrived on a certain level of stress, he took great pride in his family and the career he had chosen.

A 20-year veteran of the hotel industry, he was accustomed to the challenges associated with a new job and the stress of moving his family. He had worked hard and paid his dues to get to this point in his career, a career that began at a small resort in a small Midwestern town working various positions from bellman to dishwasher to pay his way through college. Jake established himself from the start as an individual clearly determined to succeed. An outgoing and often outspoken individual, Jake became known for fighting protocol and not hesitating to question direction especially when ethics were an issue. He quickly developed the reputation as a man unafraid of challenge, admired for the support he gave to his staff, sometimes labeled as a rebel by his peers, and often deemed difficult to control by the owners of the hotels he managed. Throughout his career he constantly challenged and pushed himself to exceed.

Jake was rewarded for his efforts with rapid advancement working for several large hotel management companies and was eventually given command of his first hotel at the young age of 26. It was at a small resort and marina, this young General Manager met an intelligent and sensitive woman by the name of Marilyn Simmons. One year later they were married and over the next few years their family expanded with the addition of their two daughters. Jake's career continued to excel with various promotions and transfers, typical of the hotel industry he had chosen.

And now, as this family of four approached downtown San Francisco, to establish a new home, their eighth such move together over the past 12 years, both anxiety and anticipation were high.

Briana, the youngest, was the first to break the silent moments of thought each shared. "Daddy, I think you should know that I need to find a bathroom very soon. I hope your new hotel has a bathroom."

Jake smiled as he glanced in the rearview mirror. "Briana, I am pleased to inform you that the hotel has over 500 bathrooms for you to choose from and I bet one of them is available when we arrive so just hold on a little longer, ok?"

"Jake; does the hotel have anything special planned for our arrival?" asked Marilyn.

"No," Jake replied, "you know I prefer to arrive unannounced. This allows me the one and only opportunity I'll have to experience the hotel as a typical guest." In fact, this had been a routine that Jake had followed shortly after his first appointment as a General Manager. Sometimes it had resulted in awkward and embarrassing moments, such as the time he arrived to find a man standing in the lobby of the hotel wearing only the current day's copy of *USA Today*. He was arguing with the front desk clerk who was demanding he produce some form of identification. There was also the incident in which two hotel restaurant waiters broke into a fight just as Jake and his family entered the lobby. It appeared the one employee had gotten to know the other one's wife a little too well over the previous months.

Jake could only hope that his arrival today would be far less eventful and he would find the hotel operating smoothly. That was probably not a realistic expectation, however, given that he had been hired because of his strong supervisory skills to address what his new employers described as a hotel 'lacking in bloody professionalism and decorum'. Little did Jake know that today would be no exception?

CHAPTER TWO

The Wilford Plaza Hotel, although presently in need of restoration, still had a grandeur and prestige about it that newer hotels had not been able to capture. As one approached this 12 story structure built in 1908 its presence seemed to capture the essence of San Francisco during a period best know for its rich and flagrant history. The Wilford had a grand history that spanned over 90 years. Built by one of San Francisco's most prominent citizens, the Wilford was viewed as one of the first premiere hotels to be constructed following the 1906 earthquake. This natural catastrophe nearly destroyed the entire city of San Francisco in a matter of seconds that spring morning in April followed by a fire of immense proportion that consumed everything in its path.

As in most societies, its residents often looked to its city fathers to see what role they intended to play in the development, or in this case, the re-development of San Francisco. One such citizen was Charles A. Wilford, a prominent land developer and speculator. Charles Allan Wilford was the only son of Elizabeth and William Wilford of Hartford, Connecticut. William Wilford had amassed a fortune as a publisher. When his son, Charles, joined his firm after completing his college education at Harvard University, Charles had plans to expand his fathers business by diversifying their holdings in real estate and property development. Over the course of the next five years, Charles nearly tripled the Wilford family fortune.

Discontent, however, began to grow between Charles and his father, who tended to be far more conservative with regards to investments than his more risk-taking son. Charles felt limited and longed to move west where he could get the jump on others buying land and speculating on future developments. One such city that intrigued Charles was San Francisco. In the spring of 1891 Charles Wilford, made the 6000-mile trek to the other end of the country in search of new opportunity.

Over the next 15 years, Charles became one of San Francisco's most prominent citizens. An aggressive developer, who had bought up much of San Francisco's downtown real estate, Charles was viewed by the citizens of the city as shrewd but always fair. What gained him the most notoriety, however, was his willingness to share his good fortune by underwriting the costs of new theaters and concert halls in support of his love for the arts.

All seemed to be going well for Charles until an unseasonably warm morning on April 18, 1906. It was at 5:13 a.m. when an earthquake of immense magnitude and destruction left the city in ruins in just over one minute. To many developers the quake spelled financial ruin. But for Charles, who had diversified his holdings outside of San Francisco, a good portion of his assets were still intact.

Although the losses Charles Wilford had experienced had been great, he also saw the quake as the perfect opportunity to play a key role in its rebuilding. Serving as a role model for others to follow, Charles was one of the first to step forward with plans to rebuild. His plans were to start with a new luxury hotel on land near what was once one of the cities key administrative office buildings. In a benevolent gesture that endeared him to the city, Charles offered to allow his new hotel to also serve as temporary offices for city officials during this critical reconstruction period.

Word of Charles Wilford's plans to build, not just a hotel but a grand and luxurious 500 room facility helped to restore the faith of others that San Francisco was truly worth rebuilding. The renewed support and recognition he received from the city for his future developments also proved beneficial in the years to come.

The Wilford Plaza Hotel, as it was so named in a grand opening gala unmatched for years to come, opened roughly two years later at a cost of just under $1 million, an extravagant cost for that time to say the least. The hotel captured the essence of hospitality in the grandest sense in one of America's gateway cities. Designed by a noted architect of that period with an Edwardian theme, the moment its guests walked through the main entrance they stood in awe of the eight massive chandeliers that hung from the 40 foot lobby ceiling each with an expansive width of over 10 feet. The chandeliers were the focal point of the lobby. Each had been hand made by Austrian craftsmen specifically for the hotel and represented one of a kind pieces never to be re-created exactly the same. All of the walls of the lobby and massive pillars that supported the 12 floors above were clad in white Italian marble that was again specifically designed for the hotel by European craftsmen. These artists carved the marble into a detailed and ornate crown molding that provided a finishing touch to this grand room. The furniture was of an Edwardian design to coincide with the hotel all tastefully complimented with lush palms and greenery common in abundance to the California area. One of the most notable features of the lobby, however, was the reflection of the brass from the elevator doors and light from the chandeliers that reflected on the highly polished marble floor.

The hotel featured 500 luxuriously appointed guestrooms, many of which offered they're own private bathrooms rather than shared facilities, more common of that time. Each guest during their stay was entitled to other rather unique services such as valet parking of guest carriages and automobiles, overnight laundry service, continental breakfast delivered at the time the guest specified. In addition the hotel featured two restaurants, an open lobby bar, men's billiards and cigar pub, tea room, barber shop, several small meeting and banquet halls and of course the grand ballroom.

The grand ballroom consisted of finely milled oak paneled walls surrounding a room large enough to accommodate over 800 people for a formal banquet. The ceiling was 30 feet high and featured its own four customized chandeliers. The focal point of the ballroom, however, was a grand curving staircase that enabled the hotel's guests to access a large balcony that surrounded the circumference of the ballroom. Hardwood parquet oak floors accented by rich full oriental rugs provided the finishing touch.

In addition to the Wilford's luxurious features, however, what established the hotel, as one of the finest was the extreme pride that was apparent in the staff that worked at the hotel. Charles Wilford had successfully instilled in these individuals that it was not just *his* hotel but theirs as well. Each demonstrated a degree of ownership in their hotel unmatched by other comparable facilities and it was their attention to service that was the ultimate hallmark of each guest's stay.

Over the years, additional hotels were built that clearly surpassed the Wilford in terms of the facilities it offered but they could not compare to the level of service the staff of the Willford provided its guests.

The depression of 1929, however, took its toll on the Wilford just as it did all other businesses during this financial crisis in American history. Charles Wilford had leveraged his investments extensively at the time of the crash and found himself, for the first time in his successful career, in his own state of depression. During a period when men had chosen suicide rather than face the loss of all they had worked for, Charles desperately sought to find a solution even if through desperate measures.

Charles needed cash and he needed it in a hurry before all was lost. The city of San Francisco was truly a melting pot of cultures and nationalities. During the years that Charles had been in the city he knew who most of the movers and shakers were. Charles also knew that most of his business associates were in the same scrape as he, but there were others with investments from overseas that he could talk to if times were desperate and Charles was convinced that time had arrived.

Charles had never spent much time in the Chinatown section of the city. He found the streets too narrow and cluttered with street vendors selling items that were foreign and, at times offensive to his senses. He entered the door of the address that had been given to him and was greeted by a man as big as the doorway. He was Asian with a dark completion and even under the baggy outfit the man wore, Charles could sense how strong he must be and what his purpose was for his employer. Charles stated whom he was and the bodyguard simply motioned for him to follow.

From the outside, the building had appeared to be a small apartment building that was weathered and blended in with all the other buildings on Grant Street. Once inside, however, the interior was decorated with fine oriental artifacts that clearly indicated the wealth and prosperity of its owner. Charles was escorted to a dimly lit room on the second floor. There seated at a large desk was a small Asian man who appeared to be in his mid to late 50's. The man stood and they shook hands. The bodyguard that had escorted Charles into the office quietly closed the door behind him.

"Ah, Mr. Wilford, it is a pleasure that we finally meet in person."

"Thank you Mr. Ma. Your office is most impressive."

"Just a few items to remind me of home. Please sir, have a seat. Can I get you something? Some tea or perhaps something a little stronger?"

"Some tea would be fine."

Mr. Ma poured tea for both Charles and himself and then resumed his seat behind the large desk. "Now, Mr. Wilford, your message indicated that you had a proposition you wished to discuss. I believe it related to the lending of some funds. My employer has indicated that he is interested in discussing such an opportunity with you. In fact, we have a proposal for you that you may find interesting."

Charles looked at the man seated in front of him debating if he should proceed but he needed money and the employer of the man seated across from him was his last resort. Charles knew that dealing with such an individual presented some key risks. "A proposal for me? I am not sure I understand."

Mr. Ma leaned forward and spoke in such a soft tone, that Charles had to also lean forward to hear him. "You see…my employer needs to ask of you a favor. In exchange for your cooperation, he is prepared to help you with your situation."

Charles stared intently at the oriental man seated across from him. "I would welcome such a discussion, sir."

For the next hour, the two men listened to what each had to offer and a deal was consummated that night. Over the difficult years that followed, while other businesses suffered greatly and many eventually closed entirely, no one seemed to question how Charles was able to make ends meet. They must have assumed that he had protected his investments somehow. Little did they know that Charles had paid the ultimate price to keep his world intact.

CHAPTER THREE

The Wilford staff continued to offer exceptional service to the limited few that could afford to stay at the hotel. Charles Wilford took good care of his loyal employees, who viewed him as their ultimate benefactor during these difficult times. All noticed, however, that Mr. Wilford clearly appeared to be burdened heavily and the amount of stress he was under was of great concern. They also noticed that he had become somewhat mysterious in his actions. One such incident involved the closing off of a section of the basement of the Wilford to all staff. There were rumors that Chinese workers entered this area during the night and worked until the following morning. The staff of the hotel was curious as to what the Chinese workers were doing but each day the areas was blocked off entirely from view and a guard was posted to make sure no unauthorized individuals entered the area. This went on for approximately two months during the Summer of 1930. And then, as suddenly as the work began, the northeast corner of the basement was reopened and all appeared exactly the same as it had before. Rumors among the staff continued for another few months but then eventually died away and the matter was forgotten.

Elma Wilford, Charles wife died during that same winter of 1930. Six years later Charles Wilford died unexpectedly from what was believed to be a heart attack. Clarissa Wilford, at age 35, then became the sole heir to his estate and all of his holdings. Clarissa had been working for her father's business on and off for the previous 10 years but clearly did not possess the keen business sense or rather the desire to continue in her father's footsteps. Upon his death, it was Clarissa's plan to divest herself of any assets she deemed as "high maintenance".

The Wilford Plaza Hotel had suffered through the depression, as did all businesses, but it clearly cost Wilford Properties more to maintain than its office buildings and land throughout the city. Clarissa, had no desire to have her time tied up with the day to day operation of a luxury hotel that was clearly draining her of money she could better use for herself. Prior to selling the hotel, she made it her goal to reduce her expenses as much as possible. She eliminated staff, cut back on the services offered and over the next few years the hotel was not maintained to the level its guests were accustomed to experiencing. The hotel developed a poor reputation in the community and was greatly in need of repair and maintenance.

Nineteen years had gone by since Charles Wilford's death and the hotel was now in terrible condition. Many of the original staff had either retired or left out of disgust by the way Clarissa Wilford was expecting them to operate the hotel. The furnishings in the guestrooms were worn and stained and offered a guest almost unacceptable living conditions. The lobby, once so grand, was now dull and lifeless. The brass elevator doors were scratched and tarnished, the marble floor had not been polished and cleaned properly in years. The Grande Ballroom could hardly be considered *Grande* with its torn rugs and scratched wood floor. As a result of Clarissa's neglect, the occupancy of the hotel became so low; it was hard to determine if it was even worth having the hotel open.

Clarissa's desire to sell the hotel was widely known and in the fall of 1955 she jumped at the opportunity when she was contacted by a group of experienced hoteliers who later purchased the hotel. Dollars were spent and, with the effective management of Hanover & Jones now at the helm, the hotel began to prosper throughout the balance of the 1950's and 1960's.

In the summer of 1969, however, poor performance from other hotels operated by Hanover and Jones combined with an economy in a state of recession resulted in the Wilford again being sold. This time to an inexperienced but wealthy Englishman by the name of James Bostwick. Mr. Bostwick had a strong desire to own real estate in America's gateway city of San Francisco. His motives were strictly to nurture his ego and status. He spent millions of dollars to renovate the hotel, often installing modern fixtures, furniture and equipment that did not fit the existing design of this historic hotel. His lack of experience in how to manage the hotel, however, ultimately led to foreclosure proceedings and he was forced to place the hotel on the market less than six years after he had bought it.

In the spring of 1975, a hotel operator from nearby Sacramento purchased the Wilford from Mr. Bostwick. At first the staff and community were again glad to see an experienced hotel man now operate the hotel. What they soon discovered, however, was that Dick Harbinger had one focus and that was to make a profit. He did invest the bare minimum in dollars needed to renovate the hotel to enhance its occupancy but over the next 14 years clearly operated the hotel as a low budget facility catering to lower rated groups and less desirable clientele. A blunt and caustic individual his "hands on, manipulative" management style resulted in a series of hotel general managers that often walked off the job in disgust of Mr. Harbinger and his questionable management philosophies.

Following the Loma Prieta Earthquake that struck San Francisco in 1989, Dick Harbinger decided to cut his losses. The Wilford had suffered extensive structural damage and it was only through his coaxing that city-building inspectors allowed to him to complete minimum structural improvements and re-open the hotel. Over the next 8 years, the hotel suffered continued losses as the economy and tourism was slow to return to San Francisco. Ultimately, Harbinger decided to place the Wilford on the market. In the fall of 1997, the Wilford was purchased by a group of Hong Kong investors known as South Harbor Investments, the hotel's present owners.

No one knew much about South Harbor Investments other than that they were a large Hong Kong operated company with real estate investments throughout the world. They were known to be highly diversified in other industries such as shipping, exports, and of course lodging.

The local media was intrigued by South Harbor's interest in the run down Wilford Hotel but soon found that obtaining a response from representatives of the company was difficult to almost impossible.

CHAPTER FOUR

Shannon Kincaid was having, what she deemed to be a typical *Tuesday from Hell.* Tuesdays were one of hotel's highest demand days each week, and today was not an exception. The Wilford Plaza Hotel was currently over-sold, or as front desk managers preferred their front desk staff to relay to the hotel guest, in a state of being 'under-departed'. Regardless of the terminology the outcome was often easy to predict in a city in which all nearby hotels were also at maximum occupancy. Someone was going to have to be 'walked', a simple term for the cruel reality that some unlucky guests was not going to be staying at the hotel as planned.

Shannon had been with the hotel almost three years and had been hired by Sam Filmore the general manager appointed by South Harbor immediately following the purchase of the hotel. She took great pride in her hotel and the front desk staff she was responsible for managing but was still trying to understand why Mr. Filmore had suddenly resigned. And then there was the accident. She was also angry at Jackson Chi, the owner's representative of South Harbor Investments that oversaw the operation of the hotel. Although she had nothing to substantiate her feelings she was convinced that he had somehow been responsible for what happened to her boss. And now that same Mr. Chi had just informed her earlier that morning that several VIP's from Hong Kong were scheduled to arrive in the next few hours and she was to make sure they had accommodations. Leave it to him to let her know only a few hours before these individuals arrive and heaven forbid he care that the hotel is full and the hotel's regular paying customers would now be relocated to alternate accommodations somewhere in the city at the Wilford's expense.

"How we coming with rooms for our Hong Kong visitors, Shannon?" said Jim Slazenger, Assistant General Manager and currently acting General Manager for the past month.

"How do you think, Jim! We're already 20 rooms over sold so why should three more rooms make any difference!"

"Well, I have some good news for you, I just got off the phone with the Hyatt and they may have screwed up and blocked a group to arrive a day earlier than planned. If so, they have rooms to sell tonight. They should be getting back to me later this afternoon."

"Thanks, Jim." The relief was apparent on her face. "I was beginning to get worried."

"Well, until we know for sure, don't take any walk-in guests and let's play hardball with the guests who are not confirmed for late arrival until I know for sure."

"Sure," Shannon acknowledged. "By the way, have you heard when our new boss is going to get here?"

"He's scheduled to arrive next week. I guess it's good he's not arriving tonight...we'd have to say 'tough luck big guy'."

"Oh yeah, and just who did you have in mind to break that type of news to him?"

Jim smiled, "why *you* of course."

"Yeah, and I'd be the first casualty to lose her job!" Shannon paused and then continued. "Jim, we haven't had an opportunity to talk much lately but I'm sure sorry our Hong Kong friends didn't consider you further to assume the position after Mr. Filmore...." Her voice trailed off as she looked down attempting to maintain her composure.

Jim placed his hand on her shoulder. "Yeah, well those are the breaks, I guess I'm not as well connected as this Jake Oliver chap."

"What do we know about him? Where did he come from? What's he going to be like to work for?"

"Shannon, it's always fun talking to you. You ask three questions in a row and I am not sure I have the answer to any of them except the first." Oliver was most recently the GM of that resort down the coast near Santa Barbara...you know the one that had the fire."

"I remember reading about that...didn't several people die in the fire?"

"Yes, and I probably shouldn't say anything but there were some questions regarding this fire incident.

"What type of questions?" Shannon asked, concern now showing by the wrinkles that had formed on her forehead at the bridge of her nose.

"Oh nothing specific, but there was some mention that fire inspection records appeared to have been doctored."

"No shit! Well I've got to go help at the desk. Thanks for getting me out of a bind and finding rooms for my unlucky late arriving guests and let's talk more before the guy with the questionable past arrives.

....

The Oliver's were five blocks away but the Wilford could clearly be seen from that distance. Painted a stark white, it stood out from the more modern buildings that surrounded it on Market Street. Even in its present run down condition, the hotel still had a presence, a historic quality about it that drew you toward it. It was as though the hotel had the ability to call out to those passing by beckoning them to come inside.

As they got closer, the wear and tear of over 90 years became more apparent. The detailed architecture, the result of craftsmen and builders working for over two years from 1906 to 1908 was clearly visible depicting a lost art that new structures did not even consider due to prohibitive costs. The detailed concrete work around each window and the intricate work on the parapet at the top of the building were the crowning feature of this grand hotel. But now it showed signs of pealing paint, mold in its crevices, and areas in which the sculpted gargoyles, designed to protect the building, had decayed and in some cases had broken free.

Badly stained and weathered window canopies gave the hotel a further dated and run down appearance. Many appeared to be torn and others were hanging awkwardly as the brackets holding them in place had broken loose from their moorings in the concrete exterior walls.

As Jake pulled his car into the adjacent parking lot he noted the cracks in the wall that had been quickly repaired over the years and hastily painted to cover them from view. Over time, however, the cracks had reappeared through the cheap and quick paint jobs that had been done exposing clearly what the hotel had endured in a city know for its unsteady ground and frequent earthquakes.

Jake was engrossed in his observation of the hotel when Marilyn spoke to him. "Jake, the hotel appears to be in far worse condition that I expected. It's worse than the other hotels and resorts you have managed. You sure about this one?"

Jake took a moment to gather his thoughts then responded. "I know it may look bad now, but after the renovation, the owners have planned, it will be brought back to the grandeur it used to be...I'm sure of it."

Just as Marilyn was about to respond, Briana interrupted. "Daddy, if we are *finally* here, I really need to use the bathroom NOW!"

Jake and Marilyn both smiled. "Come on girls, let's find one of those 500 bathrooms your father promised."

Instead of unloading the car at that time, they proceeded to the front entrance of the hotel. As Jake and his family neared the front door they overhear what sounds like an argument.

....

"Look Harry, your not listening to me. What I was saying was that the negotiations are coming up in less than a month and you need to support the changes Local #78 is recommending."

Harry studied the over-zealous bellman with caution. Harry Walters had been the bell captain of the Wilford for the past 30 years. A tall and lanky black man who, at the wise old age of 64, had seen a lot of pushy union shop stewards such as Sergio come and go but in all of his years, this guy, seemed to be sticking around for the long haul. Harry's bell captain uniform still looked as crisp and starched as it had been when he received it new six years prior. His cap placed on his head in the exact same manner each day, Harry was a proud man that took great pride in himself and the position he had elevated himself to at the hotel over the years. To Harry, the Wilford was *his* hotel and every guest that entered was entering *his* lobby. "Look, I'll make up my mind when I see what is being proposed. I'm not rushing into anything. Anyway…what is so important about my support this early?"

Sergio responded. "The staff knows and respect you Harry, they always follow your advice, if you could just…"

"Excuse me," Jake interrupted, "is it OK for me to leave my car in the parking lot down the street or is there somewhere else I should park?"

Just as Harry was about to acknowledge the guest, Sergio snapped. "I'll be with you in a minute sir."

Harry immediately stepped aside of Sergio and approached Jake and his family with a broad smile. "Sorry folks. Here to check in?"

Jake continued to watch Sergio then responded to Harry. "Yes, our luggage is in the car but first, my daughters need to find the closest restroom." Jake offered with a sheepish grin. "It was a long trip."

Harry responded with a broad smile, "I understand completely. Ladies, if you will follow me." He then held open the door for Jake and his family to enter the lobby as he gave Sergio an angry glance back over his shoulder.

As they entered the lobby, Marilyn was the first to comment. "Jake, its magnificent… the outside does not do this lobby justice."

"I thought you would like it. Wait until you see the rest, there is something about the old great ones…like this"

Harry overheard Jake's comments. "Been with us before sir?"

Jake hesitated a minute and then replied. "A…yes, about a month ago, I was up…. visiting some friends."

Harry nodded. "Well I'm sorry I missed you last time. Not too many folks come or go from my hotel without my knowledge." Harry then noticed Sarah and Briana Oliver looking anxiously at him. "Oh sorry young ladies… just down that corridor, first door on the right."

Marilyn accompanied her daughters and Harry again addressed Jake. "What brings you folks to the City?"

Jake pondered how best to respond. "We're in the process of moving to San Francisco."

"Well, enjoy your stay. If you need anything, my name is Harry and I am the Bell Captain." Harry started to leave and turned back toward Jake. "Sir, I also want to apology for my man, Sergio, he sometimes forgets who the customer is. Sorry."

Jake smiled, "no problem, Harry. I could, however, use your help getting our luggage in from the car in a few moments."

Harry nodded. "Absolutely. Sir, you go on to the front desk and check in and Sergio and I will get your belongings. What type of car you got?"

"Black Jaguar, here are the keys, its around the corner in the parking lot."

"Be right back, Mr.____?"

Jake debated how best to answer this question. "Just call me Jake."

"Jake it is. See you in a few minutes." Harry walked out the front entrance. From the motion of his hands, Jake noticed that it appeared he was already having that talk with Sergio.

Jake proceeded to the front desk to wait his turn to check in. Marilyn and the girls were still in the bathroom. A man in a dark business suit at the desk appeared to be extremely agitated. "What do you mean you don't have a room for me! I called to confirm just last week and made my reservation over a month ago! How the hell does something like this happen?"

The front desk agent, a petite young woman that looked no more than 18, was clearly intimidated by her guest. In a shaky voice that lacked the conviction of the words she was speaking she replied, "Sir, I am very sorry but we simply do not have a room. We have, however, confirmed a room for you at the Hyatt which is short cab ride away and it is a very nice hotel."

"Bull shit!" the man exclaimed. "I travel a lot and I know you *hotel people* always have a few rooms left. Listen bimbo, why don't you get your manager out here since you're too incompetent to figure this matter out!"

The man's words bit hard and even from ten feet away, Jake could see the girl was about to burst into tears. Jake stepped forward. "Hey, I was just overhearing your conversation, no room, man that's too bad." Jake saw the girl's nametag. "Hey Marci, why don't you go get your manager. We don't mind waiting." Marci departed quickly to the back room. Jake turned to address the irate guest. "Well you sure showed her. Made her cry and everything. Yeah, when there is a mistake, I always like to take it out on the hourly help. Let's face it, she didn't make the mistake, just some previous guest who refused to check out when he was supposed to and now he has *your* room. But, yeah you sure showed *her*." Jake paused to see if his words had the desired effect. From the look on the man's face, it had. Marci had overheard the entire conversation from behind the door to the back office while she waited for her manager to get off the phone.

The man looked at Jake, his face now showing signs of embarrassment. "You know, I have a daughter about her age. If I new someone was talking to her like that I'd punch his lights out." Shaking his head in disgust, "I can't believe I just did that. I really am sorry."

Jake nodded toward the front desk as Marci returned from the back room. "Don't tell me, tell Marci."

Marci approached the front desk with a sharply dressed woman in her mid thirties, who Jake assumed must be the front office manager. From the look on her face, she was clearly ready to do war as she stood across the desk from the previously angry man. "I understand we have a problem?"

Before the man could speak, however, Jake interceded. "Actually, there is no problem Miss…Kincaid? The gentleman was just about to apologize to Marci for getting so angry."

The man immediately responded. "A…Miss, I am so sorry I lost my temper. I guess it has been a long day, but I should not have taken it out on you."

Marci began to smile and the manager quickly lowered her defenses. "Mr. Mahan, we are truly sorry for the inconvenience but we honestly cannot accommodate you here tonight. I have, however, arranged accommodations at the Hyatt Regency Hotel. It is a very nice hotel and the room charges will be paid by this hotel because of your inconvenience. We can also arrange a cab to take you there."

The man accepted her offer and quickly left the hotel to avoid further embarrassment.

The manager then addressed Jake. "Hi, I'm Shannon Kincaid, Front Office Manager of the Wilford." She looked at him questioningly. "I don't know what you said to him but from what Marci told me a minute ago, the man that just left here, was an entirely different person than what I expected."

"Maybe I just helped him understand the problem a little better." He then smiled at Marci and then back to Shannon, "Well now, Ms. Kincaid, it appears that my family and I may also have a problem given what you just told Mr. Mahan."

Shannon, responded shyly, "well, let's see what we can do. Your name?"

Jake paused briefly before responding. "A...Olsen, Jake Olsen, I made the reservation last week." Jake watched pensively to see how Shannon Kincaid was going to handle the situation when a large man in a well-tailored suit approached the front desk.

Jim Slazenger had received word there might be a problem at the desk and had come to add his support. Jim assumed that Jake was the problem guest. "Sir, can I be of assistance?"

Shannon interrupted quickly. "No, Mr. Slazenger, everything is alright. In fact, this kind gentleman diffused a guest that was very upset just a few minutes ago."

Jim turned to address Jake. "Sir, I want to thank you for your patience and understanding." As Ms. Kincaid has probably told you we are currently in an embarrassing situation and cannot accommodate your reservation tonight."

At that point, Shannon again interrupted. "Mr. Slazenger, could I speak to you for one moment?"

Jim looked at her questioningly, then excused himself and both proceeded to the back office behind the front desk. Once out of view of Jake and his family who had since rejoined him in the lobby, Shannon, spoke quickly. "Jim, the reservation is for a Jake *Olsen*, his home address is in Santa Barbara, he has a wife and two kids, and Marci said he handled that irate guest like a real pro."

Jim looked at her clearly confused by the relevance of these points. "So, what are you getting at?"

Shannon continued. "What if that man is really Jake *Oliver*, our new boss, and he is attempting to surprise us by arriving a little early to look around?"

Jim considered her words. "His age is about right, and the description I got from a buddy of mine that was transferred to Santa Barbara last year fits." Jim put his hand up to his face and rubbed his chin as he looked out toward the hotel lobby. He then turned back to face Shannon. "You think so?"

Shannon looked at him with a sour expression. “I don’t think I’m willing to take that chance. I say he stays and we deal with the next guest that arrives.”

Jim responded, “I have a better idea.” He then proceeded back to the lobby and approached Jake Oliver. “Excuse me, but is it possible you’re Jake Oliver, our new General Manager?

A broad smile came to Jake’s face. “I was afraid I had given myself away. Sorry for trying to sneak one by you guys. Obviously, you are too sharp for me.” Both Jim and Jake shook hands cordially and Jake introduced his family. Marci, who had now composed herself, waved to Sarah and Briana over the counter and they both smiled.

Harry then entered, with what appeared to be, the entire contents of the Oliver car on two bell carts. Jake turned to Jim. “Are you guys that full? If so, perhaps we should go the Hyatt, as Marci suggested.” Marci immediately turned a deep shade of red with embarrassment.

Jim explained the dilemma they were in but suggested that it would be best if Jake and his family stayed at the hotel and they would take their chances the rest of the evening would go more smoothly. Shannon then excused herself to address that plan of action and assign a room.

Before the Oliver’s were escorted to their room, Jake asked if Jim and his wife would like to have dinner later that evening to get better acquainted. Jim agreed to contact his wife and suggested they meet in the lobby at seven o’clock. Marci overheard the conversation and volunteered to baby-sit after she got off from her shift. Marilyn looked at her daughters and from the look on their faces, Marci met with their approval.

CHAPTER FIVE

Jake and Marilyn met Jim and Linda Slazenger in the lobby at seven o'clock as planned. Introductions were made and the four left in Jim's car for dinner at a small Chinese restaurant, a favorite of the Slazenger's. Sarah and Briana hit it off quickly with Marci and the girls were quickly engrossed in a game of Monopoly when Jake and Marilyn left for the evening.

"Something tells me this restaurant of yours is not in *Fodor's Travel Guide* to sites of San Francisco," said Jake as Jim negotiated his car into a parking space that all, at first, thought was far to small for his late model Lincoln town car.

"I think your right about that," acknowledged Jim. "Linda and I discovered this place quite by accident while walking one afternoon. When we entered, the owner, Sue Kim, greeted us with the most perplexed stare. I first thought the place must be closed and asked her if it was all right for us to come in. Then a broad smile came across her face and she responded in somewhat broken English, 'my, you are big…my cooks better get to work!' We then experienced one of the best meals we have had and…well, we have been coming here ever since."

As Jim finished parking the car, Jake began to realize just how big Jim was. Standing at roughly 6'-1", his black curly hair was cut short and neat giving him the appearance of someone in the military. A man that had just celebrated his 49th birthday, his face showed a weathered texture of someone who had spent much of his life outdoors. He had a strong jaw line, typical of his German ethnic heritage, and a neatly trimmed mustache that was beginning to show some gray. With a broad thick neck supported by shoulders as wide as a tackle for the Dallas Cowboys, Jim's wrists and hands were easily double the size of Jake's. A man that obviously enjoyed good food, his stomach was the one area that suggested he should consider cutting back some, but he carried the weight well because of his muscular physique. It was wise, however, for someone not to misinterpret this man as out of shape. One of the most striking features, however, was Jim's eyes. Deeply set, and dark brown, they displayed a warmth and sensitivity that contradicted his intimidating appearance.

One look at his hands clearly indicated that Jim was not afraid of hard physical work with calluses and scars from years of outdoor work that coincided with one of the most diverse resumes Jake had ever seen. Jake had obtained some background on each of his key management team prior to his arrival.

The hotel industry represented a relatively new career for Jim that began ten years prior after he returned to school to get a Bachelor's Degree in Business Administration. During this return to school at the ripe old age of 35, Jim took a job as night auditor at the front desk of a small Inn in his hometown of Napa, California. He preferred working the night shift so that his days were free to attend classes and for he and Linda to build their dream home. Jim would complete his work at the hotel by seven in the morning, take a brief nap and then work on the construction of their home located on a lake, a short thirty minute drive northeast from the city of Napa. In between these long days with less than three hours sleep each day, Jim also found time to complete the necessary credits to obtain his college degree.

What was even more interesting was what prompted Jim to return to school and begin a whole new career. To understand this we must go back 16 years to a brash 19-year old. After completing two years of college, he felt that his talents could be better served as a member of the California Highway Patrol. He dropped out of college to pursue his new venture and because of his size and most visible enthusiasm; he was accepted into the police academy. Jim excelled in his new career and over the next ten years advanced to the grade of Sergeant and married his girlfriend from high school, Linda Nesbit. All was going well for the Slazenger's until a cooler than usual morning in the fall of 1985. Then his world changed.

The San Joaquin Valley in central California is noted for its thick *Tule* Fog, a common problem in the early mornings both during the spring and fall months. Jim was on patrol when he received a call that there was a traffic accident in the south-bound lane of Interstate 5, ten miles north of Stockton. As Jim approached the location he entered, what could only be described as, a dense wall of fog that obscured his view entirely. In fact, he found it difficult to see the front edge of his patrol car or even if he was on the highway. Through the fog, an image appeared. As he drew closer, the image was an 18-wheeler tractor-trailer rig pulled to the side of the road with a small Toyota wedged under the rear of the trailer. Jim turned on his flashing lights to warn oncoming cars and pulled to a stop behind the Toyota. He approached the Toyota and found a mother desperately trying to open the rear door to get to her baby son still in the back seat. The driver of the truck was attempting to access the car from the passenger side. Jim asked that both step away from the car and stand off the road away from oncoming cars. After several tries, Jim was able to pull the rear door open. Jim entered the car to get the child who appeared to be unconscious. It was at that moment that a pickup truck materialized from the fog. Jim noticed the headlights only seconds before it collided with his patrol car, pushing it into the Toyota with Jim and child inside. Seeing the truck approach, Jim just had time to cover the child with his body when the collision occurred. Jim was knocked unconscious, suffered three broken ribs and damage to his back as the roof of the Toyota collapsed from the weight of the patrol car that had now been shoved up and over the car. When the emergency rescue team arrived and extracted both Jim and the child, it was determined that Jim's heroic actions had saved the child from serious harm.

Jim spent three months in the hospital followed by another three months of physical therapy to strengthen his back. During this time, Jim and Linda considered their options. Deciding not to test fate further, Jim elected to leave the highway patrol and was placed on permanent disability. Over the next five years, Jim experimented with a variety of chosen professions that included starting a welding shop, purchasing land and setting up a mobile trailer park, forming a well drilling company, and lastly becoming a partner in an auto body paint shop. Each venture proved successful and reasonably profitable with someone eventually offering to buy him out. Although the work was hard and physical, Jim and Linda financially lived very comfortably.

In 1989, they used the income from their various business ventures and purchased land for their new dream home. Located high on a buff overlooking picturesque *Lake Berryessa*, they purchased a lot that had the remains of a home that had burned to the ground the year prior. Utilizing the existing foundation, they designed and, together with no other assistance, built their new three level home that featured panoramic views from its three tiers of decks that surrounded a house made up almost entirely of windows.

And now here was this self-made man with his diverse background and wide range of experiences, in his new role as Assistant General Manager of Wilford Plaza Hotel. Even though Jake had not yet gotten to know the man, he had great respect for all that he had accomplished.

The four entered the small Chinese restaurant that appeared to seat no more that 30 to 40 customers. A small oriental woman with graying hair wearing a plain white apron approached, "Ah…Mr. Jim and Miss Linda, so good to see you again and I see you have brought friends?"

Jim approached the woman and gave her a big hug. "Good to see you too. Sue, these are our new friends, Jake and Marilyn Oliver."

"Good to meet you…you like Chinese?" Sue Kwan asked inquiringly.

"Yes we do," acknowledged Marilyn, it fact for me the hotter the better, but for my husband…not too hot." She said with a devilish grin.

"Right this way, I have special table for you all." But as the group looked around, most of the tables were empty except for one group of eight, all of which were Chinese, sitting at a large table in the back.

Shortly after all were seated, Marilyn and Linda seemed to be immediately engrossed in a conversation that Jim and Jake soon discovered was almost impossible to join. Jim then turned to Jake and asked, "have you ever worked in San Francisco before?"

"No, this is our first time to live here, but we have visited often enough that it already feels like home."

"Ever work at a union hotel?" Jim asked as he gazed at the menu in front of him.

"No, I'm afraid that is going to be a new experience also." Jake smiled as he picked up a menu and noted that the answer to the last question somewhat displeased Jim.

Jim's sour expression to his last comment intrigued Jake. Naturally, Jake expected to be interrogated by his second in command, but he began to wonder if there was something more to Jim's questions. "Jim, you have been with the hotel since 1994. Is that right?"

"Yeah, I was hired by Sam Filmore, the General Manager...I mean, former General Manager of the hotel."

"From what I have been able to gather, Mr. Filmore was a good man, you must have been sorry to see him go?"

Jim studied his new boss closely before responding curtly. "Yes, he was. Ladies...are you ready to order?"

Jake viewed this brief dialog with Jim with concern. There appeared to be some pent up hostility with his Assistant General Manager. The question was at whom was it directed. At Jake for taking his bosses job or frustration that the owners chose to let Mr. Filmore go.

Throughout dinner, the four conversed about almost everything ranging from the Slazenger's description of their home on the lake to the best places to see in the city. The wives appeared to have hit it off immediately and the manner in which they spoke flowed easily as if they had grown up together as childhood friends. With Jim, however, his interaction was reserved and guarded. Occasionally, a humorous comment would bring a rise and a broad smile would appear. But just as quickly, he would return to being on guard. It was as though, Jim was trying his damnedest to not enjoy the evening even though it appeared he was finding this more and more difficult.

Jake decided it was time to break the ice. "Jim, I understand you have assumed the role of Acting General Manager since Mr. Filmore's departure." Jake noticed that Linda Slazenger had paused in her conversation with Marilyn and Jim appeared hesitant in how he should respond.

"Yes, Jackson Chi asked that I assume this responsibility until a new General Manager was confirmed. I guess I can back off on that task now that you are here." Jim responded a caustic tone in his voice.

"From my conversations with Mr. Cho, he spoke very highly of you. In fact, it has been my experience that the Chinese are very caution about who they trust. In your case, he gave me a raving review for how well you were operating the hotel." Jake gave Jim a moment for these comments to sink in.

"Actually, I've only met Mr. Cho one time. So I can't explain why he thinks so highly of me."

"My meeting with him was also very brief and I must admit he does come across rather aloof and mysterious. But most hotel owners that I have met over the years often appear to travel to a different drum at times." This drew a chuckle from everyone at the table.

"Jim, I too, would like to be able to count on you to assist me in the operation of the hotel and I would like to think that I can assist you in achieving your own personal career goals." The last comment got Jim's attention.

Jim chose his words carefully. "I'm glad to hear the folks in Hong Kong think so highly of me but...well...how can you assist me with my career goals?"

"Jim, any man that has the drive to become a successful highway patrol sergeant; heroically save a child from a car accident at the risk to his own life; and then proceed to be successful at a variety of new careers, is not going to be satisfied being my assistant for too long. Am I right?"

The look on Jim's face generated the results he expected. Jim briefly looked at Linda who again had paused from her conversation with Marilyn. He then turned to address Jake. "You appear to know an awful lot about me for just arriving today. But your assumptions are correct, Mr. Oliver, I give everything I do 200% effort and if that is not enough...even more. You are also correct in that I had hoped that South Harbor Investments would have considered me for the job of General Manager." At that moment Jim paused to collect his thoughts further. "But in retrospect it appears there is much, in the way of insight, I can probably learn from a man who obviously does his homework before walking into a new challenge." A broad smile came to Jim's face.

Jake returned the smile, and both Marilyn and Linda suddenly stopped talking, which prompted the men to look at their wives to see what had caused the silence.

Linda was the first to speak. "Jim, honey, it appears you may have met your match for once in your life. Maybe you should share with Jake the detective work you have done on him."

Jim looked embarrassed. "Well, I just think it's good to know something about who you are going to work with and I..."

"Jim, I'll be glad to share with you anything you want to know, the good and the bad, but I think our wives are due for an after dinner drink at the best little piano bar in San Francisco. A place Marilyn and I have enjoyed whenever we are in the city. It is located at the top of knob hill, called the *Big Four*."

With that said, Jim and Jake argued over who was going to pay for dinner, and Marilyn reminded them that it didn't matter, given that the hotel should pick up the tab. The rest of the evening proved to be enjoyable for everyone. To a casual observer the four gave the impression of two couples that had been friends for many years. They returned to the hotel just past 11 o'clock and the Oliver's retired to their room and thanked Marci for watching Sarah and Briana for the evening.

"I like them," stated Marilyn in a very decisive tone as they undressed and prepared for bed.

"Yeah, me too. It was a little shaky at first with Jim, but when I realized that he was bent out of shape for not being considered for General Manager, I think the rest of the evening went well. My hunch is that Jim is the best type of man I could have at my side coming into a new hotel, especially after the last experience."

Marilyn paused to hang up her dress, she preferred to forget about the past for the time being. "Linda, is about as genuine as they come. In many ways, the challenges that she and Jim have experienced are similar to ours. From the way she describes Jim's dealings with others, he sounds like someone who values ethics just as you do."

Jake pondered her words. "I hope your right. Because if Jim is the type of man I think he is, he has already investigated my activities over the past few years. I just hope he forms his opinions based on the facts and not just what he hears or uncovers during his research."

....

In another part of town, the Slazenger's were also discussing their evening out. "Well, what do you think Jim."

"Initially, I like them. He sure did his homework on me."

"Yes, he did. It kind of reminds you of say…YOU?

"I respect that he values gathering intelligence on the individuals working for him. I also commend him for having the keen insight to determine what my concerns were. What bothers me though is that stuff down in Santa Barbara." Jim, thought in silence as they rode the elevator up to their small apartment they had rented in the city to live in during the week.

Linda nodded as she opened the door and both entered.

Jim continued. "Those were pretty serious charges, and three people were killed."

"Do you really think Jake could have been involved in something like that?"

"It sure is difficult to imagine, given the person we had dinner with tonight. But it is still too early to tell."

CHAPTER SIX

"So what's he like?" asked Dan Kowalski, Chief Engineer of the Wilford.

"Look, I just met him briefly when he and his family were checking in but he seemed nice enough." Shannon Kincaid said as she picked up the mail from her outbox in the copy room. Both managers tended to arrive early each morning to review issues with their staff before the day got too busy.

"And that's all you have to say? Shannon, our boss is in the hotel and I thought us upper level management types should stick together and support each other." Dan gave her his 'don't forget about your old buddy look' and it appeared to be working.

Dan was 35 and divorced. His marriage had been short lived with a woman that aspired for him to be far more successful than she felt he was. Although Dan had tried to keep the marriage intact, it barely lasted three years and the divorce was rather bitter. Dan was of average height with sandy reddish colored hair, which he attributed to some Irish relatives somewhere in his family history. Built like a small tank, his years of hard physical labor were apparent with his broad shoulders, thick forearms and callused hands. Known for his keen sense of humor and generally happy good nature, Dan was well liked by staff and management alike. Rumor had it that he was a little sweet on Shannon but this had never been confirmed.

"Oh, stick together, that's a good one. Where were you last week, when I needed those five rooms back in order, I believe your staff told me you had an unexpected emergency! Let's see what was that emergency…oh yes, a FISHING TOURNAMENT!"

"Well, to some that could be considered an emergency, Pete and I have competed in that tournament ever since we were in high school," Dan responded with a slight grin on his face.

"Yes, well it is good to see you have your priorities in order. Look, I've got to go." Her hands were full and she did not notice the man entering the reception area of the executive offices as she continued to address Dan. "Hell, I tried to *walk* the guy yesterday and I don't want to make any other stupid mistakes today."

"Oh, on the contrary, Ms. Kincaid." Shannon turned abruptly and the mail she was carrying fell to the floor. Jake Oliver was dressed in a dark charcoal gray suit, freshly starched white shirt with French cuffs, decorative gold tie and polished wing tip shoes. "I know I plan to make plenty of stupid mistakes in my career and I would certainly appreciate it if you would join me by making a mistake of your own every once and awhile."

Startled, as she regained her composure Shannon replied, "a…good morning Mr. Oliver….a…I was…was the room o.k. for you and your family?"

"Just fine." Jake reached down to assist Shannon in picking up the mail she had dropped. "And please extend my thanks to Marci for watching the kids last night." Jake then turned toward Dan and promptly introduced himself. "You must be Dan Kowalski, Jake Oliver. Good to see you in so early, I was hoping we might take a walk around the hotel before the day gets too busy."

"Sure, I mean yes sir, no problem." Dan was flustered and attempted to regain his composure quickly especially in front of Shannon. "When do you want to start?"

"How about in one hour. I want to catch up on a few things first. Where should I meet you?"

Dan responded quickly. "Oh, I'll come up here to your office."

"That will be fine, see you then." Jake then proceeded to the accounting offices at the end of the hall. When he entered the office he found all of the desks already occupied. He also noted that all in the accounting office were Asian and appeared very focused on the work at hand. Jake walked toward a glassed in office located at the back of the accounting department.

As Jake knocked on the open door, a youthful looking Asian man that looked as though he was in his early twenties quickly rose from the his seat behind a large, very dated metal desk. He approach Jake rapidly "ah, Mr. Oliver, welcome to the Wilford. I apologize that I did not know you were coming to the accounting office so early, I would have made the staff more ready. I am Tony Hoy." His tie was slightly undone and his shirtsleeves rolled up to the elbow, Tony looked as though he had already put in a full day's work. As he spoke he was nervously reaching for his suit jacket to put on and look more presentable.

"Tony, good to meet you. I didn't expect to find all of your staff here so early."

"We all get here at 6:30am and usually don't leave until after 7:00pm, it's what we are used to. Please, let me introduce my staff." Tony introduced Jake to each of his clerks summarizing their educational background and specific duties for the hotel. He spoke rapidly and nervously. Although each individual Jake met appeared cordial, there was something else. What he sensed was an almost subservient mannerism and underneath that a hint of fear. But was this fear from Tony or something else? Tony was tall for his Asian ancestry with jet-black hair combed back harshly using a gel to assure it stayed in place. Jake had noticed that a carton of Marlboro's sat on the bookcase next to his desk and as Jake followed Tony he could tell he was a heavy smoker from the smell of tobacco on his suit. Tony also appeared very nervous and, although his command of the English language was good, he first addressed each of his staff in Cantonese then in English. Jake decided he would monitor this behavior more closely but for the time being chalked it up to them being nervous at meeting him for the first time.

Jake advised Tony that he would want to get together with him later in the day and review the financial status of the hotel in its entirety. He then returned to his office and was greeted by an attractive woman dressed in a black dress.

"Mr. Oliver, I am Sandra Kelly, your assistant. Welcome to the Wilford". Sandra was a petite 5'2" with olive colored skin and short strait brown hair of shoulder length. Sandra appeared to be well poised and presented herself more as a high priced attorney rather than a secretary. She apparently placed great importance on her appearance. She had an athletic build and a careful balance of make up and jewelry. She was 32 years old and divorced with a three-year-old daughter. During Jake's interview with Samuel Cho, the principal owner of the hotel, Jake had been told that 'Sandra was an extremely efficient young lady and a key asset of the hotel.' At the time, Jake thought this had been high praise coming from an owner based in Hong Kong, over 6000 miles away. In fact, Mr. Cho did not seem to address any of the other management staff with such high regard with the exception of Jim Slazenger.

"Thank you, Sandra, glad to be here."

"Please let me know if you need anything. I have tried to organize things prior to your arrival."

"Actually, the first thing I need is for you to set up a meeting of just the executive staff for this afternoon at three o'clock. Please apologize to all for the short notice but I would really like to get everyone together as soon as possible."

"Sure, I'll get right on it." As Sandra turned to leave she added, "When you are ready, I will be glad to review with you the current outstanding issues that will require your attention and where things are located in the office."

"Thanks, in fact why don't we get together after you contact everyone."

Jim Slazenger then entered the office reception area with what Jake soon learned was his usual greeting of "top of the morning, gang." He noticed Jake and approached him with a warm handshake. "Good morning, Mr. Oliver."

"In this office it's 'Jake'. And that goes for everyone else. You'll find that I am not a big fan of egos, we usually have to deal with those from our guests." This comment generated a mild chuckle from those present.

Given that the other key members of his staff had not yet arrived, Jake entered his office with Sandra to review the outstanding issues she had commented on earlier. With ultimate efficiency, Sandra had sorted and prioritized the mail for easy review by Jake. A few matters required his immediate attention and Sandra was very helpful.

A short time later, Dan Kowalski appeared at the entrance to Jake's office. "Is this still a good time?"

"You bet Dan, lets go explore."

"Where do you want to start?"

"Let's begin with your shop. Lead the way."

Jake and Dan took the back stairs by the employee entrance down to the basement level of the 90-year-old Wilford Hotel. Along the way, Jake encountered various members of his new staff and Dan did his best to remember names and introduce them to their new boss. Again, what concerned Jake was the level of tension he felt from the staff. Each individual that he met was polite but the nervous tension was quite obvious. When they arrived in the engineering department, Jake noted with great concern that the maintenance shop was extremely disorganized and cluttered. Jake had encountered this situation with other maintenance shops and this did not reflect well on Dan's leadership abilities. Jake was introduced to Dan's engineers and maintenance personnel. Again, Jake observed a high degree of tension between Dan and his staff. Jake also noted that many of these workers were casually dressed in various states of partial uniforms, improper safety shoes, and a general lack of attention to grooming and personal hygiene. Jake made a mental note that the engineering department would require some immediate attention.

As their tour continued, they visited the employee dining room. It was filthy and, in Jake's opinion, was a most undesirable room to expect his staff to eat and relax while on break. Throughout the basement corridors, Jake noted holes in the walls, ceiling tiles missing and a general lack of cleanliness in these employee only areas.

It was then that they entered the housekeeping and laundry department and Jake stopped dead in his tracks. The entire facility was immaculate, neat and organized. A short stout woman approached them with a warm smile. She appeared to be in her late fifties or perhaps early sixties with gray hair pulled back sharply into a tight bun. Her face was of a dark olive complexion and she appeared to be of either Spanish or Filipino ethnic descent. She was dressed in a uniform that resembled the other room attendants. "You must be Mr. Oliver. Welcome, I am Olivia Fernandez, Executive Housekeeper for the Wilford. You have come to see my department?"

Still stunned for words, Jake responded. "Yes, if you can spare the time."

Olivia Fernandez showed Jake her entire department and Jake shared how much he appreciated how orderly and well structured everything appeared. She then abruptly asked, "was your room satisfactory? I had my ladies put extra pillows and blankets in the room along with a refrigerator stocked with items I thought your kids would enjoy. I hope it was all right to give them some sweets, I did for my kids and they grew up just fine."

"Olivia, the room was exceptional and after reviewing your department, I can now assume the rest of the guest rooms are also in order. Sorry to surprise you by arriving a few days early."

"Oh, that was no problem. Keeps us on our toes."

Jake smiled at this woman who seemed to really be on top of matters. "Olivia, how long you have been with the Wilford?"

"I started as a room attendant at the Wilford in 1957 when Hanover & Jones owned and operated the hotel. Those were the days when someone knew how to run a hotel." Jake sensed some of the hostility that Olivia must have had during the years that followed when Bostwick, and then later when Harbinger owned the hotel.

"Olivia, my objective is to return this hotel back to the days when you were proud to work here, but I am going to need your help."

Olivia gave him a partial smile. "Mr. Oliver, I will support you any way I can, but you are going to have your work cut out for you. With these____"

"Mr. Oliver, we still have got a lot to see." Dan interrupted with a quick glance, first at Jake, then at Olivia.

Jake scanned their faces then responded. "Olivia, keep up the great work and I will see you later this afternoon to discuss the back of the house in more detail." This drew a look from Olivia that acknowledged that she too did not approve of the present condition of hotel.

Jake and Dan continued to tour the rest of the basement area. In general the entire basement needed a good cleaning and some organization. Jake noted, however, that behind the dust and clutter, the true age of the hotel was quite visible. Jake looked around with fascination at over 90 years of history. The brick walls making up the perimeter of the building were still strong and intact. By Jake's reckoning, if he had his direction right, they were now near the north side of the building. Behind this was the San Francisco Municipal Commuter Railroad. Jake was aware of this because during his interview with the owners of the hotel they had mentioned the possible plan of creating an entrance to the Muni (as it was referred to) through this section of the basement and then construct stairs to the lobby above.

Jake looked up at the ceiling in this area and noticed the light fixtures spaced evenly in all directions. The quality of the fixtures was surprising, given that this area was only viewed by hotel staff and not guests. The fixtures contained large light bulbs that illuminated the area well. "These fixtures, Dan, they must be 40 to 50 years old."

"Yes sir that would be about right. In fact, it has become almost impossible for me to find the bulbs and replacement parts for them and I have begun to change them in some areas of the basement." Dan shifted his glance from the ceiling back to Jake but noticed that he had walked away to the northeast corner of the basement. As Dan caught up with his new boss he saw Jake staring intently at the ceiling. "Sir, is something wrong?"

Jake continued to study this area intently before replying. "Odd."

"What's that sir?"

Jake now looked at Dan as he responded. "Well, look here, Dan, throughout the entire basement that we have walked so far, the light fixtures have been evenly spaced on the ceiling. But here in this area, this row of lights are located less than 24 inches from the east wall of the basement." Jake paused as he continued to study the situation and walked over to the east wall of the basement. Before Dan could respond he continued. "Dan, was this wall installed at a later date?"

Dan shook his head slowly. "Not that I was aware of, sir, but it's an old hotel and I am sure the original blueprints have not been kept up to date. But the wall looks the same. The brick, mortar. It looks like the wall was built the same time as the others and____"

"Perhaps," commented Jake quickly with a smile, "maybe we will discover a secret room or something exciting when the renovation begins." This drew a chuckle from both men and they moved on.

As they continued to another part of the basement, Jake overheard two employees talking loudly. At first, he had trouble determining where the voices were coming from but then realized the sounds were carrying from a vent outside the men's locker room. Jake entered through the door and the conversation stopped abruptly. Inside was a male employee in bell staff uniform, a second in a kitchen uniform and a third in a housekeeping uniform, perhaps a houseman or laundry worker. Jake recognized the one bellmen as the rather vocal Sergio that he had encountered when he arrived at the hotel the day before. When Sergio and the kitchen worker saw Jake and Dan enter the locker room they abruptly grabbed their belongings and departed out the door. The remaining man in the housekeeping uniform was a big Samoan with broad shoulders and thick arms that the baggy uniform could not conceal. In fact, had the argument that Jake just witnessed elevated into an altercation, there was no doubt in Jake's mind that this guy could have probably taken them all. Jake approached the houseman who remained at his locker changing clothes. "Hi, my name is Jake Oliver and you are?"

He looked to be in his early 20's with dark tanned skin that was stretched tight over a strong jaw line with a flat nose and eyes set wide apart. His thick curly black hair only added to his ominous appearance. But it was his eyes that struck Jake with interest. There was intelligence and kindness behind his tough exterior. He then responded without smiling. "Kono....Kono Hisitaki...you the new GM?"

"I guess that is one of my jobs, but sometimes I get to play referee. What was that all about?"

This drew a slight grin from Kono. "Nice to meet you sir...but I gotta go to work." Kono then departed quickly.

Jake turned to Dan. "What do you think?"

"Probably union stuff...the negotiations are less than a month away, and there is always a lot of arguments around this time. In Kono's case, he always rubs the union kiss asses the wrong way because he will not go along with their ideas...ideas that usually spell trouble for us in management."

The rest of the tour was rather uneventful and Jake returned to his office to find a message from Jackson Chi requesting they meet for breakfast the following morning. Jake had Sandra confirm that breakfast was fine and then went to Jim Slazenger's office. "You free for lunch?"

"I am always free when food is concerned. You want to eat here or go out?"

"I noticed this great looking German brew house down the street when I drove into town yesterday, let's walk." During their walk the conversation was light and both shared that their wives had enjoyed meeting each other the night before. They sat in a booth and ordered beers and bratwurst sandwiches.

At first, the conversation continued to be casual until Jake asked, "the tension level of the staff in the hotel is the highest of anyplace I have ever encountered. From what I know about Sam Filmore, he didn't run his hotels like a concentration camp, but the staff of this hotel appear like dogs that have been severely mistreated, ready to run when you approach ...scared! What's happened here Jim?"

Jim took a moment to chew his sandwich and wash it down with swig of beer while thinking of the appropriate response. "You're right that the tension did not originate from Sam, he was a good manager. The tension, you will see comes from Jackson Chi."

"Chi? He's the owner's representative and should not even be on property that much, how has he instilled such fear?"

"You haven't met Mr. Chi yet have you?"

"I'm having breakfast with him tomorrow. Care to enlighten me further?" Jake replied an edge of irritation in his voice.

Jim again considered his response carefully. "Over the past year, there have been some unexplained incidents that have occurred at the hotel."

"What type of incidents?"

"Well rumor has it that when employees have somehow warranted a personal meeting with Mr. Chi they have later been involved in unexplained accidents coming or going from the hotel."

"And what do these 'incidents' have to do with Jackson Chi?"

"I don't know," Jim said shaking his head slowly, "but on each occasion,. the employee had spoken out against Local #78. On each occasion, Jackson Chi then miraculously showed up at the hotel the following day asking to meet the employee. Later or within a few days, the employee would be involved in some type of accident. With the last two, both involved a hit and run driver and both were killed. It greatly shocked the staff.

"What did Jackson discuss with the employees?"

"We don't know," Jim responded, the frustration apparent in his voice. "I attempted to speak with them but they were too frightened and would not talk to me. But Jake, I think the staff have put together what I have just told you and they're not talking."

Jake looked into his mug of beer absorbing what he had just been told. "Jim, maybe Local #78 is behind this, but I still don't see the full connection with Jackson Chi."

"All I know is what I hear through the grapevine and your staff is more scared of Jackson Chi than their union. I should also advise you that your managers are also aware of these incidents and they are a little spooked also."

Jake paid the bill and both walked back to the hotel in relative silence. As they approached the entrance to the hotel Jake turned to his Assistant Manager, "Well Jim, I am certainly looking forward to meeting this Mr. Chi."

"You may think differently tomorrow." Replied Jim with a slight smile.

....

Each of the executive department managers filed into the small boardroom promptly at three o'clock for the meeting Jake had requested. Jake was already in the room getting some coffee and used this opportunity to better observe his new management team.

Shannon Kincaid the hotel's Front Office Manager was the first to arrive. Dressed in light gray skirt and blouse, she had abandoned the matching jacket. Earlier that morning two of her staff called in sick requiring her to work the front desk and assist with the days departures and arrivals. Shannon was in her early 30's, never married but constantly, as her co-workers would often state 'on the look out for Mr. Right'.

Appearance was extremely important to Shannon and she made it a point to keep in good shape and always dress in what some would interpret as a more 'cute feminine' manner rather than 'business professional.' The skirts she wore were often just a shade shorter than they should be, although no one seemed to complain, and her blonde hair was styled with tight curls that cascaded over her shoulders and gave her the appearance of a girl ten years younger, which was perhaps her objective. Shannon was known for her outgoing personality, but often viewed as self centered. All appeared to know who she was dating on a particular week or what bar she and her friends had frequented over the weekend. In fact, Shannon appeared to be on a quest to be liked by those she worked with and meeting a new boss was something she considered very traumatic. On each instant that Jake had spoken with Shannon, she appeared very nervous and tongue-tied. Jake recognized that Shannon's key challenge was that she appeared to wear her emotions far too close to the surface which resulted in large mood swings in her dealings with her staff and fellow managers. In turn, she was often perceived as weak and out of control at times.

Dan Kowalski accompanied Shannon as she entered the conference room and both sat together at the far end of the conference table away from Jake. Shannon was laughing from what appeared to be a joke that Dan had just shared with her. From the first few times Jake had seen Dan and Shannon together, he was convinced that, at least Dan, was interested in getting to know Shannon better. It was evident, however, that Dan probably did not fit Shannon's profile of tall, handsome, and successful, her apparent criteria for 'Mr. Right'. Shannon appeared to like Dan as a fellow co-worker but Jake thought it doubtful there was anything romantic between the two that may cause problems for the hotel.

Dan had worked for a variety of hotels throughout San Francisco over the past ten years mostly as a maintenance engineer and joined the Wilford four years prior. Dan advanced to be assistant chief engineer during his second year at the Wilford and just six months earlier had been promoted to chief following the unexpected heart attack and death of the former chief engineer. Dan's key challenge was going to be his ability to effectively adjust to his new role as a manager of his own department. He had dropped his union status with the Engineers and Maintenance Workers Union Local #12 and Jake would soon discover that Dan was having difficulty associating himself as 'management' rather than 'labor'. In turn, he was not recognized by his staff as their boss but rather 'one of the guys'.

Fred Plummer was the next to enter the room. A short plump man in his early fifties, Fred clearly looked the part as the Director of Food and Beverage for the hotel. With over 30 years in the industry, Fred viewed each of the outlets under his control as one of his own personal businesses. A man, who enjoyed good food and wine, Fred had worked for some of the finest restaurants and hotels in San Francisco throughout his career. But as times changed, the traditional formal dining atmosphere of the 60's and 70's had made way for the new 'themed' high energy restaurant / bar operations. Fred found it difficult to adjust to these changes and his previous employers chose to seek younger managers that were, as he had been told, more current with changing trends.

One year earlier, Fred had responded to an advertisement for the position of Director of Food and Beverage at the Wilford. After reviewing his extensive resume, Sam Filmore, General Manager of the hotel, at that time, was impressed with his experience but stated he simply could not afford someone of his caliber. Fred responded that money was not as important as the opportunity to direct the food and beverage operation of a grand hotel such as the Wilford. Sam studied Fred closely, concerned that his intentions were truly sincere and decided to take the chance.

Fred's presence was immediately apparent after he joined the Wilford. The level of professionalism, the quality of the food and the attention to service made dining at the Wilford again a special treat to its guests and the outside public. A food editor for the Dallas Morning News got wind of where Fred had landed and wrote a restaurant review of *Chancellor's*, the Wilford's fine dining restaurant located on the penthouse floor atop the hotel, in the Sunday Edition Food & Wine section of the paper. Following this positive review, business picked up and Fred was back in business...and so was the Wilford with regard to Food & Beverage. Fortunately for Jake, this was one department; he could afford to ignore for the time being.

Laura Sanders, the Director of Human Resources entered with Jim Slazenger. Jake had been told that Laura was extremely competent with regards to the management of her department and her dealings with the five respective labor unions that had collective bargaining agreements with the Wilford. An attractive woman in her mid forties with lightly frosted hair cut short and dressed in a well-tailored blue suit, Laura looked good for her age. She had a shapely build and dressed accordingly to show off these physical features but her face portrayed a different individual entirely. From an initial observation, Laura appeared the consummate professional. Upon closer inspection, however, this was a woman prone to regular migraine headaches, far too many cigarettes and drinks each evening, and was dealing with some serious personal issues.

Laura was in the midst of a divorce, her third in the past 20 years. A mother of four, three from her previous marriages, this divorce was proving to be one of her most difficult. What complicated matters, was that during the past five years with her, now estranged husband, he had been cheating on her. When she filed for divorce, however, she received her ultimate shock in discovering that her 18 year old daughter was his latest flame.

Jake was concerned that she could adequately dedicate herself to her job while addressing such personal challenges.

Mike Reynolds, the hotel's Director of Sales and Marketing entered the room wearing an olive colored suit, a starched white shirt and a bright gold silk tie. A man with a perpetual smile and strong handshake, Mike was an exceptional sales director. Choosing to stay in an industry that had paid for much of his education, Mike obtained a degree in Marketing / Advertising from Stanford University just prior to beginning his search for a job with a major advertising agency he was hired by the Fairmont Hotel as a Corporate Sales Manager. He enjoyed the hotel industry immensely and never pursued the career he had trained for in college. After two years he left the Fairmont to become Director of Sales of a small boutique hotel near Union Square. When the hotel changed owners, Mike considered his options and was approached by Sam Filmore to be the Director of Sales and Marketing for the Wilford. Mike was somewhat hesitant given the poor reputation the Wilford had developed in the city but was intrigued by the plans of the hotel's new owners to renovate the hotel and he decided it was worth the risk.

Mike had been well received by the staff of the Wilford and his strong management style and ability, to teach his sales managers how to effectively sell, earned him the admiration of his staff and the envy of his nearby competitors.

Jake observed Mike as he sat in a chair immediately across from him. A man, confident in his abilities, and his job, he appeared to welcome the new challenge of having a new boss.

The last managers to enter were Olivia Fernandez, Tony Hoy, and Sandra Kelly, who pulled the door and took a seat next to Jake.

Almost in unison all turned their attention to Jake and waited for the meeting to begin. "I would like to thank each of you for meeting on such short notice. The purpose of this meeting is for me to review with you some of my basic management philosophies."

"Knowing how fast information travels in the hospitality industry," Jake began studying the faces around the table, "I am not sure I have to give you much background on my past experience. But for those less informed, I am about to begin my 20th year in the hospitality industry and I know that probably comes as a surprise given how young I look." This drew some light laughter and seemed to ease the tension Jake sensed around the table. "I have managed a wide variety of hotels and resorts throughout the Country, but most of my time has been spent here in California. I must also share with you that this is my first time running a hotel in San Francisco and in dealing with labor unions. I here they are all nice guys, however, and I guess we don't expect many problems with the upcoming negotiations, right Laura?" This drew a round of laughter as Laura looked at her new boss with an exasperated expression on her face.

"This leads to the primary purpose of today's meeting. We do have some serious challenges ahead of us over the next few months. In particular I am referring to our union negotiations with Local #78 and our plans to completely renovate the hotel. Both issues can, if not properly planned, be highly disruptive to both our guests and employees." Jake paused to observe everyone's reaction thus far. The tension he observed earlier was still unmistakably present. "And lastly…the tension in this room is so thick you could cut it with a knife. Would anyone care to enlighten me? Is it my intimidating presence or is this group always the epitome of excitement." This last comment drew a tense chuckle from the group.

At first no one spoke, then Mike broke the silence. "Mr. Oliver…Jake…I think we are all just a little nervous getting used to a new GM and all."

Jake considered this for a moment but knew this was not the reason. "Perhaps, or perhaps it has to do with the sudden departure and unfortunate death of Mr. Filmore?"

This time it was Fred Plummer that spoke. "Hell, I don't mind saying that what happened to Sam sucked! He was a good manager and deserved better…just because he would not go with the flow ___"

"I think what Fred is trying to say," interrupted Sandra Kelly, "is that all of us were very close to Sam and regret that he felt the need to leave."

"No that is not what I am saying," responded Fred, but Laura grabbed his elbow and signaled him to not say any more. Jake studied the entire group's reaction with extreme interest but decided that the best way to uncover their concerns would be to meet individually. He had accomplished something; however, he was starting to get a better idea of who he would meet with first.

CHAPTER SEVEN

Jake asked Laura Sanders for the personnel files of all of the department managers for his review. He did this to better familiarize himself with his management team and took them up to his room that evening to review. All appeared to be in order for each with the exception of Sandra Kelly, his assistant. He was surprised to find little to no relevant documentation in her file. When he questioned Laura on this matter, Laura informed him that Mr. Filmore had handled the entire process of hiring Sandra Kelly personally and advised her not to worry about it.

Laura explained that Sandra had joined the Wilford Hotel on or about the same time South Harbor Investments purchased the hotel. In fact, her arrival at the hotel was somewhat of a mystery from what Jake could gather. Helen Ferguson, the previous secretary to Sam Filmore had resigned from her position very suddenly and with little notice shortly after the hotel's change of ownership. On that same day she also recommended Sandra Kelly as a possible replacement. Sam reviewed Sandra's resume during her interview and questioned her as to why someone of her past experience and skills was considering a position in which she was clearly over-qualified. Her response had been that she was looking for something with less stress so she could spend more time with her daughter. Sam still questioned this rationale but apparently decided to take advantage of this overly qualified individual that was available to start work immediately.

Jake reviewed Sam's notes in Sandra's file. It indicated that Sandra was relatively new to the Bay Area and previously had worked for several large organizations in Southern California. Her past positions had included being administrative assistant to the CEO of Consolidated Investments, a large brokerage house in Irvine as well as paralegal for one of Los Angeles' largest law firms, Stein, Johansen, and Blevens. Her most recent position had been assistant to the President of Eastern Treasures, Int'l, an international import / export consortium also in Los Angeles. All of these positions involved skills and talents that far exceeded what would be required of her as a secretary to the General Manager of a hotel.

Jake further noted that Sandra had asked Sam not to share with any of the other managers her past experience or qualifications. It appeared that Sam Filmore had honored her request. Jake later learns that her appointment raised many questions from the other managers who found Sandra pleasant to work with but very mysterious in not wanting to talk about her past. In turn, speculation and rumors ran rampant. Some of the theories included that she had been hired directly by South Harbor Investments as a kind of spy. Others came up with more extravagant theories such as she was hiding from someone under an assumed identity.

When Jake arrived the following morning, Sandra was already at her desk and was on the phone. At first she did not appear to notice Jake as he approached allowing him the opportunity to get close enough to overhear part of her conversation. To his surprise she was speaking fluent Cantonese to someone on the phone. When she observed Jake entering the office, her conversation ended and she hung up quickly.

"Good morning Mr. Oliver. You're up early this morning."

"I might say the same for you." Jake responded tentatively. "Say, why don't we grab some coffee in the restaurant and get to know each other a little better."

"Sounds good, I'll tell the operator to hold our calls."

They entered the hotel coffee shop and found a table away from the other guests. At first the conversation was light with Sandra inquiring how his family was adjusting to being in San Francisco.

Jake decided to get to the point of this meeting. "Sandra, one of the things I like to do when I arrive at a new hotel is find out a little about my staff. In turn, I had Laura pull for me the personnel files of all of the department managers. In reviewing your file...well... basically, there is not much to look at." Jake watched Sandra for any type of reaction. "Can you share with me how you came to work for the hotel and why someone who is clearly over-qualified for her position is sitting here talking to me right now?"

Sandra listened intently showing little surprise or reaction to his question. "I was referred to Mr. Filmore by Helen Ferguson, the previous executive secretary. We were friends and she told me she was planning to leave her position."

"Did Helen say why she was planning to resign?" Jake asked.

Sandra paused briefly as if gathering her thoughts. "No, only that she had some family that she needed to take care of back in Kansas or someplace in the Midwest."

"I see. Well that must have been very convenient for you given that you had apparently already left your previous position with_____?"

"That would be Eastern Treasures, Int'l. I had just left there. So yes, it was convenient."

Sandra appeared relatively relaxed but her answers were almost too rehearsed as far as Jake was concerned. "Sandra, according to your resume, the past positions you have held have required far more challenge than your present job must offer you. I would also assume a lot more pay. Why the sudden change?"

Sandra hesitated this time before answering, then spoke slowly. "Mr. Oliver, to be quite honest, I would prefer not to talk about my reasons for having to leave L.A. They were of a personal nature."

Jake tried to read what it was that Sandra was not saying. He then continued slowly. "Sandra, I realize that whatever the problem was must be awkward to talk about, but if it relates to something that could effect your present job and the hotel then I must____"

"Oh no, its nothing like that. Mr. Oliver, my previous husband was...abusive. I divorced him three years ago but he kept bothering me and Lisa, my daughter. I felt it best to try to hide and changed my name. While at my last position with Eastern Treasures, my 'ex' tracked me down and began calling me at work. My only solution was to leave and change my name again. I had some friends who put me in touch with Helen and Mr. Filmore agreed to keep my past secret. I can only hope that you will do the same."

Jake considered her words and felt her comments were sincere. "Sandra, your secret is safe with me but if you run in to problems again, please promise you will come to me. I have some friends too and maybe we can fix your problem so that you do not have to keep running. Agreed?"

A relieved smile appeared on her face. "Thank you for understanding, Mr. Oliver."

"It's Jake. Now maybe you can answer a few other questions for me."

"Sure, I'll help any way I can."

"Just how involved has Jackson Chi been with the day to day operation of the hotel?"

Sandra hesitated briefly, then responded. "Mr. Oliver, Mr. Chi has been actively involved and, if I may be so bold, is someone you should be very careful around."

"Can you be more specific?"

"No, nothing that I can exactly prove but I can share with you that those that have crossed him, are no longer working for this hotel." She responded with genuine concern in her voice.

"You are referring to Mr. Filmore, your previous boss?"

"Yes, to name one, but there have been others. I only ask that you be cautious of whom to trust and confide in. Mr. Chi has many methods of knowing what is going on in the hotel at all times. How, I don't know, but somehow he always finds out."

"Alright Sandra I will keep that in mind."

Both returned to the office to find, none other than, Jackson Chi sitting behind the desk in Jake's office using his phone. He was apparently early for his breakfast meeting with Jake.

Jackson Chi was not at all what Jake expected. Born in Hong Kong 45 years ago, much of Jackson's education had been in the United States. He had received his undergraduate degree from UCLA and his MBA from Stanford University. He then returned to Hong Kong and through family acquaintances was hired by South Harbor Investments. Utilizing his degree in Finance, Jackson advanced rapidly placing his career clearly above that of his family and friends. He developed a reputation for being extremely ruthless and often casting moral judgement aside for the betterment of the company but also conveniently to better himself politically.

Jackson Chi was rewarded for his aggressive behavior by being given responsibility for strategic overseas business ventures in which his line of accountability by-passed all conventional channels and he often dealt with the company chairman directly and *privately* on many matters. Trust and admiration were not words used by his co-workers to describe their dealings with Mr. Chi and many who knew him wondered just where or even if he would draw the line between right and wrong in his day to day actions.

As Jake entered his office, Jackson Chi initially did not acknowledge his presence and continued, what appeared to be, a rather hostile conversation most of which Jake could not understand given that it was in Cantonese. His impression was, however, that it must be his secretary or some other subordinate. The tone was extremely derogatory and demeaning.

Very suddenly, Jackson hung up the phone. It was as if his comments had been said and anything else the person on the other end of the line had to say was not important. Then his whole demeanor changed and a broad smile appeared. He approached Jake with an extended hand. "Ah...Mr. Oliver, welcome to San Francisco and to the most impressive Wilford Plaza Hotel!"

Jake shook Jackson Chi's hand and studied the man in front of him. He was approx. 5'10", with a lean build and jet black hair combed back with heavy gel. He appeared to keep in good shape and was dressed in some of San Francisco's finest threads. His suit was stylishly cut and instead of wearing a tie, wore a black silk shirt under an expensive black suit.

Jackson continued. "My apologies for using your office and phone but I had some urgent business that just could not wait. And now, let's have some breakfast and get better acquainted."

Jake nodded. "That would be fine, shall we go to the restaurant or would you prefer to go off property?"

"Oh, off property of course. My car is waiting in front of the hotel."

Both men proceeded to the front entrance and entered a black Mercedes with a chauffeur. As the car pulled away from the curb

Jackson continued, "I am so pleased to have you on board. We could not have waited much longer."

Jake looked at him questioningly, "I am not sure I understand."

"Why the upcoming union negotiations with Local #78 of course. Jake, I assume I can call you Jakc, these negotiations are of key importance to the future success of the hotel. I expect you to make this your primary focus for the next thirty days."

Jake considered how best to respond. "Jackson, I assume I can call you Jackson, I assure you that it will be my intent to place extreme importance on the upcoming negotiations. I must share with you, however, that during my initial observations of the hotel and the staff, there are several other issues to be addressed."

As Jake spoke, Jackson's head began to shake back and forth demonstrating his lack of concern with Jake's comments. "A high level of anxiety and tension is good for everyone, it keeps them focused on their job. If, however, you need me to speak to anyone in particular, just let me know."

The Mercedes pulled up to a small restaurant in Chinatown and Jackson informed Jake that they had arrived. As they exited the car, Jackson addressed Jake, "I hope you like *Congi*, it's one of my favorite breakfast foods."

Jake shrugged his shoulders. "I am always open to trying something new."

The rest of the breakfast meeting proved to be anything but enjoyable. Jackson felt that this breakfast meeting was the best time to share with Jake his many accomplishments and spoke almost non-stop about his most favorite subject...*himself!* They returned to the hotel two hours later.

Jake was dropped off in front of the hotel and Jackson indicated he was late for another meeting and quickly departed. Jake felt the purpose of the meeting was quite clear. Jackson wanted to clarify his importance and had attempted to intimidate Jake from the start. What Jackson did not realize was how much Jake loathed individuals of this type and it was quite obvious that these two men were going to clash on views often.

CHAPTER EIGHT

Jackson returned to a building roughly two blocks from the Wilford. His office, located on the 20th floor of the McKessen Building, was clearly a reflection of Jackson's outlandish tastes. It looked like a penthouse for entertainment rather than an office for business. His secretary, an extremely attractive oriental woman that he always referred to as Ms. Chuen, handed him his phone messages and faxes as he proceeded to his office barely giving her the time of day. He closed the door and quickly began going through his rolodex for a number he had not used for awhile. When he could not find the number, he yelled for Ms. Chuen. When she was informed of whom he was trying to contact, she advised him she would place the call for him. A few minutes later, the phone in Jackson's office rang and the person he wanted to speak to was on the line.

The voice said, "what can I do for you Mr. Chi?"

"I need you to proceed with the Oliver matter. Find out all you can, anything that may be useful. Is that clear?"

"Yes sir, when would you like this information?"

"Yesterday, now get to work!" Jackson hung up the phone and thought about his meeting with Jake earlier that morning. He had concerns. Jake Oliver appeared far more outspoken than he had expected. *Could he be manipulated? Would he cooperate? And most importantly, why had Samuel hired him without his knowledge?*

These were questions that Jackson must find out…and soon. Too much depended on it.

....

Later that evening, Jake shared his eventful first meeting with Jackson Chi with his wife, Marilyn. "So he is not the most warm and fuzzy guy you've ever met." Marilyn said with a sarcastic smile. "But it's not the first eccentric owner you have dealt with who has a larger than life ego!" Marilyn sat across from Jake enjoying their room service dinner in the hotel suite that served as their home until they found a new house in the city.

"Yeah, you got that right, but this guy could be the most arrogant and basically obnoxious one I've run into so far." Jake sipped from a glass of red wine as he considered all aspects of this meeting.

"You think it is more serious than just some overzealous owner's representative trying to impress you?"

"Possibly, the only purpose of our meeting this morning appeared to be for him to size me up briefly, get the point across that the union negotiations were very important to him and demonstrate just how powerful he was." Jake rolled his eyes then gave a brief, 'I'm not worthy bow' in mock respect.

Marilyn smiled. "That's right and don't you forget it." She then held up her glass and they both toasted. "To another challenge!"

CHAPTER NINE

Jake arrived at work with a specific plan in mind. After making the usual rounds of the hotel and visiting with his staff, he had Sandra contact Laura Sanders and advise her he would like to meet to review, in depth, the upcoming union negotiations and what was being proposed. In particular, he wanted to learn more about Jackson Chi's involvement in the negotiations and if specific direction had been given to Laura on this matter.

Laura entered Jake's office with several large files under her arm, a cup of coffee, and a flustered or possibly annoyed look on her face. Jake also asked Sandra and Jim Slazenger to join the meeting. All sat around a small conference table located in his office.

Jake explained that the purpose of the meeting was to get more familiar with the key concerns on the table for the negotiations and what the hotel's position should be on each issue.

"We have two primary areas of concern." Laura explained.

"First, wage increases are obviously a key issue to the workers. In general, most of the increases appear reasonable with the exception of several tipped positions. For bell staff and bartenders, the union is requesting substantial increases combined with further restrictions on the number of available shifts that can be scheduled."

Jim interjected, "our concern is the attention being paid to two positions that are already paid wages substantially higher than other positions recognized by this union. In our opinion, the union is clearly playing favorites and taking care of the positions with the loudest lobbying efforts. For example, because most of the housekeeping and back of the house food and beverage staff do not speak English, no one is taking care of their interest as compared to our rather vocal bellmen and bartenders."

Jake acknowledged this point. "Jim, this has always been an issue and, your right, it has always pissed me off that a union, designed to represent the best interest of the many, clearly benefit the few in most cases. Am I to assume, then, that our position is to dispute the larger increases proposed and suggest a compromise to take care of the some of the lesser recognized positions, such as room attendants, dishwashers, and the like?"

"Exactly," Laura nodded, "we have already put together some figures and, although the overall cost to the hotel on an annual basis will increase some, our counter proposal will benefit far more employees than what the union is proposing."

"Great," Jake responded, "let's continue with this plan. Laura, can you summarize for me the proposed increases we are considering and get them to me later today?"

"No Problem."

"What's the next concern you mentioned?"

"The union's pension fund," explained Laura, with noticeable agitation. "Over the past few years, new hotel owners have been successful in breaking away from the union. In turn, Local #78 has steadily lost its sources to fund its pension made up of an aging base of workers. This has caused the union to place higher demands on the few collective bargaining agreements they have left to make up for this loss in dues revenue. The union is expecting our hotel to help pay for the growing number of retired workers from all of the other hotels that no longer participating in the program as well as for our own retired workers."

Jim again chimed in. "Jake, there has also been quite a bit of news and controversy, lately regarding how the union's pension fund has been managed. I think they are in trouble, and they know it."

"Yes, Mr. Chi is quite concerned with this issue," stated Sandra, somewhat to herself but enough to be overheard by the group.

"Why is that," asked Jake as he looked at Sandra cautiously, "why would Jackson Chi be overly concerned with the present state of a union's pension fund?"

"I don't know," stated Sandra, who appeared to be caught off guard that she had made the comment in the first place. "All I know, is that Jackson has requested copies of all the minutes of each meeting we have had with Local #78 over the past few months."

"There is something else you should know, Jake," added Jim. "Word has it that Jackson Chi and Lou Walizak, president of Local #78 are quite the buds these days. Some of the staff have told me they have seen Chi having lunch with Walizak and that he has been seen visiting Walizak's office."

"Interesting," commented Jake, "anybody care to guess what is going on there?"

"He also gets a lot of calls from Mr. Walizak," Sandra added.

"And how would you know this?" asked Jake.

"Apparently, he doesn't believe in voice mail or something. But every time his assistant, Ms. Chuen, is not available to cover the phone, she forwards the calls to me."

Jake pondered Sandra's last statement and then commented. "I guess your ability to speak Cantonese comes in kind of handy…uh?"

This comment flustered Sandra and all she could do was nod her head slowly in agreement.

"Laura, have you summarized the proposed increases the union is requesting to the pension fund and the impact these increases will have on the hotel annually as well as over the term of the contract.

"Only some rough calculations but I can put together something more formal for your review if you would like."

"That would be great." Laura nodded as she jotted down notes of what Jake was requesting.

Jake thanked all for their input and excused them with the exception of Jim who he asked to stay. After Sandra and Laura were gone, Jake silently recalled some of the comments that had been made during the meeting. "Jim, what do you know about Sandra?"

Jim looked at him somewhat confused. "I'm not sure I follow."

"I guess what I am asking is what you think of Sandra as a team player. Is she on our team?"

Jim contemplated his next response carefully. "All I can tell you is that Sam Filmore, thought very highly of her abilities and her confidentiality. Sam was a stickler for confidentiality."

"What do you know about her background?"

"Not much really, she just sort of showed up on the scene and Sam hired her. We have all tried to find out about where she previously worked but she has always been tight lipped on the issue. I asked Sam about her one day and all he would tell me was 'not to worry, she's just a private individual'. I decided not to push it." Jim again looked at Jake questioningly. "Are you concerned?"

"Sort of, but nothing I can put a handle on at this time. Do me a favor, be careful what you discuss around her for the time being will you?"

Jim studied his new boss's eyes carefully trying to uncover what was troubling him. "Sure boss."

....

The black Lincoln Towne Car looked out of place as it approached the intersection of *Eddie* and *Leavenworth* in what was referred to as the 'tenderloin district' of San Francisco. The car pulled up to the curb in front of a four-story brick building that clearly lacked regular repair and maintenance. A small sign mounted on the building to the right of the main entrance stated, *Hotel & Restaurant Workers Union, Local #78.*

The driver of the car was a tall stocky man in his late 30's dressed in dark slacks, a pullover knit shirt and wearing a windbreaker jacket with the *San Francisco 49er's* Logo prominently displayed on the back. He got out and quickly opened the rear door on the passenger side. A shorter man, very heavy set, with short-cropped gray hair, exited from the car. He was wearing a light blue sport coat that appeared to be a size or two too small and certainly impossible to button. His dark navy blue pants, on the contrary, hung loosely with the pant cuffs slightly dragging on the ground as he stepped toward the building with a slight limp. Tucked between his teeth was what remained of his morning cigar. It was not lit at that moment which was common for the man who preferred to chew on them as much as smoke them.

He quickly entered the building and was greeted by a receptionist, a well-proportioned woman who appeared to be in her late forties or possibly early fifties with bright red hair, wearing too much make up and a dress that reveled far more cleavage than most would care to imagine first thing in the morning.

"Hi boss," she stated while chewing her gum.

"Hi Hon… what's shaken today?" Responded the man in a gravelly voice that suited his appearance.

"Skinner called and you have an envelope marked *private* sitting on your desk. A secret admirer boss?"

"You bet babe, they're lined up at the door to see old Lou," the man responded with a slight smile. "Heard from the Chinaman this morning?"

"Not so far, you want me to get him on the phone or something?"

"No, I want you to get me and Ed some coffee, pronto." The man and his driver then proceeded down the hall to a spacious but relatively cluttered office. The furniture was dark and heavy upholstered in burgundy leather that was beginning to show signs of age. On the walls were dozens of framed photographs, some in black and white others in color. Each photo featured the man who resided in the office and other individuals most would not have recognized. All of the photos appeared to have been taken at various social events with drinks and cigars in everyone's hands. Another common theme to all the photos was that all were primarily men and had the same general appearance as the man displaying the framed photos on his office walls.

Prominently displayed on the desk was a desk nameplate that read, *Lou Walizak, President*. Lou hung his sport coat on a coat rack then sat to review the phone messages waiting for his response. Vera, the receptionist entered with coffee for Lou then promptly left, closing the door behind her.

"Well Ed, its good to be back in town. I hate those fucking district meetings where everyonc trics to impress each other. Hell, I got bigger things on the plate that require my attention here."

Ed simply nodded without responding. Ed had been working with Lou for the past five years and knew it was often better to say nothing and just agree with his boss. Ed was not as dumb, however, as he often appeared. He knew Lou better than most and knew what it had taken for Lou to get to be president of one of the largest and most powerful union locals in the Country.

Lou was born, Louis Alvin Walizak 56 years prior in a small row house located south of *Mission Street*, in downtown San Francisco. The only son of Demitri and Helena Walizak, both Polish immigrants who arrived in San Francisco less than three months before Lou was born. Lou grew up in a tough neighborhood, in which respect was gained by who you knew and often, who you were willing to fight. By the time, Lou was 18, he had already served time in several juvenile detention centers and was barely on speaking terms with his father.

One of Lou's first jobs after his release from juvenile detention was working at a warehouse near *China Basin*, which was a tough industrial area of the city in those days. Lou advanced quickly with the union he was forced to join but not with the owners of the warehouse who uncovered that he was involved in the theft and black market distribution of various goods received at the warehouse and suspected that the local union was in support of this elicit activity. Lou was fired and the warehouse owners began legal action against the union. On a chilly November night, however, just as legal tensions were mounting, a fire broke out and almost the entire warehouse burned to the ground. An investigation followed, and Lou was convicted for starting the fire. The union abandoned him stating they had no involvement and that Lou had acted on his own.

Lou was sentenced to five years but released in two for good behavior. At the wise old age of 22, Lou took a job as a kitchen receiving clerk for a large hotel in downtown San Francisco. Within the next six months, he was appointed shop steward for Local #78 that had a collective bargaining agreement with the hotel. Lou climbed quickly up the ladder of Local #78 and, after only three years, accepted a full time staff position with the union.

Over the next 20 years, Lou developed a reputation as one of the toughest union negotiators in the Country. He only handled the big hotels and they usually feared sitting across the table from a man who had a reputation for being very persuasive in getting what he wanted. Always one step ahead of the law, he was often suspected but it was never proven that he was responsible for some of the untimely accidents that occurred at hotels his union had disputes with.

At the age of 45, Lou was promoted to President of Local #78, a position he had now held for the past eleven years. During this time he continued to grow stronger politically while his union grew weaker financially. In recent years, controversy had arisen regarding the management of the unions retirement pension fund. The combination of poorly chosen investments combined with an aging workforce, now wanting to cash in on their pensions, was having a depleting effect on its ability to meet everyone's needs. In addition, more and more hotels were successfully fighting off the formation of bargaining agreements with Local #78, creating challenges for new sources of funds for the pension.

Life was presently not good for Lou and he could not afford to lose all that he had worked for. He needed something to show his membership and peers that he was turning the situation around and current negotiations with the Wilford Plaza Hotel offered the perfect venue he needed to redeem himself.

"Ed, who is negotiating the Wilford contract?"

"Ah…that would be Mickey, Mickey Seleki boss," responded Ed.

"Get him in here. Have him bring the entire file. I want to know everything that is going on with this hotel. Also, I understand, they have a new GM, do we know anything about him yet?"

"I don't think so boss, he just started this past week I think."

"Then get me Jonsey on the phone, let's see what he can dig up on the *new guy*."

CHAPTER TEN

A few weeks passed and Jake had been well received by the entire staff of the Wilford. His enthusiasm and high degree of energy had restored their faith that, with effective leadership, the hotel could once again become the great prestigious hotel it used to be.

Now settled into a routine for the day to day operation of the hotel and comfortable with the hotel's planned position for the start of the union negotiations, Jake turned his attention to the scheduled renovation of the hotel. The first obstacle that he encountered was that virtually all of the development plans consisted of discussions between Jackson Chi and a local architect by the name of Ed Lee. Jake also had noted that a large amount of funds had been paid, designated as advance deposits to contractors, yet Jake had not been able to find any paperwork to support the expenditures. Jake planned to discuss this further with Tony Hoy, his controller.

Jake had Sandra contact Ed Lee, the architect of the project and arrange a time for them to meet. Ed suggested that Jake come to his office, located a short distance from the hotel in San Francisco's *Chinatown* district.

Jake arrived at ten o'clock and was greeted by a young and attractive oriental woman, who Jake later discovers is Ed Lee's daughter working for his firm during a break from college. Jake was shown to an elegantly appointed conference room to wait for Ed who, he was told, was finishing up a phone call and would be with him shortly. As Ms. Lee departed, Jake was overwhelmed with the fine oriental art present in the room. At one end of the room two statuesque bronze lions stood. Each were over four feet tall. Oriental scrolls lined another wall that appeared to be quite old and quite authentic. As a centerpiece for the conference table, two porcelain statues of ancient Chinese generals, in full military uniform stood poised ready to do battle at a moments notice. On the interior wall running the length of the room, various drawings of buildings, bridges and towers that Jake presumed had been designed by Ed and his firm, were prominently displaced. In fact, what struck Jake, was that his owners had obviously spared no expense in hiring someone of Mr. Lee's caliber to design and oversee a relatively simply project compared to other jobs Ed had undertaken.

Ed Lee entered the room silently as Jake was admiring one of the Chinese scrolls, "That particular piece is over 1000 years old and describes the development of a particular province in China we now know as Xinjiang."

Jake turned to note a small man, who appeared to be in his late forties. He was in excellent shape and dressed impeccably in a light gray suite. He approached Jake with an outstretched hand and introduced himself.

"Mr. Oliver, I am Ed Lee, very nice to meet you. I have heard many good things about you."

"Mr. Lee, nice to meet you, but I am afraid you have me at a disadvantage. No one has shared anything about you, which is the reason for my visit today," Jake pondered, questioning who had informed Mr. Lee about him and what had been said.

"Well, we shall quickly correct that matter," Ed replied with a warm smile. But first, come, I would like to show you our firm and introduce you to some of my staff. Then I have made reservations at one of San Francisco's finest Chinese restaurants, but many tourists do not know it is the finest. I hope you like Chinese food?"

"Yes, I do, and I am always open to discovering a new place to take my family for dinner."

Ed gave Jake the grand tour and introduced him to virtually every member of the firm. Jake discovered that Ed's wife was also an active partner in the business and handled most of the financial aspects of the day to day operation. Jake found her friendly but much more reserved during their brief encounter. After the tour, they returned to the conference room. One of Ed's associates had brought in the plans for the renovation of the hotel as well as soft drinks and coffee. For the next hour, Ed reviewed the plans with Jake. Ed was impressed with Jake's familiarity in reading blueprints and with his obvious experience in working with historical structures such as the Wilford.

Prior to stopping for lunch Jake asked Ed to show him the basement plan one more time. Jake studied the plans for several minutes in silence. Ed looked on trying to determine what he was looking for.

"Something wrong Jake?"

Jake looked up from the blueprints. "Oh, well, I'm not sure. It's the plans for the basement. They're incorrect."

Ed stood and joined Jake so he could view the plans himself. "I don't understand. These are the most current and supposedly up to date plans for the hotel."

Jake continued to study the floor plans. "And these plans reflect all renovations, improvements or changes that have occurred since the hotel was built?"

"Yes, my draftsmen, reviewed all records with the city building and permits department to assure they were correct. What is it that you feel is incorrect?"

"It's these walls here." Jake pointed toward the exterior walls making up the northeast corner of the basement."

Ed looked on concerned. "If these plans are incorrect, then we had better get them revised immediately. This area, in particular, is where we plan to create an entrance into the hotel from the *BART* Subway system."

Jake shook his head. "I don't know, Ed. Maybe I am mistaken, but these plans do not appear to be the same as what I visually observed during my tour of the hotel. I'll check it out again and let you know."

"Alright. Perhaps, I will also take a look," replied Ed as he continued to stare at the plans in front of him.

They both then departed for a small Chinese restaurant on Jackson Street in the heart of *Chinatown*. The restaurant was relatively plain in decor but filled with customers. Once the food arrived, it was clear why Ed liked this place over the more noted restaurants in a city frequented by tourist.

As both sipped hot tea following a superb meal, Jake inquired as to how Ed had become associated with the renovation of the Wilford. Ed explained that his ties with the owners of the hotel went back over 40 years. It was then that Ed summarized a career that Jake found absolutely fascinating.

Ed Lee was born in San Francisco, the oldest son of Chinese immigrants that had made their voyage from Hong Kong in the 1930's. Ed grew up in an ethnic Chinese neighborhood where few ever learned to speak English at that time. Ed's parents, however, wanted the best for Ed and his two sisters. All learned to speak English and were raised Catholic. Ed studied hard and attended a Catholic school while working part-time for his father who ran a fish market in *Chinatown.* Ed's hard work paid off and he was fortunate enough to receive a scholarship to Notre Dame University, to study architecture.

Upon graduation with honors, Ed's desire was strong to experience Hong Kong, the home of his parents and ethnic heritage. His father was hesitant, but finally agreed to put him in touch with some of his former contacts. Ed later discovered that these contacts of his father had mysteriously prospered after World War II and were now prominent businessmen. Ed was extended an invitation to visit Hong Kong for what started out to be a four-week visit but eventually turned into a six-year sabbatical.

When Ed arrived in Hong Kong, not knowing a sole, he was greeted by a chauffeur in a Mercedes limousine and taken to the residence of Mr. Samuel Cho, a prominent shipping magnate and developer of office buildings and hotels throughout Hong Kong and Mainland China. Ed and Samuel hit it off immediately and Ed was put to work on various developments of Mr. Cho and his partners. During the first year, Ed was primarily responsible for acting as the organization's representative in their dealings with local architects, designers and contractors. In later years, however, his position was elevated, when Mr. Cho created an internal design and construction division for what had grown to be a large conglomerate known as South Harbor Investments, Ltd.

Ed enjoyed his work for Samuel Cho and South Harbor Investments, but learned early in this relationship, that Mr. Cho was an extremely powerful man, one that many people respected but also feared. Ed could not understand what generated the fear he observed from others who dealt with Mr. Cho. For the most part he chose to pay no attention and focus on his job. But there was one incident that Ed observed, during his 6th year with Mr. Cho that clarified some of his unanswered questions.

Ed was working late in his office that evening finishing up a pressing project. He called Mr. Cho and asked if he could come to his home to review the revised plans and get his approval, so construction could begin as planned the following morning. Ed arrived, a little after ten o'clock that night and was escorted by one of the house servants to Mr. Cho's study. He was advised that Mr. Cho was still with some business associates and would be with him shortly and to wait in this room.

Suddenly, Ed overheard loud voices coming from the room across the hall that Ed knew to be Mr. Cho's personal office. There were multiple voices but all were too muffled to be clearly understood. Ed was concerned that, his friend, Mr. Cho may be in some form of trouble and stepped into the hallway to approach the office. It was at that moment that the door opened and two men came walking out. One was Mr. Cho's assistant and number two man for the entire organization, Benjamin Tsang, the other was a man, know to Ed by sight only. He was a stern looking individual, big by Chinese standards, that was always close by to Mr. Cho. All assumed he was a bodyguard of some type. The third man, Ed did not know. But what captured Ed's attention was the look of fear this man had when leaving the house with Mr. Cho's bodyguard and Mr. Tsang. As Ed observed this scene, Samuel Cho directed him into his office. He apologized for the wait and disturbance and the rest of the conversation continued as expected.

The next morning, Ed was having breakfast and reviewing the morning newspaper when he noted a photo and article on the inside front cover. It summarized the unexplained death of a businessman by the name of a Nelson Chin whose car had lost control and crashed into the Hong Kong harbor. As Ed read the article he calculated that this man had died less than three hours after he had seen him at Mr. Cho's house. Recalling the man's look of fear and then his unexpected death generated fear in Ed for the first time.

It was at this point that he decided that it was time to return home to establish his own business. Samuel Cho was concerned with Ed's sudden desire to leave Hong Kong but after he explained that his parents were of ill health and the family needed his presence, he accepted his departure.

Ed was able to get his architectural firm up and running during the first six months he was back and over the next twenty years had developed a reputation as one of the premiere architectural design firms in San Francisco and the state of California. With a staff of over 30 architects and another 20 draftsmen and support personnel, he purchased the building that housed his present office at the corner of *Kearny* and *Clay.* He considered this the best of both worlds because it was in the heart of the financial district, yet walking distance to where he grew up in Chinatown.

Jake sat in his chair spellbound as Ed brought his career to present day and paused. "Ed, that is quite a full and successful career for a man that doesn't look a day over 45."

Ed smiled at this comment. "Actually, young man, I just celebrated my 67th birthday this past week."

That drew a smile from Jake. "Ed, I'm curious. From what you have told me, obviously you had some ethical concerns with Samuel Cho, yet you have continued to work with him on projects such as this hotel. Why?"

"Jake, Samuel Cho has always been a good friend and was extremely supportive and instrumental in my career development after school. The story I shared with you was not to cast doubt in his integrity, but rather to respect that he and his partners are extremely powerful men and not to be taken lightly." Ed paused for effect. "I have no proof that Mr. Cho had anything to do with Mr. Chin's sudden accident and I prefer to not form opinions without all of the facts. This leads me to what I wanted to talk to you about today."

Jake looked at him questioningly. "I'm sorry Ed but I thought I was the one who contacted you?"

"Yes, you did, but had you not, I would have been in touch with you very shortly." Ed now studied Jake carefully. "Let's begin with your questions, such as what is going on with the renovation and for what and to whom have the recent funds been paid. Am I correct?"

"You forgot to add mind reading to your list of talents."

Ed responded with another question. "What have you found out about Jackson Chi so far?"

Jake questioned where Ed going with this conversation. "Mr. Chi and I have only met once in person and then several times by phone. I am not sure what you are asking."

"You probably already have concerns with Jackson and thought I might be a source for that information. Am I correct?" Ed stated as he poured more tea for Jake and himself.

Jake considered how best to respond. "My questions for you today related primarily to the renovation. As for Jackson Chi, I am not used to an owner's representative keeping the activities of such an extensive renovation secret from the general manager of the hotel. From a review of the plans, prior to our lunch, it appears all details have been well thought out and organized. What I am not comfortable with is that the hotel has written checks, described as advance deposits authorized by Jackson Chi, totaling over $2 million with little to no supporting documentation."

"Both of your concerns are valid Jake" responded Ed with a sincere look of concern. "You should be extremely careful around Jackson Chi and watch him carefully in his dealings with the hotel."

Jake studied Ed's face. "Are you suggesting that he may not be representing the best interest of the hotel and Mr. Cho's investment?"

"I'm only saying that Jackson looks out for Jackson first and that means that you should do the same. Get to know all of the key players, Jake Oliver, and guard you instincts in how you deal with matters. Form your trusts carefully with those around you."

On that note, Ed stood and indicated that it was time to get back to work. He and Jake drove back to his office in relative silence where Jake was dropped off at his car. As Jake was exiting the car, he turned to Ed, "When you returned to the states to set up your practice, you obviously stayed in touch with Mr. Cho and his partners in Hong Kong. Was he instrumental in helping you set up your firm here is San Francisco?"

Ed looked at him and smiled, "Jake, I had no choice but to stay in touch. It is necessary when one marries a man's daughter. Keep in touch and feel free to call me if you need clarification on anything. It may not seem like it, at this time, but I am on your side, Jake."

Jake returned to the hotel and pondered what had been discussed. It was obvious Ed Lee was well informed, but by who? He was also trying to warn Jake to be concerned with his new employer, but why? Lastly, it was clearly suggested that Jackson Chi is up to something, but what?

....

His wife, Cathy greeted Ed, as he entered his office. "So, what do you think of this new manager?"

Ed looked at her thoughtfully. "He is already asking questions, and that's good."

Ed then retreated to his office and closed the door. He dialed the number that he knew well and after several rings it was answered. "So, how did the meeting go?"

CHAPTER ELEVEN

While Jake was attempting to get his hotel in order, Marilyn Oliver had taken on the arduous task of finding a new home for the Oliver family. Taking on such a task was not new to Marilyn, over the past 12 years she had become somewhat of an expert in the field being married to a hotelier whose job often required relocation to a new hotel and new city. In fact in an odd sort of way, she actually enjoyed the opportunity to see new places and explore new areas, one of her favorite past times.

Marilyn Ann Simmons was born and raised in a small Indiana farming town of no more than 500 residents. The youngest of three with two older brothers, Marilyn often felt as if she was an only child. Her two brothers were much older and had already married and moved away before Marilyn was old enough to truly enjoy their company. Tragedy struck the Simmons's home when Marilyn was a mere 10 years old. Her father, a prominent farmer of their small community had a massive stroke while working in the fields and died. Left alone, Melitha Simmons, Marilyn's widowed mother, was forced to sell the farm and moved to the state's capital where she obtained a job as a schoolteacher at one of Indianapolis' most progressive high schools. A shrewd businesswoman, who had developed her frugal philosophies from living in the country, she invested the money from the sale of the farm wisely and purchased a modest but comfortable home conveniently near the school where she worked.

At first, Marilyn had difficulty adjusting to living in a big city but she grew to like her new surroundings and the wide variety of friends around her. These new friends were fascinating to Marilyn, in that, growing up in the small northern Indiana farming community, Marilyn had never known nor lived in the same neighborhood with people of various ethnic nationalities. Having an open mind to all that she encountered and growing up in a household that frowned on any form of discrimination or bigotry, Marilyn developed an understanding and appreciation for the challenges these individuals faced in today's society, this was truly one of her most exceptional qualities.

Marilyn's childhood passed quickly in a household with just her mother and her and the relationship that developed between them was more of good friends rather than a typical mother/daughter relationship one would expect. Marilyn had been forced at an early age to be highly independent, self sufficient, and was determined in every task or challenge she faced.

After graduation from her mother's high school, she attended a small state college and graduated with a degree in social work. During college studies she worked for a variety of charitable organizations, one of which offered a full time staff position after she graduated from college. Over the next few years, Marilyn excelled in her new position and received several promotions. It was during one of her training programs that she arranged at a small resort in southern Indiana that she met an outgoing, brash, almost too confident for his own good, man. A year later that man would become her husband.

Marilyn was a woman of small stature. At just over 5 feet tall and athletic in appearance, Marilyn enjoyed the outdoors and boating with her husband. She had blondish brown hair, cut short, dark blue eyes and a youthful face that gave most the impression she was at least 10 years younger than her actual age of 41. She was of medium build and constantly watched her weight as she got older. She maintained a good diet and most of her exercise came from chasing the girls around the house.

And now, here she was in a hotel room living in one of the most exciting cities she could imagine with her family, reviewing property listings in the newspaper and studying the various real estate publications. This had become a daily routine each morning followed by spending the rest of the day in the car with Sarah and Briana investigating neighborhoods and school districts.

On one of these mornings after roughly a week of searching out various neighborhoods, Marilyn received a phone call from a woman by the name of Naomi Shu. Ms. Shu explained that she was a realtor and had assisted the prior general manager, Sam Filmore, and his wife in finding their new home. She then asked Marilyn if she could assist her with their search for a home. At first Marilyn was somewhat hesitant but the more they spoke the better they seemed to get along and Marilyn finally agreed to meet Naomi for lunch. Marilyn arranged for Sarah and Briana to spend the afternoon with Linda, Jim Slazenger's wife, and met Naomi Shu at an upscale bistro-style café on *Van Ness* Avenue that Naomi had suggested.

Marilyn had no difficulty recognizing Naomi when she entered the café. Naomi was seated at a table by a window that afforded her a good view of the entrance to the restaurant. Naomi possessed all of the Asian features and qualities many American women would like to have. She was dark tall and thin, dressed in a black dress that was both professional but equally alluring to the men present at nearby tables. She wore little jewelry, which was not needed, with her striking facial features, long shinny black hair that ran the length of her back. Her eyes were dark and her high cheekbones complimented her appearance. At first glance she appeared to only be in her late 20's but Marilyn would later discover they were only a few years apart in age. Marilyn's first impression was that their meeting had been a mistake. Marilyn viewed herself as that of a typical housewife. Although, she had been known to get an occasional glance from an admiring bystander, she could not fathom what the others in the restaurant would think of these two women seated together and what they would have in common.

Naomi approached Marilyn almost as soon as she entered the café and introduced herself. "Marilyn? Hi, I am Naomi, thank you so much for meeting with me today."

Marilyn thought she seemed nice. "Oh, it was no problem, and besides, what does it hurt to, at least talk and a break from the kids is always a pleasant change."

Naomi recognized the hesitation in Marilyn's voice. "What do you say we have some lunch and get to know each other better. Let's start with you telling me about your two daughters…isn't it?"

By the time lunch was complete, both felt as though they had been the best of friends for a long time. Marilyn was pleased to find someone that she felt was truly genuine and sincere. As they were walking out to the car, Marilyn agreed to have Naomi assist them in finding a home.

After several follow up meetings to identify specifically what the Oliver's were looking for, Naomi began showing Marilyn a variety of homes. One home that caught Marilyn's attention was in a nicely kept neighborhood near Lake Merced south of the 'avenues', as they were called, in the southwest part of San Francisco not too far from the ocean. In fact, Naomi happened to also live in this neighborhood less than five blocks away and explained to Marilyn that she kept in contact with many of the residents in case they needed her services. Jake got away from the hotel the following afternoon and after seeing the house agreed with Marilyn that it would fit their needs. What bothered Jake was why the price of the house was so reasonable. Naomi explained, however, that the sellers had inherited the house and the one son simply wanted the cash rather than another home. Naomi was even able to get the seller to allow the Oliver's to move in during the escrow and closing on the home, in time to get their daughters enrolled in school that was about to start.

The movers successfully delivered all of the furniture in relatively good condition with only minor damages. Marilyn could accept this after the eight previous professional moves her husband had put her through since they had been married. Within two days, the house was beginning to look organized and Marilyn prepared the family's first home cooked meal, the first in over 30 days. To many, a life of living in hotels and eating all your meals at expensive restaurants each day would be the life they would dream of, but for Jake and Marilyn, the opportunity to stay home, was a welcome change.

A few days later, Sarah and Briana began school and Marilyn established a routine of dropping them off each morning at eight o'clock. The school they were attending was less than two miles away and also convenient for Marilyn to stop at a nearby grocery on the way home. All appeared to be in order as far as Marilyn was concerned. She now had a new home. Her husband had a good job at, what she was confident would be, one of San Francisco's finest hotels some day with her husband in charge. And her daughters appeared to enjoy their new school and the friends they were meeting.

....

Conveniently parked away from any nearby streetlights, a dark colored sedan sat. At first glance no one would think that there were any occupants in the car. But if one looked more closely they would see the orange glow of a burning cigarette behind the darkness of the glass. It's glow growing brighter then dimmer with each drag from the individual shrouded in the darkness.

CHAPTER TWELVE

Jake decided it was time for him to begin his own private investigation into the mysterious advance payments made to contractors. He began by first calling Tony Hoy, the hotels financial manager, to his office when he arrived promptly at 7:00am on an exceptionally foggy Monday morning. It did not surprise Jake to find Tony in his office at that time of morning. In fact, Jake was beginning to wonder if the guy ever went home and simply slept next to his blessed fax machine, the primary mode of communication with the Hong Kong office. "Tony, it's Jake, can you come to my office, I have something I want to review with you?"

Tony quickly acknowledged. "Ah yes, Mr. Jake, I will be there shortly."

Tony appeared at the door to Jake's office five minutes later. Jake motioned him in, advising him to close the door and have a seat. "Tony, I need your help."

"Certainly," responded Tony. "What is it that you need?"

Jake paused while he considered how to approach his young controller. Although Jake had only worked with Tony a short time, he felt that Tony was a hard working and basically honest individual. What concerned Jake, however, was where his loyalties truly lied. Jake assumed that Tony had been brought to the hotel in San Francisco primarily to act as a "check & balance" for the owners in Hong Kong and assure that their overseas investment was managed properly. In addition, the high degree of tension Jake had noted when

Tony was around his staff could not be overlooked. It was Jake's hunch, however, that this fear was not being generated from Tony but from either Jackson Chi or someone in Hong Kong. The big questions were who and what was Tony afraid of and if he would help him.

"Tony, I have reviewed the hotel's financial statements for the past six months prior to my arrival and I have noted some expenditures that I need your help with."

Tony shifted in his chair nervously. "I should be able to answer any question you have sir. Each of these reports were personally verified by myself for complete accuracy prior to distribution."

Jake was pleased to get this response from Tony but there was a sense of despair or rather conviction in his voice that Jake was not sure how to read. "Tony, I am not accusing you of doing anything wrong, I only want to know more about the renovation expenditures that were made just prior to my arrival. Combined, these four checks total roughly $2 million. I would also like some further explanation of how Hong Kong provides funding to cover the substantial losses the hotel has incurred during this period. In fact, if I am reading these reports correctly, the hotel has experienced a net loss of roughly $5 million during the first year of operation. That's not small change my friend."

Tony continued to shift nervously in his chair before responding. "Mr. Jake, the renovation expenditures were handled by Mr. Chi. Mr. Chi advised me to prepare the checks and to make them out to four different companies. I asked for the support documentation for these expenditures, but Mr. Chi made it quite clear that I was not to worry about this stating he would send them to me at a later date."

"So all we have is the name, address and the amount that was sent to each contractor?" Jake inquired as he leaned forward in his chair.

"Actually sir, all we have is the name of the contractor and the amount. Mr. Chi insisted on picking up the checks personally and hand delivering them. He did not give me an address or phone number to accompany each expenditure."

"But surely you had to explain these expenditures to Hong Kong when you requested funding?"

Tony gave an affirmative nod. "Yes, at first I thought so. But when I called later that evening, I was told that the funding had already been arranged and that an additional $2 million was being included in the lump sum." Jake could tell that Tony was still visibly concerned by these series of events.

"Was this normal for Hong Kong to already be aware of what funding was needed when you called?" Jake inquired observing Tony carefully.

"No, No," responded Tony urgently. "I had been advised that on the first Friday of each month, I was to fax the funding required with the appropriate documentation to support the dollars requested and then call and discuss my reports and why this funding was necessary to operate the hotel for each upcoming month."

"Tony, who do you speak with when you contact Hong Kong?"

Tony again hesitated as if choosing his words carefully looking down at his hands as he spoke. "I normally speak with Mr. Cho directly."

"But that is not who you spoke with on this particular occasion, was it?"

Tony continued to look down at his hands. "No…

I…spoke…with…a…with Mr. Tsang, Mr. Cho's assistant."

Jake contemplated his next question cautiously. "Tony, is there some reason why I should not know about these recent activities?"

Tony looked at him questioningly. "I do not understand."

"What I am saying Tony," as Jake stood and looked out the window of his office, "is that,. obviously, our discussion of these series of events is making you uncomfortable. I think you and I both know that something strange occurred last month just prior to my arrival and that you were advised to not discuss this with me." Jake came around his desk and sat on the edge across from Tony. "Mr. Chi approaches you to prepare four checks that together total $2 million with only his verbal approval and no support documentation. It is my guess that such an action was contrary to how you had been instructed to handle payments of this nature. You proceeded, however, because Mr. Chi was your boss. You were obviously concerned with how Mr. Cho would react to your actions. Your anxiety grew when you were unable to speak directly with Mr. Cho and had to deal with Mr. Tsang. Lastly, his response that he had already been advised of the necessary funding caused you further concern. Have I got it right so far, Tony?" Based on the look on Tony's face, all of Jake's assumptions were obviously correct. "Tony, what do *you* think is really going on here?"

Tony considered the question put to him. "Sir, I have already said too much. You do not know who you are dealing with and Mr. Chi is a very powerful man. We should not proceed further. I am sure Mr. Chi will eventually provide me with the documentation to support these expenditures." Tony then stood abruptly. "Is that all sir?"

Jake leaned back in his chair frustrated and confused by the response he had received from Tony. "Yes, Tony, you can go but I need two more things from you. First, I want the names of the four contractors who were paid advance deposits. Second, has it been Hong Kong's practice to send you more funding than you request?"

Tony hesitated and Jake could see it in his eyes that his mind was in a state of turmoil as to how to proceed. "I will provide you the names immediately and yes, excess funds are often sent each month." Tony then quickly left Jake's office.

Jake contemplated the information he had just been given then called Sandra into his office. "Sandra, contact Ed Lee and see if I can come by and see him around 2:00pm today."

Sandra made a note to call Ed Lee. "Early meeting?"

Jake looked up, at first confused by the question. "Ah yeah, I got in early and thought I would get to know Tony a little better. Is that alright with you?" A slight smile on Jake's face as he coaxed his secretary.

Sandra also smiled and was slightly embarrassed realizing that her question had no merit and was none of her business. "Well…yes, but I expect to be informed of these clandestine meetings in the future."

Jake watched her exit the office and his smile vanished as he asked himself, *and just how long have you been outside that door Ms. Kelly?*

……………………………………………

Tony provided the names of the contractors that Jake had requested a short time later. They were written on a piece of hotel stationary and delivered in a sealed envelope by Yuki, the accounts payable clerk with strict instructions to only give the envelope to Mr.

Oliver. This appeared to offend Sandra but Yuki insisted on following the instructions of her boss.

Jake opened the envelope and four company names were listed on the page:

- ✓ Jakovitz & Associates $500,000
- ✓ Harbinsen, Inc. $300,000
- ✓ Sunblossom Enterprises, LTD $400,000
- ✓ Wal, Inc. $800,000

Prior to Jake's meeting with Ed Lee, Jake attempted to research each company. He looked them up in the telephone directory, called directory assistance for telephone numbers, and even tried the Internet, but no information existed on these four mysterious companies.

....

Jake arrived slightly early for his appointment with Ed and this time was greeted by Cathy Lee, Ed's wife. She directed him to the conference room and was somewhat more cordial than their first visit but still reserved. It was almost as if her opinion of Jake was still undecided. After she departed, Jake noticed that the plans for the hotel were on the conference table. He quickly began reviewing the attached schedules, the RFP (request for proposal) binders and the returned proposals that had been received for the project. There was no mention of the four mysterious companies.

As Jake quickly scanned the documents in front of him, Ed Lee entered the room in the same silent manner as during Jake's previous visit. "Looking for something in particular, Jake?"

Jake spun around, somewhat startled. "Yes, yes I am. I am looking for some answers and I think you can help."

Ed motioned Jake to have a seat and poured both some hot tea. He looked troubled as he sat down. "Jake, I will assist you any way I can, but I am not sure I will have all of the answers you are looking for today."

Jake leaned across the table towards Ed. "During our previous meeting, you indicated that you were aware that $2 million, designated as advance deposits to contractors, had been dispersed from the hotel. I have the names of the four companies the checks were made out to but nothing further. I want to verify if these companies have anything to do with the renovation."

Ed smiled as he looked upon this man with a purpose. "I think you already know the answer to this question, Jake. But the answer is no."

Jake leaned back in his chair. "Well, I guess my next step is to confront Jackson Chi then contact Hong Kong with my findings."

"No Jake, not exactly," Ed responded. "There is more going on here I suspect. You are correct that, obviously the payments made to these companies have nothing to do with the renovation because I would certainly know about it. There must be a reason, however, as to why Mr. Chi wanted to refer to these payments in this manner and you must find out what that is before confronting him. Take it from one who is clearly older but not necessarily wiser, it is far better to know the answers before asking the questions." Ed leaned back in his chair smiling coyly at Jake.

"You're still speaking in riddles Ed and I am convinced you know more than your saying. If you are truly on my side, why can't you tell me more?"

"You place me in a difficult position, Jake. I want you to succeed in your quest to uncover whatever may be underfoot, but I must protect my interests and association with your employer. I will assist all I can but I regret that I am as much in the dark as you are on this particular issue."

Jake was unconvinced that Ed was truly in the dark as much as he indicated. *Had he made a mistake coming to his office today and sharing what he knew? Was Ed Lee involved in the cover up of the payments and simply stringing him along so he could warn Jackson Chi of his upcoming discussion? Was Ed Lee trying to misdirect him? Or was he truly in support and sincere in his request to help him uncover what was going on at the hotel?*

Jake did not know the answers to these questions yet but decided some caution was in order. In considering all of these factors, Jake responded. "Ed, I can appreciate your position and it has not been my intent to place you in an awkward position with Hong Kong."

Ed stood and extended his hand to Jake. "Thank you Jake, just keep me informed of what you uncover and I will assist in any way I can."

Jake left Ed's office with a revised plan in mind. He would proceed in uncovering what was going on. He would share information with Ed on a need to know only basis for the time being.

....

When Jake entered his office he was greeted by none other than Jackson Chi who appeared very agitated. Jake invited him into his office and closed the door behind them.

"Something you better get straight right away Mr. Oliver," he began even before Jake had taken a seat at his desk, "if you have a question regarding my actions, you are to come to me! All your little antics this morning have accomplished is to get everyone upset about things that are not their concern."

Jake observed that besides being extremely upset, there was something more. Jackson Chi appeared to have been caught off guard or perhaps scared. As a result, he was reacting irrationally, which actually intrigued Jake. Jake stood and looked Jackson directly in the eyes. "Mr. Chi, as General Manager of this hotel, I am responsible for all aspects of its operation. That, sir, includes the disbursement of any funds from this operation. The particular disbursements I believe you are referring to, Mr. Chi did take place prior to my arrival but it still involves the current operation of the hotel."

"It is of no concern of yours, Mr. Oliver."

"Perhaps not. Once the appropriate support documentation has been provided and these expenditures have been correctly identified maybe I can get to the task of running the hotel." Jake replied sharply with an edge of anger in his voice. "But until that time, I expect some answers."

Jackson looked as though he was about to explode. His eyes became narrow slits in a face contorted with anger and tension. For several seconds neither man spoke but then Jackson quickly regained his composure before responding. "Jake, you appear to be under the misunderstanding that *something* has occurred here and you are *implying* that I have acted inappropriately. I suggest that you be careful in making such accusations. Let me clarify that you work for me and if you want to keep it that way, you will focus on running the hotel. And that is all!" Jackson abruptly turned and stormed from the office. In his haste he slightly tripped on the carpet as he emerged from Jake's office. He briefly stumbled but regained his balance by grabbing hold of Sandra's desk. Now both angry and embarrassed he quickly departed the office ignoring the formal greetings of the staff members present who looked on awkwardly.

While Jake sat back down to consider the conversation that had just taken place, Sandra knocked on the door. "Any survivors in here?"

"Just one, but the wounds may be severe."

Sandra smiled. "Congratulations Jake, you have finally met the Jackson Chi we have all grown to love!"

That drew a chuckle from Jake as Sandra returned to her desk and closed the door on her way out. Alone in his office, he took a moment to consider what had just occurred. His day began by meeting with Tony Hoy to discuss the disbursement of funds to unknown contractors that it now appears may not be contractors at all. He then met with Ed Lee to confirm the status of these contractors and Ed suggested that Jackson Chi was up to something but would not divulge the basis for his comments. He then insisted that Jake not approach Jackson until he had more information and to keep him informed. In turn, what is Ed's involvement in this matter? Lastly, Jake returned to find Jackson Chi waiting for him clearly well informed of what he had been up to all day. Who was the informant? Tony? Sandra? Ed? Or someone else?

CHAPTER THIRTEEN

All businesses had their own internal rumor mill and hotels were no different. The news of Mr. Oliver's brief but rather vocal conversation with Jackson Chi spread like a California wildfire to every department before the day was over. And as with most rumors, variations of the truth became amplified to include a brief episode of both shoving each other with Mr. Oliver knocking Mr. Chi to the floor. Another variation explained that the argument that had occurred involved Mr. Chi bringing a prostitute to the hotel and Mr. Oliver did not approve. One theme, however, that was common to almost all of the rumors was that Mr. Oliver was tougher than the previous managers and had held his own against the evil and condescending Mr. Jackson Chi.

While two employees were discussing their opinions of what had occurred at a table in the employee dining room, a man sitting by himself at a nearby table was not impressed. In fact, Sergio Cervantes' opinion differed from the other staff of the hotel who were beginning to like their new general manager. Sergio's first dealings with Jake Oliver had been on the day Jake and his family had arrived at the Wilford. He had been the bellman arguing with his bell captain in front of the hotel. All Sergio knew was that, following some type of discussion between Mr. Oliver and Harry Walters, his supervisor, Harry had chewed him out and sent him home early that day because of his attitude.

Sergio was 27 years old, the youngest of eight children of immigrant parents that had moved to California from Ensenada, Mexico in the early 1970's. A close and hard working family, Carlos and Emalita Cervantes had always wanted the best for their children and attempted to instill sound and ethical life values. The results of their efforts were rewarded with each child becoming good citizens of the United States through hard work, honesty and sincere religious beliefs. All were now good parents to their own children and well respected in the communities in which they lived and Mr. and Mrs. Cervantes were extremely proud of their children, with one exception. Their youngest child, Sergio had been different from all the rest. At an early age, he appeared to lack respect for just about anything. He was lazy, argumentative, and often got into fights throughout his early years in school. Sergio's mother blamed his problems on his "bandito friends" as she referred to them, but his father was not as understanding.

Following an extremely violent argument that occurred between Sergio and his father, when it was learned that he had dropped out of school on his sixteenth birthday, Sergio ran away from their home in El Segundo, a suburb of Los Angeles. He hitchhiked to Oakland, where he had a buddy from the neighborhood, and for the next year, he was in and out of detention centers and had been arrested four times for petty theft by his seventeenth birthday. After undergoing rehabilitative counseling, which was his only alternative rather than spending more time in a juvenile detention facility, Sergio convinced his counselors that he was a new man. As part of a program to assist troubled teens facilitated by the Hotel and Restaurant Workers Union, Sergio was given a job as a dishwasher at the Wilford Hotel. Sergio discovered, shortly after working for the first time in his life, that being a union employee had one benefit, that he valued the most. If he made a mistake, was late for work or got into a disagreement with his supervisor, he could simply plead his case to a union representative who, Sergio felt was there to cover for him. He viewed this benefit simply as a means to do whatever he pleased and the union would protect him from being fired.

A few months after Sergio began work at the Wilford, union negotiations were up for renewal at the Wilford. A common strategy of Local #78 was to seek out hotel employees that could be used to infiltrate the staff and gather information and instill unrest as needed. Sergio was the perfect candidate. As the years went by, Sergio's name came to the attention of Lou Walizak and Lou appointed him 'special representative' to local #78, which was a creative and misleading title for basically a union spy. Lou's direction to Sergio was to keep him informed of what the hotel's management was up to and he was rewarded with under the table bonuses, kickbacks and granted special favors from the union. For someone like Sergio, life just didn't get any better.

Others around him, however, would disagree. Sergio had visibly aged hard during his 27 years. An habitual chain smoker and heavy drinker, his appearance was that of someone 20 years older. A short stocky man of only 5'5 with a paunch developed from hours of playing pool and drinking with his buddies at a local tavern two blocks south of the hotel. His hair was jet black, curly and longer than Harry Walters, his supervisor, felt was presentable for the Wilford. In fact, Harry had adamantly fought it when Sergio requested to transfer into his department as a bellmen. Harry had become all too familiar with Sergio's reputation for tardiness, absenteeism, and, of course, his habit of arguing with his supervisors.

Sergio sat at his table nursing the hangover he still had from the previous evening. He considered the employee meal not fit for anyone to consume and pushed the tray away from him as he attempted to hear what one of the front desk clerks, Devonne, was saying to Zak, a maintenance engineer. Personally, Sergio could not see what this tall bubble headed red head saw in a low life mechanic like Zak, given that they sat together each day for lunch. Perhaps Sergio's dislike had something to do with her refusal to go out with him for drinks the previous month.

"You're telling me, Mr. Oliver physically threw Mr. Chi out of his office this afternoon!" Zak said as he leaned across the table toward his luncheon date.

"All I'm telling you is that I overheard Ms. Kincaid, my boss, talking to your boss. Apparently Mr. Chi was waiting for Mr. Oliver when he returned from an appointment off the property. Ms. Kincaid said that she overheard both having an argument with the door closed." Devonne leaned forward making sure Zak was paying attention to her and then proceeded. "Ms. Kincaid asked Ms. Stick-in-the-mud what was going on but she was told not to hang around the office. Almost, like she was dismissed or something."

Zak smiled. "What's your beef with Sandra Kelly? Personally, I think she is kind of cute."

This drew the desired reaction from Devonne, who grabbed his arm stating, "*Oh really*, well maybe you should have lunch with her from now on."

Zak leaned forward, a sly grin on his face. "No, that's O.K. I guess I will just have to settle for you."

Devonne punched him across the table in the chest with a mock pout on her face. "Wow, you sure know how to make a girl feel special."

"Back to what you heard," responded Zak wanting to know more about the latest rumor. "Where did you hear that Mr. Oliver threw Mr. Chi out of his office?"

She leaned forward, glad to see he was again interested. "Well, just as Ms. Kincaid was about to leave, the door opened and Mr. Chi was walking out of the office when he lunged forward as if he was pushed."

"You really don't think Mr. Oliver would push someone do you? I mean, especially his boss."

"Well…probably not, but Ms. Kincaid said she is convinced that Mr. Oliver is the type that will stand his ground and it was her impression from the look on Mr. Chi's face, that he had clearly lost whatever argument they had."

Zak nodded his head in agreement. "Yeah, Mr. Kowalski likes the guy too. Said he is the first manager in a long time with a set of big ones and that is what is needed around here. Did Ms. Kincaid have any idea what the argument was about?"

Sergio had almost got up to leave but paused to hear more on this subject.

"Yeah, she seemed to think it had something to do with his meeting with that Chinese architect downtown. You know, the little guy that always carries what looks like a journal book of some type."

"Maybe, Mr. Oliver has uncovered something is rotten at the Wilford." Zak responded with a broad smile.

"Well, let your imagination run big boy, I have to get back to the front desk." Devonne stood, patted Zak on the shoulder then departed.

Zak watched her leave admiring that, even in the hotel's rather plain front desk uniform, she filled it out nicely. He then gathered his tray and also departed.

Sergio left the cafeteria and proceeded to the pay phone located outside the entrance to the housekeeping department.

....

It was 9 o'clock that evening and two men in Lou Walizak's office were discussing the game of pool they played earlier that evening. As was true with most organizations of this type, one advanced more from whom you knew rather than what you accomplished. The men in this room were classic examples of the "buddy system" in full action.

Mike "Skinner" Portola was a thin, lanky man of medium height with dark black hair and a perpetual 5 o'clock shadow. Skinner had gotten his name from how he had dealt with those who tried to squeal on the, less than noble, activities he performed for Local #78. Michael James Portola was born in Detroit to parents who both worked for General Motors. Growing up in a family who was active in the united auto workers union, Mike developed a somewhat skewed view of what labor unions were for. He viewed being part of a union as the perfect avenue to exploit a job for his own benefit rather than for the organization that employed him.

By the time he was 22, even with the protection of his blessed union, he had been fired and / or transferred over a dozen times and had developed quite a reputation as a trouble maker or "bad seed" as one of his employers noted in his personnel file. To escape from this reputation and start fresh somewhere else, he moved to San Francisco and got a job at one of the city's older hotels in the tenderloin district. He immediately joined Local #78 and it did not take long for him to get to know the union representative for the hotel, given the problems he immediately caused. First there were arguments with fellow employees. Next there was the food server who got into a confrontation with Mr. Portola and then was mysteriously burned the following day by hot grease that had been placed on an upper shelf in the kitchen and just happened to fall when the food server walked under it. Again, the union came to Mike Portola's rescue when all evidence pointed to him as the key suspect in the accident.

Over the next few years, Mike moved from hotel to hotel and the problems just seemed to follow him wherever he went. His reputation grew as did his case file. Then on a cold December night in 1992, the restaurant manager of a hotel was walking to his car after closing when he was attacked by someone with a knife. The scariest aspect of the attack, when relayed later at the hospital by the victim to the police was that the man who attacked him used the knife to cut up his face and kept repeating, 'I'm gonna skin you alive, mister.' The restaurant manager told the police that he believed it was a new bartender that worked for him by the name of Mike Portola but said the attacker had worn a ski mask to hide his face. He further explained that he suspected that the attack was in retaliation from an earlier argument the manager had had with him. The argument revolved around the manager scolding a waitress for substandard performance after a customer complained about the service he received. Mike Portola did not like the way the manager had reprimanded the waitress in the kitchen and began to argue and eventually shoved the manager in front of other employees. Hotel security was called and escorted Mike out of the hotel. He was placed on suspension and it was highly likely that he would have been fired for such action. The police investigated the incident and, although Mike Portola was clearly the key suspect, they could not prove it, given that Mike had the alibi of four other co-workers who swore he was with them the entire evening playing poker.

This incident got the attention of Local #78's President, who recognized that such an individual, with proper coaching, could be useful to him for future projects that may arise. A week after Mike Portola was cleared of all charges related to the attack, Lou Walizak contacted him. When Mike, now nicknamed among his inner circle of friends as "Skinner", left Lou's office that evening he had a new job working directly for the union office, although few knew exactly what his position was or his specific responsibilities.

Others now present in Lou Walizak's office included Ed Flago, Lou's driver and body guard, Sammy Smith, Skinner's partner in crime on many occasions, and Mickey Seleki, a Local #78 contract negotiator. In contrast to Skinner, Sammy Smith was a short stocky man with a barrel chest that caused his sport coat to hang open exposing a well fed belly. His hair was sandy colored and cut short almost military in fashion. Sammy had just turned 47 and had never married. Known to be a real loner, he sat in a chair by the window and said very little. Mickey Seleki had just turned 35. He was tall and had an awkward appearance about himself. He was dressed in gray slacks and a navy blue sport coat with no tie. He was beginning to show signs of being overweight due to a general lack of exercise and attempted to compensate for it by wearing clothes that clearly had come to be too tight. His hair was light brown and neatly combed. He was by far the best dressed and the most educated of the bunch.

"So what's up boss?" Skinner asked as Lou Walizak entered his office with a thin Hispanic man Skinner had never met before.

"Sorry for the short notice but we needed to meet tonight," responded Lou as he sat behind his desk. "Gentlemen, this is Sergio Cervantes, a conscientious and loyal member of our union that works at the Wilford Hotel." All nodded their heads acknowledging the new guy to their group. After brief introductions were made, Lou continued. "I have asked Sergio to keep me informed of what our new General Manager has been up to since his arrival. It is possible that this Mr. Oliver is not familiar with exactly who we are and may need to be further educated." All smiled with the exception of Mickey Selecki who looked on uncomfortably.

Skinner was again the first to speak. "Is there some reason why we are so interested in this particular hotel and GM boss?"

"For the time being, let's just say there is," replied Lou, evasive in answering Skinner's questions directly. "My concern is that Oliver may present problems if not properly dealt with."

Lou then motioned to Sergio who briefly summarized his observations of how Jake Oliver was being positively received by most of the staff. He then shared what he had overheard of the confrontation that had occurred between Jake and the owner's representative Jackson Chi.

Lou interrupted at that point "Sergio, did anyone know what the argument was about?"

"It is believed the argument had something to do with Mr. Oliver's visit to see the architect in charge of the renovation, but I have no way of confirming this." Sergio responded nervously, hoping his comments would impress the union president.

"Very well, anything else Sergio?" Lou asked, seeming to grow impatient all of a sudden.

"No, but I can keep snooping around if you____"

"Yes, that would be a good idea," interrupted Lou. "Thank you Mr. Cervantes, your efforts will not go unnoticed. Now if you will excuse us, we have some other matters to discuss."

Sergio quickly stood appearing flustered and departed quickly. Once he was gone, Lou turned to others in the room. "Gentlemen, all I can tell each of you at this time is that I have several important deals in the works and the last thing any of us need is a nosey boy scout messing up our plans." Lou turned to Skinner and continued. "Skinner, I need you to join Sammy in tailing this Oliver guy. He can fill you in on what he knows so far and we should also keep an eye on his wife's activities for the time being. Let's just find out all we can about them before we make any further plans.

Skinner looked genuinely surprised at this comment. "You mean Smitty here has already been tailing him, boss?"

"That's right, but I think this may call for your special talents," Lou stated as he walked over and patted him on the shoulder, a broad smile appearing on his round face.

What Lou was referring to was a job he had given to Skinner a few years prior. Lou had Skinner follow the wife of a department manager at a large hotel during contract negotiations for several weeks. When it was apparent to Lou that the negotiations were not going as planned he had Skinner advise the hotel manager what would happen to his young bride if he did not steal relevant documents from the hotel to get a jump on the hotel's position. Skinner advised the manager that if he failed to do what he was told, his wife would be taken for a ride she would never forget. After the manager completed the illegal activity, Skinner proceeded anyway in kidnapping the man's wife because, as he put it, she was just too good looking to pass up. Skinner was even successful in putting such fear in the minds of both the manager and his wife that both moved away from San Francisco and never attempted to file charges against him for what he had done.

CHAPTER FOURTEEN

"Working late tonight aren't we?" Asked Jim Slazenger as he stood at the entrance to Laura Sander's office.

Laura looked up startled. "What…oh, yeah, I thought I would just catch up on a few things."

Jim smiled. "I guess these negotiations do tend to get us a little anxious." He then noticed that her desk was relatively clear and she appeared to have changed into a more revealing dress and she had a little more make up on then usual. "Plans for later, Laura?"

She looked down at her desk embarrassed by his question. "Well…yes. If you must know, I have a date tonight."

Jim gave her a slight bow. "Sorry to pry. Have a great night and don't work too hard." Jim then picked up his briefcase and left for home.

………………………………………

Jake arrived home around 7 o'clock that evening the end to another long day. His concerns with the information he had gathered that day weighed heavily and his wife Marilyn had learned to read these looks well. She also new that Jake would share his concerns at the appropriate time and would not press him until he was ready.

Marilyn greeted her husband with a brief kiss at the door then returned to the kitchen. A gourmet cook by every definition, Marilyn adamantly denied having such skills. Her collection of over 500 cookbooks, a silent testimony to her desire to constantly expand her cooking expertise. Tonight, however, life was going to be far simpler. It was meatloaf night and the aroma in the house was well received by the rest of the family. "Jake, I hope you remembered that Naomi is coming over for dinner tonight."

Jake sighed, frankly he did not feel like entertaining tonight but Naomi Shu had been a good realtor and become a new friend to Marilyn. "Is this a formal evening or are we keeping it casual?"

"Oh, very casual. Meatloaf to be specific." Marilyn responded from the kitchen.

Sarah and Briana were playing in their room as Jake walked down the hallway to the master bedroom. He knocked on the door to make sure he did not embarrass his young ladies and they both responded in unison "Who.....is.....it!

Jake smiled as he attempted to think of a new and witty response to the same question he was greeted with each evening. "Tom Cruise! I was told two extremely attractive young ladies lived here and I am here to take both of you to dinner."

Jake heard both girls giggle as they prepared their response. Sarah the oldest and never at a loss for words said, "what about your new *girlfriend*?"

"Oh...her? Well, she said she thought it would be O.K. as long as your father approved." Jake responded, not having a clue who this celebrity's latest girlfriend might be.

Quick a usual, however, Sarah threw open the door responding, "Oh, it's O.K. with him, he says I can go out with whoever I want!"

Jake dropped to his knees and grabbed her before she could start running. "Oh he does, does he!" Briana laughing came running and jumped in his arms as well.

"What are you two up to?"

"Today, I am teaching Briana her multiplication tables." Sarah responded, now assuming her teacher voice and mannerisms.

"I see. And Briana, is your sister a good teacher?"

"Yes she is. Every time I get a right answer she gives me an M&M candy."

"I see. Sarah, is this the way it will be when Briana starts school next week?"

Sarah looked at her father sheepishly. "Well, not exactly."

Jake smiled then patted both on the head and advised them to save some room for dinner. He then went to the master bedroom to change into jeans and a sweatshirt. He poured himself a smooth, smokey single malt scotch, his one key vice and sat in his favorite overstuffed chair by the fireplace and began reading the newspaper. Forty-five minutes later, with his mind somewhat cleared of the days events, he joined his wife in the kitchen.

Marilyn relayed her activities of the day that included shopping for school clothes and supplies in preparation for the girls to start school the following day. Jake then described his confrontation with Jackson Chi and his unclear conversation with Ed Lee. Marilyn listened intently, her concern apparent on her face.

"What do you think is going on?" She asked as the girls turned on the television to watch the Disney channel in the next room.

"I am not sure yet, but I must admit that the more I dig the more interesting things become. Something is just not right at this hotel and I intend to ask a lot more questions. Are you concerned?"

"A little." Marilyn had to admit. "It's just that after the problems you had at your last hotel, I hate to see you getting into another mess."

"Well, that was not my choice then and it isn't this time either is it?" Jake replied with a slight tinge of annoyance at the reference to the difficulties he had experienced with his previous employer.

"Sorry," Marilyn acknowledged, "I know. It's just uncanny that, what appeared to be such a good company has to have some possible skeletons in the closet."

Jake smiled. "Yeah, I do have a knack for finding the good ones, don't I."

Just as Marilyn was putting the last of the dishes on the table the doorbell rang. Jake greeted Naomi and informed her that her timing was perfect. Naomi reminded him that she did not have far to travel given that she only lived five blocks away.

....

Jim Slazenger walked in the door of their two bedroom apartment that was less than four blocks from the Wilford. He was greeted to the aroma of lasagna cooking in the oven. "Mmmm…something sure smells good!"

"Well, it's about time you got home. Now put your butt in a chair at the table and prepare to eat at Linda's Italian bistro." Linda Slazenger said as she quickly walked from the kitchen, gave him a quick peck on the cheek and then returned wiping her hands on the apron she wore. From the kitchen she asked. "Anything exciting at work today?"

Jim dropped his briefcase on the couch and proceeded to the kitchen. "Nothing too exciting. We have a full house for the next few nights but all appears to be running smoothly, we are getting things ready for our negotiations with Local #78 and Jake met with Ed Lee today."

"Oh…he probably got told the same as everyone else."

"Now if I was in charge, I'd start knocking some heads to get some answers."

"Yes, that would be a very proper thing to do," responded Linda sarcastically. "Now with a temper like that, you are never going to have your own hotel."

"Perhaps," nodded Jim, "but I can assure you the rumors about me sure would be something to write about."

Linda looked at him questioningly. "What are you talking about?"

"Later today, Jake and Jackson Chi got in to it. We could hear them yelling at each other in the outer office. Jackson stormed out and tripped or something. By the end of the day, the word in the hotel was that Jake and Jackson had duked it out."

Both chuckled at Jim's last comment. "What were they arguing about?"

Jim suddenly grew serious. "Let's just say that the new guy is beginning to snoop around."

"Anything we need to worry about."

Jim nodded his head slowly. "Perhaps."

……………………………………

Naomi Shu returned from an enjoyable evening at the Oliver's. She lived in a modest but nicely furnished home that, as she had mentioned to the Oliver's earlier, was conveniently only five blocks away. Her familiarity with the neighborhood had been the key reason she had known of the home for sale and was pleased that all had gone as planned and that the Oliver's had chosen to purchase the home. For most realtors, they would have been excited about the commission they would be making on the sale of the home, but Naomi was more concerned with the phone call she was about to make. What also bothered Naomi, was the constant lying and the putting on of appearances she was being forced to do to get individuals to trust her and believe in her. Sometimes she wondered if she even believed in herself anymore. The Oliver's seemed like good people and she had especially grown to like Marilyn and the kids. But Naomi Shu had been given her assignment and, as usual she had performed her task with the utmost precision.

Realizing she could not avoid making the phone call any longer, Naomi dialed the number. It rang only two times and the voice that answered made every nerve in her body go rigid. The voice simply said, "Is it done?"

"Yes," Naomi responded.

"And they suspect nothing?"

"No, all has gone as planned. I will keep you informed as we discussed."

"Excellent. This calls for a celebration, perhaps I should stop by later this evening to see you?" The true arrogance of the man behind the voice was apparent through phone.

Naomi hesitated briefly before responding, "No, not tonight, I have plans to___."

The man's voice grew stern. "Yes, you do have plans. I will come later to see you." He then abruptly hung up.

Naomi stared at the phone and thought back to how she had come to this point in her life. It had been ten years earlier when she lived in Hong Kong and had accepted, what she thought would be a great job working for one of thc city's largest shipping companies. She was right out of school, 22 years old and ready to launch a career. The position she had applied for involved assisting corporate executives of the company who were relocating abroad outside of Hong Kong throughout the world. Naomi viewed this job as her opportunity to apply her education in real estate and see the world. At first, all appeared to be going as planned. Then she was informed that her job was to include various illegal and immoral actions to assure these individuals remained loyal to the organization while away from their homeland. When Naomi attempted to protest, she was politely informed of the consequences of what would happen to her if she disobeyed her instructions or attempted to leave the organization or contact the authorities. She was trapped.

When the organization began purchasing vast amounts of real estate in the United States, particularly in California, Naomi was advised to move to San Francisco and coordinate her responsibilities from there. That had been five years ago and, although she lived a comfortable life style in one of the worlds most glamorous and romantic cities, she personally did not feel glamorous and certainly not romantic with the likes of the man that was planning to call on her later that evening.

....

Laura Sanders entered the dark restaurant and was directed to a booth in the back. At first she thought she had arrived too early but then she saw the man she was there to meet. He quickly stood and helped her remove her coat as she sat across from him. He kissed her lightly on the cheek and then again took his seat and addressed her for the first time. "You look great, Laura, new dress?"

Laura blushed at the compliment. For the past few months with her divorce in the final stages, she had not felt particularly attractive and was highly self-conscious of her age. But the man sitting across from her had simply swept her off her feet. He was young, however, in fact he was almost 10 years younger and, for the time being, she had been uncomfortable mentioning him to anyone at work.

They had met quite by accident one day when Laura's car wouldn't start in a grocery store parking lot. She was about to call AAA when this good looking man walked up and tapped on the window. He had asked if she needed any help. At first Laura was going to wave him off but there was something about the way he looked at her, or rather lusted after her, that captured her interest. They began to talk and eventually, Laura chose to take caution to the wind and she let him drive her home.

The next day, she received a call from him and, after a little further coaxing, she agreed to go out to dinner. That had been roughly one month ago and now Laura was simply overwhelmed with where this new romance may be taking her. She looked across the table at the young beautiful man still asking herself why he was interested in her when he could easily take his pick of the female population. But whatever it was, he seemed thoroughly interested in her, her work, her kids, everything.

He then reached for the bottle of wine he had selected prior to her arrival and poured it into her glass. "So, good looking, how was your day at, what's the name of the hotel again, the Wilford?"

CHAPTER FIFTEEN

Marilyn's day was packed with a variety of errands to run. She dropped Sarah and Briana off at their new school. As usual it was Marilyn that was more anxiety about each starting at a new school rather than her two daughters. When they were dropped off, each walked off with their lunch and seemed to get engulfed by other kids as they neared the main entrance to the school.

Part of the reason the Oliver's had chosen this neighborhood was the strong reputation of the school and it's convenient location less than two miles away. The school covered grades 1 through 6 and featured the latest technology in educational systems as well as a large fenced in playground that was well supervised. The school had a reputation for being extremely safety conscious, which both Jake and Marilyn appreciated being in a large metropolitan city such as San Francisco.

On her way to the grocery after dropping off Jake's shirts at a nearby dry cleaner, Marilyn heard the screech of tires and horns blaring behind her. In her rear view mirror, she noted that a black sedan had apparently run the red light. Marilyn just shook her head in disgust. Since the light was already yellow when she crossed the intersection, the guy in that car was clearly running the red light. What was his hurry she wondered.

She returned to the house at 10 o'clock to unload the groceries and then got on the internet to research genealogy on her family, a favorite hobby. She had about an hour to work on her project before changing for lunch. Sandra Kelly, her husband's secretary had called her the day before and invited her to lunch to get better acquainted.

As Marilyn backed out of the garage for her luncheon appointment, she noticed a man sitting in a dark sedan at the end of the block. Although she found this a little out of the ordinary she assumed he was waiting for someone.

The restaurant that Sandra had chosen was a trendy bistro located one block off Union Square. It featured valet parking which suited Marilyn just fine given the traffic downtown. She turned her car over to the parking attendant and entered the restaurant. Almost immediately she heard Sandra call out her name and proceeded to where she was standing at one end of the bar. "Your right on time. They said they could seat us now if you are ready?"

"Absolutely," Marilyn responded.

After the waiter took their drink orders and departed, Sandra spoke. "Marilyn, I am so glad you could join me today. Are you just about settled in your new home?"

"Actually, I have to admit that it is starting to look like we have lived there for a while. So, yeah, I guess we are settled."

The waiter delivered their drinks and took their lunch orders.

Sandra fidgeted with the straw to her drink nervously.

"Marilyn, I thought we should get to know each other better. Your husband is such a pleasure to work for and he is already greatly admired by the rest of the staff."

"I'm glad to hear that." Marilyn acknowledged, as she pondered what was really on Sandra's mind. Jake had shared with her his concerns regarding her somewhat mysterious past, how she had come to work for the Wilford, and his questions regarding her true loyalties to him or someone else.

"I am a little concerned, however," Sandra continued, "your husband appears to be an honest and highly ethical individual and I am afraid that his inquiries regarding the hotel may get him in trouble."

Marilyn considered her response carefully. "Sandra, Jake has been managing hotels for a long time. A key to our relationship has always been that I have never tried to tell him how to do his job and I have no intention of starting now."

"I can appreciate that greatly," Sandra nodded, "it's just that Jake may be dealing with some very bad people."

"Who?"

Sandra again hesitated as if she was internally struggling as to what to say. "Look, all I can say is that Jake is starting to ask questions that could get him in trouble. They're not nice people and they're not ethical."

Marilyn studied the young lady sitting across from her. She seemed genuinely concerned. Could it be that she really was afraid for Jake or was this some type of warning that Jake should back off from what he was doing. And if Sandra was telling the truth, could Jake actually be in some form of danger? "Sandra, if you know something you need to discuss this with my husband right away."

"I will, but it is difficult to talk at work. All I wanted to do was have you warn him to be careful and be very careful who he chooses to trust."

Just then the waiter returned with their food. Both remained silent until the waiter departed.

"Sandra, if you know something more than you are telling me, I need to hear it."

"Marilyn, I don't know anything specific but something is going on at the hotel and I felt you should know."

Both women continued to eat their food in relative silence. Marilyn decided to change the subject for the moment and try to get to know Sandra better. Through a series of informal questions she found out that Sandra had a three-year-old daughter and was divorced. Marilyn clearly sensed that she felt uncomfortable talking about her ex-husband which coincided with what she had told Jake.

When the bill came, Marilyn was quick to pick up the check. Sandra argued. "Marilyn, I invited you, therefore, this is my treat."

Marilyn shook her head. "Well, to be honest, I am not sure what to think of what you have told me but I will share your concerns with Jake."

"Good, that's all I can ask. I just did not feel comfortable having this conversation with him at work." Both women then left the restaurant and handed the valet their parking tickets. As they waited for their cars to be brought up to the entrance of the restaurant, Marilyn happened to turn and just catch a glimpse of a man leaving a coffee shop down the street. She felt she recognized him but couldn't place where.

"See someone you know?" Sandra asked noticing the confused look on Marilyn's face as she continued to watch the man walk down the street and then turn the corner out of sight.

"No…I mean, yes, that man down the street. He looks familiar but I can't place where I have seen him." Marilyn turned to Sandra. "It's nothing."

"Well, this is my car. Thanks for lunch and please tell Jake to be careful. If I find out anything further, I will let both of you know." She then jumped in her car and drove off.

It was not until Marilyn was in her car that it had dawned on her that Sandra had turned the corner and drove off in a direction opposite the hotel. She looked forward to seeing Jake tonight and relaying what had been discussed. As she drove to pick up her daughters at school she thought. *Having her husband's secretary warn her that her husband may be in danger was a first. What the hell was going on here?*

Marilyn only had to wait a few minutes at the school before the girls ran to the car and they headed for home. She was about to turn on the street where they lived when she remembered she had forgotten to pick up the dry cleaning dropped off earlier that day. The street was relatively deserted at that time of day so she quickly made a U-turn and preceded in the opposite direction. A black sedan passed and the man driving made an effort to look away as they passed. The car caught Marilyn's eye but at first she did not know why. What struck her was that this man appeared out of place on their neighborhood street.

As she entered the dry cleaner, it all started to come together. The car that ran the red light behind her, the man she saw as she left the restaurant with Sandra, and now when she turned the car around to come to the dry cleaners. *Could this be the same man and the same car?*

When leaving the dry cleaner, her anxiety was high and all the way home she was constantly studying her rear view mirror and looking down side streets. Sarah and Briana also sense her tension.

"Mommy, is something wrong?" Asked Sarah from the back seat.

"No nothing honey, it has just been a long day."

Later that evening after the kids had gone to bed, Jake and Marilyn decided to sit out in the back yard and enjoy the cool fog as it rolled in from the ocean which was less than ½ mile away from their home. Marilyn relayed her discussion with Sandra and her suspicions that someone may be following her.

Jake initially downplayed her concerns as that of an over-active imagination following her lunch with Sandra. But he also knew his wife was not one to jump to conclusions lightly. In fact, Marilyn was more of a pessimist when it came to far fetched conclusions. She was also keenly observant knowing where the girls were at all times when we were together.

Jake pondered how best to respond. "Perhaps there is more to this than I had originally thought. Let's keep our eyes open and be careful." He commented. "Now let's get some sleep, its late.

....

In a small bedroom at the end of a hallway sat a table with electronic surveillance equipment. The operator reviewed the equipment with great frustration. The evening conversations had been quite uneventful dominated by young girls talking about their new school and the new classmates they had met. After the girls had gone to bed, however, there had been nothing. Was the equipment not functioning properly?

Then, all of a sudden there were voices again.

"It's a wonderful night out tonight," said a female voice.

"Yeah, I like the fog but it was starting to get a little too cold for me. You lock the door?" Replied a male voice.

"Of course. You get the lights."

The operator heard little after that other than the usual noises one would expect coming from a bedroom after the kids were asleep and, also dreaded not having anything to tell her employer. He would be angry and it was not good to make him angry.

CHAPTER SIXTEEN

Jake started the day by arriving far earlier than usual to review the financial records of the hotel in more depth before his accounting staff arrived. It was also his intent to do a little snooping around. His master keys opened the door to the accounting department and he began to look in various file draws. At first all appeared in order, then he discovered a locked cabinet that he was not able to access. He would bring this up with Mr. Hoy when he arrived later that morning.

Jake retreated back to his office after making a quick pass through the back of the house to conduct his usual rounds and greetings to his staff. When he returned to his office and sat down to his second cup of coffee, there was a knock at his door. Standing in the doorway was a short stocky man dressed somewhat shabbily in a dark blue suit that should have been replaced a couple of years prior.

"I heard you were an early riser. I'm Lou Walizak."

Jake stood and approached his guest with an extended hand. "Mr. Walizak, I have been remiss in not getting over to see you before now. But you know what it's like in a new job."

"Yeah, getting settled can be a hassle I guess. In my case, however, I have lived here in San Francisco my entire life and worked for local #78 the majority of that time." Lou replied proudly.

Jake smiled at the man standing before him. "Yes, there is something to be said for stability in your life. I guess for me, I am just too restless to stay put for too long. Some coffee?"

"No thanks I can only stay a moment. I just wanted to introduce myself and get acquainted with what I hope will be a new partner rather than a new adversary." Lou stared at Jake looking for some type of reaction.

"Well, we'll see won't we." Jake replied figuring he might as well goat this pushy guy some.

"Mr. Oliver, believe me when I say that my organization is here to work with your hotel in every way possible. You have been in the business for a while and you know how the game is played. You take care of me, and I will take care of you. That seems fair enough doesn't it?"

"I see, and if taking care of you is not possible?" Jake asked anticipating an interesting response.

Lou looked at the man sitting across the desk from him cautiously. "Well, that could be a problem couldn't it? Let's just say, we will cross that bridge if it occurs. But now, I must leave I have another appointment." Lou stood and walked toward the door then turned to face Jake. "One other thing, Mr. Oliver, I understand that prior to arriving in San Francisco you were in Santa Barbara…Nice town. I bet the views of the ocean from your hotel were great." Jake nodded his head slowly realizing that Mr. Walizak had apparently done a little homework. "At least when the room is not on fire."

Lou then departed as suddenly as he had appeared while Jake stood there stunned by his last remark. It cut deep into memories that Jake would have preferred to forget. Jake took his seat and looked across his desk. He was then lost in thought of the events that Lou Walizak had so abruptly reminded him about.

It was during Jake's previous position as General Manager of an ocean side resort near Santa Barbara, California that he faced one of the most difficult challenges in his career. It all started out much the same as previous assignments but into the second year, Jake began to uncover that his owners had cut corners and falsified records related to fire and safety standards. The cutbacks were all done to save money and the thought of saving lives had been clearly overlooked. The results of this decision later forced many to question Jake's own personal involvement following that terrible night in July.

It had been a typical sunny southern California day offering perfect weather for the city's annual festivities. Every 4th of July, the beach area adjacent to the resort played host to over 300,000 people coming to view one of the most spectacular fire works displays in the state. Conveniently, the resort that Jake operated was strategically located in the heart of this activity and offered all of its guests impressive views of the fireworks from the privacy of their own guest room balconies.

This past 4th of July had been no exception and the hotel had been sold out three months prior. Such an event did, however, come with its share of challenges for Jake and his staff. Increased levels of staffing in all departments were required and contrary to the direction of the resort owners, Jake substantially increased the levels of security during events such as these. The goal was for all guests to have a good time, but when unsupervised drinking was involved, Jake knew from experience that disruptions could always occur. Jake's foresight proved to be more accurate than anyone could have imagined.

The night was clear and the fireworks lit up the sky in a myriad of colors and bright flashes that generated the usual 'oohs and ahs'. Later that evening in one of the resorts bars, a few got a little over zealous. This prompted the hotel's security staff to insist that they sleep it off in their room. One young man, however, was a little more difficult. In his case he chose to take a swing at Jake while they spoke outside the *Sea Cove Lounge*. Two security officers restrained him and the hotel arranged for him to spend a comfortable night at the Santa Barbara jail.

Jake left the hotel at 11 o'clock that evening and went home for the evening. When he left, four security guards remained on watch for the night. All activities seemed to have calmed down at that point. When Jake walked in the door of his home, not only did he feel tired, but Marilyn clarified it by stating how bad he looked. Within the hour, Jake was in bed and out for what he thought was the rest of the night.

The phone abruptly rang at 2:30 am. He quickly sat up but, having been in such a deep state of sleep, he was momentarily confused by what had awakened him. Marilyn came to Jake's rescue by pointing and confirming to him that it was the phone next to the bed. As is the case for most individuals, a phone call at that time of the night or morning always generates a certain amount of anxiety but for a

General Manager of a hotel it almost always means something bad has occurred.

Jake answered the phone and was quickly informed that a fire had broken out at the resort. His chief of security further stated that the fire department was just arriving and that the resort's guests were being evacuated as they spoke.

Jake quickly dressed and arrived at the hotel less then 20 minutes later. The scene upon his arrival was utter chaos. Three fire trucks were on the scene with roughly 400 guests in various state of dress standing in the parking lot. Jake quickly located the fire chief who provided him a more detailed summary of what had occurred.

Apparently a fire had broken out in a housekeeping storage room on the second floor. A guest named John Chandler first reported the smoke. He and his family were staying in the room closest to the location of the fire. Mr. Chandler stated that when he opened the door to their room, the corridor was already filled with smoke. He quickly gathered his wife and kids and ran from the room. As they ran down the corridor he pounded on the doors of the rooms on the 2nd floor yelling 'fire!'

Another guest apparently showed the wisdom to call down to the front desk that then notified security. The first officer on the scene, quickly pulled the nearest fire alarm pull station and the horns sounded throughout the entire resort.

Jake quickly located his chief of security to confirm that the resort had been completely evacuated. He was told that both the hotel's security as well as the firemen that were now on the floors were coordinating a room to room search.

At that moment an explosion erupted from a room on the second floor. Apparently the fire had spread into that room and the heat and pressure resulted in the window of the room being blown out. Guests in the parking lot jumped at the explosion. And so did Jake.

The next 45 minutes were some of the longest Jake had experienced until he was advised that the fire had been contained. Jake was then escorted to the location of the fire. Because that particular storeroom contained various paper products used in guestrooms, the fire had spread quickly. After it had engulfed the closet and burned through the door that opened onto the corridor it flared and entered room 246. When Jake arrived, two firemen had finished hosing down the room and were beginning to remove the charred furnishings.

The fire chief walked up and patted him on the back. “Quite a mess you have here, Mr. Hotel Manager.” The fire chief was a man named Mitch Sullivan, who Jake had become a reasonably good friend with through weekly Rotary lunches that were held at the resort. Jake looked around in disbelief at how much damage had occurred.

“It sure is. Mitch, all of the guests and staff...did everyone get out?”

“We're still checking now, Jake. But we may have a problem.” The somber look on his face indicated that it must be something quite serious.

“What is it Mitch?”

“It's the sprinkler system, Jake. It didn't go off like it was supposed to. There is also the question of what started the fire. We may be dealing with arson on this one.”

Jake looked at the pipes for the sprinkler system in the burned out storage closet. Just as he started to ask Mitch another question, the radio on Mitch's belt sounded.

“Unit two to base.”

“Base. Go ahead Charlie.”

“Boss, I'm up on three. Directly above where the fire started.” There was a long pause, which prompted Jake and Mitch to look at each other questioningly. “Mitch, we have some casualties.” The finality of these words hit both men as if the walls of the corridor they were standing in had come crashing down.

Jake and Mitch quickly ran up the stairs to the 3rd floor and fireman Charlie Stein moved aside from the doorway to room 342. Inside, they viewed a mother, father and two sons. Two paramedics had apparently already tried to revive the two children but without success. They had now moved to work on the man and woman. Jake and Mitch watched helplessly until one of the paramedics looked up and shook his head somberly. Jake later learned that all had been huddled in the bathroom and apparently had been overtaken by the smoke.

Four guests died that evening and the subsequent investigation that followed put Jake in the middle of one the city's most controversial lawsuits.

The owners of the hotel immediately wanted to wash their hands of the entire matter and Jake was accused of negligence for the entire incident. Had it not been for Jake's own survival instincts and cunning, he would have ended up in jail. The press never clearly documented what happened but all of a sudden, Jake was cleared of all charges, and it was announced that he was leaving the hotel for another position.

Sandra entered the office to find her boss staring out the window lost in thought. "Jake, what was *he* doing here. Did you have an appointment with him?"

Jake continued to stare out the window as he responded. "Appointment? A…no, he just showed up to say hi I guess."

Sandra assumed that Lou's comment, which she had overheard at the door, must have disturbed him. "Jake, watch out for that snake. He is bad news and not to be trusted. In fact, he is dangerous."

"Dangerous? You mean with his bad impression of being a Mafia boss."

"Yeah, well, he may seem like a joke, but he does not play games. There have been stories of how he and his goons have harassed those who fight him."

Jake smiled trying to change the mood. "Well, let me worry about that. I am aware of Mr. Walizak's reputation for having friends in low places."

…………………………………………

In another part of town, someone else was getting an early start on the day. Ed Lee arrived at this office before the rest of his staff. He closed the door to his office and placed a call from a special phone he kept in a locked cabinet. It took several seconds for the call to be processed due to the encryption device attached to avoid the call being overheard by unwanted parties.

His call was answered promptly and Ed spoke. "He is performing as we expected…..How do you want me to proceed?….No, nothing so far….You will have to speak to him soon….yes, yes very well."

The line then went dead and Ed hung up as Cathy, his wife entered with two cups of hot tea.

"You called?"

"Yes."

"What are you going to do?"

"My options are limited. Are they not?"

"Perhaps, but you will figure something out." Cathy smiled at her husband and departed to her office to start the day.

……………………………………………

Jake walked into the accounting department and hour after his previous exploratory visit to find the entire staff now in place and diligently at work. Cordial greetings were shared as Jake proceeded to Tony's office.

"What can I do for you this morning Mr. Jake?"

"Tony, I would like to get more familiar with how this office is organized. Got some time to show me around?"

Tony gave Jake a cursory tour of the office explaining each clerk's tasks and how and where documents were filed. He quickly passed by the file cabinet Jake had noted as locked during his earlier visit to the office.

"Tony, what files are kept in this cabinet?" Jake asked watching Tony's reaction to the question.

Tony hesitated momentarily. "Mainly documents that should be secure such as blank checks, key financial records, and other such documents."

"Can we have a look?" Jake persisted.

Tony hesitated. "Mr. Jake, there are also documents of Mr. Chi's that I was told no one is to see."

"If they are so private to Mr. Chi, why are they kept in this office?" Jake continued.

"Because they involve the hotel and all such documents must remain at the hotel under my control at all times. This is a strict policy established by Samuel Cho himself." Tony replied nervously. "I insisted on it."

"Well, I am pleased to here that you firmly adhere to this policy. In turn, since I am the General Manager of this hotel, shouldn't I also have access to this information?"

"Mr. Jake, you asked me to do something that is difficult."

"Tony, let me ask you this, does Samuel Cho know about these documents of Mr. Chi's?"

"I...I would assume so." Tony responded but the look on his face contradicted his words.

"Tony, if information in those files relates to this hotel, then I must have access to this information."

Tony signaled Jake to follow him back to his office and closed the door. "Mr. Jake, I cannot show you this information. Mr. Chi has told me not show anyone."

Jake looked at Tony and saw the conflict he was experiencing internally in his eyes "All right Tony, what if, for the time being, we just keep this between the two of us. What if we meet back here around, say, 9 o'clock tonight? You could show me the documents and no one would have to know for the time being. How does that sound?"

Tony quickly considered this plan. "Yes, yes, that should be fine. I will meet you here at that time. But sir, no one can know of this." The urgency was apparent in his voice.

Jake departed the accounting department and returned to his office. As he walked, his mind speculated what information the documents would contain. He had uncovered that Jackson Chi had secret documents that may open up some doors. He had met Mr. Walizak, who could prove to be a worthier adversary than he had expected. And now he was going to play James Bond and return to his own hotel later tonight to rendezvous with his own controller.

....

Jake arrived home for dinner and found Marilyn in the kitchen. "Did you see the mystery follower today?"

"No," responded Marilyn making a face at her husband's smart-ass remark. "Today was about as normal as it gets. Dropped the girls off at school, did the laundry, took out the trash. Which by the way, isn't that your job?"

"Well yes, but James Bond does not have time for such trivial things as taking out the trash."

"Well, tell me what you found out James." Marilyn replied in mock humor.

Jake then summarized his early visit to accounting, his meeting with Lou Walizak and his plans to return to the hotel later that evening to meet with Tony Hoy. On the last issue, Marilyn's attitude changed and her face registered visible concern.

"Jake, I don't like this. Meeting your department managers after hours to view files in secret? What's really going on here?"

"I don't know, but I intend to find out." Jake then went to say hello to his daughters.

....

When Naomi Shu returned after a late dinner meeting with a couple in the final stages of making an offer on a house she was selling, she proceeded to her room to change but first stopped in the guest bedroom. The recording surveillance equipment had captured the entire conversation between Jake and Marilyn Oliver just prior to her arrival. She then picked up the phone and dialed her *real* employer. After several rings a male voice answered.

"Yes?"

"I thought you should know that something is going on tonight. Jake Oliver is meeting his controller at the hotel at nine this evening. Something about some documents in the accounting office."

"Very good, my dear. This makes up for your incompetence from the night before. Good bye." The voice on the phone hung up abruptly. She then made her a second call that evening.

....

In a bar that most would not feel comfortable even walking by at night, the man at the bar felt right at home. Skinner hated his current assignment of following a woman and her kids around all day and longed for a little more excitement. His shift was during the day and Smitty, his informal partner, covered the nights. Where was this going he thought. Although he couldn't argue that he was paid well and it sure beat the days when he actually had to work at hotels and put up with bull shit managers telling him what to do. It was just so boring sitting in a car and following someone else around all day. Granted this Oliver lady had given him quite a stir when she turned around on him on that side street before he made it around the corner. Hell he almost ran in to her and he was still concerned that she may have seen his face. Damn.

Just then his pager went off.

"Hey Charlie, hand me the phone, I gotta make a call."

"What's wrong with using the pay phone in the back?" Responded the bartender.

"Fuck you ass hole, just give me the phone," shouted Skinner.

"Yeah, yeah, here you go! And make it quick."

Skinner made the call and listened for a few minutes.

"Yeah, I got it, don't sweat it, I'll take care of it."

He then paid his tab and left the bar quickly.

CHAPTER SEVENTEEN

Jake left his house at 8:30 p.m. for the 30-minute drive back to the hotel. He did not anticipate much traffic on *Upper Market Street* at that time of night. Five blocks from the Wilford, however, the traffic came to a complete stop. At first, because of a slight bend in the street, he was not able to determine what was causing the delay. As the cars began to move slowly, however, he realized that there had been a bad accident of some type.

Flashing lights reflected off the fronts of the businesses that were now closed for the evening and lined each side of the street. Jake noticed that people were gathering at the scene. As his car neared the location of the accident, behind the procession of cars that were being diverted to the center lane by police officers, he could see a car that had apparently lost control and driven up on the sidewalk and collided with a glassed in bus stop. Suddenly there was a gap in the crowd of people standing around and he could see the paramedics and police on the scene working on, what Jake assumed was the driver of the vehicle or possibly a pedestrian that had been hit while waiting at the bus stop.

As Jake brought his car adjacent to the accident and was no more than 30 feet away, the realization of what had occurred hit him. Apparently, this had been a drive by shooting. The windows of the car were shattered and there were many bullet holes in the driver's side car door. The windshield of the car was riddled with bullet holes and the glass was distorted by the spider web cracks typical of safety glass installed on new cars. At first Jake thought the driver's side window was down but then realized that it had been completely blown away by the shooters.

Scanning the damage to what appeared to be a Honda Accord, he then noticed there was a lot of blood mixed with the glass on the sidewalk surrounding the car and, although Jake could not see much, he assumed that the injuries had to be quite serious. Probably some gang related shooting Jake thought.

Once out of the congestion he used his cellular phone to contact Tony at the hotel and advise him that he would be a few minutes late. Surprisingly there was no answer. Jake assumed Tony was running late as well.

Jake always parked in the same reserved spot on the second level of the parking garage. His space was near the stairs for quick access to the rear employee entrance. The parking garage was located under the rear wings of the hotel and consisted of four levels. The section of rooms above the garage had been added to the hotel in 1937 and extended across an alley in which all service deliveries were made for the hotel. This was somewhat inconvenient for guests to use but great for the hotel's staff and office tenants who did not want to keep their car parked at nearby lots or on the street. At night, however, the garage and alley were usually quite deserted and void of activity.

Jake pulled into the parking garage at 9:15 p.m. and noticed that many of the overhead lights on the second level of the garage were out making visibility extremely poor. He made a mental note to advise engineering to replace them promptly for security purposes.

As he got out of his shinny black Jaguar, that seemed to be absorbed by the darkness when the headlights were turned off, he heard movement nearby and turned quickly. A voice in the dark then spoke. "Nice car Mister...Oliver, right?

Jake could not see the face of the voice that addressed him but observed the glow of a cigarette in the dark. He then heard the sounds of multiple footsteps approach. At first he could still not see who the men were but as they stepped forward to within ten feet of the car the forms of three men could be seen from the little bit of light that came in from the street lamp in the alley. Two of the men appeared to be very large both in height and weight and the third was more thin and wiry in appearance, none of which Jake recognized. As Jake considered what he had done to deserve being stuck in a deserted parking garage with three goons like this he responded cautiously. "Since you appear to already know who I am, what is it you want?"

It was the smallest of the three that responded. "You know, Mr. Oliver, you keep poking your ass around places it don't belong and you may find yourself in a accident like your Chinese friend."

At first the impact of the man's words did not completely register with Jake as he glared at these men. Their faces were masked in the shadows. But as the reality of what the man was referring to hit him he felt momentarily sick to his stomach. They were referring to Tony Hoy and the accident he had just driven by had been one of his executive managers and new ally lying on the stretcher. Jake's momentary fear was immediately replaced with anger. "That was Tony…in the car?"

"Yeah, whatever his name was. Pay attention ass hole and don't think about trying to be a hero. You'll only get hurt." Said the smaller man who appeared to be the leader of this trio. "You keep nosing around and others like you and your family are going to…well let's just say…have an accident also. You got that, Mr. Manager?"

Jake considered all that was happening at that moment. "I'm not sure I know what you are talking about. What exactly am I supposed to not be doing?"

"Don't get smart!" Shouted the lead man as he threw his cigarette down sharply. "Just ask yourself this question…what are you doing here tonight?" Jake looked at the man intensely as he continued. "Get the picture *now* smart guy?"

The sound of a car or truck in the alley interrupted the sudden silence that had followed these last words. Jake then heard footsteps of someone walking up the ramp from the lower parking level and he turned to see who was approaching. When Jake returned his gaze to the three men in front of him, they had already turned and were walking down the nearby stairs. As they departed one of the guys commented. "That sure is a pretty wife and cute kids you got mister…let's hope nothing happens to them." The other two broke into laughter then disappeared out of sight into the darkness.

Jake started to walk toward them when a piercing light from a flashlight engulfed Jake and he could see nothing. Then he heard the familiar voice of Eddie, one of the hotel's security staff. "Mr. Oliver, is that you?"

Jake hesitated as he continued to look where the three men had been and then responded. "Yeah, Eddie, it's me."

"I thought I heard voices and came to check it out." The security guard looked up at the lights that were out as he quickly approached his boss. "You O.K. sir?"

"I'm fine, your timing was good, Eddie. Let's get inside, I need to check some things right away."

"Sure boss." They started to walk and Eddie again looked up. "What happened to the lights? I just checked them less than 30 minutes ago." Jake continued to walk ahead and did not answer.

They quickly entered the hotel through the rear employee entrance and proceeded to the accounting department. The door was locked but Eddie had his set of security keys with him. Jake went directly to the locked file cabinet and was not surprised to find that it was no longer locked. In the cabinet he found blank checks just as Tony had said. Another file drawer contained files with a noticeable space where several large files had once been.

Eddie observed his boss carefully before responding. "You need me any further sir?"

Jake then shook his head. "No, Eddie, that will be all, I'll lock up." As Eddie was leaving the office, however, Jake called to him. "Eddie, has anybody else been to this office this evening?"

Eddie, looked at him questioningly. "Well I'm not for sure. Ronny has been working the front, I have been walking the back." These were the terms the security staff used when referring to which officer was working at the podium in the lobby and which was making rounds of the back offices and grounds around the hotel.

Jake closed the cabinet and turned off the lights to the accounting office. He and Eddie walked to the lobby and Jake was annoyed to find that Ronny, the security guard, was not at the designated security podium at the front entrance, but sitting on the corner of the desk of the evening concierge. Yuki Somora was a cute Japanese girl in her mid-twenties. She was scheduled for the evenings primarily because of her bi-lingual skills. This enabled her to have the ability to take care of the various Japanese tour groups that frequented the Wilford.

Ronny was obviously hoping she would accept his offer for drinks when they got off in a couple of hours. The guard quickly jumped to attention when he saw his GM approach. "Mr. Oliver….didn't expect to see you back here tonight." He glared at his partner standing behind Jake. He was pissed that Eddie had not warned him over the radio that their boss was on property.

"Yeah, that's quite obvious Ronny."

"Sorry sir. What can I do for you?"

"Anything out of ordinary tonight? Any unexpected visitors?" Jake asked as he quickly looked around the lobby.

"Well actually, sir, we did have some visitors earlier." Ronny grabbed his security sign-in sheet from his podium. "A____ Mr. Chi was just here with two other men, big guys. I had never met Mr. Chi but he tore in to me telling me how he was the owner of the hotel and that he needed access to the accounting department. I told him I would have to verify this but he just pushed his way through with his friends and proceeded without me. I was about to stop them when Sam, the bartender, came out and told me to back off and explained that this Mr. Chi was really the owner and it was O.K." Ronny looked questioningly at his boss. "Did I do something wrong, sir?"

"No, you did alright. When did they leave?" Jake asked impatiently.

"They left about 10 minutes ago." Ronny replied nervously, recognizing that something was bothering his new boss.

At that moment, Jake's cellular phone rang. It was Marilyn Oliver. "Jake, find a TV quick."

"What is it?"

"The local news is covering a drive by shooting that took place earlier this evening." Marilyn paused. "Honey…I first thought it was you but…Jake…it was Tony Hoy!"

Jake looked up at the 32 foot ceiling of the hotel lobby where he was standing. "What is his condition?"

"Jake…He's dead!"

CHAPTER EIGHTEEN

The entire staff of the hotel was in a state of shock the following morning upon hearing the news. Tony had made many friends in the short time he had been at the Wilford. Jake had learned that Tony and his family had transferred from Hong Kong during the purchase of the hotel by South Harbor Investments, LTD. He had worked for the company for ten years and the general consensus was that he must have gained the respect of South Harbor's upper management to warrant his relocation half way around the world to represent one of the company's new assets in the United States.

Although it was said that he was somewhat moody at times, Tony and his wife had appeared excited and pleased with their move to San Francisco. An intense manager who often worked late into the night after all went home, his apparent dedication to South Harbor Investments was never questioned.

Jake entered the accounting office and found Sandra and several members of Tony's staff consoling each other. Jake expressed his sincere sorrow and assured them that he would ask the police to investigate the matter thoroughly. He then asked Sandra to join him in his office.

As Jake closed the door behind Sandra, she looked at him with a troubled look on her face. "It was so senseless."

"Yes, it was," Jake acknowledged as he sat down behind his desk and looked out the window.

"Sir, do you think this accident had anything to do with your scheduled meeting last night?"

Jake turned suddenly and stared at her. "How did you know about a meeting last night?" The tone of his voice appeared to startle her and momentarily she was at a loss for words.

"Sir, word is already out that you returned to the hotel last night. It is also common knowledge that Mr. Chi was here and that both of you requested access to the accounting department. Not exactly usual behavior for either of you if I may say so."

Jake realized that Sandra was well informed, perhaps too much so. "Well, yes. Tony and I had scheduled a meeting back at the hotel. I'm just at a loss to understand how the entire world seemed to also know of our plans." On this last comment, Jake studied the young woman sitting across from him. Sandra was an intelligent individual that appeared to always be one step ahead of him and far too curious. What if she was also sharing her knowledge with others. If this was the case, Jake had a serious problem that he had to address quickly. There was also the matter of the lunch Sandra had with his wife in which she indirectly warned him to be careful. Sandra knew more than she was saying and he was tired of playing games.

"Sandra, what is going on around here?

She looked up questioningly. "I am not sure I know what you ___."

"I think you do," Jake quickly interrupted, "what was the purpose of lunch last week with my wife and the cryptic warning that I needed to be careful?" Sandra looked around nervously as Jake continued. "You always appear to be well informed on everything going on around here and I think you know more than you are saying."

"Mr. Oliver…Jake, I assure you that I know nothing about what happened to Tony and the purpose of my lunch with your wife was my way of making you aware that the people we work for are not the nicest at times. I saw this while working with Mr. Filmore, although he never confided in me. But I will tell you this, I think Sam Filmore's accident was…no accident! And his sudden resignation just prior to the fire at his home….well….Jake, he was scared about something. Very scared about something!"

"Scared? Scared of what?" Jake noted that Sandra appeared to be visibly agitated, more angry rather than as emotionally upset. Was her outburst, related to her concerns for what happened to Sam Filmore or about Jake's implications that she may be involved somehow.

Sandra looked at him thoughtfully, regaining the professional composure that most throughout the hotel encountered with her. "Sir, I honestly don't know, but I would like to help you find out, if you will let me."

Jake was still uncertain of how to read Sandra's reaction to his confrontation but decided to proceed further.

"Sandra, tell me more about the fire and Sam's death?"

Sandra gathered her thoughts and then continued. "Well…no conclusive evidence was ever uncovered as to the cause of the fire. Sam's wife, Sylvia, had left their house at approx. 4 p.m. to take their new grandson back to their daughter's home across the bridge in Marin. Her plan was to have dinner up there and then return that evening. Sam had already given his notice of his intent to resign from the hotel earlier that day and arrived at his home around 6 p.m." Sandra paused showing some signs of emotion. "Well, no one exactly knows what happened next. Neighbors described hearing an explosion around 6:30 p.m. and when they looked at Sam's home it was completely engulfed in flames."

"The fire department and police were never able to determine what had caused the explosion and fire. They suspected a gas leak but stated they could not be certain. Sylvia arrived home at 8:00 p.m. and was greeted by….the horror of what had happened." These last words by Sandra were choked and tears now formed for the first time.

Jake listened to Sandra's last words in silence. Perhaps he had misread her. He reached for a box of tissue in the drawer of his desk and handed the box to her. "Sandra, your account of this incident was quite thorough." Jake was having difficulty understanding what was bothering him as he continued to respond. "In fact, you sounded more like a cop reporting on a case. How do you know so much about what happened."

Sandra gave him a weak smile and responded with a quick comeback. "Well…mostly from what I read and conversations that I later had with Sam's wife. But if I *was* a cop Jake, I do not think Sam's death was an accident."

Jake nodded his head slowly trying to absorb what had been said and determining how he should deal with Sandra. He was still not convinced that she was all that she presented herself to be.

"Jake, I know that you are beginning to suspect all is not well at the 'Wilford Manor'." This drew a smile from Jake as he nodded his agreement. "I want to help in any way I can."

"Sandra, the best way you can help me is to keep me informed.

"Jake, I will do whatever I can."

"Good. I need you to set up some appointments for me today. Lunch with Jackson Chi, Lou Walizak at 3:00, here in my office, and Ed Lee at 5:00, also here."

"Sure, I'll get right on it, I assume you have an agenda in mind? Sandra asked again with a slight smile.

"Perhaps," Jake nodded, "that will be all for now."

Sandra stood and departed abruptly closing the door to his office behind her.

Jake still wondered what Sandra's role might be in all of this but for the time being he would keep her informed on a need to know basis. He simply did not know whom to trust. He now had another concern to add to his list. If Sandra was correct and Sam's death was not an accident, then he had to play things more carefully from this point on.

Jake turned to his computer and began summarizing the events of the past few days. He had gotten in the habit of using this method to organize his thoughts. In some ways it was like keeping a daily journal but Jake found that putting his thoughts in words helped him get organized and formulate a plan. He simply noted each thought that came to mind in no particular order and then drilled down these thoughts into concise objectives. And given the series of meetings he had planned for that afternoon, he felt his thoughts and objectives should be as organized as possible.

On a blank computer page Jake summarized his findings:

SUMMARY OF ACTIVITIES – WEEK ONE

Tension Level of Staff:

- Since my arrival, staff appears on edge...almost fearful of something...but what?
- Staff fear of Jackson Chi appears evident. But why? Dollars Expended in Question:
- Advance deposits, if that is what they really are, have been made to contractors for the renovation of the hotel yet a formal bid process has not yet taken place.
- Ed Lee appears to be aware of this but continues to discuss this matter with me cryptically. It is as if he wants me to uncover what is going on but will not come right out and tell me. Where are Ed's loyalties?
- Owners may not be aware of the $2 million that has been dispersed. If that is the case, is Ed suggesting that Jackson Chi is working behind the backs of Hong Kong and Mr. Cho?
- I attempt to find out more information on the financial activities of the hotel and discover a locked cabinet containing confidential files under the strict supervision of Jackson Chi.
- When I approached Tony, the controller, he was visibly scared to have anyone know he is showing me the files.
- But Tony also appeared to have some type of conscious and whatever was in those files was eating at him.
- Conveniently for someone, Tony is a victim of what the police describe as a drive by shooting, two thugs are waiting for me in the parking garage when I arrive at the hotel indicating they are responsible. How did they know I would be there at that time of the evening?
- I am then threatened to not push things but what it is I am not to push is still unclear.
- Jackson Chi makes a surprise visit to the hotel just before I arrive last night with two men that strongly resemble the big guys I encountered in the parking lot. In turn, the mystery files are still a mystery.

Possible Informant on the Staff:

- Jackson Chi is well informed of all activity going on in the hotel.
- How did he know about my meeting with Tony?
- Jackson has an informant on the staff of the hotel...but who? One of my management team or one of the line staff?
- Sandra - Friend or Adversary?
    - Too well informed
    - Her comments that Sam Filmore may have been murdered rather than the victim of a tragic home fire is an even greater concern.
    - Her background and how she got her position is still somewhat of a mystery.
    - She doesn't quite fit in at the hotel and I am not sure why.

Union Negotiations:

- Lou Walizak stops by a week before the start of contract negotiations and appears to have done some background checks on me regarding my last job. He then drops an idle threat not to make trouble. Make trouble in what way?
- Jackson Chi seems overly interested in the upcoming union negotiations. What is behind this interest?

Jake reviewed his notes and then entered three questions:

- Who can I trust?
- What am I getting too close to that is prompting these events?
- Who is keeping one step ahead of me?

Jake then saved the document to a personal directory he had set up that required password access. In this way, he could rest relatively sure that no one would view his notes for the time being.

CHAPTER NINETEEN

Lakeside Heights Elementary School had the 'best of playgrounds'. At least that was how Sarah Oliver had described it to her parents after her first day of school. Located less than three blocks from the San Francisco Zoo, and nearby Lake Merced, this school featured a large play area for the students to enjoy during recess. Large trees surrounded a fenced in playground that gave the kids a sense of being far away from the day to day hustle and bustle of the city. Although nearby streets and busy traffic were all around the area, the large trees and ten-foot high chain link fence kept the rest of the world out of Sarah's playground.

The sun was shining and the fog had lifted an hour before the schools recess period began. Sarah exited the large double doors from the school and proceeded to a shaded area with her entourage of new friends. All the young girls appeared lost in conversation giggling and laughing about matters that no adult would most likely understand.

Standing around a picnic table located approximately twenty feet from the fence of the playground along *Lakeside Street*, the girls were so enthralled in their conversations that none of them noticed the man sitting in a car parked across the street. To the typical person passing by, the man appeared to simply be parked and having lunch from a nearby fast food restaurant. Conveniently, however, the reflection of the sun on the windshield of the car was such that the school monitors could not see that the parked car was even occupied.

In between bites of the double cheeseburger the man had purchased from *McDonald's* he raised a camera with a telephoto lens to the window and took rapid pictures of the group of girls on the playground.

"OK, let's play a game!" Shouted Sarah.

"What kind of game?" Asked a girl of similar height as Sarah but dressed more tomboyish.

"Dodge-ball!"

"Yeah, dodge-ball!" Shouted the others.

All of the girls spread out into a large circle and one girl produced a large rubber ball. She kicked the ball across the imaginary circle and the girls on the opposite side jumped to make sure it did not touch them. Another girl then chased after the ball and kicked it again this time toward Sarah and the dark haired girl with the baseball cap. Both girls easily avoided being hit by the ball and it rolled beyond them toward the perimeter fence. Sarah ran to get the ball. As she reached for the ball, she noticed the man in the car take a picture of her and then quickly try to hide the camera and look away.

Sarah quickly retrieved the ball and ran back to her friends. "Hey, come here!" she shouted and the other girls ran to her.

"What is it, don't you want to play any more?" asked one of the other girls.

"No, not that." Sarah then turned to look at the man in the car who was now turning away from her and looking down into his car. "That man over there just took my picture."

"Who is he, does anyone know him?" asked the tomboy.

All shook their heads indicating the negative. Suddenly, Mrs. Henderson, Sarah's teachers approached the group of girls. "Hi, girls, what are you playing?"

At first no one said anything and then Sarah turned to the teacher. "Mrs. Henderson, that man over there in the car just took our picture."

Mrs. Henderson turned quickly to see where Sarah was pointing and heard the sound of a car starting. The man in the car crouched down in the seat and pulled away from the curb. He turned and proceeded down a side street out of sight behind the thick trees at the edge of the playground. Mrs. Henderson looked back at the girls and lowered herself to one knee. "Come closer ladies. Did any of you recognize the man in the car?"

All shook their head no.

"Sarah, tell me exactly what you saw."

"All I saw was the man take a picture of us when we were playing. I noticed it because our ball rolled over by the fence and I went to get it."

Mrs. Henderson looked at the girls with concern visible on her face. "Sarah, was the man taking a picture of all of the girls or just you.

Sarah thought about the question and then answered. "Well, I guess it was just of me, because I was the one by the fence. I just thought he must be taking a picture of all of us playing."

Mrs. Henderson forced a tense smile. "Yes, you are probably right. But do me a favor....all of you. If any of you see a strange man again let me know right away, alright?"

All responded in unison. "Yes, Mrs. Henderson."

....

"So, Marilyn, are you and the family all settled in your new home?" Asked Linda Slazenger as they were seated at a table on the sidewalk of a restaurant at the corner of *Union* and *Pacific*.

"Yes, we're most of the way unpacked, just a few loose ends but overall the house already looks very lived in."

Linda leaned across the table and patted Marilyn's hand. "I'm glad you asked me to lunch but when you called it sounded sort of urgent. Is something wrong?"

Marilyn paused deciding if she should discuss her possible paranoia with someone she had only known for a short time. On the way to lunch after dropping the kids off at school, she had been constantly checking her rear view mirror for the mysterious car that she was convinced had been following her. But she had not seen any sign of the man or the car and was now having second thoughts of bringing the issue up at all. "Oh, it's nothing really, I...just thought it would be fun to get together and visit."

"Well, that sounds fine with me." replied Linda with a smile. "But are you sure you want to sit out here on the patio...it's a little chilly today, don't you think?"

"Oh, it's not that bad. And if you don't mind, I prefer it out here rather than inside. Is that O.K. with you?"

Both ladies then examined the menu, ordered their food and chatted about all sorts of worldly things for the next hour. By the time they were ready to leave, Marilyn was more convinced than ever that her imagination was getting the best of her. She excused herself and went to the restroom. As she returned to her seat, however, she overheard a disturbance of some type coming from a half a block up the street.

"What's going on?"

"Oh nothing," responded Linda. "Just some nut who thinks he can park in a no parking zone and eat his lunch or something. The cop is most likely telling him to move on or be towed."

Marilyn laughed as she turned to see what was happening and then froze as she recognized not only the dark car Linda was talking about but also the man sitting in the car arguing with the policeman.

"Marilyn, what is it? Do you know the guy?"

Marilyn spun around in her seat and leaned forward grabbing Linda's arm and pulling her across the table. "That man is the reason I wanted to have lunch with you today." Linda looked at her not understanding. "I think that man has been following me for, at least the past week!"

Linda looked at her questioningly. "That man? But who is he? And why is he following you?"

"I honestly don't know. But I have seen him at different times. First at the grocery last week; then when I was leaving a restaurant downtown; later when I was picking up dry cleaning; and now, while we are sitting here." Marilyn paused as she gathered her thoughts. "This is no coincidence, Linda."

"O.K, O.K. I believe you. But now what are you going to do?"

Marilyn leaned back in her chair and released her grip on Linda's arm. She was tempted to share her concerns that the man following her may be mixed up with what Jake was working on at the hotel but decides not to at that time. She recalled Jake's comments that someone in the hotel had been leaking information to Jackson Chi and although she wanted to deny that it could be Linda's husband, Jim, she decided not to say anything further until she could be sure. "I don't know," said Marilyn as she was thinking of how best to proceed. "But for right now let's______"

Their lunch was interrupted by a call on Marilyn's cellular phone. "Mrs. Oliver, this is Mrs. Henderson, Sarah's teacher. Can you come to the school? I need to speak to you as soon as possible."

....

Jake approached the table and sat down. "Thank you for taking the time to meet with me for lunch on such short notice, Mr. Chi."

"Not a problem at all, Jake. How are you doing at the hotel? The staff treating you alright?" Jackson replied as he noticed a pretty oriental girl that was being seated at a table nearby. Both men had agreed to meet for lunch at the *Harbor Village Restaurant*, which had been recommended by Jackson.

Jake noticed that Jackson was only mildly paying attention as he began to speak but was confident that he would get his attention shortly. "Actually the staff is still in a state of shock over the death of Tony Hoy." Jake paused to gather his thoughts. "In fact, that is the reason I wanted to meet with you today."

Jackson returned his gaze to Jake. "Yes, quite tragic. You have questions for me? Yes, yes, of course. What questions?"

"I need to know more about the upcoming renovation plans for the hotel."

Jackson hesitated as he formulated a reply. "Ah, yes the renovation of the hotel is a most exciting matter. But you need not worry about it at this time. I will handle all of the details." Jackson paused but not long enough for Jake to respond. "Jake, I want you to focus on the union negotiations and_____"

"Jackson," Jake interrupted. "I am already focussed on the negotiations but I must also have a clear understanding of what the renovation plans are for the hotel. I have met with Ed Lee and he has reviewed the plans but there are some additional questions I have for you."

"There was no need for you to meet with Ed Lee." Jackson asserted rather forcefully. "As I have said, these matters will be handled by me and do not concern you."

"No sir, that is incorrect!" Jake replied curtly. "Anything that involves the Wilford Hotel involves *me* as well. That is why Mr. Cho hired me!"

Jackson tensed, considering Jake's last words. *Perhaps, Samuel Cho is up to something he thought.* "Yes, yes, you are quite correct, Jake. What is it specifically that you want to know?"

Jake was surprised with the sudden change in his demeanor. He assumed his reference to Mr. Cho must have struck a nerve. "Well, for starters, why don't you tell me about some deposit checks you authorized just prior to my arrival."

Jackson stared at Jake. "Perhaps, you are not familiar with the workings of a full scale renovation of this nature. Anyway, you should know that it is quite customary for the building contractors to require advance deposits for their work."

"I am quite familiar with how construction deposits work, Mr. Chi. What I do not understand is why these deposits are being paid prior to the finalization of written contracts and why there is no support documentation to justify these expenses in the accounting department." Jake watched Jackson's facial expressions and thought he was about to blow with anger. "And lastly, I want to know why you were at the hotel the other night removing what little information we had on these expenditures from the accounting department."

"I know of no files that you are referring to." Jackson responded hotly. I was at the hotel the other night to retrieve some information that Tony Hoy had left for me. And I must admit, I thought this would be an opportune time to look around the hotel. I believe that is clearly within my prerogative as a representative of South Harbor Investments." He paused to make sure Jake was getting the drift of his message. "Unless, Mr. Oliver, you have something to *hide* that you did not want me to be aware of?"

Jake looked across the table angrily as Jackson continued. "Need I remind you that your job is to run the hotel and nothing more. Focus on these primary tasks, sir, and stop this foolishness of arranging secret rendezvous' back to the hotel at night. Do I make myself clear?"

"I did not say I was at the hotel the other night."

Jackson looked flustered before responding. "Mr. Oliver…Jake, let me assure you that I am here to support you as well as make sure that you manage the hotel effectively. I did not mean to imply that your actions were in any way inappropriate. But nor will I make it a point of informing you every time I choose to visit the hotel…no mater what time of night." Jackson then stood "And now, I regret that I must run. For some reason you feel I have over-stepped my bounds but let me assure you that your primary focus should be on the operation of the hotel. Let me worry about these other matters such as the renovation."

Jackson then summoned a waiter and spoke to him in Cantonese. "I have taken care of our lunch and now I must leave. Good day sir."

Jake left the restaurant and decided to walk back to the hotel. On the way he replayed in his mind the conversation with Jackson and one comment stuck in his mind. *Jackson obviously knew I was planning to return to the hotel the previous evening and his comment confirmed it.* Jake was bothered, however, by his use of the words 'secret rendezvous'. The last time he had heard this phrase was from his wife when he told her he was going back to the hotel to meet Tony Hoy. Was this a conveniently similar choice of words or something more?

…………………………………………

Marilyn and Linda left the restaurant and walked together to Marilyn's car. Marilyn glanced over her shoulder in the direction of the dark sedan but now noticed that it was no where in sight.

"You should report this guy or something," said Linda.

Marilyn turned and shrugged her shoulders. "And tell the police what? I have no license plate number. Hell, I'm not even sure I could describe the car or the man for that matter." She paused gathering her thoughts. "Look Linda, let me worry about this for the time being but right now I gotta go. Sarah's teacher called and said it was urgent that she talk to me." During her drive to the school, Marilyn was more alert then ever but again saw no sign of the phantom car. She arrived at the school twenty minutes later.

CHAPTER TWENTY

"Thanks for coming on such short notice, Mrs. Oliver."

"It is no problem, Mrs. Henderson what has happened? Is Sarah alright?"

"Yes, yes, she is just fine. And besides, I am probably just over-reacting anyway, but in today's society it never hurts to play it safe."

Marilyn looked on, more confused then ever. "I don't understand."

The elderly teacher organized her thoughts. "Earlier today during recess, Sarah and her friends were playing and Sarah noticed a man parked on the street that she said took a picture of her." Marilyn looked on in disbelief as she continued. "Sarah was very good in coming to me to report what she had seen. I gathered the other girls and they too had seen the man but none of them knew who he was."

"Did *you* see the man and car, Mrs. Henderson?"

"No, I'm sorry but I didn't. By the time the girls came to me the man had already driven away." Marilyn looked away, deep lines of worry now apparent on her forehead. "Mrs. Oliver, I am sorry to worry you with this but I thought you should know."

"Oh yes, Mrs. Henderson, thank you for recognizing the potential danger."

The concerned teacher paused as she debated whether to ask the next question. "Mrs. Oliver, is it possible that you are being investigated by someone?" She paused realizing how awkward such a question could be. "Perhaps, an ex-husband or something?"

Marilyn looked up at first confused. "Investigated? No, that would not make___" Marilyn did not finish her sentence as her mind began to race. *The man following her, her husband's dealings at work, what if someone had them under surveillance. But why?*

"Mrs. Henderson, thank very much for looking out for Sarah today. And please, keep me informed if any similar incidences occur."

"Of course I will. If you would like, I could refer this matter to one of our counselors."

"No, no that will not be necessary. Now if you don't mind, I am going to take my girl's home for the day. Again, thank you for being so conscientious."

Marilyn picked up both girls and took them to Linda Slazenger's house. As she departed the school with the girls, she decided that if Jake appeared to trust Linda's husband, than Linda must be trustworthy too. She called Linda from her cell phone and asked if she could stop by with the girls. During the drive, Marilyn asked Sarah to tell her what had happened during recess. Sarah was not able to tell her any more than Mrs. Henderson had except in her description of the man with the camera. Sarah explained that the man she saw was dressed in a suit coat and tie and was driving a dark green sports car. Marilyn questioned Sarah on this last point but Sarah insisted it was just like the car daddy used to have. This baffled Marilyn, in that, the car she had been seeing was a dark four door sedan. The car Sarah was referencing was an MGA Roadster Jake had owned prior to the Jaguar, when the girls were younger.

Upon arriving at the Slazenger's apartment, Marilyn shared with Linda what had happened to Sarah at school and that her suspicions were that someone was watching their every move.

Linda listened intently but still did not feel that any of it made sense. "Marilyn, I still think this is hard to believe. Did you see anyone when you left the restaurant?"

"No."

"Did you see anyone on the way over here from the school?"

"No. But if these are professionals, they are not supposed to be seen, responded Marilyn defiantly.

"O.K. if that is the case, how did you notice these professionals. Did they just simply screw up or something?"

Marilyn looked at her new friend realizing that none of what she was saying made any sense. "I don't know." But then she remembered something. "Wait a minute. When I was returning home from lunch with Sandra, I forgot to pick up the dry cleaning."

"So, what does that have to do with___"

"I was just about home when I remembered and turned around in a neighbor's driveway and drove back down the same street in the opposite direction." Marilyn looked at Linda triumphantly. "Don't you see. The guy following me did not have any time to react to my change. In turn, all he could do was try to hide his face and thus be seen. In other words, I outfoxed the professional and did not even know I was doing it. It was then simply a matter of putting two and two together of why the man and the car looked familiar."

"O.K., that makes sense. But it still doesn't explain who was taking pictures of Sarah."

Marilyn shook her head. "No, it doesn't. In fact, it suggests that there are at least two of them out there."

Both women sat in the kitchen drinking coffee as the girls watched cartoons in the living room. After a period of silence for several minutes Linda spoke. "All right, Marilyn, we have ourselves a mystery and it is up to us ladies to get to the bottom of things."

Marilyn was confused by Linda's last comment. "What do you mean it is 'up to us ladies' to get to the bottom of things?"

"Let's face it. We still don't have much to go on to prove that someone is out there, right? So let's shake the trees a little and see if we can draw them out in the open."

Marilyn was hesitant. "I am not sure I know what you have in mind."

"It's simple," responded Linda. "You and I are about the same in size and appearance. In fact, I bet your clothes would fit me."

Marilyn was confused and concerned with where this line of reasoning was heading. "Look, Linda, we are not going to play any games here. These guys may be very dangerous if they get wind we know what is going on_____"

"Yeah, but in the meantime, what are you going to do. You can't go to the police. You have no proof. All I want to do is draw them out in the open so you can get their license number. Then we let the police take over from there."

Marilyn's instincts told her that what they were planning could be a mistake but Linda had made some good points about the police not being able to do anything. "O.K. I'm in. What are we going to do?"

Given that both women were similar in overall appearance, they switched coats and Linda left in Marilyn's car to return home. The plan seemed simple enough. Marilyn and the girls would follow in Linda's car and watch for the man in the black car to follow. The man would supposedly not suspect that someone would be following *him*. In turn, Marilyn would write down the license number and let the police do the rest.

At first all appeared to be Marilyn's imagination. They were only 10 minutes away from the Oliver home and no black car had yet appeared. Marilyn was about to call Linda's cell phone number to tell her the plan was over when a black sedan suddenly pulled out from a side street two cars in front of her. She attempted to pass the cars between but traffic was heavy and the timing of traffic lights was not working in her favor.

While waiting for a light at the intersection of *Market* and *Hyde*, Marilyn tried to call Linda and warn her that the car was now tailing her but she got the message she least expected. 'The cellular caller you are attempting to reach is not available or has driven out of the coverage area'. At that moment the light changed and she proceeded as quickly as possible and attempted to catch up to Linda and the unwelcome friend following her. She now saw them up ahead and there was only one car between her and the black sedan. Marilyn had her pen and pad of paper on the seat ready when suddenly all traffic came to a stop. Marilyn watched the black car through the windows of the car that was in between them. It was then, for the first time, that she noticed that there was not just one but two men in the car and by the motion of their heads, they appeared as frustrated as Marilyn with the current traffic situation.

After several minutes, the traffic began to move slowly but just as Linda and the black sedan drove ahead, a policeman directing traffic around a construction site stepped in front of Marilyn before she could pass. He halted traffic as a backhoe pulled out on the street to push some gravel into the hole it had just dug.

Extremely frustrated, Marilyn was at a loss as to what to do. When the policemen allowed her to proceed, Linda and the men in the black car were easily several traffic lights ahead and out of sight.

Suddenly, Marilyn's cell phone rang. "Yes…Hello?"

"Marilyn, it's me Linda, I lost you back with that construction. So I decided to take a detour. I turned on Franklin and stopped at a gas station. Any sign of____"

"Linda! There are *two* of them and they were only two cars behind you! Get in the car and keep moving!"

"Alright, I will meet you at the house, did you get the license plate number?"

"No, not yet. There was too much traffic."

"Well, I will wait for you to catch up then____"

"Linda? Linda?" But the line had gone dead. Marilyn turned on Franklin and drove for roughly four blocks when she saw her car parked in a *Mobil* Gas Station. She pulled up to the car but Linda was not there. Marilyn looked around frantically but saw no signs of the men in the black car. She told the girls to stay in the car and lock the door when she got out. She walked to her car and looked inside. There in the drivers seat slumped across the passenger seat was Linda unconscious.

Marilyn used her cell phone to call 911. She then called Jake at work.

……………………………………

Shortly after Jake returned from his luncheon meeting with Jackson Chi, Jim Slazenger knocked on the door to his office. He noted that he was catching Jake lost in deep thought and when Jake did not immediately respond, he felt it best to leave and try again later. But before he could leave, Jake called out to him and asked him to come in.

"Hey, just wanted to touch base with you before your meeting with Lou Walizak. But also, I wanted to see how things went with Mr. Chi."

Jake motioned for him to take a seat and close the door behind him and smiled. "Oh, you could say that I got Jackson seriously wound up today."

Jim smiled back. "I just bet you did. So is the plan, to get all the bad guys mad at you at the same time?"

"Sort of," replied Jake. "The plan is to ruffle their feathers so to speak. Get them mad and, hope they make a mistake or say something that they shouldn't. Get my drift?"

Jim gave an admiring smile. "Yes I do boss. But you know, getting these guys mad could also be a little dangerous."

"Perhaps," acknowledged Jake as he leaned back in his chair. "But let's see what happens. These guys are up to something and I want to know what."

At that moment, Sandra knocked and then entered the office. The look of concern on her face was unmistakable. "Jake, it's Marilyn on the phone, there has been an accident!"

"Put her on!"

The phone rang once. "Marilyn, what is it?"

Marilyn explained briefly what she and Linda had done. Jake advised Sandra to cancel his appointments with Lou Walizak and Ed Lee and then left with Jim to the hospital where Linda was being taken.

....

The ambulance arrived shortly after Marilyn's call to Jake and the Emergency Medical Technicians revived Linda on the way to the hospitable. Marilyn transferred the girls to her own car and followed the ambulance.

Jake and Jim arrived shortly after the ambulance. They found Marilyn and the girls in the emergency waiting room.

"Marilyn, are you and the girls alright?" Asked Jake as he ran up to them.

"We're fine," she replied quickly looking at Jim. "And the doctors say Linda is also, Jim."

Jim looked relieved. "That's great. Where is she? Can I see her?"

A nurse entered the waiting area as they were talking and overheard Jim's question. "A...Mr. Slazenger?"

All turned to look at the nurse. "Yes, I am Jim Slazenger."

The nurse smiled. "All of you will be pleased to know that Linda is going to be fine. She has a nasty bump on the head and will most likely have a headache for the next few days but otherwise she should be fine. If you will follow me I can take you to her."

Jim left with the nurse while Jake, Marilyn and the girls waited in the reception area. Jake then sat next to Marilyn on one of the couches. "Now can you please tell me what you two were up to again. You tended to jump around on the phone a while ago."

Marilyn looked down at her hands. "It was just plain stupid. We shouldn't have tried such a stunt."

Jake patted her hand gently. "Well, why don't you start from the beginning and then I can confirm that it was probably a stupid idea."

Marilyn looked at her husband with an embarrassed smile. "It was about the guy that has been following me that I told you about." Marilyn paused for a reaction from Jake but then continued. "I decided to confide in Linda of my suspicions during lunch when I received a call from Sarah's teacher. Sarah saw a man on the street across from the playground taking pictures of her. She reported it to her teacher and the teacher contacted me. I met with Mrs. Henderson and she implied that we might be under some type of surveillance." Marilyn looked at Jake who had a skeptical expression on his face. "I know it makes no sense but I picked up the girls and took them to Linda and Jim's apartment."

Jake interrupted. "Was the man that Sarah saw the same man you have been seeing?"

Marilyn shook her head. "No, I don't think so. Her description of the man and the car are different."

"O.K. go on. Then what happened."

"Well, Linda and I had come to the conclusion that there was nothing the police could do because I did not even have a good description of the man or the license plate number of the car. So…we decided to change places."

Jake looked at her questioningly. "What do you mean change places?"

Marilyn paused knowing her comment was going to make Jake mad. "Well, we decided that Linda would wear my coat and drive my car back to the house. Me and the girls would following in Linda's car." Before Jake could comment, she continued. "The plan was for me to watch for the black sedan to appear, get behind him and write down the license plate number and then report him to the police." Marilyn looked up to see Jake shaking his head slowly.

He looked at her angrily. "And then what happened?"

"Well…we got stuck in heavy traffic. The car finally appeared but had two men in it. I got stopped by road construction and Linda and the men in the car got ahead of me. I tried to call Linda but I guess she didn't have her cell phone on initially. Then she called and told me that she had turned on Franklin Street to drive around some and give me time to catch up. She said she had pulled into a gas station. I told her to get moving and that the men in the car were behind her." Marilyn paused to catch her breath. "Then, as she was talking to me, the line went dead." Marilyn became choked up with these last words as the reality of what could have happened set in.

Jake looked at his wife, now turned private investigator. "Marilyn, do you know how dangerous this little stunt was that you and Linda_____"

"Hey guys," Jim said as he approached, "Linda is O.K. and the doc says she can leave within the next hour." He looked noticeably relieved and then shifted his gaze toward Marilyn. "I don't know what you two were up to but Linda said when we all get home you and she would explain everything."

Jake looked at his colleague with the first signs of a smile. "Yeah Jim, and you are going to love the explanation." Marilyn hit Jake in the arm in mock protest.

Across the room, a man in a sport jacket and tie approached. "Hello, are one of you Marilyn Oliver?"

Jake stood to address the man. "Yes, I am Jake Oliver and this is my wife, Marilyn. Can I help you?"

"Sir, your wife reported the accident that involved…" He looked down at a small note pad. "A Ms. Linda Slazenger. I am detective Jones of SFPD." He then presented his badge quickly as he continued to speak. "I would like to ask Mrs. Oliver and Mrs. Slazenger some questions regarding the attack."

Jim looked on and then inserted. "Sir, I don't think Linda is up to having any visitors right now."

"I see. And you are…?"

"Jim Slazenger, Linda's husband."

"Yes, of course. Well Mr. Slazenger I assure it is not my intent to upset your wife. I simply want see if she can give me any kind of description of what happed so my men can start looking for them."

Jim reflected back on his days as a cop and realized that the most opportune time to ask a victim questions was as soon as possible after the accident occurred. "Yeah, I understand. Alright follow me."

Linda sat up in bed as the congregation filed into her room. "Linda, honey, this man is a police officer and would like to ask you some questions." She nodded and Jim stepped back.

"Mrs. Slazenger, I am detective Jones. Can you tell me what happened?"

Linda debated just how detailed she should be at this time. "Well, I had pulled into a gas station and was on the phone with my friend Marilyn Oliver when a man reached in through the window and took my phone. Then another man appeared by the passenger door. He opened it and grabbed my arm. I tried to yell for help but the man standing outside my door put his hand across my mouth." Linda paused to gather her thoughts. "And then the man on the passenger side said something like, 'hey it's not her.' The other man grabbed my head sharply and turned my face toward his. He then looked across at the other guy. The next thing I know I am waking up in an ambulance."

The detective was taking notes as Linda spoke. "Ms. Slazenger, I am truly sorry but I have just a few more questions. Did you recognize the men that attacked you?"

"No."

"Do you have any idea what the men wanted? I mean, the officer on the scene indicated that your purse and money were not taken."

Linda hesitated as she looked down at her hands. "No, I don't know what they wanted."

"Can you describe them…as best you can?"

"Well, I couldn't really tell how tall they were since I was sitting in the car and they were bent over reaching in to grab me. But one was rather thin and the other much heavier. Both had black hair…the heavier guy appeared very strong. Here take a look at my arm where he grabbed me!" Linda pulled up the sleeve of her medical gown. Her upper arm had several large bruises that had already become visible.

"Mrs. Slazenger, perhaps when you are up to it we could have you look at some photos we have at the station."

"Sure, anything else?"

"Yes, just one more question." Detective Jones looked down at his notepad again. "The officer on the scene indicated that you were not in your own car but that of Mrs. Oliver. Why is that?"

Linda again looked down as she formulated how best to explain what she and Marilyn had been up to that led to this incident. "Well sir, you are going to find this rather silly but I was thinking of buying Marilyn's car and wanted to drive it to see what it was like. So Marilyn and her daughters followed in my car as we drove back to their house."

Detective Jones looked at her and then at Jim Slazenger standing at the foot of the bed. "I see…well thank you…Mrs. Slazenger. I will be in touch in a few days and I'm glad that you're alright. He then turned toward Marilyn. "Mrs. Oliver, anything you want to add?"

"No."

"Very well. Thank you for your time. I will be in touch if anything develops."

As the detective turned to leave, Jim called to him. "A detective…Jones? I don't believe I got your card."

The man turned and looked at him. "My card?"

Jim studied him carefully. "Yeah, in case my wife remembers something she forgot to tell you."

The detective nodded and smiled. "Of course, how forgetful of me. Here." He handed a business card to Jim and then departed.

After he departed Linda looked questioningly at her husband. "What was that last part about?"

"Oh probably nothing. I guess the old cop in me just came out just then and besides what was that crap about wanting to buy the Oliver's car?"

"Well, I know it was probably wrong of me to lie to the man but Marilyn never mentioned anything about a policeman at the scene. What was the cops name again?"

Jim looked down at the card in his hand. "Detective Paul Jones, SFPD."

………………………………………

Detective Jones left the hospital and walked quickly to his car. He pulled out his cellular phone and after several rings the call was answered and he spoke. “Yeah…this is Jonesy. He paused as the person on the other end of the line spoke. “No, no one was hurt but your guy's stupid stunt has gotten them all jumpy I think.” Again, he paused as the person on the other line spoke more forcefully. Jonesy started his car and pulled out of the hospital parking lot when the person on the other end gave him a chance to respond. “I just think that the two ladies were up to something and this Slazenger bitch was not telling me everything. And her husband is a goddamn watchdog. He acts like a cop or something.” As the person on the other line continued to speak for several minutes Jonesy pressed the speakerphone button on his phone to free up his hands. The voice of the man he was speaking with filled the car.

“We’re dealing with amateurs…not professionals. I’ll take care of it…now do your job and get me the information I requested or you’ll find somebody following you home tonight! Got it!!”

Before Jonesy could respond the line went dead.

……………………………………

The Oliver’s and Slazenger’s left the hospital an hour later and went back to the Slazenger’s apartment. They ordered pizza and Jake got the girls situated in the spare bedroom watching a Disney video. Jim got Linda situated on the couch to rest.

When Jake returned to the living room, Jim had opened a bottle of wine and poured a glass for each of them. Linda settled for water only, given the drugs the hospital had given her.

“Well we have all certainly had an eventful day, haven’t we?” Jim said as he reclined into what had to be his favorite chair.

Jake looked at Marilyn and Linda both sitting quietly neither saying a word. “Well, yes, I would say our two detectives have been up to a lot of things today. Don’t you agree ladies?”

Marilyn looked up with an annoyed expression. “Well, all we wanted to do was prove that I was being followed. And we did. I am just so sorry you got hurt Linda.”

"Oh, I'm fine. What concerns me though is that those guys thought I was you. And if it had been you, you might be missing right now."

All sat silently contemplating this important point.

Jim broke the silence. "Jake, what do you think is going on here?"

Jake looked up as all three looked at him for answers. "Jim, there has been some things that have happened recently that you need to know about. In fact, I need your help and you are the only one I truly trust at the hotel."

Jake then shared with all the series of events that had been going on at the hotel. He discussed his investigation of the unexplained advance deposits, Tony Hoy's willingness to help him before his death, the men waiting for him in the parking lot, and lastly how all evidence pointed to Jackson Chi who was always well informed.

Marilyn looked at her husband angrily. "Jake, you never told me about the men in the parking lot. So, Tony was not the victim of a random drive by shooting, he was KILLED!"

Jake looked at her with a serious expression. "Yes, I believe so."

"So you think Chi is up to something, but what? Stealing money from Samuel Cho?" Jim asked leaning forward in his chair.

"Perhaps, but we also have good old Mr. Walizak and Local #78. I still cannot put together the connection between Jackson and Walizak."

All sat quietly for the next few minutes and then Jim stood. "Well Jake, consider me part of your swat team. Let's get some answers."

Jake gave Jim a weak smile. "Jim, we run hotels, we're not some elite Special Forces unit. Someone tried to kidnap my wife today and they got Linda by mistake. Which, by the way," as Jake leaned over and touched Linda's arm, "I am sincerely grateful you were not more seriously hurt."

"Well then, let's add some expertise to our team." Jim said, as all looked up confused by his last comment. "First, we need to arrange for some security for Marilyn and the girls. For that task, it is time for me to call in a few favors."

He then told them about a former cop who had started his own security business. Jim did not go in to great detail as to how exactly he had become associated with this individual but indicated that the man owed him a few favors. He also added with a smile that this guy hated union thugs and would enjoy such a challenge!

CHAPTER TWENTY ONE

Jake and Marilyn left the Slazenger's apartment shortly after 10 o'clock that evening. The girls slept all the way home. All went in Jake's Jaguar. Marilyn's car was left in the parking lot at the Slazenger's for the night. After getting the girls to bed, Marilyn went to her husband and gave him a long embrace. "What have we gotten ourselves into honey?"

Jake put his finger to his lips indicating for her to remain silent. He then motioned for her to follow him to the backyard. Once outside, he explained. "Look, I may be over-reacting to all of this but earlier today, Jackson Chi said something that has been bothering me. He used the phrase 'secret rendezvous' to describe my coming back to the hotel the other evening to meet with Tony."

Marilyn looked at Jake not yet understanding the relevance of this statement.

"It just sounded out of place coming from Jackson Chi. It was as though he was trying to make a point."

"And what point might that be?"

"Marilyn, the last time I had heard that phrase was the same evening I returned to the hotel when you made the comment."

Marilyn was still confused. "Honey, I am still not understanding what you are saying."

Jake looked up at his new home than back to his wife as they stood in the middle of the backyard. "What if the house is bugged?"

Marilyn shook her head and laughed nervously. "Oh, that is ridiculous. Isn't it?"

"Maybe, but how else did they know that Tony and I were returning to the hotel? How did those men know when to wait for me in the parking garage? And lastly, how did Jackson Chi know to get his precious documents from the accounting department just prior to my arrival?"

Both agreed that it was not worth taking any further chances. Tomorrow Marilyn and girls would move into the hotel for the time being. In the morning, Jake would take Jim up on his offer to get security protection set up for his family.

....

Jim contacted his friend, Andy Baroni, and arranged for Jake, Andy and himself to meet for lunch away from the hotel. As a precaution, Jake had brought Marilyn and the girls to the hotel with him and arranged for them to stay in one of the suites. Marilyn contacted the school and advised them that they would be out of town for a few days with the girls.

Jake and Jim arrived at *Tommy's Joint*, more of a bar than restaurant located at *Van Ness* and *Geary*. To local San Franciscans, this was somewhat of a historic landmark. Some would describe it as having rustic charm. To Jake, rustic was clearly an understatement. They grabbed a table in the back and ordered a couple of beers when a man dressed in a three-piece suit approached their table. His hair was either prematurely white, or the man kept in very good condition, because he didn't look a day over 45. In reality, however, he had just turned 55. Andy had a son and daughter, the latter of which was about to give birth to his first grandchild.

Jim started to stand but the man patted him on the shoulder indicating he should remain seated. "Hi, you must be Jake Oliver," he said with out-stretched hand, "I'm Andy Baroni. Jake shook Andy's hand and motioned him to an empty chair. Andy then turned to Jim. "Jim, how long has it been, two years or is it three?"

Jim just smiled as he took a swig of his beer. "Let's just say that your hair was a lot darker than it is now when we last worked together."

"Very nice, smart ass. You're looking good yourself. Still working on that diet I see." He retorted to his old friend. He then turned his attention to Jake who was watching the banter between the two with some amusement. "Jake, Jim tells me that you may need my services?"

Jake nodded his head as he swallowed his beer. "Well, possibly."

"Alright. Why don't you tell me what is going on and I will give you some idea how I may be able to help."

The men picked up their lunch through the buffet and, for the next hour, Jake and Jim explained the series of events that had occurred closing with the incident in which the men roughed up Linda Slazenger and Jake's suspicions that his house may be bugged.

Andy sat quietly after both men finished talking. During this period, he jotted down some notes and then looked at Jim. "What was the name of the cop that came to the hospital?"

Jim reached for his wallet and pulled out Detective Jones card. "Here's his card."

"Jones, yeah I think I've heard of the guy. What did you think of him Jim?"

"Well, for one thing, he seemed far more interested in determining if Linda could identify the two guys that attacked her rather than uncovering what their possible motive was."

"Alright. Who called him?"

"Well, that is the other big mystery of the day. According to Marilyn, Jake's wife, a uniformed cop did appear at the scene. He asked some questions and then informed Marilyn that a detective Barris might be calling her."

"Yeah, Mike Barris makes more sense than this Jones guy. I'll check it out." Andy made some further notes then turned to Jake. "Jake, the first thing I would like to do is assign a couple of my guys to watch your wife and kids."

Jake hesitated before responding. "O.K…but if someone else is already watching us…well what I am trying to say…won't it get a little crowded out there? I mean, how will we know who are bad guys and who are yours?"

Andy smiled. "Jake, first of all I will personally introduce you and your wife to my men in the event they see them for some reason, but it's highly unlikely. You see, their main purpose is going to be to ferret out the bad guys as well as protect your family. And my guys are very good at what they do."

Jake nodded in agreement.

"The second matter we need to take care of is your house. I will send some guys over this afternoon. Can you arrange to meet us there? We will track down the bugs and attempt to determine who is listening in."

"But won't this call attention to whoever is behind this? I mean what is to keep them from simply packing up and going home." Jake responded.

"My men will arrive dressed as furnace repairmen. They will simply determine if the house is bugged and where they are located. Then we have equipment that will assist us in tracking where they might be transmitting to."

Again, Jake nodded appreciating that Jim had put him in touch with such a professional.

"Alright. Any other questions before we get started?"

Jake hesitated before speaking. "Andy…how much is all of this going to cost me? I mean, I have some money set aside and____"

Andy sat up in his chair and looked first at Jim then back at his new client. "Didn't Jim tell you. This one's on the house!" Before Jake could respond, Andy continued. "Jake, Jim and I go way back and I owe him in a big way. Now, if you will excuse me, I have some plans to arrange. Can my men come by your house around, say, 3:30 this afternoon?"

Jake looked on still having trouble accepting what was being offered to him. "A…yeah, no problem. I'll be there."

After Andy left Jake looked at Jim in disbelief. "Jim, I don't know what to say. What Andy is talking about is going to involve many man-hours and the costs____"

"Jake, Andy is quite sincere is his offer. So just accept it."

"But, may I ask what you did that Andy feels so obligated to help with this matter."

Jim paid the waitress and both men stood and began to walk out of the restaurant. Once on the street, Jim turned to Jake and said. "Jake remember reading up on my background and experience prior to your arrival?"

"Sure, so you knew him when you guys were cops?"

"Actually, no. I was Highway Patrol and he was walking a beat downtown so our paths never crossed."

"O.K. so how did you guys meet?"

"Remember the incident when I was with the highway patrol and I came across the kid trapped in the car with his mother screaming for me to save her son?" Jake nodded that he remembered. "Well that was Andy's wife and his oldest son, Philip."

As Jim walked off toward the hotel, Jake watched his new friend with admiration and disbelief.

....

Andy Baroni was president and founder of Baroni Security Services. He had started his business roughly 12 years prior and built it into one of the cities largest and most respected independent security service providers. His agency provided security services that ranged from the installation and monitoring of personal home security systems to providing security personnel for international dignitaries visiting the state of California. Baroni Security also had offices in San Diego and Los Angeles and Andy was working with some investors to open an office in Las Vegas in the coming year. He prided himself and his company on offering his customers reliable quality service utilizing the best-trained professionals in the industry.

Andy had learned his trade on the streets of San Francisco first as a beat cop and later as a detective in robbery-homicide. At only 5'8" tall, Andy compensated for is small stature by building up his physique through extensive exercise and weight lifting. Built like a small tank, Andy could manhandle men twice his size during his years as a cop. A highly ethical and moral individual with strong Catholic upbringing, he was admired by the public and his friends for his dedicated work as a police officer. Among some of his fellow officers, however, he was often viewed as a potential threat to those that attempted to abuse their position.

During his 20-year career with the San Francisco Police Department, Andy progressed through the ranks and was generally liked by most in the department. As with most cops, however, he made a few enemies over the years and those enemies were still out there waiting for the right opportunity to settle the score. Following a dream he had formulated during his last five years with the force, he decided to take early retirement and start his own business. Utilizing his many contacts and strong reputation for being a 'good cop', Andy was able to develop a reputable base of clients during his first year of operation.

His big break, however, came when his agency was hired to provide security for a group of African dignitaries, coming to San Francisco to speak at a large citywide convention at *Moscone Center*. During the convention, pro-apartheid terrorist attempted to disrupt the meeting but their attempts were foiled by the keen work of Baroni Security. To most that attended the convention, they were not even aware that there had been a problem, which was as it should have been. But the planners of the convention were extremely grateful, as were the operators of the convention center. From that day forward, Baroni Security was recognized as a preferred security vendor for all major conventions in the city.

In addition to providing security service, Baroni Security continued to branch into other areas of security. One such area was to provide individuals and businesses discrete and professional investigative services. This specialized trade required the use of highly technical surveillance equipment and trained investigative personnel. It was this branch of Andy's business that he planned to use to assist his newest client, Jake Oliver.

Andy called Jake to confirm that two of his best men would be stopping by his house at 3:30 p.m. He further asked that Jake be sure to be home before his men arrive. He explained that they would be dressed as *Sullivan Heating & Air Conditioning* workers but as further confirmation their names would be Greg and Tom. Jake indicated that he would be there before they arrived. Andy then asked if he could bring two other men by the hotel later that evening and introduce them to his wife and daughters. Andy explained that these men would be the two shift supervisors that would be assigned to monitor Marilyn and his daughters. Jake indicated that he would advise his wife. As Jake hung up, the reality of what he was about to embark into finally hit him.

....

Jake arrived at his home at 3:15 p.m. and fifteen minutes later a service vehicle pulled up in front of the house. On the side of the vehicle were the words, *Sullivan's Heating & Air Conditioning.* Two men came to the door.

"Mr. Oliver?"

"Yes."

"Sir my name is Greg and this is my partner Tom. We are here to look at your furnace. I believe your wife called."

Jake invited the men in and they immediately went to work. The one man, Greg, pulled out a unique looking electronic device with a small antenna and proceeded to walk from room to room. The other man, Tom opened a metal suitcase he had carried in and it looked as if he was setting up his own ham radio to begin broadcasting. After only ½ hour, Greg advised Jake he had discovered what was wrong with the furnace and said he wanted to show him his discovery. Jake proceeded with Greg down the stairs to the garage level but then abruptly turned and exited out the back door of the house into the backyard.

Once outside, Greg addressed Jake. "Mr. Oliver, I have found four listening devices, 'bugs' as most people refer to them, in your house. My partner Tom will now check the signal strength of these devices to determine the approximate range of the transmissions. This is how we will hopefully pinpoint who the listener is."

Jake listened intently, still having trouble believing that someone had actually bugged his home. "I understand. What will happen then?"

"Once we have tracked down the receiving point or at least the range of these devices we will advise Mr. Baroni and he will tell you how best to proceed.

Jake and Greg returned and Greg proceeded to go over with him a make believe estimate of what the repairs would cost. Jake then argued with him that his prices were too high. The purpose of the staged dialog was to allow Tom to trace the transmissions. When Tom nodded that he was done, Jake closed by saying that he had no choice but to accept their terms. As both men began packing up their equipment, Jake wrote down on a piece of paper the following note and handed it to Tom.

'Any idea where the listener might be yet?'

Tom took the paper and wrote below Jake's note.

'Not exactly, but they are most likely close. Possibly within 1 mile or so.' Jake nodded his understanding. Both men then left and Jake returned to the hotel. Two hours later Andy Baroni and his two surveillance supervisors, Ray Johnson and Cliff Weber met with Jake and Marilyn. Introductions were made and then all sat in the Parlor area of the suite they had moved in to earlier that day.

"Mrs. Oliver, I wanted to meet with you today for two reasons. First of all, these two men and their staff are going to make sure you and your daughters remain safe." Marilyn just nodded. "I also wanted Ray and Cliff to meet you and your daughters. It obviously helps if they know what everyone looks like, don't you think?" This drew a slight smile from Marilyn and Jake.

"Now in all honesty, you and the girls will most likely never see my team unless they want to be seen." Andy paused. "In the event they sense a problem, that is when you will see them. That's what they are there for. In addition, I would like to agree on a signal that you can give to these men if you think you are in trouble."

Marilyn and Jake looked on confused by this last comment. Marilyn spoke. "I don't understand."

"A simple signal could be you tapping your watch as if it has just stopped." Andy demonstrated by taking his right hand and tapping his fingers on the face of his watch. "Another possible signal could be you pushing your hair back as if extremely frustrated. That is providing this is not a common habit that you already have." All smiled at this moment of levity.

Marilyn considered her options. "Let's go with the watch signal that seems simple enough."

"Alright, the watch it is. Keep in mind, however, that when you give this signal my men are going to come to you. If you use this signal by accident, their covers may be blown." Andy paused again to assure this point was understood. "So use it when you need it but be careful not to cause a false alarm."

Marilyn nodded her agreement. "What about the girls? Do they need a signal?"

"No, that will not be necessary. For the girls I have arranged something better." A broad smile now formed on his face. "Beginning tomorrow, your daughters will have a new student teacher at their school who has volunteered to act as the recess monitor each day. Her name is Sally Halloran, and she is one of my best undercover officers."

Marilyn looked at Jake and then back at Andy. "Mr. Baroni, I certainly hope all of this for nothing."

Andy and the two other supervisors looked at her sympathetically. "So do we Mrs. Oliver."

CHAPTER TWENTY TWO

Marilyn left the hotel the following morning and took the girls to school. When they arrived she went inside to see Mrs. Henderson and explain what was going on but Baroni Security had already beaten her to the punch.

"Ah, Mrs. Oliver, so good to see you this morning. I was just getting to know my new student teacher, Ms. Halloran." As Mrs. Henderson turned to introduce her new assistant, an attractive brunette with short hair pulled back with two berets approached Marilyn with an extended hand. She appeared to be in her early twenties, about 5'9" tall with a rather 'tomboyish' build. "Mrs. Oliver, so nice to meet you and these must be your girls." She dropped to one knee. "Let me guess. I bet you are Briana and that makes you Sarah. Did I get it right?" Both girls nodded their heads with a broad smile.

Marilyn turned to the girls. "Sarah and Briana, why don't you run on so mommy can speak with Mrs. Henderson and Ms. Halloran." As the girls scampered off to see their friends, Marilyn continued. "Mrs. Henderson, I had hoped to be able to explain____"

"Oh, that is quite alright," replied the teacher. "I am just glad that you and Mr. Oliver are taking necessary precautions."

Marilyn then looked at Ms. Halloran questionably. "But how did… how was this arranged so quickly?"

"Mr. Baroni contacted the principal of the school and explained what was going on. Apparently, he was aware of your conversation with Mrs. Henderson and quickly supported the idea of placing me on the staff temporarily." She paused and looked at Marilyn who still looked confused. "I...I hope that was alright?"

Marilyn still could not believe how fast things had happened. "Oh...a...yes, no problem." She looked at Mrs. Henderson. "So you and the school are alright with all of this?"

"Absolutely. In fact, I will feel much better having her around."

Marilyn turned to her daughter's bodyguard. "Ms. Halloran____"

"Please call me Sally."

"Alright, Sally, what is it you plan to do if the man returns to take more pictures or if he tries to take one of the girls."

"Welcome to the age of technology, Mrs. Oliver." Sally pulled back her collar to reveal a small microphone. "I can be in contact with my office instantly and I can assure you that no one is going to mess with your daughters."

Marilyn looked at this young girl somewhat skeptically but then gave her a slight smile. "Well, I am counting on you so please don't let me down."

....

While Marilyn was getting used to life with Baroni Security, Jake now returned his focus to uncovering what the hell was going on at his hotel. In the past month since his arrival, he had been threatened, deceived and his privacy had been violated. After making his usual rounds of the hotel and reviewing the days activities, he asked Jim if he had time to go for a little walk.

Once outside of the building in the alley between the parking garage and employee entrance to the hotel Jim spoke for the first time. "Jake, it seems like the next thing we have to do is uncover who our snitch is here at the hotel."

"I agree and I think I have a plan." Jim smiled as Jake explained what he had in mind.

A few hours later Jake was working in his office reviewing the information Laura Sanders had compiled for the upcoming union negotiations. Laura had done an excellent job of presenting the financial impact the hotel would encounter if all aspects of Local #78's proposed changes to the contract were to occur. As Laura had pointed out during their previous meeting, it was quite apparent that a key emphasis was being placed on increasing the pension dues the hotel would be responsible for paying each month. In fact, as Jake reviewed the information, it was his impression that the wage increases being proposed were almost token gestures and that their real objective revolved around the union's pension program rather than taking care of the union's members financially.

Jake called Sandra into his office. "Sandra, I need you to do some research for me on_______"

Suddenly, Jim barged into the office visibly excited. "Jake, sorry to interrupt but I think I have something you have been looking for."

Jake and Sandra both looked up momentarily startled by Jim's entrance. "I don't understand Jim, what are you talking about?"

"In my hands sir is, what I think, is a copy of the documents that Tony Hoy was going to share with you the other night." Jake looked at Jim astounded by what he had just heard. He also regretted that Sandra had been present during Jim's moment of excitement. He began to reach for the manila envelope in Jim's hand when he turned to Sandra sitting across the desk listening to Jim's discovery with equal excitement.

"Sandra," said Jake in a more subdued voice, "can you excuse Jim and I, I think I need to review what he has."

Sandra looked on with an expression of confusion and a tinge of anger. "A…well…yes…sure. I'll come back later." Sandra grabbed her note pad and left abruptly.

On her way out, Jake added. "Oh…and can you close the door behind you? Thanks, Sandra."

Sandra closed the door as she was instructed and dropped her notepad on the desk. She paced around letting her hostility subside before sitting at her desk. *The nerve of the man,* she thought. *Does he not think that I am competent enough for them to share the information?* Sandra quickly gained control as Shannon Kincaid entered the office.

Shannon took a quick peak in Jim's office and then turned to Sandra. "Hi, you seen Jim anywhere?"

Sandra looked up sharply. "He's in with Mr. Oliver!"

Shannon looked on with fascination sensing that something was up. "Oh…well…I can come back." Shannon turned to leave and then stopped. "Sandra, is something bothering you?"

Sandra looked at Shannon, annoyed by her question but then quickly composed herself and gave a weak smile. "No, it's nothing. I was just in the middle of a meeting with Jake, I mean Mr. Oliver, and Jim barged right in. And then I am asked to leave!"

Shannon looked on with amusement. "Oh, they're men, what do you expect. They have no manners." Shannon waved her hand as if to dismiss the whole matter. "Don't let them get to you."

Sandra looked at Shannon and shrugged her shoulder and extended her hands with palms out. "I suppose you are right. Why should I let it bother me." Shannon gave her a thumbs up sign and departed. Sandra leaned back in her chair. She was still frustrated. *How am I to do my job if I am not part of Jake's inner circle.*

……………………………………….

"I don't know about you but boy do I feel like a heel just now." Jake said in almost a whisper after Sandra closed the door.

"Yeah, I know what you are saying," acknowledged Jim, also in a hushed voice. "Do you really suspect Sandra is the leak to Jackson Chi?"

Jake leaned forward in his chair. "I certainly hope not, Jim. Personally, I like her. She has been a great secretary and I would truly like to think she is on our side. But if she *is* the leak, I have no room for her at this Inn, if you get my drift."

Jim nodded in agreement soberly. "Well, I guess we will know soon enough after I blurted out my discovery in front of her."

Jake paused another minute and then picked up his phone and called Sandra on the intercom. "Sandra, get a hold of Chi and tell him I would like to see him right away!"

"Yes sir. Do you want him to come here or will you be going to his office?"

Jake recognized immediately the coolness in her response. Jim just shook his head and mouthed the words, *you sure got her mad!* Jake gave him a weak smile. "No…I think it would be better if I go to his office."

There was a slight pause before Sandra responded. "I see. O.K, I will contact him right now. Is that all?"

Both Jim and Jake cringed at how she asked the last question. "Yes, Sandra and thank you."

....

Dan Kowalski and Shannon Kincaid were finishing up a late lunch in the hotel's newly remodeled employee cafeteria when Jim entered and grabbed a seat next to them. Jim looked around with satisfaction that all of the tables were full with employees having lunch. Less than a month prior, almost no one even wanted to enter this room other than to grab their 'so called' lunch and then go back to their respective departments to eat.

These changes began the day after Jake toured the basement employee areas of the hotel with Dan Kowalski, Dan and his engineers were directed to give the cafeteria a complete face-lift. New ceiling tiles had been installed to replace the ones missing or stained from previous water leaks. All of the tables and chairs had either been repaired or replaced as needed. New wallpaper had been installed on three of the walls and floor to ceiling mirrors on the forth wall made the room seem 'bigger and less claustrophobic'. A television had been mounted in one corner to provide the staff some entertainment and Laura Sanders had selected new table clothes to be used rather than have the staff eat on bare tables. Lastly, Jake had insisted on a complete overhaul of the food being provided to the staff. Fred Plummer and the chef developed a set of menus for each day of the week. Jake explained that for many of the hotel staff, the hotel employee meal was the one solid meal they may have each day. So 'let's make it a good one' he told the kitchen staff.

As a result of these changes and improvements, the staff of the Wilford was now beginning to look forward to lunch and to taking breaks in this room. Another key observation was that each staff member was doing his or her best to keep the room clean and in good condition. In fact, the rest of the employee areas such as the locker rooms and service corridors were being kept cleaner with less clutter. The staff was beginning to take pride again in the hotel they worked for after so many years.

The key to getting this trend going, however, had started where it always must, from the top. Jake had insisted from the day of his arrival that he and his managers would eat their meals in the employee cafeteria whenever possible. Personally, Jake appreciated as much as the next to have a nice quiet meal and take a brief break from his day to day activities. But for the staff's attitude and morale to change, one must lead by example. The staff had taken notice of this change in management philosophy and began to appreciate what was being done on their behalf. The changes that Jake had implemented had cost the owners next to nothing, but had demonstrated that management was committed to the employees of the Wilford. Ultimately, this respect and support would carry through in the service these workers gave the guests of the hotel.

Happy employees meant happy guests and happy guests kept coming back for more. This formula for success had not been new for Jake. He had implemented similar programs at the numerous hotels he had managed over the years. What continued to amaze Jake, however, was how simple the equation was for him to understand but how difficult it often was for the owners of each hotel he encountered.

"Hey guys, lunch looks great today. How was it." Jim asked as he dug into the special of the day, meat loaf, mashed potatoes and green beans.

"It was great," acknowledged Dan.

"Yes, it was fine, but a little more food then I prefer," replied Shannon. "Can't we get Fred and the chef to offer more healthy low calorie alternatives? This skirt is already a little tighter than I would like."

Jim and Dan looked at each other and smiled. Neither man was complaining. "Yeah, I know what you mean," said Jim as he resumed eating and leaned forward so as not to be overheard. "But keep in mind that for many of the staff, this is the only good solid meal they eat all day."

Shannon and Dan nodded in agreement.

"Hey, actually I am glad I caught you two. Have you been keeping up on what Local #78 is proposing?"

Dan looked around and then responded. "Yeah, sort of."

"Well what are you hearing from the staff about the proposed changes in the number of shifts that will be offered to the bell staff?"

Shannon looked at Jim with a quizzical look. "What are you talking about? I didn't here about that."

"Oh, I thought you knew. With the new contract proposed by Local #78, you will not be able to schedule anything less than an 8 hour shift." Jim looked around and then leaned in toward Shannon and Dan. "But Jake has already had a little one on one with our negotiator. What's his name, Seleki?" Both nodded in agreement. "Well it seems Jake got the guy to back off and agree to not only 4 hour shifts if we need them but as short as 2 hour shifts as long as we notify the employee 12 hours before he arrives for the shift."

Dan listened intently. "Wow, I didn't think that hotel management and the negotiator were allowed to meet like that before the actual negotiations begin.

"Yeah, well between you and me, Jake has this little shit eating out of our hands." Dan and Shannon looked at Jim amazed by his comments as Jim excused himself and they followed. All three left the employee dining room together.

Seated at an adjacent table, Sergio Cervantes had been picking at his food as he tried to overhear their conversation. Although some parts he had missed, he had gotten the general gist of what was going on. He quickly threw away what was left of his food and proceeded to the hotel parking lot for what most assumed was a quick smoke. Once out of earshot of others he pulled out a cellular phone and pressed speed-dial #3.

"Hotel & Restaurant Workers Union, Local #78, this is Vera."

"Yeah, it's Sergio, is the boss around?"

"Sure hon, just a sec."

....

As Shannon and Dan left the cafeteria, Jim pulled both of them aside and directed them to join him up in his office. Once there and behind closed doors he explained. "Look guys, sorry to be playing something of a game with you but it was necessary." Both managers looked at him more confused than ever as Jim continued. "The story of Jake cutting a deal with the union was not exactly the truth."

Shannon sat in the chair across from Jim's desk while Dan remained standing leaning against the door. "What the hell's going on Jim?"

"Let's just say that we are playing a hunch." Jim looked at his two managers thoughtfully. "And I hope the real pigeon just took the bait."

....

"Vera, get me Seleki on the phone right now!" Shouted Lou Walizak from his office.

"What is it boss?" asked Ed Flago who was sitting at the couch in Lou's office, finishing a large stromboli sandwich he had picked up at a nearby carryout out Italian restaurant. Lou had already finished his sandwich.

"I just talked to Sergio, at the Wilford. He says that he overheard some managers talking and they are saying our man Mickey cut some type of deal with the General Manager."

"Nah, that don't make sense. Why would Mic go and do a thing like that?"

"Fuck, I don't know! That's why I want to talk to the shit." Lou stood and walked to the door of his office. "Vera, you get a hold of him yet?"

....

Jake was finishing up a phone call from a guest who had been less than satisfied with his stay when Sandra knocked on the open door to his office and stood in the doorway patiently. When he hung up the phone she spoke. "Sorry to bother you, sir, but one of your employees would like to have a moment of your time.

"Who is it?"

"He is from housekeeping. A Mr. Kono Hisitake."

Jake looked up, suddenly remembering that this had been the kid who was having the argument in the locker room during his tour of the hotel the first week he arrived. "Please, show him in."

Kono Hisitaki entered Jake's office looking more nervous and out of place than ever. He was dressed in his uniform and carried with him some rags and a spray bottle that hung from his belt. Kono looked around the office and then took a seat across from Jake. Jake motioned for Sandra to close the door and then addressed his guest. "Kono, nice to see you again. What can I do for you?"

Kono fiddled with his rags before speaking. "Well, I feel kinda stupid coming here but I just don't like what is going on." He shook his head and looked down at his hands.

Jake looked on, interested in what his visitor had to say. "Kono, first of all, I am glad you came to me to talk about whatever it is you want to discuss. If it will make things easier, let me clarify that whatever we discuss in here is between us and no one else."

Kono stared at his new boss trying to read any sign that Jake would deceive him. But all he saw was a man being extremely sincere. "Yeah…well…O.K. Look I'm here to let you know that one of the staff is going around getting everyone all fired up and saying some bad things about you."

Jake smiled. "Well, it wouldn't be the first time I haven't been liked by everyone. Why is it bothering you so much?"

"Because it sounds like bullshit to me! I mean, excuse me sir." Kono shook his head as if angry that he lost his cool in front of his boss.

"Alright, why don't you tell me what is being said and I will confirm if it is *bullshit* or not." Jake continued to smile as he used his own choice of words back at his conscientious employee.

Kono shifted in seat and Jake thought the uniform shirt the kid was wearing was going to tear at the seams. From the look of Kono's arms and upper torso, he assumed Kono must work out constantly and be on an aggressive weight lifting program. "The word is that you cut some type deal with the union and are screwing the bell staff."

Jake considered how he should best respond. He also recalled what Jim Slazenger had said about Kono one day when Jake saw him arguing with some other employees in the locker room. While Jim was the acting General Manager and was working one Saturday morning, two police officers came by asking to see Kono. Jim had been initially apprehensive as to what Kono could have possibly done but the officers quickly clarified that all they wanted to do was ask him some questions.

Jim contacted Olivia Fernandez and had her find Kono and send him up to the executive offices. Jim was also quick to tell her that Kono was not in any type of trouble but that he needed to come to his office right away. Kono arrived roughly five minutes later and, when he saw the police officers, he was clearly nervous. Jim assured him, however, that the police officers were just there to ask him some questions.

Jim stepped back into his office and the police officers questioned Kono in the office reception area. Since none of the other managers were yet at work at that time of morning, they had relative privacy. As the officers questioned Kono, Jim could not help but appreciate what he overheard.

The questions concerned a recent hit and run accident in which he had apparently been a witness. But as Jim listened to the series of questions, it was quite obvious that Kono had been much more than a witness. The accident had occurred around 10 o'clock in the evening. Kono had been waiting at a bus stop when he witnessed two women walking across the street. A car then approached the intersection and ran the red light striking both of them. Kono explained that what really got him mad was that the two 'dudes' in the car just jumped out and took off running. Kono chased down the first guy and tackled him. As he put it, 'after one blow the guy was out.' He then explained that he took off after the second guy and caught up to him just before he ran into an alley. Kono described how he grabbed the guy and threw him into a brick wall. It was at that point that he gave the officers a nervous laugh stating 'and that dude didn't get up either.'

Jim's initial assumption had been that Kono must have done something wrong when in reality the guy was a natural hero! After the officers extended their thanks to Kono, Jim also congratulated him for doing such a good thing. Kono simply shrugged his shoulders, however and said, 'It was nothing, they just made me mad after hurting those women and all.'

And now that same quiet spoken man was seated across the desk from Jake. Jake knew that if his co-workers got wind that he was in the GM's office, they would most certainly ostracize him so he decided that he should confide in him a little as to what he was up to. "Kono, I appreciate you telling me this but what your friends are saying is not exactly correct." Kono looked at him questioningly. "I can't go into all the details with you…but let's just say, I'm trying to uncover the fox in the hen house." Jake paused to see if his metaphor had made any sense. From the sudden smile on Kono's face, it appeared it had.

"Got'cha boss. If you need my help in any way just let me know. Cus' the guy that is dissin' you man just pisses me off."

Jake returned the smile. "Kono, I may just take you up on that offer. But for the time being, we need to keep things quiet. Alright?"

"Yeah, no problem. But we *are* talking about Sergio aren't we?" Jake hesitated and then nodded. "Then you should know that a lot of the staff are scared of this guy, including some of your managers."

Jake considered this last comment carefully. "What about you, Kono, why aren't you scared of the guy."

Kono, just smiled. "I do what I want, man. Not what someone tells me to do! A…except you boss."

Jake stood and leaned across his desk and both men gave each other a 'high five'.

……………………………………………

Andy Baroni's men had uncovered four well placed listening devices at the Oliver home. Instead of disabling the devices and alerting whoever was behind this crime, however, they used their equipment to jam the signal. The plan was for his technical crew to stand by and hope the individual that had placed the devices would check it out to see what the problem was.

One of Andy's technicians approached him as he sat in his office. "Hey Andy, you got a minute?"

"Sure Greg, come on in. What's up?"

"Well it's about the bugs we found at the Oliver house."

"What about them?"

"Well, they're real top quality." Greg paused deciding how best to proceed. "In fact, I thought the FBI was the only one that had these latest models." Greg's last comment got Andy's complete attention and looked up from a report he was reviewing.

Andy was now more intrigued then ever. He placed a few phone calls to some individuals that he knew with the bureau hoping he might be able to confirm if the FBI was possibly doing some undercover work and their paths had crossed. But all of his efforts uncovered nothing and he decided to drop the issue for the time being. He then turned his attention to who might have had access to the Oliver's home. Since they had just purchased the home, he decided to start with the realtor. He looked through the information one of his clerks had been able to gather on a Ms. Naomi Shu.

It indicated that Ms. Shu had rented a house roughly 6 months prior that was located only a short distance from the Oliver home. Ms. Shu was listed as being an independent realtor working for Remax, Inc. She apparently worked out of her home. What bothered Andy, however, was that when he attempted to research further on her work history, places of residence and citizenship, he continued to hit walls. In most cases the information just wasn't available for some reason or other.

Andy also had another concern. What was it that Jake Oliver was involved in that was generating so much attention. This had been his key concern ever since his initial meeting with Jake and Jim to discuss using his services. In turn, unknown to Jake Oliver, he had decided to assign one of his men to follow Jake in addition to the arrangements that had been made for Jake's family. The individual he chose was one of his best and had been advised to keep his distance. Andy did not like keeping secrets from one of his clients but, for the time being, he needed more information on Jake Oliver as well.

....

"Well, Jake how was your day?" Asked Jim as he entered his office late in the afternoon and shut the door behind him.

"Very interesting, how about yours."

"Well, I think all has gone as planned. I sure hope my great acting did not go to waste today at lunch."

"Actually, I can already assure you that you may be up for an *Oscar* with your acting debut." Jake said with a broad smile.

"Why, what has happened?"

"Well, I had a visit this afternoon from Kono Hisitake, our Samoan friend in housekeeping."

"No shit, I'm amazed he came to your office."

"Yeah me too. But his visit was quite informative. It appears Mr. Sergio Cervantes is making a lot of noise about my mysterious deal to screw him and his fellow bell staff."

Jim looked on in amazement at how fast his dirty work had taken effect. "That's absolutely amazing. What did you tell Kono?"

"Well based on what you have told me about him, I decided to gamble a little. I asked him to keep our little secret quiet for the time being. I hope we can trust him."

Jim nodded as he spoke. "Not to worry. Kono is a good man. In fact, we may be able use him later on." He leaned back in his chair. "What about Sandra? Is she our leak to Chi?"

At that moment, Sandra knocked on the door. She informed Jake that Jackson Chi would meet with him at 6 o'clock. Jake nodded his approval and she closed the door and went back to her desk.

Jake smiled at Jim. "I guess we'll have our answer to your question after my meeting but I'm inclined to think the worst at this time.

CHAPTER TWENTY THREE

Jake arrived at Jackson Chi's office a few minutes before their scheduled meeting. Ms. Chuen, Mr. Chi's secretary, greeted him. She indicated that Mr. Chi was just finishing up a phone call and would just be a few more minutes. As Jake took a seat on a comfortable leather couch situated on the wall opposite to the door leading to Mr. Chi's office, Ms. Chuen inquired if he would like any coffee or tea while he waited. At first Jake declined but she insisted that she had just made a fresh pot of tea and that he should really try it.

Jake conceded to the attractive young woman who gave him an alluring smile as she proceeded to another room. Jake had to admit to himself as she walked away in a tight and rather short dark green skirt, that Mr. Chi certainly had good taste. There was something about this woman, however, that made Jake uncomfortable. The first few times they had met or spoken on the phone, Jake merely summed it up to her good looks, but today he had a better understanding of why she made him nervous. It was her mannerisms and the tone of her voice. It was as if she was mocking or baiting him along because she knew what Jackson Chi had in mind. If Jake's feelings were correct, he only wished that *he* knew what everyone was up to.

Ms. Chuen returned with the tea in a cup and saucer of fine oriental china. Her movements were fluid and slow and Jake continued to watch her as she returned to her desk. "Tell me Ms. Chuen, how long have you been working for Mr. Chi?"

She looked down at her desk then up at Jake slowly. “I have been with Mr. Chi since I came to this country two years ago.”

“I see. You are from Hong Kong?”

“Actually I was born in Mainland China but my parents moved to Hong Kong when I was very young.”

Hoping she would be more talkative, Jake continued. “So,” he said with a smile, “how did a nice girl like you get with Jackson?”

Ms. Chuen looked down at her desk and did not respond. The look on her face was not of embarrassment but rather more of shame.

Jake decided to change the subject and pointed to a small Jade carving sitting on her desk. “What an interesting carving. Jade?”

“Yes, it was a gift from a friend who still lives in Hong Kong. This is *Kwan Koon*,” she said as if the piece of art was a real person, “he was a war general of ancient China. The significance of this piece is to basically ward off evil. Evil is always around us Jake Oliver.”

Ms. Chuen’s last comment and her intense stare caused Jake to look away momentarily. Jake gave her a slight smile. “Well, I guess he keeps rather busy around here!”

Ms. Chuen nodded her head just as the door to Jackson’s office opened and he rapidly walked toward Jake with his hand extended. “Ah, Jake, I’m glad you called and asked to meet. I was concerned after our last meeting. Please come to my office.” Both men returned to Mr. Chi’s expansive office. As Jackson began to close his door, he yelled to Ms. Chuen, “no interruptions and no calls!”

“Yes, Mr. Chi,” responded Ms. Chuen again in her cool and controlled voice.

Jake sat in a comfortable leather wing back chair opposite the desk. Jackson then sat in the other matching chair rather than behind his desk. Jake assumed it was his attempt at making their meeting less formal. He then asked. “Can I get you anything, coffee or tea?”

“No, I am fine. Ms. Chuen took good care of me.”

“Yes, she is quite efficient. So, as I said, I was a little worried following our last meeting.” He studied Jake sitting across from him. “Perhaps we have not been getting off to a good start. If so, we must change that.”

Jake was amused by Jackson’s new tactical approach. “Well, maybe so, Jackson. I do tend to ask a lot of questions at times.”

"Ah yes, and so you should. But I must say that your concerns regarding the renovation of the hotel are entirely without warrant." Jackson paused briefly as he shifted in his chair. "I should have explained matters to you from the start. It is a bad habit of mine. I just tend to go right in to things and find the whole process of having to explain my actions an annoyance. I am sure you, as a hotel manager for so many years, often feels the same. Am I correct?"

Jake was fascinated as to where this conversation was going. He then nodded his head as if in resignation to Jackson's question. "Perhaps sometimes."

"Of course you do. Well let me explain and put your mind at ease." Jackson stood and walked to the window. "There is going to be a bidding process as you put it coming up very shortly but in Hong Kong we are used to doing things slightly different than you Americans."

Jake leaned forward in his chair. "I am not sure I understand."

Jackson approached Jake and now sat on the edge of his desk across from Jake. "In our country we strongly believe in working with those individuals and businesses that have shown us favor in the past. With regard to our plans to renovate the hotel, this is also the case. The individual companies that will be awarded the bids to do our work are just such examples. Does this make sense?"

"Jackson, I can understand possibly where you are going with this but does such a practice include paying these preferred contractors in advance of them being rewarded the contracts?"

Jackson stared intently at Jake. The first signs of slight frustration appearing. "Jake, these individuals have been associated with our organization for quite some time and we saw no concern in providing them necessary front money to gear up for the work they are to perform."

"Then there should be no reason why I should not be made aware of who these individuals or companies are?"

Jackson stood up straight and was clearly agitated. "As I have said before, the renovation is not your concern." He then immediately regained his composure. "Jake, I have taken the time to share with you a little about how our organization works but now I must clarify that you do not need to worry yourself with matters that do not concern you." Before Jake could respond, he continued. "You are to focus on the upcoming union negotiations. I want them to go smoothly. In fact, unless their demands are too outrageous, I see no reason to dispute them. We want to do our best to have a good working relationship with Local #78 and for that matter all of the unions."

Jake then implemented his next move. "Alright Jackson, we can drop the renovation for the moment but as far as I am concerned, some documentation better exist to support $2 million in expenditures. Tony told me, before his untimely death, that you personally authorized these expenditures and_____"

"Excuse me Jake but I am afraid I must correct you. Such documentation does exists but records of that nature, given the sensitivity of our plans are not kept at the hotel."

Jake waited a moment before responding. "Am I to assume then that you have had the documents all along?"

Jackson looked more disturbed. Clearly he had not considered the possibility that copies of the documents that he had taken from Tony's office that night may exist "A…yes. Now if you don't mind I have a dinner engagement this evening and I must leave to ______"

"And you have the only copies of this documentation. Is that correct?"

Jackson looked as if he was going to explode. "Yes, of course, now if you will excuse me I must______"

"O.K. Jackson, I'll get going." Jake decided that he had one more card up his sleeve. "Thank you for taking the time to meet with me. At least I now know more about *Jakovitz & Associates; Harbinsen, Inc.; Sunblossom Enterprises, LTD;* and *WJC, Inc.*"

Jake's last comment clearly caught him by surprise. He apparently had not been told that copies existed. Jackson at first appeared lost in thought but then responded slowly. "Well Mr. Jake, you are certainly a persistent individual when you want to be." Jackson observed what he now considered a worthy opponent. "Good day sir. We will speak more on this matter at a later date but for the time being, your direction is to assure that the union negotiations run smoothly, is that understood?"

"Most certainly, sir." Jake opened the door to leave and noted that Ms. Chuen had changed clothes. She appeared to be dressed for a night out on the town. As Jake proceeded to the entrance to the office he commented. "Why Ms. Chuen, you look very nice." She simply bowed her head in appreciation as he departed.

....

Lou Walizak was sitting at his desk on the phone when Skinner Portola and Sammy Smith entered. He waived them to a chair briskly and then continued his conversation. "I don't care if others are going to get suspicious I want to know what is going on. Let's not forget what you have been getting paid for these past few years. I would think that you and your family have been enjoying the extra cash each month." Lou listened briefly to the person talking on the other end of the line and then interrupted. "Just do it!"

He then hung up and stared out the window. The streetlights had just come on and the fog was getting thicker by the minute. The sun had already set and as the fog rolled in, the street outside Lou's office took on the appearance of a movie set for a murder mystery. The glow of the street light dissipated and the buildings across the street appeared gray and out of focus. "Would either of you like to explain to me what the fuck happened yesterday?" When neither man responded Lou asked again. "Sometime before I get more angry!"

Skinner looked at his partner and then replied. "How were we to know the two bitches would be driving each other's cars boss?" He then continued before Lou could respond. "And besides it ain't no big deal. We just try again, that's all."

Lou turned from the window and looked at both men. "No big deal, ass hole! Didn't it even occur to either of you that Oliver's wife may have suspected something or possibly saw one or both you following her?" Lou shook his head in disgust as he continued. "That was Jonesy on the phone. He called me after he left the hospital the other day and again just now. First of all, he thinks you guys got lucky in that the other woman may not be able to identify either of you, how I don't fucking know! But he also thinks that these two bimbos may have been wise to you two jack asses and he thinks they were up to something when you guys screwed things up. In other words, he thinks Mrs. Oliver is going to be on the look out!"

Skinner was shifting in his seat nervously. "Hell, what difference does that make. I can go out there and nab the bitch right now if I want!"

"Oh really," responded Lou as he pulled a cigar from his desk and lit it. "Jonesy also told me that Jake Oliver and his assistant GM, Slazenger, met a guy for lunch the next day." The two men looked up questioningly. "Jonesy said his name is Andy Baroni of Baroni Security." Both men looked down at the floor as Lou continued. "He also said that today, this Andy Baroni guy has been asking around about him at that police station." Lou looked at his two thugs in disgust. "Is any of this making sense to you dumb shits?"

Skinner looked up quickly, an angry look on his face, "So they got some security service to help them, I can *deal* with it."

Lou continued to stare at Skinner. "Good and you better take care of it before the end of the week and if you two fuck up, don't bother to come back here because if that happens…*I'll deal with you*!" Lou's last comment appeared to have the desired effect with both men looking up suddenly. "Now go and do your job!"

…………………………………………

"I don't know how much he knows, but he knows more than I thought he did." Jackson paused as the person on the other end of the phone spoke for a long period of time. Jackson then responded. "Yes, I understand…Yes, I will keep you informed." He then hung up and dialed another number. Jackson was gathering his things to leave when Ms. Chuen looked in his office. Jackson looked at her, still annoyed by the meeting he had just had with Jake Oliver, and then waived her off abruptly.

When the phone was answered Jackson began speaking immediately. "I haven't heard from you for a few days. What information do you have for me?"

"I…I do not have anything real useful, sir." Responded the voice on the end of the line.

"Why? What have you been doing?"

"I am sorry but____"

"Enough! I do not want excuses I want information. Do you understand?" Jackson interrupted sharply.

The individual on the phone debated how best to tell Jackson. "Well, actually the equipment appears to be malfunctioning. I have been getting a lot of static and cannot make out what they have been saying for the____"

"Why didn't you tell me sooner! Is this the result of your incompetence?!" demanded Jackson.

"No…no, I'm sorry but I do not know why the system is not working properly. I will try to fix it as quickly as possible."

Jackson paced around his desk angrily. "How can I react to matters properly without information. This is what we expect of you. I would certainly hate to inform Hong Kong that you no longer want to be a part of our organization. Is that what you want?"

"No sir, please, just give me a little more time."

"Get me what I want or else!" Jackson shouted and hung up the phone, grabbed his coat and departed with Ms. Chuen at his side.

…………………………………………

"That was quite a performance Naomi. I think you truly missed your calling as an actress."

Naomi Shu looked across the room at the man sitting at the kitchen table. He removed the head set that he had been using to listen in on the conversation and walked over to a more comfortable chair in the living room. "I'm so glad you approve," she responded. The sharp tone of sarcasm now apparent in her voice. "It's not your life that is in danger here!"

The man smiled coyly. "Oh really, Naomi, we have been working together for several months now and yet you doubt my resources."

Naomi shook her head in frustration. "So what is going on *John*, why is our system not working?"

John leaned across the coffee table and grabbed a handful of peanuts that had been left out. As he chewed his snack he responded very matter-of-factly. "We are being jammed."

Naomi looked at him questioningly. "Jammed, by who?"

It appears that the Oliver's have called in a few reinforcements. But not to worry it is being taken care of as we speak."

…………………………………………

As Jake drove home from his meeting with Jackson he was disturbed. Jackson had never come right out and asked Jake about the documentation that he supposedly had. Was Sandra the leak or someone else? Jackson then went out of his way, at first, to win him over. Why would this be necessary? Jake had then baited Jackson by giving him the impression he knew all about the mystery deposits. Was that a good idea when he really didn't?

As Jake replayed the conversation he had just had he began to formulate several conclusions. The first was that, whatever Jackson was up to, it was going to happen soon given how Jackson began the meeting trying to win him over with the illusion that he was confiding in him that there would be a formal bidding process very soon. It was as if he was simply trying to buy time. Secondly, the only reason Jackson would have seen the need to win him over would have been if he feared that Jake could effect his plans in some way. But how? Was Jackson keeping something from Hong Kong? If Jackson feared that Jake might go to Samuel Cho that meant that Jackson was acting on issues that Samuel Cho was not aware of. If that was the case, Jake was faced with the difficult task of uncovering what was going on and informing his employer as soon as possible. On the other hand, if Jackson was acting on Samuel Cho's direction, than this could place him in an awkward position by contacting Hong Kong. Jake needed more information and he needed it quickly.

CHAPTER TWENTY FOUR

Marilyn Oliver was tired. She had not gotten a regular night's sleep since the incident with Linda Slazenger. She felt uncomfortable back in her new home. Wondering who was out there listening or who was waiting to possibly harm her or her family. And if she and the girls were in danger, in conjunction with something Jake was working on, then it meant that he was in danger also. Jake would say, 'don't worry, it all will work out fine.' But one thing that Marilyn felt she was an expert on was worrying and felt she could hold her own with the best of them. She viewed Jake as always being far more optimistic at times. *Someone has to worry she thought!*

Her daily routine had remained the same. The only difference, however, was that when she left the house each morning to take the girls to school, she was growing accustomed to seeing the white Ford that always followed a few cars behind. Although Andy Baroni had said that his team would be 'invisible', she had pegged them after the first few days. It was Thursday, so she assumed it must be Cliff Weber following her. She would drive to the school and Sally Halloran of Baroni Security would greet them in front of the school. Marilyn would kiss the girls goodbye and then run whatever errands she had planned. Although a part of her greatly disliked being followed everywhere she went, another side of her appreciated the feeling of security knowing that someone was looking out for her and her kids. And she had to admit that Andy Baroni's crew were being true to their word in keeping relatively invisible. At the most she only caught an occasional glimpse in her rear view mirror but then again she knew what to look for. The plan was for the bad guys not to know they were there and get caught so that the Oliver's life could return to normal.

....

Earlier that morning, Cliff Weber arrived for his daily shift at 5:00 a.m. He alternated every three days with his partner Ray Johnson. Cliff had been with Baroni Security for five years and liked what he did. With his blond hair and lean features, he looked like he belonged on a beach working as a lifeguard rather than working for a security service. He was dressed in jeans, tennis shoes and a white sweatshirt with the words *University of San Francisco* embossed on the front. To most he looked the part of a typical San Francisco tourist. Although following around a housewife as she ran errands was not the most demanding of tasks, he figured there were far worse jobs that he could be assigned. Always good-natured, Cliff liked to laugh and have fun but took the job of providing security very seriously.

Standard procedure called for Cliff to arrive in one of Baroni Security's company cars, usually a plain white Ford sedan. Word was that Andy had cut a great deal for the lease of all of his company vehicles. Cliff parked a block away and around the corner on a side street. He walked to a car parked two blocks from the Oliver home. The car had a good view of the Oliver home and, with the use of binoculars, the security officer seated in the front seat could clearly make out each of the Oliver family.

Pete Salis was drinking his coffee when he heard the sudden rap of someone's knuckles on the driver's side window. Pete turned to see Cliff holding a bag of donuts up to the window in an alluring manner. Pete laughed at the site and rolled down the window. "Hey, I'm sorry man but you better beat it. My supervisor will be here any minute." He than smiled broadly. "Oh, but you can leave the donuts."

"Yeah, very funny," said Cliff in as serious a tone has he could muster so early in the morning. "Now get your butt out of the car and go home, it is clearly past your bedtime and you must be suffering from some form of delirium."

Pete looked at him with a confused look. "Delirium?"

"Yeah that rare infliction in which you think I am going to share my breakfast!"

Pete reviewed that all had seemed quiet enough with no signs of sinister cars driving by or following the Oliver's when they left or returned to their home. He left and Cliff settled in to his breakfast of donuts and the two cups of coffee he had purchased on the way.

At 8:30am, he saw the garage door open at the Oliver home and a few minutes later, a dark red Toyota *Camry* backed out onto the street. Cliff put down his coffee and started his car. He then picked up his radio and logged in. "This is perch one. Mamma and her chicks are leaving base now. Do you copy."

On the frequency Cliff was using only two other officers were on the same frequency. One was Sally Halloran who simply tapped her microphone hidden beneath her blouse twice signally that she had received the message.

The other was an officer that had been assigned to follow Jake. "That's a roger. Papa is already at the roost."

"Understood. Stand by for further updates," responded Cliff as a broad smile appeared. He had always thought the use of codes, such as these, sounded so ridiculous.

Cliff followed Marilyn Oliver as she took her two daughters to school. He was glad that it had worked out to have Sally at the school to cover the girls. It clearly was the best way to protect them. But Andy had surprised both he and Ray Johnson by adding an officer to follow Mr. Oliver, given that, to the best of their knowledge, Mr. Oliver was not aware that he had security protection. It was not normal practice for the individual hiring their services to be watched without his knowledge but he assumed Andy had his reasons.

"This is perch one, the chicks have arrived. Momma is again on the move."

Again, Cliff got his required two taps from Sally Halloran acknowledging that she received the message and that the kids were now her responsibility for the day.

And thus, another day of security was underway for Cliff Weber and his team.

....

"So, how did your meeting go with Chi last night?" Asked Jim Slazenger as he entered Jake's office and closed the door.

"Well, it was certainly interesting." Jake then summarized what had occurred the evening before.

Jim leaned back in his chair and sipped his coffee listening intently to what was said before responding. "So basically we are still in the dark about Sandra."

"It looks that way. Jackson never came out and confronted me about the make believe documents that we led Sandra to believe we now have. But, I still think that Sandra is not what she makes herself out to be. I just have a hunch that____"

A sudden knock on Jake's door cut him off. Sandra opened the door. "Excuse me gentlemen, but Mr. Oliver, you have visitors." She then pushed open the door and Ed Lee entered followed by the principal owner of the hotel, Samuel Cho, Chairman and Chief Operating Officer of South Harbor Industries, LTD.

Both Jake and Jim stood abruptly to greet them. Jake walked from behind his desk and extended his hand. "Mr. Cho, it is good to see you again." As they shook hands, Jake briefly looked at Ed Lee questioning the purpose of the unexpected visit.

"Thank you, Jake. I thought it was time I come to visit. I hope this is not a bad time?"

Jake studied both men intently. "Of course not." Jake noticed Jim standing to the side patiently. "Mr. Cho, Mr. Lee, I don't think you have both personally met my Assistant General Manager, Jim Slazenger."

"Ah, Mr. Jim, my sincere thanks for taking such good care of the hotel for me before Jake's arrival. I have heard many good things about your work," replied Mr. Cho as he extended and shook Jim's hand.

Ed Lee stepped forward and also shook Jim's hand and then returned to his stance next to Mr. Cho.

Jim was embarrassed by Mr. Cho's comment. "Thank you sir, your comments are greatly appreciated."

Mr. Cho turned to Jake. "Jake, I hope we are not interrupting anything too important but we were hoping to be able to meet with you for a little while."

Jim caught the cue. "Actually, I was just leaving gentlemen. Please, make yourself at home." He departed and Jake motioned for both gentlemen to have a seat.

Sandra asked if she could get them anything. Both Samuel Cho and Ed Lee accepted her offer of hot tea, Jake indicated that he would stick with his cup of coffee.

"Jake, sorry to drop in so unexpectedly," continued Mr. Cho, "but I felt it was time we had a little talk. As you are no doubt aware by now, Ed has been keeping me somewhat informed of your activities." Jake nodded his head, his reaction apparently easily read by Mr. Cho. "Don't be upset with Ed, Jake, he was only doing what I had asked of him."

Ed now spoke for the first time. "Jake, as I told you, Mr. Cho and I go back many years."

Mr. Cho added. "Actually, Ed has told me that he is quite impressed with your knowledge of construction and architecture and even more impressed with your…how should we say it…*investigative skills*?" Jake was now intrigued. "Jake, I would like to hear more about what you have been doing at the hotel since your arrival."

Jake tried to read what Mr. Cho was digging for and he had a pretty good idea. "Well, let's see, as you know, I have been at the hotel for just over two month. Upon my arrival I encountered extremely high levels of stress from the staff but overall they seem to be responding to some changes I have made. I have met with Ed on several occasions to review the renovation plans for the hotel and I have had the great pleasure of meeting Mr. Lou Walizak, president of Local #78 who is about as offensive as one would expect." These comments drew smiles and a little chuckle from both men.

He then continued. "Oh, but I think I have forgotten to mention that your controller, Tony Hoy, has been killed. There appears to be some possible misuse of funds, although I have nothing to support this claim and I was threatened by men waiting for me in the hotel's parking garage and lastly, someone tried to kidnap my wife the other day! The agitation in Jake's voice was now clearly noticeable.

With these comments, the smiles on both men's faces quickly vanished. Ed looked over at Mr. Cho and then spoke. "Jake, I have informed Mr. Cho about Tony Hoy and some of your suspicions. From our preliminary conversations, Mr. Cho thought it best to come to San Francisco and share with you some further information regarding South Harbor Industries and what is expected of you at the Wilford Plaza Hotel." He then turned to Samuel Cho who looked on with keen interest.

Mr. Cho stood, walked to the window in Jake's office and looked out on the busy traffic on Market Street. His hands were clasped behind his back as if he were about to preside over a jury for opening remarks. "Jake, I want to assure you that no one wants any harm to come to you or your family. We are greatly disturbed by the death of Tony Hoy and we support your concerns regarding what you referred to as a 'possible misuse of funds.'" He then turned and looked at Jake seated behind his desk. "In fact, I want to clarify that we are counting on you to investigate this matter thoroughly for us and to uncover what is going on."

Jake looked at Mr. Cho and Ed Lee. A thousand questions were now coming to mind. "Mr. Cho, I don't understand. If Ed has informed you of my actions, you also know that I suspect that Jackson Chi may be involved and he works for *you* sir. If you suspect something why do you need me to ______"

Mr. Cho abruptly interrupted. "I have suspected for some time that Mr. Chi has misused our money, Jake. We need to know what he has done with it and why he has chosen to take such risks."

His last words 'why he has chosen to take such risks' set off alarms in Jake's head that he recognized probably had more serious implications. "Yes, I understand," responded Jake. "But why can't you just confront him and____"

"It is more complicated than you understand," replied Mr. Cho, a slight tinge of irritation in his voice. He then returned to his chair and leaned towards Jake. "Jake, Jackson Chi has been involved in many dealings with our organization and his knowledge could become a problem if not…how should I say…handled correctly." Jake considered just how serious these 'dealings' could be as Mr. Cho continued. "Why don't we get some lunch and we can discuss this matter further."

Jake, Ed Lee and Samuel Cho left the hotel and drove to a restaurant in *Chinatown.* Jake did not notice the name of the restaurant but, as with the time that he had gone to lunch with Ed previously, there were many customers, most of which were Chinese.

When the three men entered the restaurant they were greeted by an oriental woman who appeared to be in her early sixties and clearly recognized who Mr. Cho was. She quickly approached them, spoke some words in Cantonese and then lead them to a private dining room that consisted of one round table big enough to accommodate 8-10 individuals. Ed Lee spoke to her briefly, again in Cantonese and then she departed. A few minutes later, a waiter brought in hot tea and later various dishes all meticulously prepared. Since neither man had ordered as best as Jake could tell, the restaurant was apparently taking certain liberties in choosing what they would eat. During lunch, the conversation seemed to revolve around the food and how Jake and his family were getting acquainted in their new home. After the last dish was cleared, however, and the waiter was excused, Mr. Cho resumed the conversation that had begun back in Jake's office.

"Jake, we require your help."

Jake sipped his tea and then responded. "For me to assist you, I need to have a better understanding of some things. First of all, up to this point, I feel like I have always been behind the eight ball so to speak. Jackson has always been one jump ahead of me. Someone within my hotel is keeping him informed of my activities."

"And do you have any idea who this informant may be?" asked Mr. Cho with what appeared to be genuine interest.

Jake considered how much he should tell these men at this early stage of conversation. "No, I'm afraid I don't at this time." The silence that followed suggested that neither felt Jake was leveling with them completely. Jake stood fast, however, and remained silent waiting for the next question.

"Jake, we need you to uncover what Jackson Chi is up to. If it endangers my organization he must be stopped."

Jake shook his head slowly. "Mr. Cho, what you're asking has nothing to do with the operation of the hotel. If you are that concerned, you need to contact the authorities and_____"

"Maybe I am not making myself clear," interrupted Mr. Cho, "you really have no choice." The finality of his last words hit Jake as if he had just been thrown into a pool of freezing water.

Jake looked up sharply. "What is that supposed to mean?"

Ed Lee now spoke. "It means, Jake, that you must now listen very closely to what we are about to tell you."

CHAPTER TWENTY FIVE

Andy Baroni was reviewing the security reports from his men when Ray Johnson, one of his supervisors entered his office. Ray held up his hands and had two cups of coffee. Andy smiled and motioned him to sit. "Ah… a man who comes bearing gifts. Have a seat Ray."

"Thanks. Going over our reports on the Oliver's?"

"Yeah, looks like things have been rather quiet. No signs of anything out of the ordinary?"

"No, nothing really. There was a car we thought was a little too common that showed up on several different shifts but we checked it out and it was nothing."

"Who was the car registered to?"

"Some guy named Nelson Smythe, a government worker of some sort. We checked him out but he appeared to be clean with no visible ties to our union friends."

"What department did he work in?"

"Overseas Currency Administration or something like that. Apparently a new guy, not much history with the department."

Andy nodded as he continued to review the reports in front of him. "Well, let's keep an eye on him. You know how hunches often prove to be the real thing when you least expect it.

Ray finished his coffee and stood. "Well, I gotta run boss. I'm relieving Cliff a little early today. He has some hot date or something like that tonight."

"Alright, keep your eyes open on this one. It just doesn't make sense that the bad guys would pack up and go home. I also expected some type of reaction from the person with the big ears now that we have been jamming their signal for the past few days. They're bound to make some type of move soon."

"Yeah, makes sense." As Ray was leaving his office, he encountered two men who had just entered the office. Andy's secretary, Millie was out to lunch so Ray interceded. "Can I help you…?"

Both of the men were dressed in business suits and were not overly friendly. The man in the lead appeared to be in his mid forties with dark hair that was cut short, almost in a military style. He had an arrogant determined expression as he addressed Ray. "Andy Baroni, where can I find him?"

Ray responded in kind. "It depends on who is asking. I still need a name Mr.____"

Andy overheard Ray's question and walked to the door of his office. "I'm Andy Baroni?"

The lead man stepped forward and shook Andy's hand. "Mr. Baroni, my name is John Garrison and this is Skip Henderson. Can we have a moment of your time?"

Andy scanned each man's appearance and demeanor and after a brief glance toward Ray signaled them to come into his office. Ray looked to see if he should stay but Andy waved him off and shut the door. He returned to his desk and looked at the two men sitting across from him. "Now what can I do for you, Mr. Garrison? And lets start with who you work for."

"Mr. Baroni, we understand that you have been making some inquiries regarding surveillance equipment, may we ask why?"

Andy was intrigued that his few calls had generated such interest. These men could have had FBI tattooed on their forehead it was so obvious. Andy leaned back in his chair as he responded. "You know, I do believe I just ask a question and instead of a response I was asked another question. Why don't we begin again. Let's begin with the two of you producing your FBI identifications pronto, comprende?"

John Garrison, the man who appeared to be in charge, glanced toward his partner and they presented identification that confirmed Andy's suspicions that they were with the FBI. "Look Baroni, we are not here to play games," replied Garrison. "Why have you been asking questions about surveillance equipment and if we have any covert operations underway?"

Andy realized that he must be on to something for these guys to come to him. "Gentlemen, given that my business often requires similar talents as yours, I just thought it would be a common courtesy that we make sure no one steps on the others toes."

Garrison again looked over at his partner trying to decide how best to proceed. "Mr. Baroni, I appreciate your interest but surely you realize that we cannot divulge information regarding an ongoing investigation."

Andy nodded his head slightly as if he understood and then hit them with anther question. "You know, I find it amazing that my few calls to the bureau regarding a particular type of listening device has prompted you two to come to my office this afternoon. What else got your interest?"

Garrison smiled and leaned forward in his chair. "You know, Baroni, you may be as good as I have heard."

"Well, I assume that is a complement. Now, what the fuck is going on!"

Garrison again looked at his partner and then responded. "What exactly is your interest in Ms. Naomi Shu?"

....

Jake looked angrily at the two men sitting at the table with him. His mind raced with the realization of whom he might be dealing with but anger and frustration then took over. "Alright, gentlemen, what the hell is going on around here?"

Mr. Cho was the first to respond. "Jake, we have been observing Jackson Chi for some time. And as you have said, he *is* well informed."

"And the two of you know who that individual is?"

Ed chimed in. "We don't know who Jackson's contact or contacts are but we are confident that you will find out." Ed sipped his tea and then continued. "Jake, my suspicions are that you already have someone in mind. Can you share with us who that individual is?"

Jake shook his head slowly. "No, no one in particular. So the verdict is still out. Would you care to share with me, who has been keeping the two of you informed?"

Mr. Cho now responded. "Jake, it is necessary that I keep informed of activities that effect my investments."

The anger was still apparent on Jake's face. "And I guess simply asking your appointed General Manager is out of the question?" Jake retorted.

Mr. Cho smiled. "Jake you are taking this all wrong. Let me____"

Jake interrupted. "Mr. Cho, you said a few minutes ago that I would have 'no choice' but to help you. What did that mean?"

Samuel Cho leaned back in his chair with a satisfied look on his face. It was as if this was the line of questions that he had intended for Jake to take. "Jake, to explain, it is best that you understand a little more about my organization."

....

"Naomi Shu?" Andy Baroni responded as if the name was not familiar to him.

"Don't play games with us Baroni. What is your interest in the background of Ms. Naomi Shu?" Responded John Garrison, now as direct and intense as ever.

Andy was now beginning to piece things together. He decided it was time to provide a little more information and then ask the questions. "This is very interesting Mr. Garrison." Andy stood and walked over to a side table to get some water. He gestured to see if either of his guests wanted some and then continued. "I have a client. This client suspects that his house is bugged. We check it out for him and what do you think we discover?" Garrison and Henderson looked around the office nervously. "Not only do we find the house has bugs, but highly sophisticated devices commonly used by who?" Andy paused for effect. "Why, our own FBI!"

Andy walks back to his desk but does not yet sit down. "Now we know that these bugs have a limited range so our listener has to be close by." Andy takes his seat and is now ready to drop the big one on his guests. "So, then I ask myself, who had access to the Oliver's house just before they moved in. Low and behold, I discover that a one, Ms. Naomi Shu was the realtor that sold them the house and guess what? She just happens to reside at 1322 *Woodcrest Drive*, an address that is located only a short distance from my client and safely within the range to listen in with electronic ears. And now, you two waltz in my office interested in both my inquiries regarding your little toys as well as a woman I would like to know more about. Coincidence…my ass!"

Garrison now stood. "Alright, Baroni, you get your fucking merit badge for this week but you are a little off base. We have been watching Ms. Shu for some time."

"Watching for what? Doesn't she work for you guys?"

"I am afraid we can't say." Andy shook his head in disgust. "But we can tell you that if you will cooperate with us, we may be able to assist you with your client, Jake Oliver."

This last comment got Andy's attention since they obviously knew who Andy's client was.

…………………………………………

Jake's mind was spinning with a thousand questions. "So it was your people that tried to kidnap my wife?"

This question drew a stunned look from both Ed Lee and Samuel Cho. "Absolutely not! We had nothing to do with that incident. In fact, we are at a loss to understand who might have been behind it. Not even Jackson Chi would have anything to gain by such a move."

Samuel Cho continued. "Jake, South Harbor Industries has many interests. These include the construction and management of office buildings and hotels such as the Wilford, here in San Francisco, gaming and casinos operations and a fleet of shipping lines. We are a diversified company that has holdings on every continent in the world. In turn, it is critical that we maintain a balance within our organization to assure profits are maximized and our investments are protected." Jake listened to this rudimentary business 101 lesson wondering where it was leading. Samuel Cho obviously sensed that he was not maintaining Jake's interest. "Many of our business deals generate an immense amount of cash that must be *handled*… properly."

His last comment recaptured Jake's attention and also concern. "Perhaps you should explain just how this cash is to be *handled* properly."

Samuel Cho smiled coyly. "Jake, your hotel represents an important element of that very process."

Jake listened to the words of what he had already begun to surmise. He felt frustrated and angry at what he was being told. He then looked at both men and clarified his understanding. "You mean, sir, that you are using my hotel to launder cash from your overseas operations."

Samuel Cho looked on and a stern look appeared on his face. "Call it what you will, Jake. The point is that much is at stake here and you are most certainly involved."

Jake looked down at the table. "Why are you telling me all of this? What is keeping me from walking out of here and going to the police."

Samuel Cho smiled. "A very good question, Jake. Maybe it would help if we told you that your name and signature currently appears on documents that can link you to approximately $6 million in, how did you put it, *laundered* money?

Jake was confused by his employer's last comment. "What are you talking about? I have signed no such documents."

"Oh, but you have sir. In fact, we currently have documents that, if turned over to your authorities would put you away in jail for many years." Jake looked on questioningly. "In other words, you would not be around to see those two daughters of yours grow up. Now would you?"

Jake shook his head in confusion. "I don't know what you are talking about. What documents and how can I be implicated in what has occurred?"

"Ed, can you explain the process for him?"

Ed Lee had been sitting quietly through most of the conversation but now leaned forward with the mannerisms of a man about to discuss a topic he clearly was not proud of. "Jake, your job profile fit what South Harbor needed." He paused as he organized his thoughts. "The problems you encountered at your last job. The fire, the falsified inspections, the entire incident made you the perfect candidate to meet our needs. In addition, your employment history described your pattern of breaking from established company protocol, a manager who 'bucked the system'. These factors were South Harbor's reasons for selecting you, Jake."

Mr. Cho chimed in. "It was determined that you could easily be set up to take the fall for us if we ran into trouble. And now, Jake, we plan to get the bonus of you helping us uncover what, our friend, Mr. Jackson Chi has been up to." Ed looked at Jake whose intense stair prompted him to look down at the table. Samuel Cho instructed Ed to continue.

"In the event, the authorities start investigating the hotel and South Harbor Investments, this plan represented their parachute so to speak. They will simply implicate you as being behind the laundering of overseas cash. They would then decline any involvement and offer to cooperate entirely with the authorities."

"Our losses would be great but minimized." Samuel Cho continued. "The false documents would tie you to a small loss to us but substantial enough to satisfy your law enforcement. In turn, we would suffer only the minor inconvenience of having to secure a new location in the world to handle our money."

"So you see Jake," Cho continued, "as far as the police would be concerned, you have already committed the crime and your questionable past will only help solidify their case. We, of course, would express our complete ignorance to your activities and let you take …what is the word…*the rap* for the crime."

The true seriousness of what these men were telling Jake began to take effect. Jake spoke now only slightly louder than a whisper. "What is it that you want?"

Samuel Cho tapped the table next to his empty cup of tea and Ed Lee quickly picked up the pot and filled his cup and Jake's. "Jake, I realize what we have told you may come as quite a shock but all is not lost. All you have to do is uncover what Jackson Chi is up to and we will take care of matters from there. As for your position, as long as we are safe from the authorities, so are you, providing you cooperate when asked to do so." He sipped his tea and then continued. "Is that too unreasonable?"

……………………………………

Agent Garrison looked at the president of Baroni Security with intense frustration. Garrison had spent two years developing this case and now some wise ass rent-a-cop could destroy every thing.

John Winston Garrison, was the youngest son of a family of eight that grew up in central Kansas. Contrary to many families in that part of the country whose focus revolved around farming and agriculture, the Garrison household was rather unique. Paul Garrison, John's father was a doctor and his mother, Emily was a registered nurse. Both parents were highly educated and assured that all of their children were afforded the same opportunity.

As each of John's older sisters and brothers graduated from college and launched into successful careers as doctors, lawyers, business executives and the like, John's interest was in law. Unfortunately, contrary to his father who looked forward to his youngest son pursuing a degree in law and setting up a successful practice, John's sought his education in law enforcement. This clearly angered his father, who felt that such a career was a waste of John's talents. In turn, the two men grew distant from each other.

After advancing to the rank of detective with the Kansas City police department, however, it was apparent that John Garrison had a natural talent for solving the more difficult cases. His successes became well publicized in the local papers and this recognition began to break down the barriers that had been created between he and his father.

John then decided to expand his career by joining the Federal Bureau of Investigation in 1984. Considered by some within the Bureau to be somewhat unconventional in his thinking his efforts were rewarded by continued advancement and increased responsibilities. In the summer of 1996 he was assigned as Assistant Director to the San Francisco field office, a promotion that was envied by many throughout the country.

Agent Garrison attributed his success to two key factors. His willingness to constantly challenge himself and the fact that he truly enjoyed his job and the satisfaction gained from putting the 'bad guys' as he referred to them away.

Garrison then turned to the other man with him, Skip Henderson, who spoke for the first time. "Andy, I am the director of our San Francisco office and Agent Garrison has spent the past two years working this case. I am about to share with you some information that involves the security of the United States." Andy walked over to his desk and sat down. "Are you familiar with a man by the name of Samuel Cho?"

Andy shook his head. "No sir, I am not."

Skip then took off his coat and asked "can we get some coffee, this is going to take a while." Andy called his secretary, Millie, who had returned from lunch and within a few minutes, a fresh pot of coffee was brought in and set up on Andy's credenza.

Once Millie was gone, John proceeded. "For the past two years we have been investigating a Hong Kong based operation known as South Harbor Investments, LTD. A man known as Samuel Cho, a wealthy businessman who resides in Hong Kong runs this limited partnership. From what we have been able to gather, the manner in which he accumulated his wealth is open for discussion but it appears that he and his partners prospered in the years immediately following World War II." John looked at Andy and then asked, "are you following me so far?"

Andy nodded an affirmative and John continued. "South Harbor Investments owns various real estate and businesses throughout the world. One such piece of real estate that resides here in San Francisco is the Wilford Plaza Hotel." Andy sat back in his chair as the pieces of the puzzle began to fall in place. "Ms. Naomi Shu has worked for South Harbor for the past ten years. They recruited her young, if you get my drift. Ms. Shu has no love loss for her present employers but her options for leaving don't exist." Andy understood what John meant by this comment. "In turn, we recruited Ms. Shu to also work with us this past year."

Andy leaned forward and spoke. "So *you* guys bugged the Oliver home?"

"No stupid. Remember that Naomi Shu is still working for the bad guys. She was directed to set up the Oliver's in the home they are now in. This is her specialty with the organization. We simply assisted her to keep her in good graces with her employer. In turn, she shares what she knows."

"So you have no interest in Jake Oliver?"

"We didn't say that did we?" Garrison responded in an irritated tone. "We are curious, however, why an organization hires the guy and then bugs his house. Maybe there are concerns with Oliver, we're not for certain."

Andy stood and walked to get a cup of coffee. "O.K. guys. I'm not here to screw up your investigation. Jake Oliver hired me after someone tried to nab his wife and possibly his kid. My only concern is to take care of my client."

Skip Henderson again spoke. "Look Andy, as far as we can tell, Oliver is clean but most likely up to his eyeballs in shit with a company that he may not even know anything about. We want Samuel Cho the head of this monster. But we cannot have you and your men fuck things up."

Andy nodded his acceptance. "Alright, what do you want me to do?"

CHAPTER TWENTY SIX

Jake returned to the hotel alone and after signing a few purchase orders and checks that were waiting for him on his desk he decided that he needed to collect his thoughts. As he packed his briefcase, Sandra Kelly knocked on the door. "Sir, can I speak with you for a moment?"

Jake looked at Sandra but his mind was millions of miles away. "A…actually Sandra, I need to run a few errands and will most likely be gone the rest of the_____"

"Jake, please. I really need to speak with you."

Jake looked at his young professional assistant and leaned back in his chair. "Alright, Sandra, what's up?"

"Sir, I have gotten the impression, that I have upset you or angered you in some way. If I have, I am truly sorry. But what is it that I have done?"

Jake looked at her cautiously. His head was pounding and he needed time to think. "Look, Sandra, I'm not upset. I just have a lot on my mind and____"

"Sir, I can help you in your dealings with Mr. Cho."

This comment caught Jake off guard. "What exactly are your talking about?"

"I know that Samuel Cho specifically sought you out to be the new GM of this hotel. I thought this was a rather strange request but I assisted them in locating you at the hotel in Santa Barbara. They were very interested in information regarding the problems you had at the hotel."

How long ago was this?" Asked Jake.

Sandra thought for a moment. "Oh, about two months before you came on board."

Jake nodded. Samuel Cho had been in contact with him also around the same time while he was at his last job. It was all part of their plan. Jake walked around his desk and sat in the chair next to Sandra. "Sandra, listen to me. I apologize if I have been...a...somewhat distant, but believe me, I do appreciate your concern but please bear with me just a little longer."

....

The two FBI agents left Andy Baroni's office and proceeded to their car. Once inside, Garrison spoke. "What do you think Skip? Can we trust him?"

"Actually, he seems like a good guy. His record as a cop was spotless and his reputation in his work with the local police both in L.A. and here in San Francisco are good. How much more time you need?"

Garrison shook his head. "I don't know, maybe another couple of weeks, maybe more."

"Any word from our contact inside the hotel?"

"Nothing too exciting...but I will keep you informed."

Skip Henderson considered Garrison's words as they drove back to their office. "You still want to make the move with Oliver?"

"Yeah, I think we need him." Garrison responded slowly as if he was considering his options.

"Then make the move with Oliver soon, John, and make sure Ms. Shu doesn't jump ship or double cross us."

"Yeah, I'll take care of it."

....

Naomi Shu arrived at her home at 7 o'clock that evening. It had been a long day of dealing with two couples that she had shown numerous homes to throughout the city. It was hard for her to relate to the people that had enough money to seriously consider some of the outrageously priced homes that existed in the city. But such prices existed when demand to live in one of the most beautiful and romantic cities in the world exceeded the supply of houses available.

Naomi kicked off her shoes as soon as she entered her house and proceeded to her bedroom. The first thing she was going to do was get out of her work clothes and take a long hot bath, one of her favorite methods to relax.

Naomi unzipped her skirt and let it fall to the floor. As she finished unbuttoning her blouse, she was grabbed from behind and thrown on to her bed. She turned to see who had attacked her but it was too dark since she had not yet bothered to turn on the light. She could only make out the silhouette of a man's face from the light that filtered through the window from the outside street light. "Working late tonight, aren't we Ms. Shu?" The voice spoke in precise Cantonese. Naomi was overcome with panic and could not initially speak. "Come, come, Ms. Shu, is that any why to greet the man that pays for this house?"

Naomi now began to compose herself. She pulled her blouse together and responded. "I…I didn't know you were coming."

The man now went over to the nightstand and turned on the lamp. He took a moment to gaze at Naomi in her partial attire. "Of course you didn't." His eyes drifted down the length of her shapely physique on the bed. She still had on black stockings and a garter belt and her blouse was unbuttoned and hung open except where she held it closed firmly. "Put on some clothes and join me in the living room."

Naomi looked at him questioningly. "What do you want?"

"I said get dressed!" The man responded abruptly. He then turned and walked out to the kitchen and fixed himself a drink. As Naomi quickly dressed and went to the bathroom to compose herself, he continued to speak. "Do you remember when you joined us Naomi?"

Naomi stared at herself in the bathroom mirror. "Yes, I remember very well."

"And when I brought you to San Francisco?" He asked more deliberately.

"Yes, it was five years ago." Naomi responded as she entered the living room to find him sitting in one of the wing back chairs by the fireplace.

The man looked at the ice cubes in his glass as he spoke. "Five years, and you would think in that time, you would have some degree of loyalty to me."

Naomi looked at him confused as to where he was going with this dialog. "I don't understand."

"I think you do." As he looked up from his drink. "Why didn't you tell me Samuel Cho was in town?"

Naomi looked at him with a blank stare. She was surprised to hear that Mr. Cho was in San Francisco and confused as to why he thought she would know of his visit. "I…I knew nothing of his visit. How could I have____"

"Because, if you were doing your job of listening to the Oliver's you would have known!" Shouted the man angrily. "Jake Oliver must have know he was coming to town. He has probably said something." The man stood and walked across the room toward Naomi. "Your job was to keep *me* informed, remember!"

Naomi backed up slightly as he leaned toward her. "I…I told you, the equipment it____"

"Why haven't you fixed it?"

"I…I have not been able to get into their house." Naomi looked around nervously. "There was nothing I could do and____"

The man suddenly slapped her across the face knocking her against a wall. "You have failed me Naomi." He stooped down with his face less then a few inches from hers. "Do not fail me again." He said barely above a whisper.

The man then stood and looked around the house. "I think we will pass on going out tonight. I hope that is alright with you?" Naomi remained speechless sitting on the floor. He walked to the front door and turned just before he left. "By the way, when did you start smoking?"

Naomi looked at him entirely confused by his question. "I don't smoke."

"Ah…I see. Then why is the ash tray full on the kitchen table?"

Naomi realized that the cigarettes were from the FBI agent that John Garrison had sent to check out the surveillance equipment. He had been somewhat of a flirt actually and she had also thought he was rather cute. When the agent had not been able to find anything wrong with the equipment from the receiving end, they had talked for a while the afternoon before. Naomi had to answer the man's questions carefully. She knew how dangerous he was. "One of my neighbors, Sally Kingsley, was over and we were visiting. She is a chain smoker."

The man stared at her intensely and then responded. "Yes of course. Well I must be going." As he began to close the door he added with a smile. "Oh, by the way, I enjoyed the little strip show earlier. Pity though, I should have waited a little longer and gotten my money's worth."

When the door closed, Naomi brought her knees up to her chin, huddled on the floor against the wall and began to cry. Naomi hated the man that had just left and she hated the people she worked for. And she hated her life. Naomi knew that her decision to assist the FBI was extremely dangerous but she had to change her life or end it. There was no other option.

John Garrison had introduced himself as someone who had just moved to the city and was looking for a new home. At first it all proceeded as planned. In fact, she found Mr. Garrison attractive and he appeared to be single and straight, two key requirements often hard to find in a liberal city like San Francisco. He was easy to talk to and asked her questions about where she was from, how long she had been in San Francisco and how long she had been in real estate.

But just as she was beginning to relax around this man, his next question brought a lump to her throat. He asked how long she had been working for South Harbor Investments. She initially tried to deny that she knew what he was talking about. Garrison then proceeded to recite her entire history from the day she had joined South Harbor Investments and when she had moved to San Francisco.

Before Naomi could react, he then explained that he was with the FBI and that he knew what illegal activities she had done for the organization. He said that if she would assist them in exposing what South Harbor was up to, he would arrange for her a new identity and a real life that she had never had. He also made it clear that her other option was to either go to jail or be deported. The latter of which Garrison knew had the least appeal, given that if the organization thought she had said anything she would be dead within 24 hours. Naomi had no choice but to cooperate.

....

Jake arrived at home to the smell of something great cooking in the kitchen. He entered the kitchen to find Marilyn in her cooking garb. The kitchen looked like the site of a mad scientist's experiments. "Something smells real good." Jake said as he walked up behind her and kissed her on the back of the neck. "But I am afraid to ask what got sacrificed."

Marilyn elbowed him in the gut. "Yes, well, I may not be the neatest and organized cook, but the end result is always worth it."

Jake raised his hands in the air in mock surrender. "No argument there. Where are the girls?"

"They're in the back yard playing with some neighbor kids they met at school. In fact they live in the house just two doors down from here."

"Well that's good." Jake then placed his briefcase on the couch and fixed himself a drink.

Marilyn noticed he appeared to be off in some other world. She checked her dinner and then came out to join him. "So, how was your day?" Jake looked at her, wondering how or even if he should explain. Marilyn then realized what he might be thinking. "Oh, it's alright honey, two guys from Baroni Security came by and removed all of the bugs. Andy called me beforehand and explained that it would be no problem, given that they had been jamming the signal for the past couple of days. Whoever was listening clearly had to know that the gig was up."

"The gig is up? Picking up the lingo rather quickly are we?" This drew a smile from Marilyn as she returned to the kitchen to double-check the items cooking. Jake was somewhat disturbed that Andy had not informed him of this change. He then recalled there were over a dozen phone messages sitting on his desk that he had not bothered to look at after returning from his meeting with Samuel Cho and Ed Lee. For all he knew, Andy may have tried to contact him.

Marilyn returned and took a seat on the couch. Jake continued. "Well, it has been a disturbing day and I don't really know where to begin." Jake paused as he tried to decide how much he wanted to explain to his wife. But they had been a team for over 12 years and he had always found Marilyn to be a great sounding board and source for good ideas. And tonight, he needed some good ideas.

Jake fixed himself another drink and for the next hour he reviewed what had transpired and closed with what his possible options might be. What disturbed both Jake and Marilyn, however, was Mr. Cho's comment that neither he nor Jackson Chi was behind her attempted kidnapping. This left good old Local #78 as the culprits, but why?

CHAPTER TWENTY SEVEN

Briana Oliver stood outside the bus with her friends. Today they were going on a field trip to the San Francisco Zoo. All of the 35 kids were excited and jumping up and down. The fact that it was a rainy day sure didn't seem to bother them. Each child had been issued yellow rain slickers and blue umbrellas. Sally Halloran, however, was not excited. Several key security concerns existed. First, Sally knew that her ability to contain and protect these girls was limited in a large and spread out area such as the zoo. And most importantly, as Sally looked at the kids jumping up and down in front of the bus, all she saw were 35 seven-year-old kids of approximately the same height, all wearing the same yellow rain slicker and carrying the same blue umbrella.

In addition, the two Oliver girls would be separated and that would require additional personnel from Baroni Security. Sally had placed the call to her supervisor, Ray Johnson. Ray had arranged for a second female officer to accompany her with the Briana's class to the zoo. Another female officer was assigned to remain at the school with Sarah Oliver. A key concern, however, was that the second officer, assigned to Sarah Oliver was relatively new and inexperienced.

....

Marilyn backed out of the garage and looked down the street. She didn't see the white sedan that she had come to recognize. She wondered where Cliff was. He had followed them earlier that morning when she took the girls to school but as Marilyn turned the corner and proceeded on her rounds of various errands. She caught a glimpse of the car and sighed in relief. She proceeded to a drug store a few miles away to pick up some photos that she was having developed. At a traffic light, the security car was two cars behind Marilyn. She looked in the mirror and noted that the man driving had dark hair but that was all she could make out with the rain coming down and the condensation on the mirror and windows. Although Marilyn found this odd, given that Cliff typically worked on Tuesdays, she did not give it much thought assuming that he had traded shifts with someone else.

....

The first grade class of Lakeside Heights Elementary School arrived at the zoo at 10 o'clock in the morning and quickly exited the bus in an orderly fashion. The children were advised that they must stay together and listen to the volunteer parent chaperons that also accompanied the kids. Sally Halloran and the other officer, Janice Keller, scanned the area and agreed that one would stay in the front of the group and another in the back.

They proceeded into the park and all appeared to be going well until they came to the gorilla cages. The kids went wild and all took off running toward the exhibit. The group was now extremely spread out and intermingled with the other customers of the park. Sally and Janice quickly scanned the group to make sure that none of the kids were wandering off. They then noticed one solitary yellow rain coat walking off with a man in jeans and a dark windbreaker jacket.

....

Marilyn left the drugstore and walked to the dry cleaner that was located in the same shopping complex. While in the dry cleaner waiting for her clothes, she looked out to the parking lot but did not see Cliff's car anywhere. She knew it was ridiculous to keep looking for the security officers. They had told her that most of the time, she would never see them but she liked to be sure. Marilyn left the dry cleaner and walked to her car. She again did a quick scan of the parking lot but saw no one. She placed the clothes in the trunk when a man suddenly stepped out of a car parked next to her.

"Excuse me, Miss?"

Marilyn jumped back not knowing what to do. The man seemed to realize that he had startled her. "I…I'm sorry, I didn't mean to startle you. I was just wondering if you had any jumper cables." He motioned with a wave of his hand at his car. "My battery is dead."

Marilyn still did not know how to react or to believe the man. All she could manage to do was shake her head no and say. "A…no, I'm sorry." She then quickly got in her car and drove off. After a few minutes, her breathing began to return to normal and her mind began to race. *Where was Baroni Security?*

……………………………………

Sarah Oliver was talking with her friends in the school corridor when a woman approached and asked to speak to her. She walked away from her friends a short distance and the woman introduced herself.

"Hi Sarah, my name is Tammy Daing and I will be filling in for Sally today."

Sarah looked at the woman questioningly. "But Sally said a woman named Kelly would be here today?"

Tammy was annoyed with the little girl in front of her. "Look, I don't know. All I know is that I was told to be here this morning and keep and eye on you. So don't give me a hard time, O.K?"

Sarah nodded her head and then asked. "Can I go now?" Tammy nodded and Sarah returned to her friends looking back several times as she walked away. Tammy simply shook her head and walked off to introduce herself to some teacher she was supposed to check in with named, Mrs. Henderson. But first she had to make a quick phone call.

……………………………………

"Security two to one" radioed Janice Keller to Sally Halloran.

"This is one, go"

"Over by the flamingos, we got one of the kids walking off with a white male in jeans and blue windbreaker."

"Yeah, I copy. Converge immediately!"

Both women officers ran to the man with the child. Sally grabbed him, threw him to the ground, and pinned his arm behind his back. Janice grabbed the child. It was then that both women realized that the child was a boy and he was screaming not to hurt his 'daddy.'

The parent chaperons gathered the other children and Briana's teacher ran to them. The man on the ground was now yelling. "Let go of me! What the hell is going on?"

Sally continued to hold the man, "Who are you and why were you taking that child."

The man turned his head to see as best as he could. His face was pinned to the wet asphalt. "That child is my son. And I just wanted to visit with him."

The teacher, Karen Jones nodded. "Yes, that is Mr. Pieser, I believe. Mr. Pieser, the school has been advised that you are to stay away from your son."

"Yeah, well…I just wanted to talk to him." Said the man struggling to get free but Sally held on tight.

"Well, you can explain that to the police mister." At that moment two police officers appeared on the scene and took the man away. Sally turned the man over to them and then quickly scanned the area to make sure Briana Oliver was safe and accounted for. "Is everyone else here?" She called to the parents to the group.

"A…Ms. I think we are missing one." Yelled a mother in the back of group.

……………………………………………

Marilyn arrived at the grocery and entered the store. This was her weekly shopping for the entire week and she was in the store 45 minutes. When she emerged from the store, she did a quick scan of the parking lot and was pleased to see the white security vehicle. This made her feel at ease. She proceeded to her car continuing to scan the other cars for no more surprises such as the episode back at the dry cleaners. All this business was making her jumpy and she didn't like it.

Marilyn had placed her groceries in the trunk and was returning the cart to one of the designated areas in the parking lot when her cell phone rang. She fumbled for her phone just as she saw the Baroni Security vehicle pull up behind her car. The officer, a man she did not recognize got out of his car and called out. "Mrs. Oliver? We just received a call from the school, can you come with me please?"

Marilyn looked at him as she answered her cell phone. "Mrs. Oliver, this is Andy Baroni, are you alright?"

It took Marilyn a moment to register two conversations at the same time. One conversation was coming from her cell phone and the other from the officer standing in front of her. "A…yes, in fact one of your officers is here now and____"

"Mrs. Oliver, that's not one my guards, get in your car and drive away ____" The phone was grabbed from her hand.

The officer standing in front of her terminated the call. "I am sorry but, as I was saying Mrs. Oliver, you need to come with me immediately. There has been an accident."

……………………………………

"Briana, where were you?" Asked Sally Halloran, not wanting to alarm the small child after their brief frantic search.

Briana looked around and wondered why everyone was looking at her. "I…I just went to the bathroom." She pointed to the restrooms located next to the Gorilla exhibit. "I didn't mean to do anything wrong but I really had to go!

Sally knelt and gave the little girl a hug. "It's alright, we just didn't know where you were. At that moment, Sally's radio beeped. It was followed by a call from the base office.

……………………………………

When the connection went dead, Andy Baroni slammed down the phone and picked up his radio. "Code Red! Code Red! Abduction is currently underway. Proceed to last known location of Mrs. Marilyn Oliver. 1526 Sanders Street, Murhpy's Dry Cleaning. Pronto!"

Andy paused and then continued. "Base to Officer Halloran"

"Halloran here."

"Sally, we think they are making a move on Mrs. O. Are the little one's alright?"

"A…sir, I can only comment on the youngest. We had a little scare but all is fine."

"Who is with the oldest"

"The new officer, what's her name, Kelly or something."

Andy then looked at a roster in front of him. "Base to Kelly Masterson, report!" After several moments of silence he looked at his assistant. "Millie, get me the school on the phone! What's her name…Henderson?"

A minute later Millie called to Andy from her desk. "Andy, Mrs. Henderson is on line two."

"Yes, Mrs. Henderson, this is Andy Baroni, did my officer check in with you this morning?"

"Yes." Replied Mrs. Henderson. "In fact, I was just about to contact you."

Andy held the phone close. "Why is that?"

"Well, your replacement officer, Ms. Tammy Daing, she is not getting along too well with the kids."

Andy stared at the phone in disbelief. "Mrs. Henderson, please listen very carefully. The woman there is not one of my officers but an imposter. Where is she now?"

The reality of what Andy had just told her took her breath. "Oh my, well she is in class right now but they are due to break for recess in the next 20 minutes. What do you want me to do?"

"Nothing." Responded Andy, I will be there personally but please do your best to make sure she does not leave with Sarah Oliver."

Andy ran out the door of his office shouting orders to his secretary to have back up officers meet him at the school immediately.

……………………………………

Jake had remained relatively low key focusing on the day to day issues of running a hotel while he juggled the new developments that had arisen. His owners had basically set a trap to uncover a problem in the ranks and used Jake to be the broom to clean up the mess. He was considered a disposable commodity and had clearly been set up from the start and this aggravated him tremendously. With over 20 years in this industry, he should have noted the signs better.

Jim Slazenger knocked on the door. "Hey, hey, got a minute?"

Jake looked up from behind his computer screen. He had been entering the latest developments in his computer journal as he organized his thoughts. He quickly hit the minimize button and waved for Jim to enter. "Come on in. What's up?"

Jim plopped down in one of the chairs across from Jake. "You've been kinda quiet today. Something bothering you?"

Jake smiled. "Oh, I guess I just got a lot on my plate right now."

"No doubt about that!" Jim looked at Jake with genuine concern. "Alright, how about dinner tonight, you, Marilyn and the girls? I've found a new restaurant. It's called *Max's Diner* and wait until you see what their desserts look like." While talking, Jim held up his hands to demonstrate that the desserts were over 8 inches tall.

"Sure, I'll give Marilyn a call and_____"

"Excuse me Jake," interrupted Sandra who opened the door suddenly without knocking, "Mr. Baroni is on the line and he says it is urgent."

Jake immediately reached for his phone and punched the active line. "Yes Andy what is it?"

"Jake, we may have a problem. One of my officers has not checked in for over an hour. I contacted your wife on her cell phone to advise her that we could not reach our officer. She told me that my officer had just pulled up to her car. Then the phone line went dead."

"Is Marilyn alright?"

Andy paused. "We don't know yet. I have several units out looking for her by retracing all the places she typically goes."

Jake was standing now and pacing behind his desk. "What about my girls?"

"Briana is fine." Again Andy paused. "But, we may have a potential problem at your daughter's school with Sarah."

"What do you mean?!" Jake yelled into the phone.

Andy paused as a loud truck drove by. "Sir, we suspect that an imposter is currently there posing as one of my officers." Before Jake could respond he continued. "I am on my way there right now and we will take care of things."

Jake stood there and held the phone as his mind was racing. The reality that someone may have just kidnapped his wife and that an attempt was underway for one of his daughters was overwhelming. "Andy, how did this happen?"

"Jake, I don't have the answers yet but I plan to very shortly."

Jake felt helpless. "Andy, I am on my way and will meet you at the school. You have my cell phone number. Call me if you find out anything."

"Yes sir." Jake hung up abruptly.

"What is it Jake?" Jim asked seeing the tension in Jake's face. He had risen from his chair and was standing next to Sandra. Both looked concerned and recognized that something was terribly wrong.

Jake was already putting on his jacket and looking for his car keys. "The guard watching Marilyn has not checked in, Marilyn may be in trouble and someone may be trying to take my daughter, Sarah, as we speak!"

Sandra heard the phone ring and returned to her desk to answer it.

Jake was starting to walk out the door when Sandra interrupted. "Jake, there is a man on the phone. He won't say who he is but told me that you would want to speak to him."

Jake stopped, looked at Jim, then at Sandra and then returned to his office. "Put it through now." Jake picked up the phone.

"Mr. Oliver, we have someone who belongs to you." The voice paused for effect and then continued. "No harm will come to her as long as you cooperate. Is that understood?"

Jake debated how best to respond. "I don't know what you are talking about."

The voice laughed. "Oh, I think you do. That's why you hired the rent-a-cops to keep an eye on your wife and kids. Guess they weren't so good after all."

Jake's voice grew stern. "What is it that you want?"

"You will be informed later. I just wanted to introduce myself. But listen very carefully. If you go to the police, she's dead! Do you understand?"

"I want to speak to her." Jake responded quickly.

"No," responded the man on the phone.

"If I don't talk to her, I'll assume that you have already killed her and I *will* go to the police. And then, I will hunt your ass down. Now, do you understand *me*!" Retorted Jake angrily.

The voice now hesitated. "I'll call back and you can speak to her then."

"I speak to her now or I go to the police!"

Jake could overhear muffled voices on the other end of the line. "O.K. Mr. Oliver. Talk to your wife." Jake could again here muffled voices and then in a shaky voice Marilyn spoke. "Jake?" Jake's grip on the phone tightened and it was visible to Jim and Sandra with his knuckles turning white and his jaw becoming tight.

"Marilyn, are you all right?"

There was a slight pause and then she responded. "A…yes. Are the girls O.K?"

Jake debated how best to respond. "I think so. Look Marilyn I will____"

The man was now back on the line. "Alright, you spoke to her. Now do what we tell you or this lady is going to get hurt. Understand?"

Jake was almost in shock at what was happening. "Yeah, I understand. What do you want from____"

The man interrupted abruptly. "I told you that we will get in contact with you. But, again, go to the police and she is dead. Don't forget it!"

"I will contact you later this evening and advise you of what I want on your cell phone, so keep it on and wait for instructions." The line went dead with no further words.

Jim was standing across the desk from Jake throughout the phone conversation. "It was them?"

"Yeah, they have Marilyn." Jake looked down at his desk. "Was I right to ask to speak to her?"

"Absolutely! It is the only way you can know if she is still alright."

Jake grabbed his car keys. The deep lines of concern etched on his face. "Look, I gotta get to Sarah's school."

"Jake, you have to get the police involved," replied Jim almost in a whisper.

Jake shook his head sharply. “No, not yet!” Jake then ran out the door.

He exited the rear employee entrance of the hotel and ran up the stairs to the second level of the parking garage. As he approached his car he was too preoccupied with what had happened to notice the two men getting out of their parked car a short distance away.

....

Andy arrived at the school and was greeted by Ray Johnson who was standing out in front. “Is she in there?”

“I’m afraid not, Andy. Seems our mysterious woman posing as one of our officers flew the coop.”

Andy slammed his fist against his car. “How did she know?”

Ray shook his head. “We don’t know for sure but we think she must have observed us pulling up in front. The students said she excused herself stating she had to go and then just never returned. It turns out that the classroom she was in is located right in front.” Ray pointed toward the window.

“Damn. Sarah Oliver is alright?”

“Yeah, she is fine.”

Just then both men’s radio’s sounded. “Base to P-One.”

Andy grabbed his radio. “This is P-One, go.”

“Andy we are at the 7-11 at the corner of Market and Hillside. We found officer Weber tied up in the men’s restroom.”

“Is he alright?”

“He has been beaten up pretty bad and we have called for an ambulance.

“Very well. Keep me informed. P-One out.”

....

Sandra approached Jim as Jake ran out of the office. Tears had already formed in her eyes. “Is it true, Jim, has someone kidnapped Marilyn Oliver?”

Jim raised his hand signally her to be quiet and then motioned her to come to his office. He closed the door behind him. Neither one noted the individual standing in the adjacent office who had overheard what had just occurred.

CHAPTER TWENTY EIGHT

Jake ran to his car and was placing the key in the door to unlock it when he heard footsteps behind him and turned quickly to see who was approaching. Two men in suits stood less than ten feet way. The one on the left spoke first. “Mr. Oliver, can you come with me, sir? We’re with the FBI.” The man flashed a badge of some type that Jake did not have a chance to look at closely. “Please sir, can you step over to our car?”

Jake looked at each man questioningly. “Am I under arrest?”

“No sir. We just want to speak with you.”

Jake hesitated. “Look, I have a problem at my daughter’s school and____”

“Sir, it will only take a minute. Please.” The man again motioned toward a dark *Crowne Victoria* backed in to a parking space near the wall. Jake proceeded with the men and was directed to step into the back seat while the other man held open the door.

Once inside the car, Jake encountered another man. He too was dressed in a dark suit and appeared to be in his mid forties. Jake also observed that, even though the man was dressed like a typical businessman, he could not help but notice the man’s gun in a shoulder holster visible where his coat hung open. This man sat quietly until the door was shut. “Mr. Oliver, my name is John Garrison with the FBI.”

Jake looked around nervously. "Can I see your badge? The other two guys merely flashed theirs quickly and I want to make sure I know who I am talking to."

John reached into his inside coat pocket and handed Jake his badge. It read, *John Patrick Garrison, Deputy Director, International Affairs, Federal Bureau of Investigation, San Francisco Field Office.* Jake handed it back and then leaned back in the seat and John continued. "Mr. Oliver. I felt it was time we have a little talk."

....

Sandra left Jim's office and went to the restroom to compose herself. While she attempted to make herself more presentable, Laura Sanders and Shannon Kincaid entered. Laura noticed that Sandra seemed upset and was the first to comment. "Sandra, are you alright?"

Sandra turned away and dabbed her eyes with a tissue. "Yeah, Yeah I'm fine. I just…I just found out a good friend of mine may be trouble."

Shannon looked at her with concern. "Anyone we know?"

Sandra shook her head no. "No, but thanks for asking." She left the other two women and returned to her office.

After she departed Shannon turned to Laura. "What was that all about?"

"Who knows. Let's face it, she is always so secretive around here."

Shannon nodded. "Yeah, maybe, but she really seemed upset. Maybe she will tell us when she is ready." Both women smiled at each other and then also departed.

....

"Mr. Oliver, I am not sure how best to explain this to you. The FBI has been watching South Harbor Investments and the activities of Jackson Chi for some time." John Garrison looked for some type of reaction from Jake. As he continued he noted that Jake seemed distracted and distant. "It's also my hunch that you too, suspect something is not right in the hallowed halls of the Wilford Plaza. Am I correct, Mr. Oliver?"

Jake did not respond as Garrison continued. “In fact, we think you know that your Chinese buddies are up to something and have been conducting your own informal investigation.” Garrison continued to watch Jake attempting to get the desired reaction. When he saw what appeared to be a man rapidly attempting to process the information he was receiving he again continued. “Jake, we need your help.”

Jake looked at him. “My help…how?”

“Jake, we need you to provide us with the necessary documentation to clarify what illegal activities your employers are up to.”

Jake stared at the man seated next to him. “And how do you know that I am not involved? In fact, how do I know that you have not been watching me and that I am being set up to take the fall for whatever you suspect is going on at the hotel?”

Garrison leaned back in the seat, pulled out his cigarettes and lit one before he responded. “Why would we want you Jake, have you done something wrong that you want to confess?” The sarcasm in his voice annoyed Jake.

“I just want to know why you have chosen me. I am not involved in anything and I'm not sure I know what you are talking about.” Jake stared at John with an intensity that indicated to John that this was not a man that would be manipulated easily.

“Jake, to be honest, at first, we did suspect that you may be involved. The sudden accident that took the life of Sam Filmore and then your quick appointment certainly got our attention. After observing your actions, however, we now suspect that you too feel that your employers are up to something. All I am suggesting is that we pool our efforts.” John Garrison paused at that point to allow his words to sink in and there was silence in the car for a full minute before Jake responded.

“Look Mr. Garrison, I can appreciate your concerns, but honestly, I'm not exactly sure I know what you want me to do?”

Jake's attempt to side-step the issue aggravated Garrison. He tossed his cigarette out the window and leaned forward toward Jake. “Look, Jake, don’t fuck with us. We know you suspect something. If you choose not to help us, then you will go down with your Chinese buddies. Is that what you want?”

Jake's anger also became apparent. "What I want is to get out of this car. I have an emergency that requires my attention NOW!"

John studied the man sitting across from him. Jake was certainly more strong willed then he suspected. But deep down, he needed the assistance of someone from the inside and Jake was his best opportunity. He then considered his next response carefully. "Look, Jake, I think you are an honest man that has chosen to work for some individuals that turned out to be some crooks. You need my help and I need yours. Here is my card. Take it. Think about my offer but don't take too long or you are going to go down with them."

Jake took the FBI agent's card and stared at it for a few seconds before responding. "Can I go?"

John waved toward the door and one of his men opened it from the outside. Jake got out, ran to his car and quickly departed.

John pulled out another cigarette and lit it as one of his men stuck his head in. "So, is he going to play ball?

John shook his head and said, "I honestly don't know."

....

Andy Baroni called Jake on his cell phone. Jake answered immediately. Andy advised him that his daughter, Sarah was fine and briefly summarized what had occurred. He then expressed his concerns for the safety of Jake's wife and what he knew so far.

"One of my supervisors, Cliff Weber assigned to follow Marilyn this morning, was found beaten and tied up in the bathroom of a 7-11 approximately 4 blocks from your home and his car is missing. We immediately began to search for Marilyn by back tracking all of the areas that she typically frequented. We found her car abandoned in a grocery parking lot. Most likely I was on the phone with her when she was abducted. I called her when we lost radio contact with our man to warn her that there may be a problem. It was then that she indicated that she was fine and that one of my guards was approaching her at that moment. I then quickly advised her that the man approaching was not one of my guards when the line went dead."

Jake listened intently as he swerved to an alternate lane to avoid stopped traffic in front of him. "Andy, I am about 10 minutes away from the school, where are you?"

"I'm at the school and will wait for you."

Jake continued his rather hurried drive to the school. When he arrived, Andy was waiting in front with several others of his staff. At that moment, Jake had one objective in mind. To make sure his daughters were safe and to wait for further instructions from the kidnappers. He also needed time to think and plan how he was going to proceed.

Jake parked his Jaguar in the loading and unloading zone area in front of the school. Andy walked with him as he proceeded to Mrs. Henderson's office and explained that he needed to pick up Sarah and Briana. Briana and the other girls had just returned from their trip to the zoo and Sarah had assumed that her mother was on her way to pick her up. Sally Halloran brought the girls out to meet Jake in the parking lot. Both girls were confused as to why their father had come to pick them up and not their mother. Jake hugged each and as they climbed in the back seat, Sally approached Jake.

"Jake," Andy continued. This is Sally Halloran. She has been watching the girls here at the school."

"Sir, I am sorry about what has happened and____"

"Sally, Andy tells me that you did a great job of handling a situation at the zoo earlier today."

"Oh well, it was nothing, turned out to be an unrelated issue."

"Yes, but you didn't know this at the time. Thanks."

"Jake." Andy said. "We need to discuss matters and____"

Jake looked around before responding. "Andy, I need to go now and get the girls settled. I will call you later this evening."

Andy nodded in understanding and stepped back as he quickly jumped in his car and left. He pulled out his radio as Jake drove away. "P-One to Pappa Watch."

"This is Pappa Watch, go ahead P-One."

"It took Mr. Oliver, a long time to get here this afternoon, anything out of the ordinary?"

"I don't know. Per your instructions I have been keeping my distance on him so I cannot watch him all of the time."

"What do you mean?"

"For instance, when he parks in the parking garage behind the hotel each morning. I see him drive in and then walk out to enter the hotel."

"What's your point?"

"Today, he was in the parking garage almost 10 minutes before he drove out. I mean he walked in, but it took him a long time to drive out?"

Andy listened to the guard he had secretly assigned to follow Jake. "A...10-4 Papa Watch. Stay with him but keep your distance. Remember we are looking for someone that may be tailing him."

"Roger. Papa watch out."

Andy then keyed his radio again. "P-One to Base."

"Go ahead P-One." Responded his dispatcher Betty, who had been with him since the formation of his company. "Betty, what is the latest on Cliff, is he going to be alright."

"That's an affirmative. Doc says he just has a big bump on the head and a lot of bruises."

"That's good to hear. Tell him I want to talk to him as soon as possible. Also have Ray meet me back at the office as soon as possible."

Andy had just put down the radio when Betty's voice came back on calling for him. "Andy, I have Mr. Oliver on the line requesting to speak to you immediately!"

Andy looked at Sally and then responded. "Put him through!" There was a slight pause followed by a few clicks on the radio. "Jake, this is Andy. We need to ______"

"Andy listen to me, I am on my cell phone because I still do not trust the phones in my home."

"Alright, where can we meet?" There was a pause while Jake was apparently thinking. "Andy, can you call Jim and see if Linda can watch the girls for awhile?"

"Sure, no problem."

"Good, I will drop off the girls at Jim and Linda's apartment and then meet the two of you at 7 o'clock at Schroeder's. Jim knows the place."

"You bet. See you there at seven."

....

The girls knew that their father was upset about something and this caused them to both be upset as well, even though neither knew specifically why. Jake explained that all would be all right but neither girl felt the tone in his voice matched his words. When they arrived at the Slazenger's apartment, Linda was already there and assured Jake that they would be fine.

Jake then drove to the German pub that he and Jim had visited during his first week at the hotel. When he entered the restaurant and his eyes adjusted to the dark interior, he spotted Andy and Jim sitting in a booth in the back. Jake sat down next to Jim and across from Andy.

At first there was a brief moment of silence. Andy began. "Jake, have you heard from the them?"

Jake signaled the waitress to bring him a beer and stared at Andy angrily. "How the fuck did this happen?! Where were your guards?"

Andy looked at Jake clearly understanding why he felt the way he did. "Jake, you have every right to be mad." He paused briefly as he decided how to proceed. "Jake, at 10 a.m. this morning, my guard, Cliff Weber did not report in. We attempted to contact him but there was no response. I had teams search the areas that your wife frequented. I then called the school and Mrs. Henderson informed me that someone other than my assigned guard was at the school. I immediately advised my officers to go to the school and I contacted your wife on her cell phone. She stated that one of my guards was just approaching her when the line went dead."

Jake took a swig of his beer. "What happened to the individual at the school?"

Andy shook his head. "She must have spotted my officers when they arrived and skipped out. We are still looking but she appears to have vanished." We found out that the officer that was supposed to be there received a call stating that she was not needed for the day. She is new and failed to confirm this call per standard operating procedures. Sorry." Andy looked down at the table.

Jake looked at Jim and then back to Andy. "Look Andy, I'm sorry I was angry a minute ago but what about my wife?"

Andy looked up and continued. "We found her car in the parking lot of the Safeway grocery. The doors were unlocked and the groceries she had purchased were still in the trunk. The officer assigned to watch her was found badly beaten and tied up in the bathroom of a 7-11." He paused again. "Jake, whoever did this cased us out real good. It was well planned and I am embarrassed and sorry for letting you down."

Jake was not sure how to respond.

Andy continued. "Jake, my entire organization is at your disposal. I want to help. Have you been contacted yet?"

Jake recapped his brief conversation with the kidnapper and Andy concurred that speaking to Marilyn was a good move and something that Jake should insist on each time he is in contact with them.

Jim spoke for the first time. "Jake, how did your meeting go with Samuel Cho and Ed Lee?

Jake was caught off guard by Jim's sudden change in the subject but decided that, until he mapped out a real plan, the fewer that knew what was really going on the better. "Basically, not much was discussed. Cho expressed his concerns with the upcoming negotiations and questioned if Jackson Chi was providing assistance or was a hindrance." Jim nodded and Jake continued. "I decided not to share my concerns about Jackson for the time being."

Jim looked on as his boss finished speaking. He was beginning to read his new boss better and clearly sensed there was more to this meeting that Jake was not sharing with him.

There were a few moments of silence and then Andy spoke.

"Jake, has anyone else been in contact with you?"

Jake looked at him, at first not sure how to respond. "A…no, why do you ask?"

Andy leaned forward with his elbows on the table. "I did some snooping around. Looks like the FBI has been keeping an eye on your employers, Jake, especially your Mr. Cho. Seems they suspect your owners are conducting some illegal activities with the Wilford as the front."

Andy studied Jake's reaction and noted that none of his information appeared to come as much of a surprise and this disturbed him greatly. "So, gentlemen, you appear to be working for some rather despicable individuals that have captured the attention of the FBI for some time. Andy observed as Jake stared into his beer sitting on the table in front of him and then continued. "Jake, any of this come as a surprise?"

Jake looked up suddenly at Andy's question and then at Jim who was watching him with equal fascination. He decided that now was not the time to share all he knew with his new partners. He then simply responded. "It would certainly make sense."

Jim was still trying to grasp the magnitude of what Andy had just said. "Does the FBI know about Marilyn being abducted?"

Andy continued to watch Jake. "No, not that I could tell." Both Andy and Jim sensed there was more that Jake was not saying but neither decided to push the matter. Jim was the first to speak. "What are you going to do, Jake?"

Jake looked at each man. "Guys, I need some time to figure things out. If I need your help, can I count on both of you?"

Andy then spoke, "Jake, I would like your permission to have my men try to find your wife."

Jake was hesitant. "Andy, my concern is that these guys have your team pegged. Your actions could be mistaken as the police and get Marilyn killed. I can't take that chance."

"Jake, I can assure you that my team will be invisible."

"Andy, they clearly noticed your men and just kidnapped my wife!"

"Jake, they noticed my men because they were supposed to be visible to deter such action. Obviously, I underestimated them…it won't happen again."

Jake looked at Jim who nodded that he supported Andy's involvement. "Alright Andy, but please use extreme caution. These guys sense they are being chased, and _____" Jake's voice broke off as he considered just how serious the circumstances were.

They sat in silence for nearly 60 seconds when Jake turned to Jim. "You up to helping further, big Jim, knowing the type of people we are dealing with?"

Jim replied, "you couldn't keep me away."

As Jake stood to leave Andy spoke. "Oh, there is one more thing. We tracked down the surveillance equipment used to bug your house. We suspect that a Ms. Naomi Shu put the bugs there. I assume you know this woman.

Jake turned and quietly replied. "The realtor that sold us our house…why am I not surprised."

"Guys, we need to agree to keep what we know under our hat for the time being. I have a plan but I need to think it through further before I discuss it with each of you. Andy, find out where my wife is and how to get her back. I am counting on you so please do not let me down. Jim, I will need your assistance in uncovering what Jackson Chi is up to and how Local #78 is involved. We've got some loose lips at the Wilford that need to be closed as soon as possible."

All nodded and left. Each knew what they had to do and what was at stake.

CHAPTER TWENTY NINE

Marilyn awoke in a large bedroom of a house somewhere outside the city. At least she assumed it was outside the city because it was so quiet. Her guess was that she was out in the country but the only window had been blocked from the outside to keep her from seeing out. She could not tell if it was day or night. At first she heard no sound at all from within the house. Then faintly she could hear muffled voices. She could not make out what they were saying. It sounded like two voices but that was all she could determine. Her hands and feet were bound tightly with rope to keep her from moving.

The only memories Marilyn had of what had happened to her were now somewhat vague. She remembered walking to her car and putting her groceries in the trunk. She remembered a Baroni Security car pulling up behind her and the officer getting out. She then remembered getting a cell phone call from someone and then she woke up in this room. Her immediate concern was that the kidnappers had not elected to gag her or cover her eyes. That detail she recalled from watching television. If her abductors were allowing their faces to be seen, then they had no intention of ever letting her go. This revelation enhanced her anxiety further.

Her head began to clear and she had a pounding headache. The smell of rubbing alcohol or something like it was noticeable on her clothes. The only contact she had had with anyone since her abduction was what she remembered vaguely when one of her abductors, wearing a ski mask, had entered the room and thrust a cellular phone at her.

It had been Jake on the phone and she vaguely remembered saying that she was alright. Then the man had grabbed the phone from her and left the room abruptly. She knew it was a man because she heard his voice speak on the phone as he walked away. *But was she alright? And what about the girls? Jake had hesitated when she asked if they were o.k.*

The door to her room suddenly opened and another one of her abductors entered with a hood over their face. This one was different in build to the man that had given her the phone earlier. This one was shorter and clearly slighter of build in appearance. He wore dark black dress slacks and a dark knit sweater. He appeared to have a white turtle neck shirt on under his sweater. He left her some food then began to leave without speaking.

Marilyn attempted to sit up in bed and called out to him. "Wait, please, how can I eat with my hands tied?"

The man stopped and looked at her but still said nothing. He then reached in his pants pocket and pulled out a pair of handcuffs. He then untied her hands and attached one end to Marilyn's wrist. The other was attached to the steal headboard of the bed. This allowed Marilyn to have one hand free. Her abductor then promptly left closing the door behind him. During the entire process, no words were spoken. Marilyn continued to stare at the door as it closed. Something was bothering her about the man that had just entered. His movements, appearance and that no words were spoken just seemed out of place.

Actually, eating was the farthest thing from her mind at that moment. She was frightened and wondered if her children and Jake were safe. It then dawned on her that on both occasions the kidnappers had disguised their identity by wearing masks. This, at least, gave her some degree of hope that she may survive this ordeal.

Marilyn then reviewed her surroundings further. The only way out of the room was the one door. The heavy boards across the window made this exit impassible. The room was sparsely decorated with only the one window. A small bathroom was located across the room and Marilyn preferred not to think about how that would be handled when the time came.

She sat on the bed and lifted the cover off the plate of food on the tray in front of her and discovered that her abductors were not exactly cooks. On the plate was a *McDonald's* Big Mac and fries. As she nibbled on some fries that were cold, she began to ask herself what her husband had gotten involved with that would result in her kidnapping. *What did the kidnappers want her husband to do? Jake and her were not wealthy by any means and had no real money to speak of personally, so she immediately deducted that this crime related to her husband's job some how.*

Marilyn again leaned back against the headboard. She was extremely tired and did not know why. She suspected that she had been drugged and this accounted for the loss of time and memory she was experiencing. She resigned that all she could do was wait. She had confidence that Jake would figure a way to solve this problem. He always had in the past no matter how difficult or seemingly impossible the problem was.

....

As Jake drove back to the Slazenger's apartment with Jim, his cell phone rang. He quickly answered it and the same familiar voice he had spoken with less than four hours earlier was on the line. "By now, Jake Oliver you must know that we are serious. Are you ready to cooperate?"

Jake's anger was building but he kept telling himself that he had to keep in control. "What is it that you want?"

"It is quite simple." Jake could here other voices in the background as he spoke. "Starting next week, negotiations begin with Local #78. All you have to do is agree to their terms and your wife will be released."

As Jake listened he noticed some things. The man's voice for instance was almost too precise with no apparent accent. The method in which he spoke suggested an educated individual, possibly foreign. This was no small time thug. The guy was too cool and rehearsed. "Am I just supposed to agree to everything they ask? Can you be more specific?"

"You have been questioning funds appropriated for the upcoming renovation of the hotel. You have also had concerns with the union's proposed increases in pension fund dues."

Jake's mind was racing for a response to throw the guy off balance. "So, you work for the union." It was not a question but rather a statement.

The comment seemed to have no effect. The voice on the other end of the phone said nothing initially. "You will not question the deposits made to contractors and you will support the union's proposed increases to the pension. Any questions?" The voice paused but Jake did not respond. "Understand this Jake Oliver. Play games with me and your wife dies." The line then went dead.

"That was him?" Asked Jim as they drove in silence.

"Yeah, all he wants is for me to approve the pension increases and back off looking into the mystery renovation deposits."

"How are the two connected?" Asked Jim more to himself than to Jake.

"That is what we have to find out as soon as possible, my friend. It all sounds far too simple."

....

Jake picked up the girls and drove home. Although he did not want to worry the girls, his silence caused both to be concerned. Sarah was clearly aware that something was wrong and was the first to ask. "Daddy, what has happened to Mommy?"

Jake looked over at his eldest daughter and smiled. "She has gone away for a while, sweetie, that is all I can tell you at this time."

Sarah looked at Jake intently as he spoke. "Is she alright?"

Jake choked back his response. "I hope so. I really hope so."

When they arrived at home. Jake prepared dinner consisting of hot dogs and chips. Although this represented one of the girls favorite meals, he recognized that it was not one of the more nutritious meals typically served in their household but they enjoyed it and then went to their rooms to do homework and play, not necessarily in that order.

Jake poured himself a drink and sat down to review what his options might be. He got out his laptop computer and opened the file entitled *Wilford Issues*. He entered his password to access his personal files and reviewed what he had written previously before entering the latest developments to date:

- South Harbor Industries is operating the hotel as a front to launder illegal money from its oversees operations.
- I have been set up to take the fall for them with forged documents if anything goes wrong.
- The owners want to use me to uncover how and why Jackson Chi has been skimming money from them.
- Marilyn has been kidnapped and they want me to cease investigating Jackson Chi and support the union's request to increase the pension fund. How are the two related?
- The FBI wants both South Harbor Industries and Jackson Chi but apparently does not have enough to arrest either one. In turn, they expect me to assist them.
- Who abducted Marilyn:
    - Local #78 – Lou Walizak?
    - Hotel's Owners – Samuel Cho?
    - Hotel's Black Sheep – Jackson Chi?
    - Someone else?

Jake paused as he typed in the last statement. If he could wave a magic wand, he would find out where his wife was and get her back. This was his key concern. Once this was accomplished he would focus all of his energies to find the necessary documentation to bury Jackson Chi and then leave it up to the FBI to go after Cho and the rest of the Hong Kong investors. Jake simply wanted to get his family back together and then get the hell out of Dodge, so to speak.

But what about South Harbor Industries forged documents with his name on them and how could the FBI help under these circumstances.

....

It was just past 10 o'clock when Jackson entered the restaurant in the old Italian section of San Francisco. He proceeded to the back and found Lou Walizak seated in a booth.

"Hey Chi, have a seat." Lou said with his mouth full of pasta as he motioned for Jackson to have a seat. "I didn't think this was your type of restaurant but what the hell."

Jackson, appeared to ignore Lou's wise remark. He looked at the two other men seated at the adjacent table. Jackson recognized them as two of Lou's men. "We need to talk...privately."

Lou finished chewing his food and took a long drink of his red wine. He looked at Jackson and then motioned to Ed Flago and another man, named Nick that sometimes filled in for Ed as Lou's driver and bodyguard. The two men stood promptly and walked outside to have a smoke. As they walked away Lou again addressed Jackson. "Alright Chinaman, you wanted privacy, so you got it."

Jackson looked around as he sat down in the seat across from Lou. "Why was the Oliver woman kidnapped today?"

Lou stopped eating and looked up quickly. "What are you talking about?"

"You fool, it was not necessary. I had everything under control and_____"

"Control! Look Chi, I don't know what the fuck you are talking about but I didn't take the broad." Retorted Lou as he banged down his fork. "The negotiations are less than a week away and your General Manager has been asking far too many questions. My men were planning to make the move in the next day or two but someone must have beat us to the punch."

Jackson stared at Lou. "If you did not do this, then who?

"Hell if I know, this is the first I've heard about it. Maybe your buddies in Hong Kong uncovered what you've been up to and decided to set you up to take the rap." Lou smiled, emptied his wineglass, and started pouring another from the bottle on the table. "We both have a lot at stake here partner. I just wanted to make sure it's not me that takes the "rap" if you know what I mean."

Jackson shook his head slowly. "Whoever has taken his wife wants Jake to do something." Jackson looked far off as he spoke. "We need to find out who is behind this. If this should get back to either one of us____"

"Relax, it won't. I'll have my guys dig around and determine who is behind this and let you know."

"But if something goes wrong____"

"The only thing that will go wrong is if you don't keep your end of the bargain. Understand my Chinese friend?"

Jackson looked at what he considered to be a slob of a man. He was stuffing his face with food that Jackson found truly offensive, he was vulgar and uncultured. He questioned how he could have gotten involved with such an individual but he had and there was no choice but to proceed ahead as planned. Jackson stood. "I must go."

"See you around, Chi. And don't worry. It will all work out and you and I will get what we want." Lou waived his now full glass of wine in the form of a mock cheer. Jackson turned to leave and Lou added. "On your way out, can you send in my boys?"

Jackson did not respond as he walked away. He exited the restaurant and saw Lou's two thugs leaning against the building smoking and leering at Ms. Chuen seated in the back seat of his limousine that was parked at the curb. He waived to them stating that their boss was calling and proceeded to the car.

When Ed and Nick were seated, Lou spoke. "Ed, get in touch with Skinner. Tell him I need to see him pronto."

"Sure boss. Anything else?"

"Yeah, I would like to eat in peace. Now get out of my face and find me Skinner, now!

....

As the limousine pulled away from the curb, Jackson appeared lost in thought. Kim Chuen, dressed in a black evening dress, sat comfortably in the back seat next to Jackson. She poured him a brandy as the car pulled away from the curb. She knew that during times like this it was better to say nothing. It only angered him. Jackson's mind was racing as he pondered the day's events. *Why was Samuel Cho in town from Hong Kong and why had he not been notified of his visit? Was Lou telling the truth that he did not kidnap Jake's wife? If not Lou, than who was behind the kidnapping? Did what happened to this woman really concern him? The key was to minimize his personal exposure. Lou would have to be dealt with at some point, of that he was quite certain.*

CHAPTER THIRTY

The alarm clock went off at its usual time of 5:30 a.m. but the man lying in the bed next to it was already awake. In fact, he had slept very little since Marilyn's kidnapping two days earlier. As he laid in bed he thought. *Was she alright? Was she still alive? I can't think that way. I have to keep focused. Today, we are going to get some answers to what is going on and I am going to get Marilyn back.*

Jake got the girls ready for school, fed them breakfast and then arranged to drop them off with Sally Halloran an hour earlier than normal at the school so he could get to the hotel early. Sally also agreed to bring the girls home after school and stay with them at the house until he returned that evening.

He arrived at the hotel at a little after 8 o'clock, and proceeded to his office. He was not surprised to find Sandra Kelly already at her desk. He asked her to forward her phone and join him in his office. She entered and closed the door behind her. "Sandra, there have been some developments. As I am sure you are aware, someone kidnapped Marilyn and attempted to take one of my daughters yesterday." Sandra nodded her head and Jake noted again a certain inner strength about her that he could still not place. It was as if she sat there ready and prepared for whatever assignment he had in store for her.

Jake continued. "I have always trusted my instincts when all of the facts could not be gathered and I have decided that I can confide in you on this matter."

Sandra again nodded and replied quietly. “I will help you in every way possible, sir.”

“My guess is that Jackson Chi may be involved, and it’s his relationship with Local #78 that we need to focus on.”

“Sandra, ultimately my plan may be to bring down the entire organization.” Jake looked on. “If this is the case, my actions, and yours by helping me, may put your job and life in jeopardy.”

“Sir, if the hotel’s owners are behind these events, then working for them is the last thing I want to continue doing. So, what exactly is your plan?”

Jake stood and paced nervously. “Actually, I’d rather not go into the specifics just yet. But I need your help with an important element of the plan. I need you to find out who has been communicating with either Local #78, Jackson Chi or possibly both from within the hotel. My guess is it has to be someone who is close enough to monitor my actions.”

Sandra smiled. “No wonder you suspected me. My first thought was that I would be the most likely candidate.”

“Yeah, and I’m banking that my instincts are correct and your not. If I’m wrong, well the plan just failed.”

Sandra stood and walked over to him. “Sir, I can assure you that your plan is still intact. Let me do a little snooping around and I will get back to you.” She started to leave but then stopped and turned. “Sir, about your wife, have you notified the authorities? I mean, the FBI is supposed to be involved when there is a kidnapping.”

Jake looked up sharply. “No. Sandra, the FBI will be involved in my plan but for the time being, absolutely no word about this to anyone. Understood?”

“Understood.” Sandra again started to leave but stopped. “Sir, what changed your mind? I mean…about me?”

Jake looked at her and smiled. “Let's just say that you passed the test.” She first looked confused by his remark and then smiled. “Alright, if you say so.” Just as she walked through the door she added. “And by the way, I never did buy Jim's story about the copies of the files!” Jake's smile vanished. *Had he made a mistake?*

....

Andy was no fool. He had quickly concluded that someone had tipped off the bad guys that his agency was watching the Oliver's. That someone was clearly providing the kidnappers detailed information on his operation and this had made him appear as a fool and let down his client, Jake Oliver. One of his guards had been taken out and this led to the abduction of Marilyn Oliver. Another one of his guards had been easily conned by a simple phone call and the imposter had come far too close to getting Jake's daughter. Andy was embarrassed by these series of incidents. He had underestimated whom he was dealing with. This would not happen again.

Andy had lots of friends with the SFPD and it did not take him long to find out that no detective was investigating the incident with Linda Slazenger. In fact, his contacts seemed to be caught off guard by his question. Someone had gone to a lot of trouble to make sure that this incident never got any further than the patrol officer that responded to the call. Then there was the matter of what detective Paul Jones, who was assigned to Vice, was doing at the hospital that afternoon stating he was investigating the incident. And now, based on the information that Andy had just received from his phone call, it appeared that detective Jones had not taken any action and filed a report on the incident, which was standard operating procedure.

With a little further detective work, through some other less dignified friends that Andy had, he uncovered that detective Jones, who most referred to as "Jonesy", had been doing some ad hoc work outside the police department for some local unions. Andy was not a betting man but he was willing to bet his next paycheck that one of those unions was Local #78 and that Jonesy was providing information and inside support to the bad guys.

Andy assigned one of his men to tail Jonesy and, as luck would have it, by the following day Jonesy paid a visit to the Local #78 main office on *Levenworth*. For Andy, it was all starting to come together. All that he had to do was turn the table to his advantage.

A special meeting was called that included each of Andy's supervisors. At this meeting, Andy outlined what he called "Operation L-78". The objective of this new operation was quite simple. Use the known suspects to uncover the unknown suspects that will lead them to the hostage, in this case, Marilyn Oliver. Granted, Andy did not know for sure that Local #78 was behind the kidnapping but he placed a lot of trust on his gut instincts and they had never let him down yet. Perhaps that was what he liked about Jake Oliver. Most men in his situation would have been a basket case and panic stricken but not Jake Oliver. He was a fighter and instead of laying down, he was determined to fight to get his wife back. Jim Slazenger had called in a big favor for his new boss. That meant that Jim was supportive of Jake and so was he.

....

Jim Slazenger caught Jake walking through the lobby toward the rear of the hotel and called to him. "Hey, where you off to?"

Jake turned and waited for his Assistant General Manager to reach him before responding. "I am on my way to pay Mr. Ed Lee a visit."

"I see, well I was hoping you might have the time to fill me in on your conversations with the big guys from yesterday."

Jake hesitated. "Yeah, in fact I have a lot to fill you in on, but first I need to go. Let's plan on meeting later this afternoon."

Jim hesitated. "Sounds good. I'll man the fort here."

Jake patted Jim on the shoulder and proceeded out the rear entrance of the hotel toward the parking garage. He didn't notice the white Chevrolet *Caprice* parked in an adjacent parking lot with a sole occupant behind the wheel. The occupant had conveniently parked in a space that afforded him an excellent view of any person coming or going from the rear entrance of the hotel. Jake proceeded up the stairs to the second level and began to walk to his car when a dark four-door sedan pulled up and blocked the path to his car. Two men in suits got out and the one on the driver's side, opened the rear door and motioned for Jake to get in. Jake recognized the car and the men from his previous encounter and got in as he was directed.

"Nice to see you again, Mr. Oliver." Replied the man seated in the back seat.

Jake looked idly out the window. "Do you always make it a point to pounce on unsuspecting citizens in parking garages, Mr. Garrison, or am I just being treated special?"

Special Agent John Garrison gave Jake a slight smile. "We need to talk." He turned to the driver of the vehicle. "Larry, let's go."

Jake looked around. "Where are we going?"

"Don't worry, Jake, you're not under arrest or anything like that, I just need some time to talk to you."

"But I have an appointment to go to and I____"

"This will only take a few minutes." The car pulled out of the parking garage and proceeded down the alley to 8th street and turned right. None of the occupants of the FBI car noticed the white sedan that pulled out the parking lot across the street.

"It's been a few days, Jake. Have you considered our request regarding South Harbor Investments?"

"Yes, I've given it some thought. But I need some more time."

"How much time?" asked Garrison impatiently.

"Another two or three days."

"Why the stall, Jake, what's going on?"

Jake looked directly at Garrison. "Look, I'll play ball but it's going to have to be on my terms." Garrison began to speak but decided it was best to remain quiet as Jake continued. "Later this week, I will share with you my complete plan but for the time being, I need you to cool it. Is that clear?"

Garrison nodded his head as he responded. "Alright, one week max."

The car had just complete a five block circle and was now pulling back into the alley behind the Wilford and drove Jake to his car. As Jake was getting out, Garrison again spoke. "Jake, where has your wife been these past few days?"

Jake froze momentarily but then responded. "Visiting some friends? Why do you ask?"

"Jake, if she is in trouble, we can help."

"Actually, Mr. Garrison, I'm counting on that."

The FBI vehicle pulled away and Jake got in his car. He then proceeded to Ed Lee's office downtown.

....

Andy Baroni was just about to walk out of his office when his secretary called to him. "Andy, important call from Ken."

Andy returned to his office as she put the call through. "Ken, what's going on?"

"A dark sedan, just gave Mr. Oliver a five minute ride around the block. Apparently they were waiting in the garage and picked him up on the way to the car."

"What can you tell me about the car."

"Standard government issue."

The FBI, Andy thought. "Good work, Ken, where is Oliver now?"

"I am following him at the moment. Looks like he is heading towards the financial district or Chinatown, I'm not sure yet."

"Stay on him."

"Roger that." The phone line went dead and Andy held the phone for a second as he thought. *So the FBI made contact with Jake again. Was Jake involved in something else that Andy was not aware of?*

As Andy placed the phone handset back in the cradle it suddenly rang again. Andy picked it up and heard Jim's voice. "Andy, it's Jim. Jake wants to get together this evening. Will that work for you?"

"Sure, what time?"

"Not sure yet but I will let you know later this afternoon."

"Sounds good, Jim. I have some news to share and a lot of questions for Jake."

....

Jake arrived at Ed Lee's office just as an afternoon shower began. The rain hit quickly and Jake cursed himself for not keeping an umbrella in the car. He parked and ran to the building entrance. His hair was wet and his suit would need a trip to the dry cleaners but actually, he enjoyed the outburst. The rain was like a quick slap in the face. Jake needed to be alert and quick thinking when meeting with Ed Lee.

He walked in to the entrance of Lee & Associates Architects and was again greeted by the pretty oriental receptionist. She immediately recognized Jake. "Ah, Mr. Oliver, welcome. I will let my dad know you are here. Please proceed to the conference room. If, you would like to freshen up, the wash room is straight down the hall."

Jake smiled. "Thanks. I think those are Asian manners trying to tell me, that you're soaking wet and need to clean up before meeting my boss."

Jake's comment caused her to giggle as he walked down the hall. A few minutes later, Ed Lee joined Jake in the conference room and both sat down and had some hot tea that had just been brought in by the receptionist.

She departed quickly and closed the door behind her. "Jake, I am glad you came over this morning. I wanted to explain further about my association with Samuel Cho.

"Ed, contrary to what you may think, I am not upset with you. You have always leveled with me as best you could. In fact, in retrospect, you were giving me all the hints, I just wasn't quick enough to pick up on them."

"Ah…don't underestimate yourself, Jake. I certainly do not."

"Ed, I wanted to meet with you to clarify just exactly what Mr. Cho expects of me."

"All he wants is for you to uncover what Jackson Chi is up to. We have already identified advance deposits that we think aren't real deposits. We also know that both Jackson and the union seem far too interested in the pension fund. Perhaps this is the direction to proceed."

"Perhaps," indicated Jake as he considered his next question.

"Jake, I want to assure you that Mr. Cho had nothing to do with the abduction of your wife."

Jake stared at Ed. "Alright, so you know about this. Look Ed, I may not agree with Mr. Cho's business practices but he doesn't strike me as the type of man who goes around abducting women."

"You are correct on this point, Jake." Ed sipped at his tea before continuing. "He can be a fair man. Do what he asks and the company will take good care of you. I regret that it was necessary for him to share with you the steps he has taken to control your actions but he felt it was necessary to properly ensure your cooperation."

Jake considered Ed's words in silence for a few moments. "And if I do not cooperate?"

Ed looked at him gravely. "Jake, Samuel is very powerful and he got that power in ways that most would not consider the most conventional. You have heard the phrase, desperate men, will take desperate measures? Samuel Cho took desperate measures to establish his fortune, and I can attest, from first hand knowledge, that he will take whatever actions necessary to protect his empire."

Jake sipped his tea clearly understanding Ed's reference that Samuel Cho was not to be underestimated.

………………………………………

Jake returned to the hotel and spent the rest of the afternoon reviewing the present labor contract with Local #78 and the plans for the renovation. He knew there was some connection but it wasn't obvious yet.

Just prior to calling it a day, Jake contacted Jim Slazenger and Andy Baroni and arranged for them to come to his house later that evening after the girls were asleep. He then packed up for home to relieve Sally Halloran from her extended duties of babysitting. When he arrived and entered the house, he found his two daughters and Baroni's female security officer all sitting on the living room floor engrossed in an intense game of Monopoly. Briana, really didn't understand the complete workings of the game but she enjoyed playing with the little houses and motels.

Jake dropped his computer case and a pizza on the kitchen table and joined them in the living room. Briana noticed her dad first. "Daddy, your home!" She ran to him and jumped into his arms. Sarah quickly joined her sister in the daily hug ritual, which Jake valued more than ever during these difficult few days.

"Hi, Sally, everything go alright today?"

"Just fine, sir."

"Well thanks for working the extended shift today. Care for some pizza before you go?"

"No, but thanks for the offer. Besides these guys had me beat at this game anyway." Both girls giggled.

Jake visited with his daughters as they ate dinner. It was difficult getting the girls to settle down but he finally got them in bed by 9 o'clock.

Jim and Andy arrived a few minutes later and all proceeded to the dining room table where they could talk and not wake up the girls. Just as Jake was getting some beers from the refrigerator, his cell phone rang. Jake quickly handed the beers to the men at the table and then answered his phone.

"Just checking in Mr. Oliver." Jake waived his hand signaling that the kidnapper was on the line. "Tomorrow the negotiations begin. Just agree to the terms and everyone goes home happy. Understand?"

"I want to speak to my wife." Responded Jake impatiently.

"Don't get demanding Mr. Oliver. It may not be too healthy for the Mrs."

"Same deal as yesterday. Either I speak to her or I assume the worst and the deals off!"

The voice on the phone was silent for almost 20 seconds. Jake could here what sounded like a door being unlocked and then he heard Marilyn's voice.

"Jake?"

"Yeah, its me honey. How are you?"

"A…I'm alright. What is going_____"

The cold steel voice that Jake was becoming far too familiar with was now back on the line. "Alright, you have spoken to her. Satisfied?"

Jake's mind was racing. "If I do what you want, when will Marilyn be released?"

"We discuss that later. Do your part and she lives. Fail and she dies. No mistakes, Mr. Oliver, your wife is counting on you." The line then went dead.

"That was them?" Asked Jim as Jake walked back into to dining room. Jake simply nodded, his mind turning over what the man on the phone had just said to him.

Andy and Jim remained silent while Jake gathered his thoughts. "Gentlemen, this guy is really starting to piss me off." The determination in his voice was quite apparent.

Jim stood, walked over behind Jake and patted him on the back. "Well then, its time we start kicking some butt, gentlemen."

Jake seemed to snap out of his previous trance. "Your right about that, Jim, so lets get to work. Negotiations with Local #78 start tomorrow. Our kidnapper is quite insistent that I cooperate completely with their demands. That would suggest that the union is responsible for my wife's kidnapping."

Andy interrupted. "Or we are being led to believe that they are responsible." Jake and Jim both looked across the table somewhat confused.

"Andy, you have information to suggest otherwise?" Asked Jim.

"No, not completely. But it just seems too obvious, in my opinion that these bozo's from the union would kidnap your wife and then make it so obvious that you are to agree with the proposed terms."

"Perhaps," Jake acknowledged. "But for the time being, unless we have something more substantial we will proceed with this assumption. Agreed?" Andy and Jim both nodded as he continued.

"I am assuming that I will learn rather quickly what the key issues are with Local #78 when we meet. My goal is to determine what relevance Local #78 has to do with Jackson Chi and if there is a connection with the mystery advance deposits given to contractors for the renovation."

"What if this connection is not as obvious as we assume?" Asked Jim as he finished his beer and went to the refrigerator to get seconds for all of them.

Jake drank the last of his first beer and gladly accepted the second bottle in Jim's hand. "That is why we need to rattle the bushes, so to speak." Andy and Jim both nodded. "Jim, do you think you could persuade our big Samoan friend, Kono, in housekeeping to put a little pressure on the union's snitch, Sergio. We need to know if the union has Marilyn and, if so, where she is being held."

Jim smiled. "Jake, I can almost assure you that Kono will have the little shit tweetin' like a bird."

"Good, but we also need to cut off the inside communication to the union. Perhaps…"

"Perhaps, Sergio will need to take a little vacation until this matter is resolved."

"Jim, you must have read my mind. We need to keep Lou Walizak in the dark as much as possible."

Jim held up his beer in the form of a toast. "Consider your assignment understood and accepted."

Jake then turned to Andy who had been sitting patiently waiting his turn to speak or be spoken to.

"Andy, my initial thoughts are for you and your team to find out where Marilyn is being held once we confirm who is responsible. It will then be up to you to come up with a plan to get her back safely."

Andy nodded and then responded. "Jake, has the FBI been notified yet regarding Marilyn's disappearance?"

"No, not yet."

"But you have been in contact with them?"

Jake looked at Andy sharply. "What are you talking about?"

Andy considered his words carefully. "Jake, yesterday, I was visited by a Mr. John Garrison and his supervisor, a Skip Henderson. Apparently my inquiries with the FBI regarding the surveillance equipment used in your house hit a nerve. After a little persuasion, they shared with me that they were investigating your employers from Hong Kong." Jake looked on fascinated by what Andy had uncovered.

"Jake, they plan to take your guys down and you with them if your not careful."

Jake stood and walked over the window overlooking the street in front of his home. An elderly couple Jake recognized as living several doors down was taking their usual evening stroll. "Andy, I must commend you thus far. Yes, Mr. Garrison of the FBI has contacted me. He wants me to help set up my owners or he plans to implicate me with them."

Jim now also stood. "Jake, if what the FBI is saying is true and South Harbor Investments is conducting illegal activities, why wouldn't we want to help them?"

Jake turned. "It is a little more complicated than that, my friend." Andy and Jim looked on as Jake paused. "As you are aware, I met with Mr. Samuel Cho and it appears that all is not well internally within South Harbor Investments." Both men looked on confused. "And they appear to have their own agenda and internal strife to deal with." Andy and Jim still did not understand.

"Also, they say they have documentation that, if sent to… say… the FBI, would implicate me as their sacrificial lamb. I am not exactly sure what it is they have but I must consider all the options before I seek cooperation with the FBI. There is also the issue of Marilyn's safety. Notifying the FBI could cause the kidnappers to panic and cut their losses. I am not going to let that happen."

Jim and Andy listened in silence as they began to understand that Jake was clearly juggling a three-ring circus.

"So gentlemen, as you can see, I need your help. Your actions may mean defying the FBI and I am not exactly sure what type of trouble this may get both of you in. But I do have a plan once I get the answer to a few of the big questions. Are you guys still with me?"

Jim and Andy nodded their agreement as they got up to leave. Just as they were walking out the door, Jake called to Andy. "By the way, Andy, did John Garrison tell you that he had spoken to me?"

Andy looked around and then responded. "A…no, Jake, he didn't." Andy hesitated not sure how Jake would react to his next comment. "Actually, sir, ever since you hired me to watch your family, it didn't make sense not to keep an eye on you as well. I regret not telling you about this before now."

Jake frowned and then continued. "So you have been having me followed?"

Andy looked down, clearly feeling awkward with the situation as Jake spoke. "Forget it Andy. Actually, I guess it's nice to know that I've had some back up these past few days." Andy gave a sigh of relief just as Jake continued. "At least now I know there is not someone else out to get me driving a white Chevy *Caprice.*."

Andy looked on in amazement. "Remind me to fire my best man for being pegged by a real *pro*!"

As the door closed and Andy and Jim walked to their cars, Jim spoke. "Never underestimate this guy, Andy. That is why I have grown to like him and stand behind him."

"No argument there, buddy. Guess it is time we both go to work on our assignments."

…………………………………………

At that same moment, in a small little restaurant in the San Francisco suburb of *North Beach*, a couple was just sitting down to a late dinner. The man was dressed in a nicely tailored light gray double-breasted suit, pale green shirt and bold green and burgandy paisley tie. The woman was dressed in a black dress that possibly was a little short and a little too tight for a woman of her age but she was an attractive woman and no one in the restaurant was complaining. The two together, however, seemed out of place. The man appeared more reserved and formal while the woman less polished and professional.

"It was great hearing from you this afternoon."

"I'm glad. I was just pleased that you were able to meet me on such short notice." Replied the man in a voice that suggested that he was well schooled, probably from the East Coast.

"Boy, what a day. I never thought I would get everything ready for tomorrow." Said the woman as she sipped the glass of wine the waiter had just poured.

"Oh, what's going on?"

"Tomorrow, union negotiations begin with Local #78."

"Local #78?" Replied the man questioningly.

The woman just smiled coyly. "Oh, I should probably refer to them as the Hotel & Restaurant Employers Union, Local #78. This labor organization represents most of the employees at the Wilford."

"Ah, I see. Do you expect there will be difficulties in the negotiations?"

"Well, I'm not for sure. I have reviewed with Mr. Oliver, that's my boss, everything that I can think of to prepare."

"So Laura, this Mr. Oliver will simply follow your recommendations on this matter?"

Laura Sanders laughed lightly. "Yeah, if only it was that simple. I have advised him that the union plans to propose substantial increases to the union's pension fund dues. That will probably be the biggest issue to agree on."

"Do you expect him to dispute and fight the union over these issues."

"I would hope so. Their demands are outrageous. Don't get me wrong. He seems to welcome my input but I think he will probably do whatever he feels like once the negotiations begin."

"This negotiation process seems quite exciting. Tell me more."

Laura looked across the table at the dark handsome man she was dining with. She was completely enthralled that this younger man was so interested in her. Perhaps this was going to be Mr. Right some day she thought. "You can't really be interested in all of this?"

The man leaned forward and placed his hand on hers. "I am, really. By the way, did I mention how beautiful you look this evening?"

Laura smiled and blushed. "Yes, you did but you can say it again as much as you like."

CHAPTER THIRTY ONE

Jim Slazenger arrived at the hotel at 6:45 a.m. and proceeded to the housekeeping department located on the basement level of the hotel. He found Kono Hisataki alone in a storeroom getting some supplies for the room attendants.

"Kono, can I speak to you for a moment." Jim said as he entered the storeroom.

Kono immediately looked around to see if anyone was watching. "Mr. S? This is not a good place to____"

"Sorry Kono," Jim interrupted, "but I need your help."

Kono looked at his assistant general manager. There was a certain look of desperation in Jim's eyes that he had not noticed previously. "Sure boss, what's up?"

Jim looked around and then continued. "I need you to put a little pressure on our friend Sergio."

Kono just smiled. "Man, that is not a favor, it would be a pleasure." The look on Jim's face, however, suggested that something was seriously wrong.

Jim continued. "Kono, I need you to keep what I am about to tell you completely confidential." Kono just nodded as he continued. "Several days ago, Mr. Oliver's wife was kidnapped. I don't know for sure who is responsible but there is a possibility that Local #78 may be involved. If this is the case, our friend Sergio may be able to shed some light as to where she is being held."

Kono stared in disbelief at what he was hearing. "Jez, boss, I…a…what do you want me to do?"

Jim explained what he had in mind keeping his voice low. Kono was to try to find out if, in fact, the union was behind the kidnapping and inform Jim of what he found out. When Jim had finished talking, Kono looked at his boss, puffed out his cheeks and exhaled deeply.

"You got it boss, so you want me to squeeze him for the info we need but not show our complete hand, right?"

"Kono," Jim acknowledged, "I couldn't have said it better. But there is one more thing. We need Sergio to…how should I say, be out of commission in reporting to the union."

Kono nodded slowly. "You want me to knock him off?"

"No, nothing that extreme. We just need Sergio to take a little trip and be out of touch for a while."

Kono just smiled. "Piece of cake. That little shit will be to scared to go to the bathroom after I finish with him."

Jim smiled and returned to his office as the rest of the housekeeping staff began to arrive for the day's work. Kono then set out on his special assignment.

……………………………………

Laura Sanders arrived early to make sure the room was set as she had specified. As a veteran of several previous collective bargaining sessions over her fifteen years in the hospitality industry she had learned a few things about the art of negotiation and the psychology associated with the environment for the negotiations. Everything from lighting, the placement of seats around the table, the direction in which each participant would face and the view or sights visible to each. All were important in creating the type of environment conducive to successful negotiations.

Fred Plummer, the hotel's Director of Food & Beverage entered the boardroom with two of his banquet staff. "I figured that you would be here, Laura. A tad anxious are we?"

"Gee, I can't imagine why. Word from other hotels is that Local #78 has been extremely difficult to deal with all year. I have a new GM and I don't have a clue how he intends to act. And lastly, I'm a little hung over if you must know the truth."

Laura's last comment drew a chuckle from the large elderly man as he placed a tray of glasses down on a side table. "Been doing a little partyin'?"

"No, not exactly." Laura was suddenly embarrassed but did not know why. Fred Plummer had always reminded her of her father who had long since passed away. "Let's just say that I have a new interest in my life these days."

"Ah, I see, anyone I know?"

"No, he does not work in the industry."

"What then, does this gentlemen caller do?"

"Well, I'm not sure exactly. He says he deals with overseas imports but I'm afraid I don't know much more than that."

"How did you meet this mysterious stranger?"

"Well, he just sort of appeared." Laura, was suddenly growing impatient. "Alright, you dirty old man, enough about my evening activities. Let's review the set up of the room."

"Very well, Miss Nervous Nellie. I just happened to bring along the banquet event order for this function. Let's see…Conference Table to accommodate 12 people. Conference table is to be set to one side of room, so that one side of the table will have their backs close to the North Wall with the full-length mirror. The banquet chairs are as you specified the oldest and least comfortable we have. How we doing so far, my dear?"

"Sounds good Fred. You know, I don't care what everybody says about you." Laura gave the elderly man a sly grin. "You know why I like this set up don't you?"

"I bet it has a little to do with the ancient Chinese study of *Feng Shui*. Am I correct?"

"You're on the right track. Psychologically, individuals placed up against a mirrored wall will eventually feel intimidate and uncomfortable but won't exactly know why. They will feel crowded and backed into a corner. The idea of the wobbly chairs combined with our plan to keep the air conditioning set just a little warmer than usual, should prompt them to be very anxious and in a hurry just to end the sessions as soon as possible. And that would be just fine with us, Fred."

"Well then," responded Fred, "you will probably appreciate some of the extra touches I have added. For instance, each of the chairs closest to the mirrored wall side of the table are missing at least one of the of the feet on the chair legs. This will make whoever is sitting in these chairs, rather uncomfortable and irritable even though they may not know why or what is causing their irritation. In addition, I have arranged for those spot lights on the ceiling." Fred stood and walked directly under one of the many adjustable spot lights mounted on a bar that hung six inches from the ceiling. "These lights will shine directly into each of the union representatives while seated at the boardroom table. Laura smiled as he continued. "You forget, my young thing, that this old fart has been around a while also. In fact, I have negotiated some pretty good settlements in my day."

"Yes, Fred, I'm sure you have. But we better get cracking on finishing the set up. Our guests will be arriving within the hour."

The weather outside had changed substantially from earlier that morning. The temperature had dropped in the past hour to a rather chilly 55 degrees. The fog had blanketed the entire city and light drizzle had saturated the streets and sidewalks.

Lou Walizak entered the lobby of the Wilford Plaza Hotel. He was dressed in his usual attire of navy blue slacks, a light blue shirt, open with no tie and a dark blue sport coat. He also wore a wrinkled black full-length trench coat. Most notable, however, were Lou's shoes that were brown, dull and badly scuffed. The shoes did not match the rest of his outfit but clearly fit the man wearing them.

Flanked on his right was Ed Flago his driver, dressed in dark slacks and a short windbreaker coat, that appeared wet and saturated from the drizzle outside. On Lou's left was Micky Seleki, the only one of the three men that appeared ready to attend a meeting. He was dressed in light gray suit, white shirt and maroon tie. He carried a large briefcase, similar to those carried by attorneys.

All three men proceeded through the lobby and were directed to the Charles Wilford Library. This room, used as a boardroom for meetings and small group gatherings, was located in the rear of the building off the main lobby. The entrance door, made of three-inch thick carved mahogany, was propped open. As the three men entered the room, all three instinctively followed the decorative woodwork from floor to ceiling around the four pillars in the room. It was an impressive room, rich in history and depicting the ultimate in quality and sophistication. There were floor-to-ceiling bookcases that ran the length of the room along the wall to the left as one entered the room and also along the back wall. The books on these bookshelves contained a detailed history of the Wilford Plaza Hotel as well as other landmarks of San Francisco.

On the wall to the right, was a full-length mirror that ran the entire length of the room, making the room appear much larger than it actually was. Situated somewhat askew in the room was a large mahogany boardroom table and twelve chairs. Lou noticed immediately that the chairs clearly did not go with the rich table they surrounded. They were common stackable banquet chairs and not rich leather, high back swivel chairs one would expect in a room of this nature. Lou also noted that the table had been placed off center in the room, which he assumed was due to the decorative pillars they had to work around in the center of the room.

Lou took in the entire set up of the room and slowly proceeded toward it when Laura Sanders introduced herself and directed them toward the side of the table closest to the mirror. Lou was not particularly pleased with this arrangement but noticed that all of the other seats had materials placed in front them indicating that someone was already seated there.

Just as Lou was removing his trench coat and taking his seat, he looked toward the entrance to the room and recognized Jake Oliver entering followed by a large bear of a man and a small attractive woman. Lou recognized the woman as Jake Oliver's assistant that had been seated outside his office during his previous visit. The large man, he presumed was Slazenger, the assistant general manager of the hotel. A man that his informers had told him could be difficult to deal with at times.

Jake proceeded toward the table and extended his hand. "Lou, good to see you again." His candor and reference to Lou by his first name caught him by surprise.

At that same moment, several more of the Wilford's management staff entered and took their seats around the table. Jake waited for all to be seated and then began. "Why don't we begin with introductions." Jake motioned with his hand as he introduced each of his management team. "Jim Slazenger, the Assistant General Manager; Sandra Kelly, my Administrative Assistant; Dan Kowalski, Chief Engineer; Laura Sanders, Director of Human Resources;

Shannon Kincaid, Director of Front Office Operations; Olivia Fernandez, Executive Housekeeper; and Fred Plummer, Director Food & Beverage. Sadly, we are without a Controller at this time." This comment caused all to momentarily look down in silence.

Lou looked around the table and smiled. "You seem to have come with reinforcements Jake and clearly have us outnumbered."

Jake smiled back. "Actually, I was afraid that you might feel that way so I have taken the liberty of inviting in several of our union members to sit in on the negotiations."

Lou looked at him with a confused expression just as the rear service door to the Library opened and four members of the Wilford staff entered, in uniform, and sat at chairs that had been placed along the back wall. "A…this is rather unusual and not typical of ____"

Jake interrupted. "I just thought they should have the opportunity to hear and see first hand, how you and your associates plan to negotiate a new collective bargaining agreement that affects their well being and livelihood. Are you saying that you would prefer that they not be present?"

Lou hesitated as Mickey Seleki interceded and looked quickly over at four of his union members. "A…no, Mr. Oliver, we have no objection. It has just been our past experience that these matters can often drag on for some time and usually, it has been cost prohibitive for the hotel to have some of its employees being paid just to sit in meetings."

Jake nodded his head as if in complete understanding. "Mr. Seleki, I assume? Thank for being concerned with my labor costs, but given that these meetings involve their wages and benefits, I feel strongly that they should remain and I am prepared to incur the expense associated with this time."

The four employees, a housekeeper, a bellman, a waiter and a cook, all looked on in silent fascination waiting for the president of their union to respond. "Well said, Mr. Oliver. I too, have no objections to my constituents being present and," Lou waived his hand in their direction, "hearing what we have to say." Lou paused for effect before proceeding. "I would have preferred, however, that my shop stewards be selected for such a task or, at least, some of my members with say, a longer history with Local #78."

Jake could easily interpret what Lou was suggesting. He wanted his loyal union members, such as Sergio Cervantes, and others that had been properly conditioned to edit and filter out what Lou felt was appropriate to share with the rest of union members. "Yes, I can see your point exactly. But we felt that these individuals encompassed the key positions your union represents." Lou was about to again counter when Jake continued. "So, they will have to suffice."

Lou looked at his new adversary intently before speaking. "We should proceed then."

As Mickey Seleki handed out copies of the proposed changes that Local #78 wanted to implement. Lou and Jake continued to keep eye contact for the first several minutes. Both men were sizing each other up and trying to determine what each one had up his sleeve. Lou presented himself as confident and determined but in reality, he was frustrated and concerned. *This Jake Oliver character is already testing my patience with his little stunt of bringing in workers to observe the negotiations. This is clearly going to cause some problems given the primary issues that I planed to pursue.*

Jake, watched the man seated directly across the table from him. *Was this the man that had arranged for my wife to be kidnapped?* Part of him wanted to reach across the table and beat the truth out of him, but he knew that he had to be patient. In any battle, the cool head always wins by thinking out each action and making the right strategic moves at the right time.

....

One of Jake's strategic moves, in fact, was currently underway in the basement of the Wilford almost directly below where the negotiations were being held. Sergio Cervantes had arrived at the hotel earlier that morning in an exceptionally positive state of mind. He had done what Lou Walizak had requested of him and kept his leader informed of the activities within the hotel. Given the importance that had been placed on him to get this information, there was little doubt in his mind that his actions would result in a promotion within the union. Perhaps to a full time staff position. Yes, Sergio was exceptionally pleased with himself and, as far as he was concerned nothing was going to ruin his day.

Sergio decided it was time for a smoke break and walked toward the back alley, where other employees went to smoke. He was surprised that there were no others outside but it did not matter. He had few friends that he socialized with in the first place. He lit his first cigarette when he heard the rear entrance door open and someone exit. Sergio started to turn around when someone grabbed him by the back of neck with a grip that felt like a vice.

"Hey Serg, we need to have a little talk." Sergio turned slightly and recognized the big man standing behind him. Everyone on the staff knew who Kono Hisitake was. But no one feared him. The word was that Kono was a friendly guy, a team player, something that Sergio could not relate to, but certainly not someone he should fear.

"Hey Kono, what's up man?" Kono just looked at him intently and then pushed him forward toward the parking garage stairwell. "Hey, come on, what are you doing. I got to get back to work and_____"

"Shut up and walk, ass hole!" Kono said in an intense whisper as he continued to push Sergio through the door into the parking garage. Sergio walked in the direction he was being pushed and the first hints of fear began to set in. *What had he done to piss off this big guy.*

Once they were out of the alley, Kono pulled the door closed behind him and then let go of the little Hispanic standing in front of him. Somewhere during their short walk, Sergio had lost the cigarette he had just lit. Sergio looked around nervously, not sure what was about to happen. "Hey man, if you are looking for 'some', I don't deal man, but I can put you in touch with those that can and_____"

Kono shoved Sergio up against the concrete wall and walked toward him. His face was only three inches away when he spoke. "Listen carefully, little man. I am going to ask you a few questions and you are going to answer them, understand?"

Sergio could only nod his head indicating that he understood.

"Someone has nabbed Mr. O's lady. I want to know who and where she is or I start breaking a few bones." The intense look in Kono's eyes indicated that he meant every word he was saying.

"A…look, I don't know nothing about this, man. I _____"

Kono shoved him roughly against the wall. The force temporarily knocked the wind out of him. "That was not the right answer, ass hole, you want to try it one more time?"

Sergio tried to catch his breath before speaking. He was now sweating profusely even though the temperature in the stairwell was only 55 degrees and damp. “Kono, I’m serious, I don’t know where she is. It wasn’t us. Really!”

“Who’s us? Tell me what you do know. My patience is wearing thin.” Kono grabbed Sergio by his collar with one hand and lifted him off the ground and held him against the wall.

Sergio shook his head back and forth. “Man, I can’t say anything, they’ll kill me!”

Kono leaned forward, his breath now stung Sergio’s eyes. “What the fuck do you think is going to happen to you if you *don’t talk*?”

Sergio attempted to look away but Kono was standing so close it was not possible. Kono could tell he was gathering his thoughts and was about to talk. “Look, all I know is what I hear around.” Sergio looked at Kono and it was obvious he needed to continue. “Some guys that work for the union. I guess they were supposed to nab her but someone else did it. Walizak was pissed man. That’s all I know.”

Kono considered what he was being told. *What did he mean, someone else?* “You fuckin' with me, man?”

“No, really!”

“You said that some guys with the union were going to kidnap Mrs. O, maybe they did and you are such a piss ant in the organization that they didn’t tell you.”

“No, I was there when they told Walizak. He came unglued and ripped them new ass holes.”

“Why was the union wanting to kidnap Mrs. O?”

Sergio looked at him somewhat dazed. “Leverage, I guess. They're up there now in negotiations. I guess they just wanted to make sure Mr. O cooperated.”

Kono considered how he wanted to proceed next. “So, your job for these guys was to be a stoolie, a snitch, right?”

Sergio looked down. “Yeah, sort of.”

“Well, guess what?”

Sergio looked around nervously. “What?”

Kono looked around and then pushed him up against the wall again. “You’re going to take a little vacation. In fact, I strongly suggest you take a trip to Mexico and visit the family or your cellmate buddies. Whoever you got down there, you need to go see them starting today."

Sergio shook his head. "I can't do that. I_____"

Kono punched him in the stomach and he bent over sharply at the waist as he tried to catch his breath.

"Look, this is not an option. You want to walk out of here? You get lost. Any further conversations with your buddies at Local #78 while the negotiations are going on and you are going to experience a little *accident*. You know how that works...don't you? Maybe next time we have this meeting on the roof. I understand that you don't particularly like heights?"

Sergio looked up at Kono's last words. If disappearing for a short time meant getting this big guy out of his face, it seemed like a small price to pay. Besides, he could still save his reputation with Local #78, in fact protect it. If something goes wrong, they couldn't blame him, if he was away. He could come back in two weeks, and everything would be back to normal.

"Alright, I'm outta here."

Kono grabbed him and shook him. "Make no mistake, I get word that you are snitching and I kick your royal ass from the 12th floor. Comprende?"

"I understand." Sergio looked down at the floor. "What do I tell my sup?"

"Tell him you feel sick and have to go home. If I find you still on this property 30 minutes from now, we take a walk again."

Sergio nodded and both men exited the parking garage stairwell and returned to their jobs. Sergio was true to his word and was most convincing to his supervisor, Harry Walters at the bell desk.

Kono, called Jim Slazenger's office but got his voice mail. He figured he was in the negotiations and would catch him when they broke for lunch. He was disappointed that he was not able to find out where Mr. Oliver's wife was but perhaps his information would prove useful somehow.

....

The negotiations ended at noon the first day and it was everyone's consensus that all needed some time to review the proposed changes that Local #78 had introduced.

Jake quickly scanned the document and, as he suspected, the emphasis was clearly on the pension fund. The wage increases being proposed were surprisingly reasonable. Jake would use this to his advantage to uncover why the pension fund was so important at this time.

Jake, Jim, Sandra and Laura returned to the executive offices. After they entered Jake's office and the door was shut, Jake spoke. "Well, guys, no big surprises so far. Laura, you pegged them right on what their key demands would be."

"Well, we might as well thank, Mickey Sileki for that, sir. Most of the time, he is a pretty decent guy to work with. He shared with me some of the key issues last month. I guess he figured the more time we have to plan and address what they want, the quicker the negotiations will go."

Sandra then spoke. "Great idea having some of the staff sit in on the meetings, Jake."

"Thanks. I just thought that our staff should see just how hard their union is fighting for them. Today, they got an initial taste of what the union's priorities are. And these priorities had very little to do with increasing wages or the benefits that would support them directly."

"Their presence certainly didn't sit well with Lou Walizak," said Jim as he leaned back in one of Jake's office chairs.

Jake laughed briefly. "Yeah I'd say Lou was a little pissed about that one. Well, let's get back to running the hotel everyone. We've only got the rest of today to prepare before we resume negotiations tomorrow and we need to be on our toes. I don't think we want to underestimate our union friends." All nodded in agreement except Laura who appeared lost in thought.

"Laura, everything alright? You were sort of quiet this morning." Asked Jake.

Laura looked up suddenly. She quickly scanned the others in the office then focused on Jake. "A...yes sir. Sorry, I guess I'm just a little tired." All looked on concerned. "No really, everything is fine. I guess I was just out too late last night."

This comment drew a reaction from all three. Jim then asked. “A date perhaps?”

Laura looked embarrassed. “Well, yes, sort of. I mean, yes.”

“Jim smiled. “Anyone we know?”

“No.” Replied Laura quickly. “And now can we talk about something else.”

Jake smiled. “O.K., let’s stop picking on her. Laura, get some rest this evening. I need you in top form tomorrow.”

“Yes, sir. Not to worry.” All proceeded out of Jake’s office and Sandra followed Laura to the bathroom.

“So, when and where did you meet this guy?” Asked Sandra as they walked down the hallway.

“Actually just a few weeks ago. We just started talking at a bar one night and one thing led to another, I guess.”

“What’s he do?”

“He is into shipping, imports, something like that.”

“Is he from here?”

“Well, he lives here now. But no, I think he was originally from England. He has sort of a regal accent and has traveled the world extensively.”

Sandra smiled. “What do you guys talk about, or is this strictly a physical thing?”

Laura looked at her in disgust. “No, it is not a physical thing! At least not yet.” She said with sly grin.”

“Well, then do you talk about travel or what?”

Laura pondered the question. “Well, its funny actually. He always seems so interested in what I do. I guess I have been spending too much time talking about myself because, I really don’t know much about him.”

Sandra nodded and then excused herself. She returned to her desk and noticed that Jake and Jim were not in their offices. She assumed they must be at lunch. She quickly scanned the area and then pulled a cell phone from her purse and made a call.

....

Lou Walizak, Ed Flago and Mickey Seliki left the hotel without speaking. Lou and Mickey waited in front for Ed to pull the car around and then they departed. Lou was the first to speak. "What the fuck was that all about back there?"

Mickey responded. "Sir, what do you mean?"

"I mean, what was this shit about having some of our members present in the room. He is just trying to make us look bad."

"Well, sir, technically there is no reason for them not to be there."

"Well, understand this! Find a way to get them out of there or maybe I'll figure out a way to assure that *technically* you are not there. Got it, Mr. Seleki?"

Mickey looked down and nodded his head. "Yes sir."

Ed pulled the car up in front of the union office. Lou advised Mickey to get out and get to work on tomorrow's meeting. He then advised Ed to continue to drive and pulled out his cell phone. He dialed a number and waited. The phone was answered by a soft female voice. "This is Walizak, Chi there?"

After a few moments, Jackson Chi was on the line. "Chi, what the hell is going on!" Lou shouted. "Oliver, sure doesn't seem too intimidated for someone whose wife is missing."

"What happened?" Replied Jackson. Lou summarized the first meeting and expressed concern that they may have problems.

"If your men had done their job correctly, we would not have such worries." Retorted Jackson in disgust.

"Don't lay that shit on me, Chinaman! You and I know that someone else is playing games here. Whoever is behind his wife's kidnapping is our bigger problem."

Jackson considered Lou's words. "Perhaps."

"Perhaps, my ass! Someone's messing with us and you need to find out who."

"Just stay calm. I will find out who is behind this and all will proceed as planned. You do your part and I will take care of the rest."

"You better!" Lou threatened and hung up the phone. Jackson shook his head. He had clearly made a mistake dealing with a man such as Walizak but they were so close in accomplishing what he wanted. Jackson hung up the phone and returned to reviewing the documents on his desk. He did not notice that Kim Chuen was also placing the receiver for her phone back on the hook in the other room.

....

Marilyn had drifted off to sleep and awoke suddenly. She had lost track of time and was not certain how long she had been asleep or even how many days she had been in captivity. Her captors, had continued to treat her reasonably well providing her meals and allowing her to go the bathroom at regular intervals.

With the windows to her room covered, she could not tell if it was night or day. She sat up in the bed as best she could, struggling to keep upright, with her hands tied behind her back. Once she was settled, her mind began to clear. She remembered her last encounter with, who she now thought of as the *Head Kidnapper*. He had come into the room and suddenly shoved a cell phone up to her ear. It had been Jake on the line asking if she was alright. *He had sounded worried. But of course he was worried. She had been kidnapped, and what about the girls? Were they alright or had something also happened to them?*

The door suddenly opened and the kidnapper she had nicknamed, *Bashful,* entered carrying a tray with a cover on it. Again, the same as all of the others, this individual wore a hood and black non-descript clothing. This person's movements were fluid and made no sound at all.

The tray of food was placed on the bed and one of Marilyn's hands was untied and the other handcuffed to the bed frame. Without a word spoken, *Bashful*, motioned toward the bathroom. Marilyn shook her head indicating not at this time. *Bashful* then departed, the sound of the door being locked had become another ritual. Marilyn lifted the tray cover and, to her surprise, it was not *McDonalds*, but a deli sandwich of some type. At first she had not bothered to eat what the kidnappers gave her but later decided she needed to keep up her strength and her hope.

As she ate her new sandwich, she reviewed what she knew. She knew there were a total of three kidnappers. The head kidnapper was definitely a man. She had heard his voice when speaking to Jake on the phone. This man was approx. six feet in height and appeared to be in good shape. This was obvious from the all black outfit he usually wore when he entered the room. The other two kidnappers, on the other hand, were much smaller in build and stature. Neither one ever spoke. If Marilyn had to guess, based on the movements and mannerisms, they were most likely women. So a man and two women in a house of unknown location were holding her. But wait, there had been a sound. She had heard it on several occasions. She knew this sound but could not place it. She must pay attention and focus on this sound the next time it occurred. It could be a key to where she was being held. How this would benefit her she was not sure but she decided that she had to keep her mind active and alert to assure she was ready to escape if the opportunity arose.

CHAPTER THIRTY TWO

Jake started his day with his usual walk of the hotel. Besides the serious problems he was dealing with, he was pleased to note that he hadn't lost his touch when it came to managing a hotel. The improvements that he now observed during his walk were substantial. The employee dining room had been renovated and cleaned up. It resembled a restaurant for guests rather than an employee dining area. The entire basement was neat and orderly and the staff friendly and talkative. Everyone that Jake encountered greeted him with a smile and pleasant exchange.

It was also no surprise that the occupancy and average rate of the hotel were up substantially from the budget and sales bookings had been strong under the direction of Mike Reynolds and his sales team. It was just unfortunate that a hotel as grand in history as the Wilford was now owned by individuals such as Samuel Cho and company, who were using this landmark to launder money for their illegal operations around the world.

As Jake returned to his office he pondered how best to proceed. Jim had met with Kono after his little exchange with Sergio but he had not been able to uncover that the union was behind Marilyn's kidnapping. Was he wrong? And if not them, who? Jake entered the executive office foyer and was surprised to find Ed Lee sitting in the outer office. "Ed, this is a surprise, what brings you here this time of the morning."

"I was hoping to have a moment of your time," replied Ed, a somber expression on his face.

Jake offered him some tea while Jake poured himself another cup of coffee and then motioned him to his office and closed the door. Once they were seated, Ed spoke again. "Jake, I have some information regarding the contractors that Jackson paid advance deposits to." Jake looked across the desk as his interest was peaked.

"I have also been able to determine what these contractors were hired to do."

"Well, you have my attention, sir."

Ed stood and walked to the window in Jake's office. He seemed uncomfortable and acted as if he was out of his element, if that was possible, for someone as poised as Ed. "Actually, Jake, it was you that pointed me in the right direction."

Jake continued to study Ed's movements. "I don't understand."

"It involves the plans for the renovation. When we were reviewing them you pointed out that the basement plans did not match the 'as built' plans or that of the present layout of the basement. This bothered me some because I always pride myself on making sure my drawings are correct. In fact, I researched the hotel extensively and I was confident that the plans were correct. But then you pointed out this discrepancy. It pointed out my carelessness in not personally inspecting each of my projects more thoroughly. This morning, I arrived early to see for myself. As you noted, the walls making up the northeast corner of the basement are not as they appear on the plan. This is a critical error, given that the only scheduled renovation work to take place in the basement happens to be in that very area."

Jake nodded his understanding. "Yes, the entrance to the BART subway."

"Correct. So then I simply started putting two and two together." Ed turned and began pacing slowly back in forth in the office. His hands were clasped behind his back. "The names you gave me of contractors that were supposedly given advance deposits, initially did not ring a bell with me. But after a little digging here is what we have." Ed looked at the whiteboard mounted on the wall over the small conference table in the office. He motioned toward it. "May I?" Jake nodded and he proceeded to list the four contacts and the deposit amounts.

Jakovitz & Associates	$500,000
Harbinsen, Inc.	$300,000
Sunblossom Enterprises, LTD	$400,000
Wal, Inc.	$800,000

"When you first gave me these company names. I was not familiar with their relevance. So I did a little research and discovered some interesting findings."

"Wal, Inc. is the parent company of Concrete Surfaces, Inc., which is the parent company of non other than Kaiser Construction. The contractor that is scheduled to do all of the demolition work for the hotel. I took the liberty of contacting the owner, a man by the name of Bud Bell. Mr. Bell was, at first, hesitant to speak with me until I told him whom I represented. Well, he must have gotten confused because he explained how his team was ready to begin demolition of the basement wall within the week."

Jake asked. "Next week? But we haven't yet gotten any permits or approvals from the city. And besides, why would we want to start this project when we have more visible and relevant work scheduled for the rest of the hotel?"

"Jake that was my point exactly, but please listen. There is more. The next two, *Jakovitz & Associates* and *Harbinsen, Inc*, both turned out to be front organizations hired to complete the project on the subway opening. After you dig through the paperwork, you uncover that both organizations have a common member on their board of directors. Care to guess who?"

"Well, my crystal ball is a little rusty but…I'd have to guess, Jackson Chi?"

"That is correct, sir. Now for the grand prize, we have *Sunblossom Enterprises, LTD*. I researched this company thoroughly but initially found nothing. But after your visit when you mentioned the error in the basement plans, it came to me. *Sunblossom Enterprises* was hired by Charles Wilford in 1929 to do some remodeling work. The records indicated that the work involved some office remodeling and apparently back then, no one questioned a cost of $100,000."

Jake stood and approached Ed. "Wait a minute! $100,000 was a hell of a lot of money to spend back in 1930."

"You are correct again, my friend."

"Who is *Sunblossom Enterprises*?" Asked Jake.

"*Sunblossom Enterprises* proved to be another front company for several other smaller operations, but this one was rather unique, in that one of the principal owners of this company is a businessman from Hong Kong." Ed paused as he saw Jake's mind racing and then continued. "Non other than Benjamin Tsang, Deputy CEO of South Harbor Investments."

Jake sat back down and leaned back in his chair. "So, we may have a connection between Jackson and Benjamin Tsang?"

"It is quite possible." Replied Ed soberly. "The fact that Benjamin is on this company's board is no surprise since *Sunblossom* has served as a front organization for South Harbor at times over the years. What is unique, however, is the connection of *Sunblossom* with the Wilford 70 years ago!"

Jake sat pondering what he had just been told in silence for several minutes. Ed sipped at his tea waiting for him to speak. "So what have we got, Ed? Jackson Chi and possibly Benjamin Tsang have arranged payment to companies that they control in one way or the other. From your conversation with Mr. Bell, it would appear that these funds are being paid for actual work to be performed, specifically work on the basement subway entrance. Lastly, is it just coincidence that Benjamin Tsang is associated with an organization that was linked to the Wilford 70 years ago?" Jake walked around to the front of his desk and sat on one corner. "And then we have Charles Wilford, founder of the hotel spending an unexplained amount of money in 1929 supposedly for work on the hotel." Jake paused and Ed sat patiently waiting. "Ed, you're sure there is no record of such work being performed with the city? No permits, plans, anything?"

"None." Responded Ed simply.

Jake paced back and forth in his office thinking. Suddenly, it was evident that things were starting to come together. "O.K, the connection is the basement."

Ed smiled. "Possibly, what are you thinking?"

Jake's mind was racing. "We have old man Charles Wilford having some renovation work done that may have costs as much as $100,000 in 1930. Yet your records indicate that no such work took place. Or I should say, at least no work that the city was aware of. Correct?" Ed simply nodded his head.

"So," Jake continued. "We have money being allocated for some purpose that someone has gone to a lot of trouble to disguise for renovation work but may be used for some other purpose."

"Or," Ed added. "We have payments made for renovation work to be done that no one is to know about."

Jake looked at Ed with fascination. "And you believe that the work done back in 1930 and the work now being planned without our knowledge both relate to the basement?"

Ed gave Jake a knowing smile.

Jake then returned to his chair and studied the elderly Mr. Lee. "Ed, why are you…."

"Providing assistance?" Interrupted Ed. Before Jake could respond, he continued. "Perhaps we face a common enemy, Jake Oliver." Jake simply nodded his head in agreement. "Also, consider this, all of the contractors mentioned above are union. South Harbor Investments has always tried to put all work out to bid to both union and non-union contractors, skewing its decisions toward Chinese run operations."

Jake nodded slowly. "And I bet that if we do a little more checking, all of these contractors have close ties to our friend Lou Walizak."

Ed again smiled. "I would not be surprised."

Jake again stood and walked over to the white board where Ed had listed the contractors. "So let's condense this a little further. We have, at least one contractor paid to open up the basement area and supposedly create a hotel entrance into the BART San Francisco Subway. It just so happens that this is the same area of the basement that we suspect has been changed sometime throughout the Wilford's history." Jake finished making this notation on the board and then continued. "Then we have knowledge that $100,000 was spent for some unexplained work on the hotel in 1930." Jake quickly scrawled another note on the board and looked over at Ed. He then drew circles around each these three statements and drew lines down from each until they converged at the bottom of the board and wrote in big letters: NORTHEAST CORNER OF BASEMENT!

"Ed, it would appear that Jackson Chi, Lou Walizak and possibly Benjamin Tsang are interested in this particular area." Jake pointed at the words on the board with the marker in his hand. "Now we have to uncover why and what is so important that individuals have been killed and others, namely my wife, has been kidnapped."

....

Andy was growing tired of staring at the various security reports in front of him and let his mind drift as he stared out the window of his office. From his office window he could see the Bay Bridge clearly now that the fog had receded in the late morning. A sudden knock on his door brought him back to reality. He looked up and saw Ray Johnson standing at the door. "Got a minute?"

"Sure Ray, what's up?"

"Well, I did some follow up work on the car."

Andy looked at him with a confused look. "What car?"

Ray began to organize the papers in his hand as he responded. "You may recall that our guys continued to notice on several occasions around the Oliver home?" Andy nodded as he recalled their previous conversation and motioned for him to take a seat. "Well, we saw the car again, yesterday, and Cliff was able to get a better look at the guy. It was driven by a male, dark hair, appeared to be in his early to mid thirties, wearing a business suit." Ray again shuffled the papers in his hand. "Well, if you recall, we traced the plates to one Nelson Smythe. He was listed as a government worker, with International Currency."

"Yeah, I remember. You think he's up to something?"

Ray rubbed his forehead as he pondered where to begin. "Well, it was just a hunch or rather a bad feeling. When Cliff brought him up again, I pulled my notes. What bothered me was that the address we had on him was across the bridge near Sausalito. That puts our friend kinda far from home and his office is downtown in the financial district."

Andy nodded in agreement. "Makes sense, what else you got?"

"Well, I did a little more digging on Mr. Smythe's government work. Turns out that he just moved here to the City last month. Transferred from the Hong Kong Embassy."

"Alright, but_____"

Ray quickly continued. "Oh, there's more. Turns out he lives in a reclusive house in the headlands area of Marin County." Ray looked at his boss and knew that he hadn't yet peaked his interest. "Well, I just thought that a house like that seemed awfully high priced for a government worker. So I dug a little further with some friends I have in the title office in the city of Marin. It appears that our friend is renting this remote home from a company, Sun Blossom Enterprises. What bothered me was why a company would own a home in an exclusive area such as this."

"Is there a principal contact person?"

Ray looked down at his notes. "A…yes sir…a Mr. B. Tsang."

"Where does Mr. Tsang reside?" Asked Andy

"We have an address in Hong Kong." Andy then smiled and looked up from his desk. "What is it boss?"

"It may be nothing but Mr. Oliver's employers are from Hong Kong and well, I just think it seems coincidental." Andy stood and approached Ray. "Good work Ray. Let's send someone up to take a look at this home. Maybe we'll get lucky and see something."

"You bet, boss and thanks for the time."

Andy picked up the phone and dialed the number prominently displayed on his desk blotter. When the operator answered, he asked for Jim Slazenger and was connected promptly. Jim picked up on the second ring. "Jim, it's Andy. I may have something. Does the name B. Tsang from Hong Kong mean anything to you."

Jim sat up in his chair. "It sure does! Benjamin Tsang is the number two honcho with South Harbor Investments. How did you get that name, Andrew?"

"Maybe we need to get together with Jake and talk."

…………………………………………

The Asian woman dressed in black slacks and a black turtleneck sweater was seated in an overstuffed leather chair in the far corner of the living room. Her knees were tucked up under her chin and she rocked slowly contemplating the mess she had made of her life. Across the room her friend Tamara Su a.k.a. Tammy Daing, sat in silence. The sudden sound of the phone ringing startled both women and they sat up as the man from the other room entered. He glanced quickly at each of them as he answered the phone.

"Progress report." Said the voice on the telephone.

"All is proceeding as planned. My source assures me that he will cooperate."

"And they suspect the union is behind the abduction?"

"How can they not, sir."

"And the authorities? Are we certain that Oliver has not sought their assistance?"

"I have continued to check his house and do not think that he would endanger his wife by going to the FBI. He still has the amateur security around but they are of no concern."

"You are certain of this?" Said the voice impatiently on the phone.

The man looked at the girl named Tamara seated on the couch as he responded. "I am certain, sir. How much longer does this go on?"

The voice on the phone then grew angry. "As long as it must! You will be informed when I deem it necessary. Is this understood?"

"Yes sir," responded the man, now embarrassed at being scolded in front of his two underlings.

"Keep me informed." The phone went dead. The man looked quickly at the two women in the room and continued to talk into the dead phone to save face and not let on that his employer had hung up on him.

Tamara, was the first to speak after the man hung up the phone. "When will we be able to get out of here? This living in the wilderness away from the city is getting to me. No excite…ment." The seductive grin on her face sent the man the signal she wanted to see.

"Not much longer, my princess. The two of you just continue to do as you're told. Any problems with our package?"

Now the other women spoke from the chair across the room. "No, in fact she has been very cooperative. Is she going to be let go?"

The man turned around and stared at her intently. "Why is that your concern, Cynthia. Just make sure she never sees either of your faces."

The man walked to another room and a few minutes later returned dressed in a conservative dark suit. Tamara, walked up to him and straightened his tie with a look of disgust on her face. "You are going out with *her* again?"

"What I do is my concern." Replied the man sharply. "Besides, my dear, you should worry more about *your* well being. I could have easily told him how you fucked up with your task of impersonating the security guard at the school. If you had succeeded in getting the kid I would not have had to clean up your mess by taking Oliver's wife."

Tamara looked away indignantly. "All I needed was a little more time and____"

"Time!" The man laughed. "If I had not contacted you and told you to get out of there, you would have been staring at the head of Baroni security and your sweet little ass would be in jail right now." Tamara shook her head angrily.

"We will need to go out for groceries and food for Mrs. Oliver." Stated Cynthia Yee to change the subject.

"Very well. One of you go, but be careful you are not followed or observed."

Both women nodded as the man walked out the front door of the house.

....

Jake and Ed sat in silence as they considered all that had just been discussed. Jake finally broke the silence. "Ed, why was the Wilford purchased by South Harbor Investments?"

"Why? I don't understand."

"I mean, why the Wilford. With Samuel Cho's financial resources, they could have purchased a hotel of far better quality that was performing better. Why take on the headaches associated with a 100 year old hotel in need of extensive renovations, facing union negotiations and the like?"

Ed considered Jake's questions a moment. "Your points are well taken Jake, but I am afraid I do not know for certain. But I can ask Samuel if you wish."

Jake considered this option and then a plan began to formulate. "Yes, Ed, I would like you to do that very thing. Ask Samuel Cho why the Wilford Plaza was purchased."

Ed then excused himself and returned to his office. Jake walked over to Jim Slazenger's office and knocked on the open door. "Hey, got a minute?"

Jim looked up from the papers on his desk. "Yeah, in fact, I was just about to come find you. Andy may have something. He is on his way over and you may be surprised."

Jake looked at his Assistant with an amused expression on his face. "Today, Jim, nothing seems to be surprising me much."

CHAPTER THIRTY THREE

Andy Baroni met with Jim and Jake and summarized what his man had uncovered concerning Nelson Smythe and his connection by renting a house from a company controlled by Benjamin Tsang from Hong Kong. All agreed that the coincidences seemed too fantastic not to investigate further. Andy was glad they were in agreement, given that he had already advised Ray to dispatch a team to check out the house in the Marin headlands.

For this task, Ray Johnson contacted his partner Cliff Weber and teamed him up with Janice Keller, a relatively new member of the Baroni Security team. Andy had been hesitant to approve using Keller at first but she had handled herself well at the zoo with officer Halloran.

Ray's thought for the operation was for Cliff and Janice to appear as a couple out sightseeing. After they were given their instructions they departed immediately to beat the rush hour traffic across the Golden Gate Bridge.

"I'm sure glad Ray and Andy allowed me to work this assignment."

Cliff looked over at his new female partner, her auburn hair seemed to glow in the afternoon sun. "Glad to have you as a partner." Both smiled. They had noticed each other in passing and each sensed that there was a possible attraction. "Besides, I have a personal beef with these bad guys and my head is still sore from the bastard that clubbed me."

"I know. I guess we all have a beef with this bunch since they have taken us for fools so far." Janice looked out the window of the car and took in the view of *Alcatraz* that could clearly be seen as they drove north across the bridge. "So, you know your way around over here?"

Cliff nodded as he exited off of Highway 101 and took the first exit after crossing the bay. He pulled up to a stop sign and then turned left. "Sure, I used to come this way with my family and we would tour Muir Woods. Later…well later, let's just say that I have explored a number of these mountain roads."

Janice understood Cliff's reference and wasn't going to let him get off that easy. "So, what you are saying Cliff is that you and your dates used to come over here and what…watch the submarine races? Or something like that?"

Cliff shook his head in disgust. "Smart ass, I am not going to dignify your question with an answer."

The two security officers drove for another 20 minutes following the directions that Ray Johnson had written down on a piece of paper. They drove by the driveway entrance to the home the first time. Then turned around and drove past a second time, trying to take in as much of the surroundings as possible. They found an area to park off of the road a short distance away from the driveway that placed them between the house and downtown Sausalito. The assumption was that, if Marilyn Oliver was being held captive in the home, the abductors would need to occasionally make runs to the closest town for food and supplies. Their hunch was confirmed less than 20 minutes later.

A light blue Honda *Accord*, pulled up to the road from the house's long driveway and then turned towards town. The person driving the vehicle appeared to be an Asian woman in her mid 30's with long dark hair. She was alone. Cliff and Janice considered following her but decided to stay and observe who came and went from the house first.

Roughly 40 minutes later, the woman in the light blue Honda returned. Several bags of groceries were observed in the back seat. The woman glanced toward where Cliff and Janice were parked but all she saw was a couple catching an afternoon kiss.

"Well this undercover stuff does have its benefits." Said Janice as the two of them released each other from their choreographed embrace.

"Yeah…well…I'm glad you enjoyed it," replied Cliff. "She looked our way and…." Cliff blushed. "Well…let's hope she bought it."

……………………………………

Marilyn had grown to recognize each of her abductors by their mannerisms and actions. Even though neither woman had spoken, Marilyn was now convinced that the two of them were women. She could also sense that one was clearly more sympathetic to her plight than the other. The man, on the other hand, was all business and she had come to the conclusion that this was the individual that she needed to fear the most.

Marilyn had renamed her two abductors as *Nice Lady* and *Impatient*. The actions of each were quite apparent. *Nice Lady*, always seemed to be a little more conscientious and caring of Marilyn's needs such as when she needed to go to the bathroom, or uncovering her food. She also made sure she could reach everything alright. The other, *Impatient*, simply threw the tray of food on the bed, roughly cuffed Marilyn's hand to the bed frame and always seemed put out if Marilyn requested anything.

The male abductor, who appeared to be in charge, was gone most of the time. Marilyn could hear his car come and go from the house but could not hear any other cars from the street. She therefore deducted that the house was set back away from the street. On occasion she also noted another car by the different sound it made, that she presumed belonged to one or both of the women when they came or went. These trips normally proceeded a meal period. Each of these trips took roughly 30-45 minutes, which suggested to Marilyn that the house was not too far from a town of some type.

Suddenly the door opened and Marilyn waited to see which one she was getting for dinner. It was *Nice Lady*. Marilyn had decided shortly after her abduction that, if possible she should try to gain any sympathy that she could and use this to her advantage. *Nice Lady* was her best bet.

"I'm glad it's you this evening. The other woman is not very nice." Stated Marilyn attempting to get a rise out of the woman dressed in black with a black hood. "You don't like what is going on, do you?" Cynthia Yee looked at Marilyn Oliver but still said nothing.

Marilyn decided to continue. "I have two daughters, 5 and 7. I bet they are very worried about me." Cynthia continued to set up the tray of food in front of Marilyn and tried not to look directly at her. "Can you imagine what they must be going through?" Cynthia looked up suddenly and her eyes locked on Marilyn's stare as she lay handcuffed to the bed. Marilyn thought she could see Nice Lady's eyes tearing up so she continued.

"You have a child or children. Don't you?" Cynthia backed away and walked toward the door to leave quickly, still saying nothing. Marilyn continued. "Can you imagine what your child would be doing right now. Probably crying and asking where her mommy was."

Cynthia's hand was on the door knob but she had stopped and was frozen in place. Her head dropped slightly and Marilyn thought she could here soft sobbing from under the hood. Marilyn remained silent, waiting for *Nice Lady* to make the next move. Suddenly and very softly Marilyn heard her abductor speak for the first time. "I sorry for you. I sorry for your children. But there is nothing….nothing I can do."

The voice sounded Asian, Marilyn thought, her English was broken and her accent resembled others Marilyn had encountered from the east. "Just tell me why? Why am I being held? Are my daughters safe?"

Cynthia turned slowly and began to approach the bed when the door suddenly opened and *Impatient* stood in the opening. She grabbed *Nice Lady's* arm roughly and signaled with her other hand to her mouth to remain silent. Both women abruptly left and locked the door behind them.

Marilyn leaned back against the headboard of the bed and sighed as she considered what had just occurred. She was getting through to one of them. Perhaps her college study in sociology was finally paying off. She began to doze off when she again heard the sound of a foghorn in the distance. She was near the bay. Perhaps not as far from home as she originally thought.

....

Jake leaned back in his chair and looked over at the clock sitting on the bookcase on the far wall of his office. It had been a long day but he felt it had been somewhat productive. Ed Lee had shed light on the mystery advance deposit issue and, as Jake liked to think of them, the bad guys were starting to surface.

He began packing up to head home when Dan Kowalski walked in carrying a piece of paper. "Oh, Jake, glad you're still here. I was just about to put this on your desk. It's a fax." Dan handed a single piece of paper to Jake.

Jake looked at the paper with a confused expression. "I don't understand. Is this all there was?"

"A…yes sir. That's all there was. I assumed you would know what it meant."

"Very well. Thanks Dan." Dan started to leave and Jake again spoke. "Working late tonight, aren't we? What are you still doing here?"

Dan turned to readdress his boss. "Oh, I got behind on some paperwork and well…well, I just needed to catch up. In fact, I better be going."

Jake watched his chief closely. He seemed nervous about something. "Everything alright, Dan?"

"A, sure boss. Just ready to get going." Jake didn't buy his excuse, but he had enough on his own plate to get involved in the problems of one his managers. Jake simply nodded and Dan left the office.

He then looked down at the paper he was still holding. It was a fax that simply said. *Deliver to Jake Oliver immediately* in bold print followed by a three-word message. YOU HAVE MAIL. Since this phrase typically referenced messages on the internet. Jake opened up his internet provider and saw a message waiting for him to view. It was simply entitled "Urgent!" He did not recognize the sender's address.

He opened the message and began to read. The first page of the document simply stated a cryptic message that said, 'Your answer lies in why the Wilford was purchased.' Jake considered the meaning behind this statement and then scrolled down to the next page. The information that someone had sent him was remarkable. He again referenced the sender's address for any clues but it was just a series of numbers.

Jake read further. The message provided detailed information of investments Jackson Chi had made that coincided with the union's pension fund investments. It further supplied Jake with specific transactions, dates and implicated Lou Walizak as well.

Then Jake noted that the mysterious author of this message referenced an attachment. He clicked on the attached document and a photocopy of a report appeared on his screen. As he read the contents of this document he suspected that it was pages from some type of audit that had been done on the union's pension fund. Jake scanned the document quickly but the key points suggested that the fund had experienced extreme losses over the past year and was currently under-funded.

Jake leaned back and absorbed the information in front of him. *Who was providing this information? How did this individual have access to information that had been kept from public knowledge up to this point?* The answers to these questions, Jake thought, would have to come later. He then hit the print icon to generate hard copies of this most vital information. He waited several seconds for his printer to be prompted. When nothing happened. He quickly reviewed the printer settings on his screen and realized that this confidential document had just been sent to the network printer located in the copy room. Jake ran out of his office to the copy room a short distance down the hall. When he turned the corner, he almost ran into Rick Kowalski who was standing at the copy machine. Jake quickly scanned the room and noted the last of 8 pages of information being printed on the printer directly behind where Dan was standing.

Dan was momentarily startled when Jake appeared in the doorway. "Mr. Oliver…Jake, you startled me."

"Sorry Dan, I accidentally printed some documents to the network printer behind you. Mind if I pick them up?"

"Oh, I hadn't noticed. Sure, in fact, I'm through here." Dan departed to his office with a large stack of papers in his hands.

Jake quickly grabbed the pages from the printer grateful that Dan had apparently not seen them yet and returned to his office. He stashed the documents in his briefcase and then departed for home.

Laura Sanders overheard the commotion and got up to see what was going on when her phone rang.

"We still on for this evening?"

"A…oh, yes," replied Laura. Just catching up on some things."

"Is something wrong?"

"A…no. It's just that I just saw my boss and he seemed…well… he seemed flustered or something."

"Well, you can tell me all about it when we meet later. Can we get together in about two hours at Kuletto's?"

"Can we meet sooner?" Asked Laura.

"I would like that but I still have some matters to take care of before our dinner. I will see you at 8:30."

CHAPTER THIRTY FOUR

Naomi had just arrived home and cautiously entered her home. It was a little past 7 o'clock and it had been a long day. Her main objective was to block out her thoughts of work, take a long bath and then go to bed early. She needed to relax. Ever since the episode with her employer the week prior, she had been on edge. Actually, the tension she felt went back much further than the past week.

Here she was playing both sides of the fence. Her employer expected information and not providing what he wanted was the most dangerous thing she could do. The FBI, on the other hand, had put her in a dangerous situation as well but the potential reward of freeing herself from the *organization* was worth the risk. Wasn't it?

Naomi proceeded to the kitchen to listen to the messages on her voice mail. There were several messages from her real estate office advising her of clients that had called. The last message was a male voice that identified himself as Ken Eastwood and indicated that he would be stopping by around 8:30p.m that evening. Naomi turned off the machine and slammed her fist on the counter. *Why tonight, she thought?* The man named Ken Eastwood was a code name that she and John Garrison had agreed to. *His message could only mean that he needed more from her. What should she do?*

Naomi sat down in a nearby chair and considered her options. Up to this point, she had protected herself by only giving the FBI as little as possible. She had never given out her employer's name nor shared with John Garrison that her employer was responsible for Mrs.

Oliver's kidnapping. But she had grown to like the Oliver's and Marilyn could have easily become a close friend if things had been different.

Then there was the incident last week. Her employer had always been a little rough at times but the last incident, the intensity in his voice and the look in his eye. Naomi now feared for her own safety and feared that he had no intention of allowing Marilyn to return home alive. She had to help, even if her own safety was in jeopardy.

A knock on the door brought her back to reality. Was Garrison early she thought as she walked to the door. "Who is it?"

"I have a flower delivery for a Ms. Shu?" Naomi looked out but all she could see was a man holding a large vase of flowers that blocked his face and most of his upper torso.

Naomi unlocked the front door to accept the delivery when the man thrust his way in using the flowers to push Naomi back into the house and onto the floor. The man quickly closed the door and dropped the flowers on Naomi as she lay on the floor stunned by the sudden action.

"Hello, Naomi. Remember me?"

"What is going on?" Naomi started to get up but the man used his foot to push her back to the floor.

"What is going on? Nothing…that's the problem my sweet thing!"

Naomi, now realized that something was terribly wrong. "What is it? What do you want?"

"We are going to have a little talk and I strongly recommend that you have the right answers." He now grabbed her arm and dragged her roughly over to a chair in the kitchen. "Why have you not been able to correct the problem with the listening devices at the Oliver home?"

Naomi's mind was racing. "I…I have tried but with Marilyn Oliver gone, I have not had the opportunity or reason to go to their home and replace the devices." He considered her words when Naomi continued. "Is Marilyn alright, you haven't hurt her or____"

The man slapped her harshly across the face. "You will not ask me any questions. Is that understood?" Naomi nodded her head as she rubbed her cheek where she had been hit. "Someone was checking into to my background the other day. Perhaps you are working for someone else and your loyalties have strayed?"

Naomi's look must have told him the answer he suspected. He grabbed her and lifted her out of the chair and threw her across the room. When he reached for her again, Naomi slashed out with her hands and her long nails scratched his left hand. This infuriated him further and he began to beat her severely.

Thirty minutes later, he looked at his watch. "Pack up your bags. This operation is now closed. You will be sent back to Hong Kong." He then grabbed her by the hair. "You know you cannot run, because we can find you anywhere. Cooperate and all will return to as it was. Fight us and you die!" He then left as quickly as he had arrived.

Naomi was barely conscious. Her face and mouth were already very swollen and it was difficult for her to move at all. After what she thought was several minutes, she began to crawl toward the cordless phone that was sitting on the coffee table in the living room. After losing consciousness completely twice it was almost an hour later when she awoke and reached for the phone and placed a call to John Garrison. She told the dispatcher to find him stating it was an emergency. Naomi began to drift back into unconsciousness when she heard Garrison's voice on the phone.

"John?" stated Naomi, the pain and fatigue in her voice was quite apparent.

"Naomi? What's wrong? Where are you?"

"John, please come. There is much I must tell you."

"I am on my way. Naomi, what has happened?" Garrison waited but there was no response. "Naomi?! Naomi?!"

…………………………………………

"What are you doing?!" Yelled Tamara after she had pulled Cynthia from the room where Marilyn Oliver was being held.

"Tamara, listen to me! This is wrong! She is a mother, she and her daughters they…"

"You are a fool, Cynthia! You have let her get to you. Do you realize what will happen to you if he finds out?"

"What *is* going to happen to her? You *really* think he is going to let her go?"

Tamara shook her head and walked away. “I don’t know. Damn, why couldn’t you just do what you were told.” Tamara paced around, her frustration with her friend was quite apparent. “What did you say to her?”

Cynthia thought for a moment. “Nothing really. She knows that you and I are women. She considers me more considerate and caring than you.”

“*Considerate! Caring!* I don’t have time for this! Look, no more conversations. Alright? I won’t tell Nelson about this and you won’t either.”

Cynthia nodded her head in agreement and looked down.

Tamara then picked up her jacket and purse and started to walk for the door. “Where are you going?”

“I need some air and to get the hell out of here. Do what your told. I will be back later.”

Tamara stormed out the door to her car. She drove the car fast and erratic as she headed into downtown Sausalito. She parked on a side street and walked into *Houlihan’s Bar & Grill*, which was located at the water’s edge of the San Francisco Bay. The air was cool and crisp. The fog had drifted in giving the view of the bay a dark and foreboding look.

She found a small table in the bar near a window and ordered a Vodka and Tonic. When the drink came she asked the waitress to get her another. Tamara needed time to think. Cynthia had been a childhood friend. Both had grown up in the poorest section of Hong Kong. The only thing that both of them had going for them was their good looks. Nelson Smythe had noticed her first in a bar where she was sitting with some friends, one of which was Cynthia. At first he had seemed charming with his English mannerisms. He bought all of them drinks and it was quite clear that he had money and knew how to spend it.

His offer had been quite simple. Come work for him ‘entertaining’ as he put it and you will never have to return to the life you and your friends currently have. What he had left out, however, was that over the years, you would lose all of your dignity, self worth, and become property that is completely under his control.

Tamara looked down at the second drink that had been brought to her table. The look of despair or anger must have been apparent on her face. She had been so absorbed in her own thoughts that she had not noticed the handsome guy that had sat down at a nearby table by also by himself. He had blond hair and looked like a surfer type.

"You know, you stare any harder into that glass, you are going to fall in and I will have to jump in and save you."

Tamara looked up momentarily startled and then smiled.

"Hey, that's a lot better. The smile does wonders."

Tamara continued to smile. She really didn't feel like talking but he was good looking and she simply wanted to escape from that house and the woman she was holding captive in it. "Thanks, I guess, I needed a compliment."

"Well, I'm glad I could help. You waiting for someone?" Asked the man as he looked around the crowded bar.

"No. Would you care to join me."

The blond-haired man jumped up from his seat. "Ask a silly question and you got my attention." Tamara smiled and waived him toward the seat across from her. "My name is Cliff."

"Tamara. What are you drinking, Cliff, I'm buying."

"Oh no, I insist. It was me that pushed my way up to this table."

The two continue to talk for the next hour as Janice Keller maintained her lookout in the car parked on the street. From the car she could see her partner Cliff Weber conversing with the attractive oriental woman. She had called in their actions to Ray Johnson and he had approved of them taking the covert action.

Earlier, Cliff and Janice, while staked out down the street had noticed a man fitting Nelson Smythe's description leaving the country house. Unfortunately, they had no backup and debated if they should follow him and leave the house unattended. They decided that it would be best to stay with the house, get back up in place and then wait for the next opportunity. That opportunity had come approximately an hour later when an Asian woman, different than the one they had observed leaving the house earlier left in the same car and headed toward town. With a backup team now in place to continue to watch the house, Cliff and Janice had followed the late model Honda into downtown Sausalito. When they observed the suspect entering the bar, Cliff proceeded to go in and attempt to find out more information.

As Janice watched the two, a slight tinge of jealousy arose. Cliff certainly was a good actor. Or was he enjoying his covert role just a little too much. Janice tried to shake off these feelings of her partner but vowed that he better come out of this with some useful information.

....

Laura Sanders arrived at *Kueletos* a few minutes early. She was glad they had chosen this restaurant. It was one of her favorites. *Kueletos*, an Italian Bistro, was one of San Francisco's more trendy establishments. The women dressed to attract attention and the men dressed to impress. When one looked around the crowded establishment it was easy to see that both genders were accomplishing their objective.

Laura had changed from her work clothes into a simple but provocative black dress. She felt sexy and secure in this outfit. It fit her well and, in her opinion made her look thinner and younger, two issues she was always concerned about. The waitress returned with the martini she had ordered and she took a sip. What a day she thought. The union negotiations were finally underway and initially had started out positive, at least for the hotel. Jake Oliver seemed to be handling himself well and that little maneuver of having some of the employees sit in and observe the activities was a great move.

But enough thinking about work, she thought. Here she was all dolled up waiting for her younger man to appear and she was nervous. But why, Robert had always been kind, sensitive and caring to her in the past few weeks that they had been together. But there was something else. There was an intensity about him that she could not explain and this feeling always kept her off balance. Maybe it was the mysteriousness of not knowing everything about him. But what was the rush, she thought. This man had clearly swept her off her feet and she was loving every minute of the attention he was giving her. Laura smiled as she picked up her drink.

"What are you smiling at, lovely lady?"

Laura looked up and her man had arrived. He was dressed in a nicely tailored Italian suit and as far as Laura was concerned, he was the most handsome man in the place. "What am I smiling about? Well, its this guy I recently met by the name of Robert Samuelson."

"Oh, I see. Well, may I join you for a while before the guy arrives?" Laura again smiled as the man she knew as Robert kissed her on the check and then sat down and ordered a glass of red wine from the waitress.

"So, tell me about your day. The negotiations began today didn't they?

Laura was momentarily caught off guard by his questions. She did not expect to start off talking about her work. "A…well, yes. The first meeting was today with many more to go I am afraid. But we don't have to talk about work."

The intense stare of the man sitting across the table mesmerized her as he spoke. "Your work is important to you and that makes it important to me." He paused and continued to stare at her. "Tell me what happened at the meeting."

Laura was prepared to do whatever her man asked of her. They ordered dinner and for the next thirty minutes, she summarized the first day's events and how, in her opinion, Jake Oliver had won the first round of sizing up the competition. When she finished the man known as Robert leaned back in his chair. Laura noticed that he seemed troubled about something.

"Is something wrong, Robert?"

"No, sorry. I guess it has just been a long day. So it sounds like your boss, this Jake Oliver, has his own agenda. Isn't he following your recommendations?"

"My recommendations?" Laura was confused by the question. "Well, yes, I guess. But he is still the GM and it's his call how best to negotiate each issue."

"I see." Robert appeared to be deep in thought. "So, you think Jake Oliver plans to rattle a few cages with the union, eh?

Laura smiled. "Well, I guess he may." Robert raised his left hand to signal the waitress for an after dinner drink. It was at that moment that Laura noticed for the first time the scratch across the top of his hand.

"What did you do to your hand?"

"Oh this? It was stupid actually. I was carrying a box out to my car earlier today and I scratched it on the door of the car. A piece of chrome trim must have come loose and unfortunately my hand found the rough edge."

"I bet that one hurt? They are long scratches and look deep."

"It's nothing really."

Laura then leaned toward him across the table. "You sure it wasn't some jealous woman that I should know about?"

Robert returned the devilish smile. "There is only you, my love, only you."

....

Jake had finally gotten the girls to sleep. Both had been particularly wound up that evening and Jake had to conduct some serious negotiations with these two feisty young ladies to get them to finally go to bed. He closed the door to their room as quietly as he could when the phone suddenly rang. Jake ran and caught it on the second ring. He hoped that it would not awakened the girls.

"Jake? It's Andy. Sorry to call so late but I think we have something."

"What is it?"

"I have a team watching the house in Marin County that we suspect may be where Marilyn is being held. So far they have observed two women and one man coming and going. The man, who matches the description we have of Nelson Smythe, left before we had a backup team in place so we were not able to follow him when he went out this evening. A woman then left the house around 7:30 p.m. She went into downtown Sausalito and entered a bar. One of my supervisors did a little undercover work."

Jake listened but was anxious for Andy to cut to the chase. Andy must have sensed this. "Well to make a long story short, he struck up a conversation with the woman and the name she gave him was Tamara Daing." Andy paused, quite pleased with what had been uncovered.

Jake on the other hand, had not recognized the relevance of this discovery. "Andy, I'm not sure I understand. How is this relevant?"

"Oh, I'm sorry, let me explain further. Remember the woman that impersonated one of my agents at your child's school?" Before Jake could respond Andy continued. "Well the name she gave the teacher was Tammy Daing and the descriptions match also."

"So it is beginning to look like Mr. Nelson Smythe is our kidnapper and…this Tammy Daing works for him or something?"

"That's my guess Jake. Look, the purpose of my call, is that I think we have enough to make a move."

Jake's mind was again racing. He wanted to get his wife back as soon as possible and her safety was paramount. "Andy, good work! How much time do you need before your men make a move?"

"Well, of course, time is of the essence, but to get everything set, my thought would be to storm the house the day after tomorrow in the morning. Making a move at night is not that critical, given the number of trees close to the house. My men can practically walk in the front door before those inside suspect anything. My other thought is that if we wait until…perhaps mid-morning, Smythe will be out and about and that will only leave the women in the house to deal with. This should minimize any risks to Marilyn. Of course, if we hear trouble before that, we may need to move immediately."

Jake hesitated and then responded. "Alright Andy, you're the expert on this sort of thing. Let's plan on hitting the house at around 10 o'clock the day after tomorrow. That will allow me time to make some moves of my own."

Andy listened pensively and then responded. "Anything, I should be aware of boss?"

"Let's just say that its time we spring our trap and nail all the bad guys involved."

………………………………………

John Garrison and two other FBI agents arrived at Naomi Shu's home twenty minutes after he received her call. He and his men entered the house cautiously not knowing what to expect. After ringing the bell and calling to Naomi, they broke down the front door and found her lying on the floor with the phone was still in her hand.

Garrison signaled two agents to search the house and ran to her. She had been severely beaten about the face and head. His concern was that there was far too much blood. She appeared to be unconscious at first but when he felt for a pulse there was none.

Garrison dropped his head and thought. *She was young and pretty with so much to live for. Whoever had done this was because of him. She had been helping him!*

One agent returned to the living room and saw his supervisor leaning over the woman on the floor. “All clear sir. No one else in the house.”

Garrison looked up suddenly. “Get a team over here ASAP! This woman was murdered and I want the bastard that did it!” The agent nodded to the other agent that had also returned to the living room and both men returned to their car to call in the crime as directed by their supervisor.

Skip Henderson, entered the home as the two agents were leaving. “Dead?”

Garrison now stood and nodded his head. “Yeah, and whoever did this sure took out his frustrations on this defenseless woman.”

“Think they found out she was helping us?”

“What do you think, Skip? God damn it!” Agent Henderson nodded his head and waited for Garrison to continue. He had decided that any further questions might be a bad idea at that moment.

“It’s time for some answers, Skip.”

“Where are you planning to look, John?”

“We are going to start with our friend Jake Oliver. He seems to be in the middle of this goddamn three-ring circus. It’s time he shared with us what his employers are up to because I’m getting tired of cleaning up after them!”

CHAPTER THIRTY FIVE

The girls were procrastinating and Jake knew it. Unfortunately, it was Marilyn that had devised the unique psychological methods of getting them dressed and off to school on time. But this morning, Jake had his work cut out for him.

"Come on girls, I need both of you dressed and sitting at the breakfast table in five minutes. No excuses."

"But daddy," protested Sarah, "I want to wear my red shirt today. Don't we have time to wash it."

"No, I'm sorry but we don't. You will just have to wear something else."

"Daddy," asked Briana, "when is Mommy coming home?"

"Very soon, I hope." Jake gathered his two daughters and they all sat down on Sarah's bed. "Look girls. I know it has been tough the past few days but I need each of you to be strong and help me out. Alright?" Both girls nodded their heads indicating they understood. "Good, now are we going to get ready for school or…is the tickle monster going to have to come visit!"

Both girls jumped up immediately and ran off laughing. Jake followed them down the hall to the kitchen and poured each a glass of orange juice when the phone rang. Jake told them to go ahead and eat their cereal while he answered the phone.

"Jake? This is John Garrison. We need to talk right away." The tone in his voice was tense and serious.

Jake walked off into the living room away from the girls. "Actually, Mr. Garrison, I was planning to contact you this morning."

"Look Jake. You're playing with some real bad asses here. Your realtor, Naomi Shu…is dead." Garrison's words hit Jake like a sledgehammer in the face. "Jake, you still with me?"

Jake continued to gather his thoughts for a few seconds before responding. "Yeah, I'm here. I will drop off my daughters at school in the next 30 minutes. Let's meet at the *Lakeside Café*. It's just down the street from the school at____"

"Yeah, we know the place," interrupted Garrison. "See you there at 0800."

……………………………………

Jake walked into the coffee shop and saw John Garrison and another gentlemen seated in a booth in the back. He walked toward them and took a seat next to the man he had not yet met.

"Jake this is agent Henderson." Jake nodded at both men as Garrison continued. "These guys are real serious and they're killing people. Are you with us or are you going down with these low lifes?"

"What happened to Naomi?"

John looked up at the ceiling as he responded. "Someone used her head for a punching bag. You want me to go into details."

Jake shook his head indicating that the details were not necessary. "Why was she killed?"

Henderson responded to this question. "We don't know for sure, Jake, but it's possible that they found out that she was working for us."

Jake considered his comment carefully. "So, you recruited her to help you and she gets killed. You guys sure have some great motivational recruiting techniques."

John Garrison leaned across the table. "How long do you think it will be before they don't need your wife, Jake?"

Jake stared at agent Garrison intensely. "So you know someone has kidnapped my wife."

"Yeah, we know. Why didn't you come to us sooner?"

"Probably for the same reasons as what you have just told me." Both agents looked down as Jake continued. "But, actually, gentlemen, I am now here to ask for your help."

Jake then explained what Andy Baroni and his team had been able to uncover and described how they had the house, where they thought Marilyn was, surrounded.

When he finished, Garrison was the first to reply. "Jake, *we* will take care of this. And we don't need Andy Baroni and his team to____"

"Baroni Security is in on the rescue!" Interrupted Jake. "They found her and they will get her back!" The two agents looked at the man seated at the table with them. The look of determination he had was so strong that neither man wanted to challenge him further. Jake continued. "Look, gentlemen, I can provide you with the information you need to uncover what is going on."

Jake's comment peaked both agents' interest. He then explained the plan he had in mind. As he spoke, Henderson looked over at Garrison. Each was impressed with what Jake had been able to uncover and supported his plan.

Jake then stood, "And now gentlemen, it's time we all go back to work. I only have one more question. Who do you have inside the hotel working for you? I may need their assistance."

Garrison looked over at his supervisor who nodded his approval. Garrison then answered Jake's question. Jake gave him a knowing smile and then departed.

....

Jake called the hotel on his cell phone and advised Sandra that he would be in about 11 a.m. after a morning appointment. Sandra informed him that Laura Sanders had already been by the office twice to see him. He confirmed that he would not be in until 11 a.m. and that she would have to wait until then.

He then called Ed Lee and informed him that he was on his way over and wanted to speak with him right away. Jake arrived at Ed Lee's office at 9:30 a.m. When Jake entered the main entrance to the architectural firm, Cathy Lee, Ed's wife was there to greet him.

"Good morning Jake."

"Good morning Cathy. The boss got you working the front door today?"

"It would seem so. My daughter has returned to school and we have not yet hired her replacement. Ed will be with you in just a minute. Is there anything I can get you while you wait?"

Jake looked around anxiously. "A...no, thank you." Cathy started to walk into a back room when Jake called to her. "Actually, Cathy, you may be able to answer this question. How long as Benjamin Tsang been with South Harbor and your father?"

Cathy Lee turned and looked at Jake with a combined look of pride and amazement. At that same moment, Ed Lee entered the reception area from the conference room and she addressed her response to her husband. "Jake Oliver appears to be on the right track and it is time for you to fill in the blanks."

Jake looked at Cathy, confused by her cryptic response. Ed motioned him into the conference room and shut the door behind him. "Perhaps if I understood better what the nature of your questions were about, I might be able to respond more accurately."

"Actually, I only have a few questions. How long has Benjamin Tsang been with Samuel Cho and what is their relationship at this time?"

Ed walked over and poured himself some tea. He motioned to Jake who declined. "Benjamin joined South Harbor in the mid 70's if I recall. Samuel was looking for someone to groom to handle the day to day operations of the organization so that he could devote more time to strategic planning for South Harbor Investments."

"And their current relationship?"

Ed smiled as he sat for the first time. "Well, on the surface, one would think that the two men were the best of friends depicting two partners that compliment each other's talents."

"And within the organization?"

Ed was clearly gathering his thoughts and Jake sensed that whatever response he got was going to be censored to some degree. "Jake, all large organizations of the size and scope of South Harbor must deal with internal strife." Ed paused and Jake remained silent. "But tensions between Samuel and Benjamin have been brewing for some time. From such tensions, rumors often develop. Now we all know that the accuracy and credibility of such rumors must be taken into consideration carefully."

Jake leaned forward across the conference table toward Ed. "Tell me about the rumors, Ed."

"It has been said that there is a power struggle, of sorts, between Samuel and Benjamin that has been growing more intense over the past few years. It is suspected that Benjamin has strong desires to take over South Harbor Investments but no one is quite sure how he plans to accomplish this task."

"How?"

Ed stood and walked over to the side table to get some more tea. "Business is handled somewhat different in Hong Kong, Jake. One can assume power in many ways. It is not as simple as your Italian Mafia. Benjamin cannot not simply arrange for Samuel Cho to just disappear because he still requires the approval of the board of directors before he can assume the role vacated." Jake nodded his head as he began to understand. "For such a shift in power to occur, Benjamin would have to first politically destroy Samuel Cho."

"Possibly a scandal of some type such as the misuse of funds or a partnership with a disreputable union."

Ed smiled. "Now you are getting the drift of things."

"But I guess I got in the way of that, didn't I?"

Ed sat down and leaned back in the conference room chair. "Samuel Cho wanted a man to run the hotel that was not scared of ruffling a few feathers. But also one with a high degree of ethics to uncover what was going on. You fit his needs on both issues."

"Samuel Cho is one to talk about ethics. He is currently attempting to blackmail me to launder illegal money from his operations. Ed, I find it hard to believe that____"

"Don't be too hard on Samuel, Jake. I don't condone what he does for a living. That is why I chose to return and not work for him further. But he chose the right man to operate the Wilford. He needed you to flush out what Benjamin was up to and now it appears quite obvious that he is working with Jackson and possibly Local #78 to disgrace Samuel."

Jake looked out the window at the light rain that had started since his arrival. "No, Ed I don't think that's all that is going on here." Ed looked on confused by Jake's last statement.

"I must go. Thank, you for seeing me." Jake walked to the door and was about to leave when he suddenly stopped and turned to face Ed. "Ed, did you ever find out whose idea it was to purchase the Wilford?"

Ed was more confused than ever. "Who's idea?"

"I mean, why did South Harbor purchase the Wilford, a run down hotel in San Francisco? As a front for its operation? Why not another?"

Ed shook his head. "Well, I am not sure I know for sure. But my guess would be they wanted a business that would not attract a lot of attention and…" Ed paused realizing his explanation made no sense. The Wilford was still a recognized hotel with a rich history. And its disputes with Local #78 certainly didn't fit the profile of keeping out of the public's view.

Jake could see Ed's internal conflict. "Ed, you don't believe that explanation any better than I do. What I am getting at is who, within South Harbor, specifically recommended that they buy the Wilford?"

Ed thought for a moment and then looked up suddenly. "I reviewed my notes from when Samuel first contacted me and ask me to look at the hotel." Ed paused as he recalled the entire conversation again in his mind and then continued. "He said that Benjamin Tsang had recommended it as a good investment."

Jake just smiled and nodded his thanks as he left Ed's office. As he walked out the door the cool rain hit him in the face and he found it refreshing. Jake now had a plan and needed to put a few more pieces together before he made his move. His first task was to get back to the Wilford. He needed to do some quick research before the next negotiation meeting began later that afternoon.

Jake arrived at the hotel and quickly proceeded to his office. He signaled Jim Slazenger to join him along with Sandra Kelly who was just returning with the morning mail. When both were seated, Jake reviewed what Andy and his team had uncovered concerning where Marilyn may be held. He then reviewed some of the specifics of his plan.

Jim and Sandra emerged from Jake's office. Both looked stunned and amazed by what they had just heard. Sandra returned to her desk and began to sort the mail. As Jim started toward his office he stared at Sandra for a moment. She looked up and smiled. Jim just shook his head and smiled back and the walked off.

Jake had quickly cleared his desk of all non-emergency issues and turned to his computer. He logged on to the internet and began his search for information. He began with a general search of historic events that occurred in Hong Kong from 1925-1935. The web site he found accessed relevant articles from the local papers of that time. Jake was thankful that someone had taken the time to translate these articles into English. Jake continued to narrow his search and 20 minutes later, the first part of his puzzle was uncovered.

The event that caught his attention occurred in the spring of 1930. The article on the screen had been translated from a local Hong Kong paper. It addressed the theft of ancient Chinese artifacts that had been on display from the mainland. The items had been on loan to a local Hong Kong museum. The rest of article indicated that, initially, authorities had no specific leads as to who was responsible for the theft. Great suspicions, however, revolved around how the thief or thieves had accessed the building.

Jake clicked a button at the bottom of the screen that indicated a web link to similar and / or follow up articles on the same subject. Jake read quickly and he was amazed by the information before him. One article indicated that authorities suspected the thieves may have had assistance from someone working at the museum. Another article referenced that the security hired to watch the items had been drawn away to another disturbance. A later article then suggested severe negligence on the part of the security firm and that they were under investigation.

Jake noticed a quote from the founder and principal benefactor of the museum. His name was Chiang Moy Soon. The article went on to say that he was a prominent businessman and a key financial supporter of the museum and the arts community. It further stated that he had used his political influence to arrange for the exhibit to be at the museum. Later in the article, however, it referenced that the Mr. Soon was suspected of being tied to organized crime and then went into detail on his vast empire consisting of shipping, gambling, and large sums of Hong Kong real estate.

Jake continued to review the articles on the stolen exhibit when he came across a front page headline. The article described the sudden and mysterious disappearance of Mr. Chiang Moy Soon. The story indicated that servants, who had been dismissed the night before, returned to Mr. Soon's home and found much of the interior destroyed and Mr. Soon missing. They also noticed that his bed had not been slept in. A company spokesman said that he was missing when he failed to be present at a very important meeting involving the purchase of another company earlier that morning. The authorities indicated that an extensive search was underway.

In a later article, a spokesman from Mr. Soon's primary company, South Harbor Investments, indicated that they were greatly concerned for Mr. Soon's safety. The spokesman further stated that no one had contacted them indicating that they had abducted their leader. He appeared to have simply vanished.

Jake continued to view different documents and eventually came across a follow up article dated three weeks after the disappearance of the exhibit. This article suggested that there may be a direct connection between the stolen exhibit and the disappearance of Mr. Soon. The article indicated that new evidence from the on-going investigation suggests that Mr. Chiang Moy Soon may have personally arranged for the security that had been hired to protect the exhibit. Such a menial task was severely questioned for a man of Mr. Soon's power. The article further stated that an anonymous source had suggested that Mr. Soon was experiencing some financial difficulties and implied that he may have arranged for the exhibit to be stolen with the intent of selling off the priceless artifacts to the highest bidder.

The last few articles specifically captured Jake's attention. It stated that Mr. Soon may have been the target of a 'crime syndicate shifting of the guard' as the article stated. The article indicated that a key suspect in the investigation of Mr. Soon's unexplained disappearance was his second in command, a Mr. Samuel Cho.

Jake leaned back in his chair and considered what he had read over the past hour. *We have an exhibit of Chinese artifacts disappearing during the spring of 1930. We have the founder of South Harbor Investments mysteriously disappearing two weeks after the artifacts. The authorities think that Mr. Soon may have been involved in the theft of the exhibit. And lastly, there is strong evidence that Soon's disappearance may have been the result of a power struggle in which Chiang Moy Soon was pushed out of power by none other than Samuel Cho!*

The last article that Jake pulled up on his computer screen summarized a long and ruthless career for Chiang Moy Soon and his rise to power following World War One. The article indicated that he was one of Hong Kong's most powerful and wealthiest men at the time of his disappearance. It referenced that Soon's companies were in constant battles with the port authority over illegal imports and exporting practices. Later in the same article, it referenced that the acting Chairman of the Board was Samuel Cho. It then described Samuel's rapid rise through the ranks of South Harbor Investments. The article closed with a reference that, although Samuel Cho was a key suspect in the disappearance of Mr. Soon, no direct evidence had yet been discovered.

Jake quickly jotted down some notes and dates from what he had uncovered in such a short amount of time. He then picked up the phone and called Andy on his cell phone. Andy answered promptly.

"Andy, it's Jake. All still quiet at the house?"

"So far so good. All three suspects that we have identified are in the house as we speak. We also have surveillance with long range listening devices but have not yet heard a voice that we can match with Marilyn.

Jake held the phone and sighed deeply. "Will you be set to move in tomorrow morning as we planned?"

"Yes."

Jake then explained to Andy his plan and the timing of events to follow. When he added that the FBI would be working with him, Andy laughed. "I'm willing to bet a hundred bucks that they didn't like the idea of working with me any better than I will like working with them."

"You're right about that but they provide the legal basis for us raiding the house. So you get to keep your money." Just before hanging up Jake paused before he continued. "Andy, are you sure your men can pull this off and get Marilyn back safe?"

Andy remained silent on the phone and then responded. "Sir, we will do everything we can."

"That's all I can ask, Andy. I'm counting on you partner."

"I know sir." Both men hung up the phone.

Jake looked at his watch and realized that in less than one hour he would again be face to face with Lou Walizak and if his plan failed, he might lose Marilyn, his job, and Sarah and Briana's father may be sent to jail.

....

Jake entered the meeting room a few minutes past 2 o'clock. All individuals that had been at the previous meeting were again seated awaiting his arrival.

"Sorry for the delay, ladies and gentlemen. Shall we get started?"

Laura began by summarizing the minutes of the previous meeting. As she spoke, Jake focused his gaze on the heavyset man seated across the table from him. Lou Walizak appeared uneasy and kept looking away not able to maintain eye contact with Jake for more than a few seconds.

Jake then noticed Laura Sanders seated next to him. She looked different but, at first, he could not place it. Maybe it was her outfit or possibly how she had done her hair. Maybe it was the glow in her face. Or maybe it was the new man in her life that had put the bounce in her voice. Was her new love interest just a coincidence?

When Laura finished, Jake addressed the others in the room. "Unless there are any questions, corrections, deletions or revisions to the minutes of our last meeting, I would like to begin. But first, would my distinguished guest, Mr. Walizak like to make any opening remarks?"

Lou had been leaning over whispering something to Micky Selecki, his union representative. Upon hearing his name, Lou quickly sat up in his chair.

"Thanks, Mr. Oliver. Yes, I would like to clarify a few issues that arose the other day." Lou looked over nervously toward the hourly staff members of the Wilford who sat quietly in chairs along the wall. These were his constituents and it was important that they did not lose faith in his abilities.

"The other day, some of you may have been led to believe that I objected to you, my fine constituents, being present at these negotiations. I do not! My only concern was that much of what is discussed must be drilled down, so to speak. It takes time before plans are finalized and officially presented to all of you in the form of a collective bargaining agreement. My concern is that things said during the process of negotiations may be taken out of context and interpreted incorrectly. In turn, negative impressions may be formed of this administration. I, therefore, recommend that if questions arise you should seek out your respective shop stewards at the hotel. They will be glad to clarify any concerns you may have."

Jake smiled at Jim Slazenger, seated two chairs down. His disgust at Lou's feeble attempt to spin a positive impression out of his negative actions the other day was expected. "Lou, your concerns are admirable." Replied Jake, a tinge of sarcasm in his voice. "In fact, your concerns with our well being are always appreciated." This comment drew a slight chuckle from the other department managers seated around the table.

Micky Seleki was the next to speak. "A…today I thought we should discuss scheduling and minimum shift requirements. Specifically, we want to make a few changes that____"

"Mr. Seleki?" Interrupted Jake. "My apologies. But I was hoping that we could start out today's meeting with a little discussion about increases being proposed to the union pension fund."

Seleki looked over at Lou Walizak who was now staring intensely at Jake while he leaned back in his chair. He then glanced over at Seleki indicating his approval for him to proceed.

For the next hour, Seleki reviewed the proposed increases for the pension fund. The increase in monthly dues that both the hotel and the employees would have to pay were substantial. Jake continually asked questions during Seleki's well-rehearsed and clearly well scripted dissertation and his questions had the desired effect in causing unrest among the employees present. Lou noticed the whispers among his members and the looks of concern with the proposed increases. Increases that would result in their net pay decreasing. He was losing their support and he knew it.

"So, let me get this straight, Mr. Seleki." Jake replied. "You are telling us that the sole reason for requesting the proposed increases to the pension is the need to increase funds to support the past and future retirees of Local #78 who will be drawing from this fund?" Jake's question was designed to specifically call attention to this issue.

"And, what is causing these increases at this time? Do you expect a big infux of retirements over the next few years?"

"A...Mr. Oliver. I am afraid it is a little more complicated than that." Replied Seleki nervously.

"Oh, I see. Let me direct my questioning another way. Perhaps you can tell us how the current funds have been invested during...say...the past year?"

Before Seleki could respond, Lou Walizak stood. "Nice try, Oliver, nice try. We know what you are trying to do here!" Jake remained poker-faced while Lou continued. "How the fund has been managed is not in question here."

Jake leaned across the table. "Well, maybe it should be, Mr. Walizak."

Lou's frustration was reaching its boiling point. His face reddened and his thick neck strained against his shirt collar. He looked quickly around the room. "Mr. Oliver, I am very disappointed. We came here in good faith to discuss the well being of these individuals." Lou now motioned, with his hand toward the gallery of hotel employees. "But it appears that you have your own agenda to support management, not the worker!"

Jake remained seated. "All I am asking is_____"

"This meeting is done for today!" Interrupted Lou. He gathered the papers on the table in front of him and the representatives of Local #78 left the meeting room with no further words said. Once they left the room, the employees in the room were immediately engrossed in conversations among themselves.

Jake and the other department managers departed leaving them to contemplate what had happened.

Shortly after Jake sat down in his office, Jim Slazenger entered and plopped down in a chair. "Damn, that was fun! It was great to see that guy squirm."

"Well, let's see what happens next. I just hope we get the reaction we want and not the one we don't want."

Jim nodded, as a more somber mood now set in. "It won't be much longer, Jake, and you will have Marilyn back safe and sound."

"I hope so, big guy. I certainly hope so."

CHAPTER THIRTY SIX

Jackson Chi had just returned from a late lunch to his office. As he shook off his umbrella from the rain outside, he glanced toward Ms. Chuen seated behind her desk. “Any messages?”

“Yes, Mr. Walizak called a few minutes ago. He wants you to call him immediately.”

“Immediately! Who does this man think he is?” Ms. Chuen simply looked down at her desk and said nothing. Jackson stormed into his office and slammed the door behind him.

He sat down at his desk and began to review faxes that had arrived from Hong Kong the night before. Suddenly, there was a knock at the door. Ms. Chuen entered and informed him that Lou Walizak was again on the phone and insisted on speaking to him. Jackson nodded and waived impatiently for her to put the call through.

Jackson let the phone ring several times before answering it to demonstrate that he was in no hurry and would not comply with this slob’s demands.

“Chi, where the hell have you been?”

“My activities are of no concern to you. What is it that is so urgent?” Jackson replied, clearly irritated.

“Listen, Chinaman. I just left the negotiations at the Wilford. Oliver must be on to us!”

“What are you saying?”

"I'm saying that for the past hour, I sat there and listened to Jake Oliver beat around the bush. He targeted the pension fund first thing. Then he drilled my staff as to why the pension fund was in such poor financial condition. He suggested that perhaps the administration of the fund should be reviewed."

"He knows nothing you fool!"

"He knows and I suspect that tomorrow he is going to drop the bomb on us! In fact, I thought he might try it today so I stopped the meeting and we walked out."

Jackson contemplated Walizak's last words. "He was bluffing. He must have_____"

"The hell he was! I think someone has provided him with information on our use of the funds and he has now put two and two together."

"How could this be possible?" Replied Jackson in disgust.

"We have a snitch in one of our camps, ass hole! That's how!"

Jackson remained silent as his mind considered this possibility. "If this is the case, then we may have a situation here."

"A situation! Is that what you call it? Listen Chi, this is a hell of a lot more than a damn *situation*!"

"Listen to me, Walizak! This is just a minor setback. We are making assumptions with no basis in fact. What about your sources in the hotel. What are they telling you?"

Walizak shook his head as he reached for the second drink that Seleki had made for him in the car as they drove back to his office. "My sources have dried up. I'm blind as a bat at the moment!"

Jackson considered this development. "Well, my friend, I suggest that you become "un-blind" as soon as possible. We need to know what Jake Oliver is up to. Find a source. Find out what he knows. I thought this was what you were known for Mr. Walizak, getting inside information and using it on your opponents."

"Don't get smart Chi. I'll do my part. You do yours! Put a muzzle on this guy and find out who is leaking him information!" The phone went dead while Jackson was still holding the phone in his hand. He replaced the phone and leaned back in his chair. If what Walizak said was correct then they both may have a serious problem.

Jackson stood and walked over to the window. As he looked out at the traffic and busy sidewalks 15 stories below, he called to Ms.

Chuen in the outer office. Kim Chuen entered without making a sound and approached his desk. She was dressed in, what could best be described as a smart but sexy business suit.

"Yes Mr. Chi."

"Ms. Chuen, I just received a disturbing phone call. Where are the files that I recently gave you from the Wilford?

"I will get them for you sir." Ms. Chuen then turned to leave. Jackson watched and admired the tight fitting skirt and shapely legs. Suddenly he called to her. "Have we had any visitors lately?"

Kim Chuen hesitated at the doorway and then turned to look at her employer (and forceful lover) who was still standing by the window. The light from outside casts his face and body in a dark silhouette. "Visitors? I don't understand."

"Have you been spending your time with anyone else I should know about?"

"No sir." She responded quietly.

"If I discover that your loyalties have strayed…"

Ms. Chuen simply bowed her head and then returned to her desk closing the door behind her.

Jackson returned to his desk and sat in silence. He considered the loyalty of the woman on the other side of his office door. He had been introduced to her while out drinking with some business associates in Hong Kong. She and several of her friends had been arranged by one of Jackson's long time college friends to accompany these young executives and of course entertain them later as desired. Young professional businessmen, such as Jackson, were aggressive individuals climbing their respective corporate ladders to success and, as had Jackson, all come from wealthy families. They were arrogant, spoiled and were used to getting everything they wanted.

Jackson noticed Kim Chuen the moment she entered the nightclub and approached the table with four other women. She had only been 18 at the time but there was a certain manner about her. The way she carried herself. She had an air of confidence and the looks to back it. Her hair was shinny black and straight, cut short. The blue dress she wore clung to her trim figure and the way she walked further accented her beauty. As the evening progressed Jackson was convinced that she recognized the effect her appearance and mannerisms had on men and used this unique talent to her advantage.

Jackson soon became mesmerized with this young Chinese beauty and they saw much of each other while he was in Hong Kong. Differences in their social classes, however, did not allow their relationship to ever become public. Jackson later married a woman of proper upbringing but continued to keep Ms. Chuen well cared for as his Mistress.

When South Harbor insisted that he transfer to San Francisco, he went to considerable trouble to arrange for her to also join him and he set her up with a luxurious apartment on Nob Hill. He then purchased his own residence for he and his proper wife in Pacific Heights. Conveniently, for Jackson, Ms. Chuen's residence was a short distance away.

His superiors with South Harbor frowned on Jackson's dual lifestyle but his Hong Kong friends, several of which also had mistresses on the side, admired him. Contrary to his friends, however, Jackson knew that his actions were beginning to take their toll. His wife, from an arranged marriage, obviously knew of his extra curricular activities and was growing tired of looking the other way or pretending not to overhear his associates reference Ms. Chuen at social functions.

These factors currently weighed heavily on Jackson, who had come to the conclusion that he must maintain his marriage to assure further career advancement. Ms. Chuen was beginning to effect his marriage and possibly the actions he was presently taking against South Harbor.

Jackson leaned back in his chair and thought. *Would she risk betraying me after all that I have done for her?* As far as he was concerned she owed him for the lifestyle she enjoyed and most importantly he was confident that she feared him too much to betray him. And confidence was not something that Jackson Chi lacked. Someone was playing games with his welfare, however, and they would pay.

His cell phone rang and he was momentarily startled. When he answered the phone, the voice on the other end began to speak in Cantonese. "I will be arriving tomorrow in San Francisco and we must talk."

"Tomorrow? I was not aware that you were planning to come to the states at this time."

"Actually, it was Mr. Cho's idea. I agreed to come along. We will arrive around 10 a.m. your time. Mr. Cho will proceed to the hotel and I will inform him that we have some business to discuss and come to your office."

"Very good sir."

"All is proceeding as planned?"

Jackson hesitated. He did not want Benjamin Tsang upset with him. History had demonstrated that such actions were not wise and often not safe. "A…yes sir. All appears to be proceeding as planned."

"Good. Then I will see you tomorrow." The phone went dead while Jackson was still holding the phone for the second time that day.

What was happening here, Jackson thought. *Was he being double-crossed? What if Samuel Cho got wind of what was happening and Benjamin Tsang was now simply covering his tracks by making him the fall guy. What if Tsang has cut a deal with Lou Walizak and put all the guilt on him.*

……………………………………

Lou slammed the phone down and leaned back in the spacious rear seat of his Lincoln Towne Car. Chi was an arrogant bastard! He knew he should not have teamed up with him but the money seemed ripe for the taking. And the best part was that the money was dirty and needed to be laundered. The guys in Hong Kong weren't going to complain. How could they?

Ed Flago sat quietly behind the wheel waiting for the light to change. "Back to the office, boss?"

Lou snapped out of his moment of thought. After leaving the Wilford, he had advised Micky Seleki to go back to his office and prepare for tomorrow's meeting. Micky had initially protested stating that they should discuss what had happened. Lou cut him off and told him that he had other matters to address. He then contacted Jackson Chi. What he had to say to Chi did not concern Micky Seleki. In fact, Seleki had been kept out of almost all of Lou Walizak's dealings. He did not trust the young hotel representative and had often questioned where his loyalties truly lie when dealing with the hotels assigned to him. But Ed Flago was loyal to him and was involved in all of his business dealings.

"Yeah Ed, back to the office. And get Skinner on the phone. Tell him that he and Smitty are to get their butts over there immediately."

"Yes sir. You got a plan boss?"

Ed never got an answer to his last question. The rest of the drive to the Local #78 headquarters was in silence while Lou considered his options. He needed to know what was going on inside the Wilford. *Where was that damn Sergio and what had happened to him? Why had he suddenly disappeared?*

Ed pulled the car up to the building's rear entrance and Lou got out and went inside. He breezed by his assistant, Vera, and slammed the door to his office behind him.

A few minutes later Ed entered and approached Vera's desk. "What's with him?" Asked Vera.

"Ah, nothin. Just a bad day at the negotiation table, that's all."

"Well, maybe. But I sure don't recall seeing him so riled up over any negotiations in the past like that."

Ed just smiled. "Maybe he's just losing his patience."

Ed went to get some coffee and roughly 30 minutes later Skinner Portola and Sammy Smith arrived. Vera waived them in to Lou's office. Ed Flago followed and took a seat by the door. No words were spoken. Both men were a little hesitant. The failure to kidnap the Oliver woman, as directed, had greatly angered their boss. Lou was not seated at his desk when they entered. He had gone to the bathroom through a door off to one side of his office. Both men took a seat on the well-worn leather couch as the door flew open and Lou emerged.

"Hi boss." Said Skinner. "You wanted to see us?"

"Yeah guys. I have a task I want you to perform and this time you better not fuck it up!"

"Won't happen, sir." Replied Smitty who rarely spoke. "We won't let you down."

Lou stared at both in silence. The tension in the room was high and both men seated on the couch recognized that their boss was very upset about something. "Gentlemen, I need some answers and I need them fast." Skinner and Smitty sat up from their most common slouching positions in preparation to receive their instructions. When

Lou was done, he waived them off indicating that their meeting was now over.

After Lou's henchmen left the office, Ed walked up and took a seat in a chair across the desk from Lou. "You, think they will be able to find out what we need before tomorrow?"

Lou clipped the end of a fresh cigar and placed in his mouth and began to light it. "Maybe, but I have a back up plan. It's time to call in an old favor, Ed. And I know this individual will not let me down. He wouldn't dare."

....

Skinner and Smitty walked out of the building without speaking. Once outside, Skinner lit a cigarette and looked up at the gray sky. The rain had stopped and it looked like it was going to be overcast the remainder of the afternoon. It would be dark in less than an hour. Smitty watched his partner as he spoke. "Well, what do you think. You gotta plan?"

Skinner just smiled and blew smoke in Smitty's direction. "Yeah, I gotta plan. We are going to enjoy this one." Both men then proceeded down the street as Skinner relayed to his partner what he had in mind.

....

Andy walked in carrying a small stack of papers in one hand and coffee in a Styrofoam cup in the other. "Sorry we're late." Accompanying Andy were a man and woman.

"No problem." Replied Jake. "We were just getting started."

Andy and his associates sat down at the conference table. Also seated at the table were Jim Slazenger, Sandra Kelly, and agents John Garrison and Skip Henderson. Jake recognized the man that entered the office with Andy as Cliff Weber one of the men assigned to watch his wife. He had not yet met the young woman seated on Andy's right. All were seated around the conference table in Jake's office as agreed upon at 5:30 p.m.

Jake remained standing and now walked up to the table to address his guests. “Well, I guess we can get started. Andy, why don’t you bring us up to speed on what we have.”

Andy began to spread the papers he had brought with him out on the table. “O.K. This is a layout of the house and grounds. After sneaking up and attaching a few well placed bugs, we suspect that Marilyn is being kept in this portion of the house.” Andy pointed with a pencil he picked up from the table. He then looked across the table. “To tell you more about the situation, I have asked the two officers in charge of the surveillance to be here today. Let me introduce Cliff Johnson and Janice Keller.” Both nodded to the group seated around them.

Cliff began. “We have been monitoring the house for the past 48 hours. During this period of time only three individuals have been observed coming and going from the house. Two females, one with long dark hair and the other with short dark hair. Both appear to be Asian. The third suspect is a man. He is roughly 6 feet tall, in his mid to late 30’s, and Caucasian. At each sighting, he has been dressed in a coat and tie. This is the man we are reasonably sure is Nelson Smythe, if that is his real name. The night before, we did not have our entire surveillance team in place when Smythe departed in the early evening. We made the call not to follow him and officer Keller and I continued to watch the house. A short time after his departure, the woman suspect with the long hair departed the house and we followed her. Our back up had arrived and continued to watch the house. The woman drove into downtown Sausalito and proceeded into a bar known as *Houlahan’s.* I radioed in our position and was approved to enter the bar. My task was to attempt to strike up a conversation and see what I could find out.”

Jim then interrupted. “Sounds like that was a tough task!” This drew a slight chuckle from the others around the table with the exception of Janice Keller.

Andy then stood to get some more coffee and gave Jim a mock look of disapproval. “Proceed Cliff.”

“Well, we kinda hit it off right away. She identified herself as Tamara Daing. Said she was house-sitting for a friend and feeling cooped up and decided to get out for the evening.”

Andy then interrupted. "I'll take it from here Cliff. The suspect, Tamara Daing fits the description to a tee of the imposter that was at the school and tried to abduct young Sarah Oliver. She even used the same name, which I think is kind of amazing. We ran a check on her but found nothing. So we suspect the name is false but it does link her to our friend Mr. Smythe and supports our theory that she was involved in Marilyn Oliver's abduction."

"What time did Smythe leave the house last night?" Asked John Garrison who had been listening intently.

Cliff looked through his log sheets, as did Janice Keller. Janice was the first to respond. "He left at 6:30 p.m. Is that relevant?"

"It could be." Garrison replied. "It makes him unaccounted for when Naomi Shu was beaten and later died from her attack." All looked down at the table instinctively. "So this guy may be our murderer as well." Garrison stared across the table at Jake. "That also means, Jake, that we need to move quickly and that your wife is in great danger."

Jake nodded and leaned forward in his chair. "Yes, I agree. At this time, I want to share with each of you the sequence of events that are to occur tomorrow. My plan is based on several key assumptions but I am confident that if these assumptions are correct, Marilyn will be safely rescued, the bad guys get put away and you, Mr. Garrison, get what you want. All looked on and listened carefully to Jake's plan. Andy Baroni looked over at the two FBI agents seated across the table and they nodded that they were equally impressed by the plan.

Just as Jake was concluding his talk, his cell phone rang. Before Jake answered it he stated. "My only hope is that I haven't pissed off Mr. Smythe with today's antics at the negotiation meeting." He flipped open the phone and the man's voice that Jake had come to recognize far too well spoke immediately. "Working late, Mr. Oliver?"

Jake looked around the table as he responded. "Well, I still have a hotel to run. I want to speak to my wife."

"No." Responded the man curtly. "Tomorrow you are going to move the negotiations along, I am not a patient man. I realize you need to put up a front of some sort but let's not over do it."

These last words caused Jake to smile, which confused the others around the table as he stood and walked toward the window. "Well, I'm glad you approve, bastard! Now, why can't I speak to my wife?"

"Do as you're told and she will not be harmed. But do not underestimate me, Jake Oliver. You would certainly not want to underestimate me." The phone line then went dead.

Garrison was the first to speak. "That was our man?" Jake simply nodded. "Why the smile?"

Jake returned to his chair at the conference table as his mind raced. "He didn't know about today's meeting yet. His information pipeline must have a flaw." Jake glanced at Jim and both men smiled.

"Maybe not a flaw." Replied Sandra Kelly seated in the chair next to Jake. "Maybe he just hasn't received his update for the day yet."

Jake looked at his assistant with a knowing smile. "Perhaps you are correct, Sandra."

"I'm afraid that both of you just lost me." Stated Garrison seated across the table.

Sandra smiled coyly. "Let's just say, I happen to know that someone from this office has a date later tonight. And my guess is that her new boyfriend is our Mr. Smythe."

Andy then spoke. "If that's true, we will be able to confirm that. I have two men following him at all times."

"Where is he now?" Asked Jim Slazenger.

Andy picked up his radio and called the two officers assigned to tail Nelson Smythe. They informed him that he had left the house approximately 45 minutes ago and drove into San Francisco. They observed him park his car on the street near the intersection of Sutter and Hyde, he was presently sitting in his car at that moment.

When Andy signed off from his radio call, Jake spoke. "No wonder he wouldn't let me speak to Marilyn. He was calling from his car."

....

Laura was tired and frustrated. The negotiations had gone to hell in her opinion and she was concerned with what her boss was attempting to prove. After work she had run home, fed her kids dinner and arranged for a friend to stay with them for the evening. She had agreed to meet Robert Samuelson a.k.a Nelson Smythe at the same bar they had first met. Although the bar was one of San Francisco's more trendy establishments its entrance was located at the end of a dark alley off of *Kearny Street*. It was a little past 7:30 p.m. and for a weeknight, the area was surprisingly deserted.

Laura parked her car around the corner and was just proceeding down the alley when two men appeared from the shadows and grabbed her. The one man quickly covered her mouth to keep her from screaming. She fought and struggled with all of her might as she attempted to free herself but the two men were much stronger. They pulled her into an inset area of the alley hidden in the shadows and slammed her roughly into the brick wall of a building.

The taller of the two and the one that had covered her mouth released his hand from her mouth slightly and then leaned in so that his face was less than an inch from hers. His breath smelled of beer and stale cigarettes. "Got a message for you bitch." The man said in a harsh whisper. "Your boss is causing problems and we need to know why."

Laura stared wide-eyed at her attacker and at first no sound came from her as she tried to speak. "I…I don't know what you___"

The man again slammed her against the wall. Her head hit the hard brick that time and she felt a searing pain run down her neck and back. "Why is Oliver asking about the pension fund?"

Laura then realized that this was not some random mugging. This was related to the union negotiations. "I…I don't know." She replied, her voice shaky and scarred. The man grabbed her shoulders and squeezed hard. "I don't know!" She cried out. "He hasn't told me anything!"

"What does he know?"

Laura shook her head. "I don't know what you____"

Laura braced her self for the impact as the man brought his hand back and prepared to slap her across the face but something stopped him. Suddenly the man was thrown backwards against the wall on the other side of the alley. The man's partner, the shorter stockier man ran to assist but was kicked abruptly in the face. He fell to the ground with his hands to his face, which was bleeding profusely. Both attackers quickly scrambled to their feet and ran out of the alley then there was silence.

At first, Laura had not been able to focus on what was happening. Then she heard her name. She looked into the darkness. The only light came from a light located roughly 50 feet further down the alley. The silhouette of a man stood in front of her.

"Laura, are you alright?"

Laura recognized the voice. "I…a…Robert?"

The man stepped closer and Laura could now clearly recognize that her man, Robert Samuelson, had come to her rescue. "Maybe we should get you to a doctor?"

Laura was now again aware of her surroundings and shook her head. "No, I'm alright. But how did you____"

"That's not important. Let's get out of here and get that drink." He helped her into the bar and they sat at the only table available, which was near a window. Robert did not like to be seated in a visible and, what he considered, vulnerable location but it was the only table available.

When their drinks came and Laura had a swig or two the reality of what had happened set in. "Back there, Robert, you handled those two guys ….like a real pro. It was like something from a movie and____"

"It was nothing. Did they say what they wanted."

"What they wanted? Oh, yes. They wanted to know about the negotiations and why Mr. Oliver was asking about the pension….and what he knew." Laura's voice faded off. It was obvious that she was still shaken by the incident.

Robert Samuelson looked at her intently confused by her last comment. "The negotiations? What exactly happened today?"

Laura briefly explained how Jake had challenged the union in their handling of the pension fund. She then summarized how Lou Walizak had walked out of the meeting and how employees present in the room had reacted surprisingly positive to the confrontation.

While she spoke, he found it difficult not to hide the anger he felt for Jake Oliver. He put his feelings aside, however, and asked another question. "What did Mr. Oliver say were the reasons for his change in tactics?"

"That's just the thing. He didn't tell me anything. In fact, I tried to see him immediately following the meeting but he explained that he did not have time to see me. He spent the rest of the day behind closed doors." Laura waived to the waitress to bring another round of drinks. She then leaned across the table and took his hand. "But enough about me. Back there in the alley. Where did you come from? And seriously, where did you learn to fight like that?"

Smythe's mind was racing as he thought how best to answer her question. He decided that he did not have time to play games with this bimbo and pretend to be her new lover any longer. "Laura, I need to tell you something and hope you will not be hurt." The look on Laura's face answered his question. "Laura, my name is not really, Robert Samuelson and in the interest of national security, I cannot tell you my real name. I am on temporary loan from my office in London and working with your FBI." He stopped at that point to allow her to absorb what he was saying and then continued. "We are investigating the activities of your hotel's owners and their dealings with Local #78. That is the reason for my particular interest in the negotiation meetings.

Laura looked down at the table not able to establish eye contact with a man she realized she had known nothing about. "Then all of this…I mean…you and I and…it was all a game?"

"A game? Oh, Laura, most certainly not a game. I have seriously grown close to you but I could not allow our relationship to go any further under a veil of lies." Nelson Smythe looked across the table hoping these words would convince her that he actually cared for her. He would still need her for information a little longer. "Laura, I need to know. Will you help us?"

Laura took a long drink and then looked up. "I guess I should have know better to think that a guy like you would be interested in____"

"In a beautiful woman? Laura, I am not proud of what my job makes me do at times, but please give me a little more credit. I am not *that* good of an actor." He reached out and took her hand and she smiled for the first time that evening. "But Laura, I do need your help."

Laura looked at the man seated across from her as if they were meeting for the very first time. Even after being told Smythe's creative lies, she was still attracted to him. Slowly, she finally answered. "Yes, I will help. What do you want me to do?"

Smythe mentally patted himself on the back for pulling off the ultimate scam. With a big smile he said. "Great. Well first, I am going to buy you a good dinner. And while we eat, maybe you can again summarize exactly what happened today at the negotiation meeting. We will begin with Jake Oliver's interest in how the pension fund has been financially managed. Tell me exactly what he said today."

....

"What do you make of that, Sam." Asked Charlie Winston, one of two Baroni security guards assigned to follow Nelson Smythe.

"Damn if I know, Charlie. The bad guy comes to the rescue? Wait until Andy hears that one."

The two Baroni security guards had located a small coffee shop across the street that afforded a good view of Smythe and another woman seated by the window.

"Nice of them to sit by the window, eh"

"Yeah, it sure was. But I'll be damned if I know how Andy was able to describe the woman he would be meeting with such accuracy."

Sam simply smiled. "I keep telling you, Andy Baroni is a damn mind reader!"

"Yeah, sure. So our mission here must be strictly for confirmation of facts that Andy already knows."

"What do you make of that little scuffle with the two goons bothering the woman. Our perp here just ran to the rescue. A regular god damn hero!"

"A hero that kidnaps and kills people. Let's not forget that. Now, are you going to eat that piece of pie?"

CHAPTER THIRTY SEVEN

Lou Walizak, seated in the back seat of his car, stared at the two men in the car with him. The men recognized the contempt and anger in his eyes as he alternately looked at their injuries. It was the following morning and Lou was on his way to the Wilford to resume negotiations. They drove on in silence for several more minutes before Lou finally spoke. “So, you mean to tell me that one guy was able to kick both of your asses?” Lou shook his head in disgust and continued before either had the opportunity to respond. “One guy! And he just appeared out of nowhere?”

Skinner was the first to respond. “Look boss, I don’t know where he came from but he…he knew what he was doing. I mean, he handled himself real well.”

Smitty now chimed in. “That’s right boss. He moved like he had some type of special training…or something and _____”

Lou interrupted and bit down hard on his cigar. “Alright, enough. And the bitch didn’t tell you anything?” Both shook their heads without speaking.

“Ed, pull over. The fearless twosome are getting out.” Ed pulled to the curb. They were only a few blocks from the Wilford.

As both men slowly got out of the car, Skinner turned and leaned back in through the rear window. “So boss. What are you going to do?”

Lou leaned back in the seat and puffed on what was left of his first cigar of the day. “Look, don’t worry about it. Just be ready for the next time I need you." Skinner simply nodded and walked away from the car. He was amazed that he was being let off the hook so easy.

Ed Flago pulled back out into traffic and then looked in the rear view mirror at Lou. "Boss, what are we going to do, if you don't mind me asking?

"Remember the old favor I said I was going to call in last night?"

"Yeah, you find out something?"

"Yeah, I found out something, alright. I am not sure what I am going to do about it but, at least, I know what Jake Oliver knows about our dealings with the Chinaman."

"So, you think we've been double-crossed?"

"Oh, we've been double crossed alright. I think either Chi is trying to pull a fast one or he has someone setting him up. In either event, we're going to get the short end of the stick unless we can come up with a plan."

Ed simply nods, recognizing that this was one of those moments in which it was better that he say nothing and let his employer contemplate his situation in silence.

They pulled up to the front of the Wilford. Harry Walters the hotel's bell captain was standing outside by the door and opened the rear door for his union president. "Good morning Mr. Walizak. Ready for today's meeting?"

Lou maneuvered his way out of the car, grabbed his briefcase and simply nodded at Harry and proceeded toward the meeting room where the negotiation would take place. Ed parked the car around the corner from the hotel. Before he joined his boss, however, he decided to smoke a quick cigarette, since they were actually a little early for the meeting.

....

Lou met Micky Seleki at the door and they took their seats at the table. They quietly mapped out their strategy. Or, as it appeared to the members of the staff that had been invited to sit in on the meeting for that day, Lou was doing the talking and Micky was doing the listening. No one attempted to interrupt the two men and quietly took their seats without saying a word.

Jake and the other department managers entered a few minutes later and all took their seats at their pre-assigned locations. Lou continued to lean toward Micky and speak in low tones appearing not to notice the management of the hotel seated across from him.

Jake decided it was time to get the meeting underway. "A…Mr. Walizak, if we could get started?"

Lou leaned back in his chair and looked across the table at Jake and his team. He studied the individuals carefully making a point of establishing eye contact with each. Several of the hotel's managers, looked away. Good, Lou thought. Let them know who is boss in this arena. "Where is your assistant manager, a…Mr. _____"

"Slazenger." Prompted Micky Seleki quietly.

"Yes, Mr. Slazenger, your Assistant Manager. Why isn't he here today?"

Jake had watched Lou the entire time noticing his attempts to intimidate his staff. "Mr. Slazenger had some other matters to attend to today but I will let him know that you missed his presence." The other managers chuckled at this comment.

Micky Seleki was the next to speak. "Well, if we could begin. Yesterday, Mr. Oliver, you appeared to have some concerns with the union's retirement pension fund. I would like to clarify to all present that our reasons for requesting the proposed increases are quite necessary. I would also like to clarify that we take great offense at your suggestion that these funds may have been mismanaged."

"Mr. Seleki." Jake replied. "It was not my intent to accuse the union of any wrong doing. I simply felt that, given the substantial increases being proposed, perhaps an audit of the pension fund would be in order to protect all concerned."

Lou was the next to respond. "Mr. Oliver, I think you have been reading too many sensational fiction novels or should I say e-mails?"

The managers and employees in the room were confused by Lou's last comment but Jake understood the hidden message. *So, Jake thought, he knows about the mysterious e-mail message I received. How is that possible? Did the message come from him? But that would not have made any sense. No, Lou had somehow been informed about the message and the only way that could have been possible was from one of his managers seated at that table. Why did Lou want me to know he had a source. Obviously, to intimidate me.*

Laura decided it was time to assert herself. "Perhaps we should cover the other outstanding issues and reach some agreement before we tackle what appears to be a key concern."

"I agree with Ms. Sanders." Chimed in Micky Seleki.

All agreed. For the next hour, they reviewed a variety of issues. In Jake's opinion many of the issues discussed didn't even warrant getting together for a meeting. As it approached time for them to break for lunch, Jake decided it was time to proceed with his plan.

"Alright, I think we are making real progress." Stated Laura. "Perhaps we should break for lunch and then____"

"Laura," interrupted Jake, "before we break for lunch, I want agreement on one more issue. "Lou, let's agree that an audit will be conducted of the union's pension fund by an independent public accounting firm."

Laura was completely thrown off guard by Jake's sudden request. She started to lean toward him to speak privately when Lou responded. "Mr. Oliver, are you accusing us of something that I should be aware of?"

"To put it simply, Mr. Walizak, yes." Everyone in the room was completely silent and looked on in amazement at the dialog that was taking place.

"Why you pompous, arrogant, son of a bitch! I am not going to sit here and listen to this bullshit. Let's see how well you can run this hotel once I call a strike."

"A threat, Mr. Walizak."

"No, a fact, Mr. Oliver." Lou looked around the room. "All of you heard what was said. Local #78 has come here today, to negotiate a new collective bargaining agreement with the Wilford Hotel, a landmark of San Francisco for over 90 years. And now you have some hot shot GM with a past perhaps all of you should know more about." Micky Seleki grabbed Lou's arm and attempted to stop him before he continued but it was of no use. "Mr. Oliver was GM of the a resort in Santa Barbara. Last year that same resort had a fire. Several guests and one employee were killed and your GM is currently under investigation for his mismanagement of this serious disaster." The staff seated around the room looked on absorbing what was being told to them. Quick glances first to Jake and then to Lou gave him the prompting he needed to continue.

"Now, he is messing with your livelihoods and is attempting to discredit one of the nations best and largest unions. As your duly elected president, I cannot stand by and watch your jobs be put in jeopardy by this mad man!"

Jake now stood and walked to the head of the conference table. "Perhaps, Mr. Walizak, you could share with everyone how you have been using the pension fund for your own personal gain."

Lou also stood and began to gather his things. "You're through here, Oliver. I will not stand here and listen to_____"

"Sam Filmore found out about your activities. Didn't he? That's why he had the accident. He was about to expose you." The room grew completely silent as everyone stared at Lou waiting for a response.

"Lies, all lies."

"During the past 12 months, dollars have been siphoned from the pension and placed in high risk investments. And the companies behind these investments can be traced back to you, Mr. Walizak, and a few other partners." Jake's last comment was enough to push Lou over the edge.

"This meeting is over." Shouted Lou and began to walk from the room.

"Actually, you are quite correct." Replied Jake. "I believe you will find that there are some men waiting for you outside. They too have some questions concerning your business dealings."

Lou turned and stared at Jake. The hatred in his eyes was enough for Jake to determine that he had hit on all of the right nerves. Just then two FBI agents entered the meeting room and approached Lou Walizak.

"Mr. Walizak, you are under arrest." The agents cuffed him and escorted him from the meeting room. Lou looked around franticly but said nothing. Everyone in the room sat in silence stunned by the actions that had just occurred.

Jake looked around at the faces of his staff and fellow managers and then his gaze stopped on Micky Seleki still seated across the table. Ed Flago had followed the agents as they escorted his boss out of the room leaving Micky alone at the table. "Mr. Seleki, I have been told that you are a fair and respectable man. Can we request an extension so that you can revise the terms and conditions proposed for this hotel's collective bargaining agreement?"

Micky looked at Jake not sure how to respond. "A…yes, Mr. Oliver. I think that would be the best course of action. I will need to contact our district personnel, given what has just occurred."

"Very well then." Jake looked around the room. "And now, ladies and gentlemen, I think it is time we call this meeting to an end so that we can get back to running the hotel." He then left the room and returned to his office. As he passed Rick Kowalski he paused and leaned down to whisper to him. "Rick, can you join me in my office now." The firmness in the tone of his voice, caused Rick to sit up in his chair and his heartbeat doubled. Jake left the room and Rick followed behind.

As soon as Jake was gone the entire room erupted in individual conversations. Some questioned Lou's reference that Jake was under investigation for the fire at his last hotel. Others wanted to know more about Jake's accusation that their president may have misused their pension fund. Laura looked at her fellow managers and to the most part they sat quietly completely flustered by the events that had just unfolded. She was also angry that Jake Oliver had not confided in her of his plans to make such a spectacle of what she sincerely felt were *her* negotiations.

Laura gathered her materials and left the meeting room without speaking to any of the other managers. Sandra followed a short distance away as she also returned to her desk. Laura entered her office and quickly closed the door behind her. Sandra was not surprised when she saw the light on her phone light up indicating that Laura was placing a call.

In her office, Laura found her purse and the card that Nelson Smythe (who she still knew as Robert Samuelson). She dialed the cell phone number he had given her and he answered after the first ring. "Yes," replied Smythe.

"Robert? We need to meet right away. I am so confused and____"

Laura, not on the phone. Meet me at our usual spot and you can tell me everything."

"Alright, I will leave now. How soon can you get there?"

Smythe considered how he should answer. In reality he was only a few blocks away waiting to meet with Benjamin Tsang when he arrived from Hong Kong shortly after lunch. He was looking forward to being able to advise his employer of the latest developments. "Actually, I had some errands to run and I am close by. I will meet you there in about 15 minutes.

Laura grabbed her purse, made a quick stop by the women's restroom to make sure she looked presentable and then proceeded out to her car that was parked on the first floor level of the parking garage.

She entered the parking garage when Sandra Kelly appeared from behind a column. "Hi, Laura. Going somewhere?

Laura was startled and looked at Sandra with confusion. "Sandra? What are you doing out here?" It was then that she saw that Sandra was not along. Two men in dark suits stood in the shadows behind her. They approached.

Laura looked anxiously at the two men who stood a little too close for her liking and then back at Sandra. "Sandra, what is going on? Who are these men?

"Laura, these men are with the FBI and they would like to ask you some questions about your friend Nelson Smythe."

Laura shook her head. "I…I don't know a Nelson Smythe."

Sandra walked up to her and stood less then two feet from her. "Nelson, or whatever name he gave you is the mystery man that appeared in your life recently."

"But I don't understand. How are you involved?"

Sandra reached in her purse and pulled out her identification. It read *Special Agent Sandra Kelly, FBI District Office, Los Angeles.*

"Your with the FBI?" Laura asked in amazement.

"Yes, and we need to know everything you can tell us about the man that you have been meeting each evening."

"But, I don't understand! Robert is one of you!" Sandra and the two men all looked on in confusion.

"What do you mean?" Asked Sandra.

"I mean, he said he was working for the FBI on special assignment. He said he was investigating the hotel and its owners. In fact, I am on my way to meet him right now. He wanted me to keep him informed of what occurred in the negotiations."

Sandra directed Laura to a nearby car and they got in the back seat. The two other agents sat in the front and they pulled out of the parking garage and proceeded to the San Francisco office downtown. As they drove, Sandra continued her questioning. "Laura, first of all, this man is not working with or for the FBI. I need you to tell me everything you can about our friend. What you talked about, what he asked, and any other issues that you consider relevant."

"What about my meeting with him?"

"I'm afraid that Mr. Smythe is going to get stood up."

Laura simply nodded her head and began reviewing her involvement with the man she knew as Robert Samuelson. A man that two days ago was a new potential lover and now the reality of those fun filled weeks was completely gone.

....

Jake returned to his office. On the inside, he was nervous and his stomach was in knots. The first step of his plan had gone as suspected. As he started to take a seat, there was a knock on the door. "You wanted to see me Jake?"

Jake looked up at Rick Kowalski standing at the door. The guilt on his face was quite apparent. "Yeah Rick, come in and shut the door behind you." Rick nervously complied and took a seat across the desk from Jake. "Rick, you want to tell me about your conversation with Lou Walizak?"

Rick looked away and could not keep eye contact with his boss. "Sir, I am sorry."

"Why, Rick? Of everyone on my team, I certainly would not have suspected you."

"Sir, you don't understand. I had no choice."

"Care to explain?"

"A few years ago, after my divorce, I kind of flipped out a little." Jake stood and poured some coffee and returned to his seat as Rick continued. "Well, I ran up some debts and needed cash quick. Remember, at this time, I was still paying dues and a card holder in Local #78. Through some contacts, I helped rough up some members that Lou felt were not getting with the program. In turn, he somehow took care of my past debts. It came with a price, however, Lou made it real clear that I owed him a favor." Jake continued to look on in silence. "Well, he called in that favor last night. I debated about simply saying that I didn't know anything but did not want the bastard's 'favor' hanging over me any longer. So I told him about the strange fax you got. I figured it could not do that much harm. Clearly, I was mistaken."

Rick paused trying to read how Jake was accepting his explanation. Jake now stood, looked at his watch briefly and then walked to the window as he spoke. "I am disappointed that you did not come to me with this, Rick." Rick looked down. Personally, he was also disappointed with his recent actions.

"I guess I seriously screwed up boss."

Jake shook his head. "I guess we all screw up occasionally. In your case, however, you sought help from the wrong individuals." Jake returned to his seat and leaned across the desk. "Rick, I need to know that I can trust the managers that work for me and that their loyalty to the hotel will never be compromised. Can you meet those requirements?"

Rick looked up quickly. "Yes sir! I have certainly made some serious mistakes in judgement but I have grown to respect your high degree of integrity and the pride that you have restored in the staff...and in me. I want to continue to be a part of your team, sir, and I can promise you that I owe no other debts and my loyalty is true."

Jake smiled at his chief engineer. "Alright. Now get out of here and earn your keep for the day."

Rick stood quickly his enthusiasm was genuine. "Yes sir. Thank you sir." He quickly left and Jake was confident that his first stop would be the front desk to see Shannon Kincaid. That would obviously be another issue that Jake would have to address if their relationship became too apparent and disruptive throughout the hotel.

Jake again looked at his watch. Andy should be making his move to rescue Marilyn any time now. It was imperative that Baroni Security and the FBI rescue Marilyn shortly before Smythe began to suspect that something was wrong. He then happened to look toward his computer. At the bottom right edge of the screen was the symbol indicating that he had mail. He clicked on the icon and noted several messages that he deemed not urgent from friends and department managers of the hotel.

He then noticed another message from the same e-mail address that had provided him the information he needed on the pension fund.

He opened and read the message quickly. He then leaned back in his chair and smiled as he thought. *Whoever you are, your timing is impeccable.*

Jake stood, put on his jacket and proceeded out the door. He had an appointment he wanted to get to and was quite confident that the others at this meeting would not welcome his presence.

CHAPTER THIRTY EIGHT

The rumor mill throughout the hotel remained true to form and it did not take long for word of the events that took place at the negotiations to reach Jackson Chi. Jackson slammed down the phone so hard it startled Ms. Chuen seated at her desk. He began rummaging around his desk and then yelled. "Ms. Chuen? I need Lou Walizak's cell phone number. I had it right here and I don't understand what_____"

Jackson looked up and Ms. Chuen was standing in front of his desk with the phone number on a piece of paper in her hand.

Jackson grabbed the number from her and immediately started dialing the number. Ms. Chuen turned and started to leave when Jackson called to her. "Wait. I need you to find out if anyone has recently inquired about my accounts. You know which ones."

"Yes sir. What is it that you want me to find out?"

"If someone has inquired about them! Whatever they could find out. Damn!" Jackson was so agitated that he dialed the number incorrectly and an ice cream store somewhere answered. He again slammed the phone in the cradle and began to dial again.

"I will see what I can find out." She said as she returned to her desk and accessed her computer. *What an ignorant man, she thought. Benjamin Tsang will be here in less than an hour and he is still trying to cover his ass.*

The phone rang several times and Jackson was about to hang up when it was answered. Jackson did not recognize the voice. "Walizak?"

"No, Mr. Chi, this is Ed Flago his assistant."

"Ah yes, Mr. Flago. You were at the negotiation meeting?"

"Yes sir."

"And Walizak is under arrest?"

"For the time being."

"What can you tell me about the meeting?"

For the next few minutes, Ed summarized the dialog that took place between Lou and Jake. Jackson hung up and contemplated how to proceed. If the FBI had not yet traced Walizak's activities back to him, it was simply a matter of time. And then there was Benjamin Tsang to deal with who would be arriving at his office in less then 30 minutes. He had to consider his options and most importantly he had to figure out how Jake Oliver had obtained such detailed information. Even Walizak was not aware of everything that had been planned and Jake Oliver was far too knowledgeable for his comfort. *Had he been double-crossed by Benjamin Tsang himself? Had Samuel Cho discovered his activities, confronted Benjamin Tsang and then been double-crossed? Or, had someone else set him up? Someone with direct access to his business dealings?*

....

Earlier that morning, Cliff and Janice sat in their assigned car and observed Smythe leave the house roughly an hour earlier. Two officers had tailed him and had just reported that he was presently sitting in a restaurant in downtown San Francisco. If they were going to make their move it had to be now.

They both looked up as a white Ford Explorer approached with two individuals in it. They recognized Andy's SUV. The sports utility vehicle pulled up next to them and two men got out. They walked over and got into the back seat of the car.

"Hi guys. You remember Jim Slazenger from the hotel?" Cliff and Janice both nodded toward Jim as Andy Baroni continued. "O.K., what do we have?"

Janice responded. "The suspect we know as Smythe left the house at 11am and we have two men on him. He is presently at a restaurant in the city. He appears to be waiting for someone."

"He doesn't know he is being followed?" Asked Andy impatiently.

"We don't think so." Replied Cliff. "We have been taking the usual precautions. In fact, this is the fourth team we have had on him and all teams have been keeping their distance.

"Alright. So to the best of our knowledge, we just have the two woman in the house watching Marilyn Oliver?"

"Looks that way sir." Replied Janice.

Andy looked at Cliff. "You've coordinated with the FBI?"

"Yes sir. They have given us four men who are presently stationed in the woods surrounding the house. They all reported in just before your arrival. All appears quiet. Perhaps too quiet."

Jim now spoke for the first time since getting in the car. "You're concerned that something may have already happened to Mrs. Oliver?" The concern in his voice was quite apparent.

Janice looked down and considered how best to respond. "We have to consider that possibility sir. It is…it is possible that they may have killed Marilyn in the past 24 hours. I mean, we understand that Mr. Oliver has not spoken to her and____"

"But we are going to approach the house with the assumption that she is alive and being held captive," interceded Andy.

Both Janice and Cliff looked down at their notes. "Of course, sir."

Jim broke the silence. "Look guys. I tend to be the eternal optimist at times like this. So what's the plan here. Do we go in with gun's blazing or do you have a well executed plan in mind that even James Bond would be proud to be a part of?"

Jim's levity released the tension that had developed. Andy smiled and began to describe what they had in mind. When he finished, Jim nodded his approval.

……………………………………………

Tammy threw down the magazine she had been reading and stood impatiently. "I can't stand just sitting around the house in the middle of nowhere!"

"Patience, Tammy, it's not all that bad. We've certainly had worse assignments."

"Cynthia, you have to be kidding. Here we are, out in the woods babysitting this woman, while Nelson plays 'lovey dovey' with some older woman. Face it! This entire situation sucks!"

Cynthia looked at her friend impatiently. They had been friends for many years and she recognized what was really bothering her. Tammy always wanted to be in the spotlight, the center of attention, and what was really bothering her was that she did not like Nelson Smythe being with another woman. "Tammy, why don't you see what we can fix for lunch while I check on Marilyn."

"Marilyn? Listen to you. Remember what Nelson said. Don't get close to her. You know what we may have to do?"

Cynthia shook her head as she got up from the chair located by the window and started to walk down the hall to where Marilyn Oliver was being kept. "No! I refuse to think that it will come to that. She cannot identify us. She doesn't know where she is. Why would he____"

"It could happen, so deal with it." Interrupted Tammy curtly. Now, don't forget your mask and gloves." Tammy walked into the kitchen to prepare lunch while Cynthia walked to the end of the hall and stopped outside the door to the room where Marilyn was being kept. She did as she was told and put on the ski mask and gloves and then opened the door and entered the room.

Marilyn was lying on the bed. Her hands were handcuffed to the steel headboard. She looked toward the door in anticipation of which abductor she would be dealing with. It was *Nice Lady*. The one that she was convinced was sympathetic to her situation. During each encounter, Marilyn had been playing on this individual's sympathy and guilt in the actions that had been taken. She was confident that she was getting to this person and felt that was good. Concerning the other woman abductor, however, Marilyn had some fears. This individual appeared extremely impatient and volatile. In fact, Marilyn was convinced that *Impatient* might actually harm her if she did not get away soon. *Nice Lady* had interceded during a previous encounter. The third abductor, the man in charge, appeared cold as ice and there was no reaching him.

Cynthia approached Marilyn and undid the handcuffs. She motioned for Marilyn to use the bathroom if she needed to. Marilyn stood, stretched and walked toward the bathroom.

Cynthia was caught off guard when Marilyn spoke. "You know, my husband is not going to do whatever it is that your boss wants. He has too much integrity and pride to succumb to his demands. Do you understand me?" The masked figure, at first did nothing, but then Marilyn thought she saw a slight nod of understanding. "What will happen to me then? Are you going to kill me? Would you do that to me?"

Cynthia's heart was now reaching out to Marilyn Oliver. She hated what she was doing but she had no choice. Marilyn knew that she was getting through to this woman. Her mind was racing as she continued. "You don't want to be a part of my murder, do you?" Asked Marilyn.

The masked woman now walked over and sat on the bed. Marilyn approached and sat down next to her. "He's gone now, isn't he?" Before Cynthia could acknowledge, Marilyn continued. "Let me out of here now. You don't want to be a part of this. Let me go and I will tell the authorities. They will be able to make concessions for you. The masked figure turned and Marilyn was convinced that this abductor was going to speak to her for the first time.

Before any words were spoken, however, the door to the room burst open and the other woman abductor stood there. Tammy was also wearing her mask and gloves. She stared in amazement that Cynthia seated next to Oliver woman on the bed and she was not handcuffed. The anger and disgust she had at that moment was quite apparent in her eyes and her body movements and blurted out. "What the hell is going on?"

Cynthia looked toward the door and spoke. "This is wrong, Tammy. We must let her go." Marilyn sat quietly and listened. The accent of their voices was clearly Asian.

"Shut up, you fool. Stop talking and secure her to the bed now!" Shouted Tammy as she shook her head in anger and approached Marilyn. She roughly grabbed Marilyn's arms and handcuffed them to the bed frame. She then grabbed Cynthia's arm and forced her to stand and exit the room with her. The door to the room was slammed shut as they departed and Marilyn could still hear them arguing loudly.

Marilyn leaned back against the headboard and pondered what had just happened. She was obviously getting through to *Nice Lady* and, in turn, causing distrust among the two women. Her only hope was that they might make a mistake that could be used to her advantage.

....

"What the hell did you think you were doing just a minute ago!" Shouted Tammy as she pulled off her mask and gloves and threw them harshly in the chair next to her.

Cynthia shook her head and looked down at the floor. "I just want to know why we are doing this. Why torment this woman? She has a family and____"

"It's our job, damn it!"

"No! We don't have jobs here, Tammy! We are basically prostitutes doing whatever he demands in fear of what will happen to us if we say no!"

....

"Sir, we have activity and loud voices inside. Some type of disturbance."

Andy and Jim ran to the technician that monitored the surveillance equipment that was tapped into the house where Marilyn was being held. A directional microphone was also aimed at the house. "What type of disturbance, Sal."

"Hard to tell, boss. But it is two woman yelling. Unfortunately, I can't make out everything they are saying, but tensions seem high. Should we make our move, sir?"

Andy looked at Jim and then grabbed the radio on the table next to his electronics expert, Sal Salinas. "Base leader to teams Alpha and Bravo, do you copy?" Promptly, Andy heard two sets of double clicks on the radio indicating an affirmative from each of the teams that were in place and ready to raid the house once the word was given. "Proceed as planned. Base leader out!"

....

Jake left the hotel and drove down *Market Street*. When he was stopped at a traffic light he looked at his watch and then took a deep breath. He pulled out his cell phone and dialed the number he had programmed earlier that morning.

The call was answered on the first ring. “This is Jim.”

“It’s about time. Is everything set?”

“Actually, Jake, we just initiated the raid just a few minutes ago.”

“Something happening in there?” The anxiety in Jake’s voice was noticeable.

“We heard some arguing of some type and did not want to take any chances.”

“I don’t like it, Jim. Where is Smythe?”

“He left earlier, as we had hoped.”

“Call me as soon as you have Marilyn.”

“I will, Jake. And don’t worry.”

“Yeah, right.” Jake laughed nervously and then hung up. He should be there he thought. But, his plan required Andy to make his move at the same time as his meeting if he truly wanted the element of surprise.

....

Tammy had made herself a drink and returned from the kitchen. She plopped down in an overstuffed chair and looked across the room at Cynthia who had not said a word for the past few minutes. “Look, maybe things will work out and the Oliver woman will be let go.”

Cynthia gave her a defiant stare. “You don’t believe that any more than I do. We are just kidding ourselves. Well, I will not be a part of murder!” She then stood and started to walk down the hall toward the room where Marilyn was being held.

Tammy jumped up and ran toward her. “What do you think you are doing!” She shouted as she grabbed her outside the door. The two women began to struggle when suddenly the entire house seemed to come crashing down around them. Glass was breaking and smoke filled the house. Before either woman could react and determine what was happening, men dressed in black and wearing gas masks harshly threw them to the ground.

Both women were face down against the carpet in the hallway and could not see much. Their eyes watered and it was difficult to breathe. They could hear what sounded like a dozen men throughout the house with doors being kicked open and the continual yelling of the words, 'clear', obviously signally that there were no other hostile individuals to deal with. Then a man's voice yelled from the room that Marilyn was in, 'hostage located'!

Marilyn, was scared. She had heard the scuffle outside her door, then what sounded like an explosion. She stared at the door and then noticed what looked like smoke seeping under the door. Panic now set in as she feared that the house was on fire and she was chained to the bed and helpless.

She then heard the sound of male voices followed by a thunderous crash as the door to her room was kicked open and two men dressed in black with gas masks entered and quickly scanned the room. Then one man came to her and quickly freed her from the handcuffs and helped her to her feet. Another man appeared and helped her put on an extra gas mask that he brought with him. Then the two men helped her out of the house. As they walked out of the room that had been her prison for the past four days, Marilyn saw her two woman abductors lying on the floor face down and handcuffed. The two men in black quickly escorted her out of the house and, once out in the brisk afternoon sunshine, they removed their masks and all took in a breath of fresh air. Marilyn squinted in the bright light and coughed to clear her lungs of, what she would later learn was teargas. Her eyes would continue to water for the next few hours.

Just as Marilyn started to ask questions of the two men that had rescued her, a white Ford Bronco drove up the driveway and came to a stop in front of them. Marilyn looked toward the vehicle and saw Jim and Andy get out and run toward her. "Marilyn!" Said Jim as he reached her. "Are you alright?" Andy was at his side and remained silent awaiting her response.

"Yes, I think I am. Thanks to all of you. Where is Jake?"

"Actually," replied Andy, "this rescue was arranged by your husband."

Marilyn looked at both men confused by his comment. "Come on, Marilyn. Let's get out of here," said Jim. "Jake is anxious to know that you are O.K. and you have two little girls that will be glad that their mommy is safe and sound."

....

Jake parked his car on the street and walked toward the McKesson building for a meeting that he had not been invited to. His cell phone rang and he answered before the second ring. "Jim?"

"No, this is your wife." Tears formed in Jake's eyes as he heard Marilyn's voice.

"Are you alright, honey?"

Marilyn now began to cry. "Yes, I'm O.K. Are the girls alright?"

Jake regained his composure and responded. "You bet they are and anxiously awaiting you at home."

"Well. I am on my way. Where are you?"

Jake considered how best to respond. "I'm just taking care of the bad guys that did this to you." Sensing what Marilyn was probably thinking he added. "Don't worry. I will be home shortly and we will be a whole family again."

Marilyn began to cry again and nodded into the phone. Even though no words were spoken the message was loud and clear. "Yeah, me too. Jim and Andy will take care of getting you home. Is Jim with you?" Marilyn handed the cell phone back to Jim.

"Yeah, boss."

"Jim, how did it go?"

"A real precision operation, Jake. Maybe the FBI and Baroni Security should work together more often." Jake could hear Andy laughing in the background.

"Who did we get?"

"The two woman. One was the alias, Tamara Daing and the other identified herself as Cynthia Xhing. They are being quite cooperative and talkative so far. In fact, we should be able to find out some useful information. They are both requesting some degree of consideration if they cooperate and the FBI appears willing to listen."

"What about our friend, Mr. Smythe?"

"Well, we may have a problem there. Andy's men lost him downtown about 10 minutes ago. We have therefore cleared out and hope to nab him when he comes back here."

Jake was concerned by this development. It had been his plan that Smythe would be away from the house when the raid took place. He had thought it would make it easier to get Marilyn out safely. But now he was still on the loose and had to suspect that something was up when Laura Sanders did not show up for their luncheon date. "Alright, Jim, keep me informed if he shows up."

"I will. Jake, you need my help with the rest of the plan?"

"Don't worry. I brought some back up if I need it." Jake hung up the phone and proceeded toward the main entrance of the building. He had a very important meeting to attend and was quite certain that what he had to tell the men upstairs would be quite enlightening.

CHAPTER THIRTY NINE

Benjamin Tsang stood in the doorway of the office and quietly observed the attractive Asian woman seated at the reception desk. As he approached her desk he had to admire Jackson's taste in female companionship.

Ms. Chuen looked up, startled that she had not noticed his approach. She stopped working at her computer and stood abruptly. "A…Mr. Tsang. So good to see you sir." She nervously looked down. Benjamin remained silent as she continued. "I will notify Mr. Chi of your presence." She then quickly turned and proceeded to Jackson's office and entered without knocking.

A few seconds later, Jackson appeared in the doorway and approached his boss with an extended hand. "Ah, Mr. Tsang, you are here earlier than I expected. Please. Please come in. Ms. Chuen, get us some tea and bring it to my office."

"Yes, Mr. Chi, right away."

Benjamin entered the office and Jackson closed the door behind them. He looked at the back of the man and contemplated what this visit was all about. *Benjamin's presence could not have been at a worse time. The union negotiations were not going as planned and Jake Oliver appeared far too close to uncovering what was going on. Could Benjamin have found this information out and come to Jackson with a revised plan. Or was he here for something far worse.*

Benjamin sat down in one of the comfortable leather chairs in front of Jackson's large desk. He motioned for Jackson to have a seat.

Jackson was smart enough to know that every effort should be made to demonstrate his respect so he sat down in the other seat in front of his desk rather than behind it. Jackson wanted to keep the meeting as positive as possible. As Jackson took his seat, Benjamin spoke for the first time. "Things have been going as planned?"

Jackson hesitated. "A…yes. Well…I mean basically everything is going as planned."

Benjamin leaned back in his chair and gave Jackson a hard stare. "My sources tell me otherwise."

Jackson looked at him nervously. *Who were Benjamin's sources and what exactly did he know.* "Sir, I am not sure I understand."

Benjamin stood and walked over to a bookcase located along one wall of Jackson's office. "Explain to me how the kidnapping of Oliver's wife took place."

Just as Jackson was about to respond, there was a light tap on the door and Ms. Chuen entered carrying a tray with a pot of hot tea, cups and saucers. She placed then on the corner of Jackson's desk and quietly departed.

Jackson's mind was racing as he responded to Benjamin's question. "Actually, sir, we are not exactly sure what happened." Jackson looked at Benjamin but his expression remained unchanged, so he continued. "We know that the Oliver woman was kidnapped but we, that is, Lou Walizak and I do not know who is behind it."

Benjamin shook his head in disgust. "Listen to yourself!" The anger in his voice concerned Jackson. "This Union thug is playing you for a fool. Obviously, he is behind the kidnapping and has lied to you."

"No, I do not believe so. If this was the case, than Jake Oliver would be cooperating fully and_____"

"What do you mean?" Interrupted Benjamin. "Jake Oliver is not agreeing to the proposed terms of the contract?"

Jackson shook his head and looked down at the floor, frustrated that he had spoken so quickly without thinking. But he had no choice but to continue. "No sir. Jake Oliver is demanding that there be an audit conducted of the union's pension fund. We also suspect that he may know of our joint ventures with Local #78. We suspect that he may have knowledge of the companies you told me about and the monetary disbursements that have been made to them."

Benjamin reached for the tea on the desk and poured a cup for both of them. “How could that be possible?” The anger that had been in his voice was now replaced with one of concern.

“I do not know, sir.” Jackson looked down into his cup of tea.

Benjamin shook his head in disappointment. “Let’s remember what we are trying to do here, my friend. Our objective is to create suspicion among South Harbor’s board members regarding Samuel Cho’s handling of the Wilford, one of our key overseas investments. Only in this way, will they begin to doubt his abilities and demand a change in leadership. Obviously such a change will benefit both you and I. Is this plan not clear to you?”

Jackson stood impatiently. “Yes, yes of course. But sir, someone is undermining us, I think.”

“You think!” Benjamin also stood. “Jackson, you are a fool! Of course, someone is attempting to undermine our plans. My question to you is who?” Before Jackson could respond he continued. “Start with telling me how and why you think Jake Oliver is not cooperating. Would he seriously risk the life of his wife?”

Jackson looked at him in frustration. “How can I possibly answer your last question when we don’t even know who took Oliver’s wife!”

“Obviously, your friend Mr. Walizak is lying and *his* people have her.”

“Again, I do not think so. I just spoke to one of his men. The FBI has arrested Walizak and he is being questioned for the mismanagement of the pension fund and his choice of investments in your chosen companies. Sir, it is only a matter of time before he implicates us.”

“Us, Jackson? I think not. You see, if there is a problem, it will only be you that takes the fall you incompetent fool.”

Jackson’s anger began to flare. “What are you saying?” Suddenly Jackson heard the door to his office open behind him. “Not now Ms. Chuen!”

“I’m afraid I’m not as good looking.” Replied Jake Oliver who stood in the open doorway. “It sounds like you two have a few questions that I can probably answer.”

Jake walked over to the desk and poured himself some tea. Both Jackson and Benjamin stared at him in silence. They were clearly confused by his presence there. Before either could reply, Jake turned toward Jackson and continued. "Let me help you out on this one, Jackson. Your buddy Mr. Tsang is the one that has double crossed *you.*" Jackson looked on with a confused expression. Benjamin Tsang locked on to Jake with a cold and calculating stare.

Jackson recalled Benjamin's words just prior to Jake walking in. His mind quickly replayed what had been said. He then turned to Benjamin. "What is he talking about? Are you behind this?"

Benjamin placed his cup of tea on the desk and approached Jackson. "Don't be a fool. He knows nothing."

Jake simply smiled and sat down in Jackson's desk chair, putting his feet up on the desk to demonstrate his complete lack of respect for the men in the room. "Jackson, have a seat while I tell you a little story. Oh and Benjamin, please feel free to jump in any time, if I miss a key point." Benjamin remained standing and actually appeared fascinated with what Jake had to say. Jackson unfortunately looked more confused than ever. Jake again motioned for him to have a seat but he also declined.

"Let's see if I got it right. You formed a partnership, so to speak, with Lou Walizak of Local #78. My guess is that Mr. Tsang suggested this collaboration. The plan was for you and Walizak to skim money from the union's pension fund and invest them in some selected organizations, four construction companies to be specific. My guess is that Mr. Tsang also suggested these organizations to you." The look on Jackson's face, provided adequate confirmation that his initial assumptions had been correct. Jake looked at Benjamin. "How am I doing so far?"

Benjamin simply raised his cup of tea. "Oh please, Mr. Oliver, continue. I am intrigued."

"In fact, one company, Sunblossom Enterprises, was very important to Mr. Tsang for reasons that I will get to in a minute." This comment clearly drew concern from Benjamin and he slowly took a seat as Jake continued. Jackson also took his seat.

"At first, I was a little confused as to why Lou Walizak would join forces with Jackson but, again, my guess is that Jackson was able to convince him that the investments would be a sure thing. Demonstrating your willingness to also invest in these companies using excess funds wired to the hotel from Hong Kong probably did this. And this was certainly easy to arrange, wasn't it Jackson, given that Mr. Tsang was the one that approved the amounts of these transfers. And let us not forget, that this was dirty money in the first place!"

Jake took a sip of his tea and then continued. "You disguised these, so called investments, as advance payments for the renovation. My guess is that you probably figured that even if Samuel Cho discovered what was going on, he would not do anything openly. In fact, you two probably assumed that all you would have to worry about was dealing with him internally." This comment clearly caused both men to feel uneasy.

"Now, at first, I assumed that the two of you were simply embezzling money from Samuel Cho and South Harbor. I thought maybe you were planning to go into business for yourself. But that seemed too obvious. The other dilemma was that the earlier shortfalls in the pension would eventually stand out and be questioned. And that would not look too good for our friend Mr. Walizak. I then considered that perhaps this union boss was not as dumb as he acted and started to put some pressure on you, Jackson, to help him out of his mess. If that was the case, that was probably when the two of you cooked up the plan in which the union would suggest substantial raises in the pension fund dues. The tough part, however, would be to assure them that the hotel, and most importantly, the GM, would agree to the terms of the new contract. Jackson tells Walizak, 'no problem, the GM will do what I tell him.'"

Jackson looked on nervously and Jake continued. "You approached Sam Filmore, the hotel's previous hotel manager, but my guess is that he was already having concerns with South Harbor and getting wise to your activities. Then, quite conveniently, there is a fire at Sam's home and now the hotel needs a new GM. What fortunate luck for the two of you!" Jackson and Benjamin shifted nervously in their chairs.

"But a little problem arose, didn't it gentlemen. Samuel Cho stepped in to hire the new GM for the hotel and, my guess is, that he did so without consulting with either of you. Am I right?" Both Jackson and Benjamin said nothing.

"By the look on your faces, I'll take that as a yes. Well, all of a sudden, you have me to deal with. Jackson and Lou Walizak do a little research on my past history and figure there is enough dirt to make me comply with your demands. When that doesn't seem to work, however, you plotted to kidnap my wife or possibly one of my children. Now that part bothers me greatly gentlemen and that created a big problem for you." The cold stare that Jake assumed when these words were spoken made both men feel even more uncomfortable. "The first attempt was poorly planned and failed. I assume that these were some goons hired by Mr. Walizak."

Jackson stood and subconsciously paced nervously. "This is ridiculous! Everything you are saying is complete conjecture. You have no proof or_____"

"Sit down, Jackson." Stated Benjamin Tsang. "I am enjoying Mr. Oliver's fairytale."

"But Mr. Tsang, we____"

"Sit down, now!" He demanded. Jackson complied and Jake continued.

"Now this is the part that had me a little confused at first. There was the strange man hanging around my daughter's school. Then there was the woman impersonating a security officer at the school. I was confused why you and the union had suddenly turned your attention to kidnapping one of my children. Then my wife was later kidnapped, but this time, it seemed far too well planned and executed. My question was why wasn't this done the first time. It didn't come to me until later that someone else was behind the kidnapping. In fact, this new someone first targeted my daughters but settled with my wife. This was someone who clearly had a lot more at stake and did not have the confidence that you, Jackson, and Lou Walizak could pull it off, with the security I had hired to protect my family. How am I doing so far, Mr. Tsang?"

"You have me completely enthralled, Mr. Oliver. In fact, I can hardly wait to see how this epic novel ends." Replied Benjamin Tsang with a smug look and tight smile on his face.

"Glad to hear that I'm holding your interest, Benjamin, and I hope you enjoy the ending as much as I will." Jake's sarcasm angered him but he said nothing more as Jake continued.

Jackson now spoke in a soft voice. "You are suggesting that Mr. Tsang is responsible?"

"You see, Jackson, Mr. Tsang probably lost confidence that you and Lou Walizak could pull off the kidnapping but that worked into his rather complex plans. He therefore arranged for my wife to be kidnapped and his plan was to convince everyone that the union was behind it."

Jackson looked at Benjamin. "Is this true?"

Before Benjamin could respond, Jake continued. "Oh, there is more, Jackson. "Approximately one hour ago, Baroni Security and the FBI successfully rescued my wife from a country house in Marin County. The kidnappers were working directly for Bejamin Tsang. We know this because we were able to identify an individual we know as Nelson Smythe snooping around my house. Baroni Security followed Smythe to the house where we suspected she was being held. The clincher was that the house was rented. Care to guess who the owner of the house was?"

The slight smile that had been on Benjamin Tsang face began to fade. "A very good story Jake but, again, you have no proof and no direct connection to me."

Jake smiled. "Well, you see, Benjamin, that is where you are mistaken. It appears that during the rescue of my wife, two woman were arrested and they are being quite cooperative as long as they receive some degree of immunity for their crimes and receive consideration. And I must say, they are chirping like little birds right now." Benjamin Tsang was agitated by this last comment and stood.

He continued to stare angrily at Jake. Jackson stared at his employer as his anger began to build. "Why, Benjamin? Why did you kidnap the woman? We had a plan. And why the game earlier acting as if you knew nothing about this?"

"The answer is simple." Replied Jake. "You were being set up to take the fall."

Jackson turned sharply and addressed Jake. "Set up, how?"

Jake leaned back in his chair and crossed his arms. "I have some very detailed information concerning the money that you and Lou mishandled with the Union Pension Fund. Ironically, similar information was anonymously sent to the FBI just yesterday and Lou Walizak is already in custody. They will be coming to visit you very shortly. This information also implicates you in money laundering activities involving the Wilford Hotel and South Harbor Investments.

Obviously, this charade was designed to implicate Samuel Cho. Sort of like history repeating itself. Don't you agree, Benjamin?"

Jackson stared at Benjamin angrily. "Why am *I* being set up?" Demanded Jackson.

"Actually." Replied Jake. "You're not the only one being set up. Care to enlighten him, Benjamin?"

"Jake Oliver has conjured up this entire pack of lies. And I think we have heard enough."

Jackson shook his head and shouted. "But how does he know these things?

"It doesn't matter." Replied Benjamin.

"But how can you say that. If, what he says is true then____"

"It does not matter!" Shouted Benjamin angrily.

"But who provided Jake and, as he said, the FBI, with the information he is speaking of?" Demanded Jackson.

Benjamin shook his head. "Obviously, he is lying!"

"Actually, Jackson, that question bothered me some at first. But after giving it a little more thought the answer was quite obvious.

"I still don't understand." Replied Jackson. "Who?"

Jake continued. "An interesting question, Jackson. You see the FBI approached me to help them catch Samuel Cho. My guess is they recently found someone else to help them inside the organization. Or was it you, Benjamin, that approached *them*?"

"Mr. Oliver," replied Benjamin Tsang without still acknowledging Jackson's question, "you have presented a most impressive synopsis. In fact, I am quite intrigued with your assumptions and the conclusions that you have drawn, many of which are correct to some degree. I find it curious; however, that you have overlooked that it is you that will be implicated in the money laundering scandal. We have gone to great efforts to assure that your name appears on these documents." Benjamin now walked over to the window and peered down at the people on the sidewalk below.

"The plan was really quite simple," continued Benjamin, "the ultimate objective was to disgrace and embarrass Samuel Cho. He must lose face. The board would then demand change. I agreed to cooperate with the US authorities in return for immunity and the promise that I would arrange for South Harbor Investments to sell off its holdings on US soil.

"But that was not the only objective here, was it?" Asked Jake.

"What are you talking about?"

"Why the Wilford? Why did South Harbor Investments choose the Wilford?

Benjamin smiled. "This was explained to you by Samuel Cho during his last visit, Jake. We bought that old run down hotel for only one purpose. To launder our funds. Do you think we would actually look at that place as a sound investment?"

Jake was pleased at how he had led Benjamin to this point in the conversation. "Then why are you planning to renovate the hotel. Why not keep it run down. Wouldn't that make it easier to justify the need for cash infusions from Hong Kong each month?"

"I don't see where this is leading and___"

"A simple question." Interrupted Jake. "Wasn't it you that personally suggested the Wilford to Samuel Cho? All I am asking is why?"

Benjamin hesitated momentarily. "Samuel Cho needed a business in the United States to launder South Harbor's funds. I simply found a suitable business."

"Buzzzzz, that's not the correct answer, said Jake sarcastically, "care to try again?"

Benjamin was puzzled. *What else did Jake know and how could he have found out.*

Jake noticed that Benjamin's mind was racing. "Mr. Tsang has played everyone for a fool, Jackson. He has conducted this entire series of events with two ultimate objectives in mind. To disgrace Samuel Cho so that he could assume leadership of South Harbor Investments and what is buried behind a wall in the basement of the Wilford. The look of astonishment on Benjamin's face provided Jake confirmation that his assumptions were on track.

Jake walked over to the desk and sat on it. "Let me tell each of you another bedtime story.

In 1930 an exhibit of ancient Chinese artifacts were stolen from a museum in Hong Kong. After an investigation, Mr. Chaing Moy Soon, one of Hong Kong's most prominent and yet most questionable businessmen of that time was implicated as a possible suspect. Before the Hong Kong authorities could question Mr. Soon he too mysteriously disappeared."

Benjamin Tsang moved restlessly. "I do not see the relevance of this *story*, as you called it."

"Patience, Benjamin. As I was saying, Mr. Soon's disappearance received quite a bit of publicity. You see, Mr. Soon was the chairman of a newly created organization known as South Harbor Investments and after it was believed that he was dead or had fled from the country, the company's board of directors appointed a new chairman, a man by the name of Samuel Cho."

Jackson sat back in his chair, fascinated by where this story may be going. Benjamin, however, was highly agitated and Jake wondered how much longer he would be allowed to continue..

"A very sensational rendition of the history of South Harbor Investments, Mr. Oliver but I think we have heard enough." Benjamin was looking around the office as if he was expecting someone.

Jake continued. "Oh, but there is more. Right around the time the artifacts were stolen a ship left the port of Hong Kong bound for the United States, San Francisco to be specific. This ship arrived here two weeks later and the men on board unloaded an unidentified cargo. The cargo was trucked to an unknown location and placed in a room that had been created in the basement of a building."

"What is this fantasy you are describing?" Demanded Benjamin.

"This is not fantasy, Mr. Tsang, as you are well aware. The men from the ship were told not to discuss the cargo or its location. Two men boarded the ship in San Francisco for the trip back. The night before the ship put into port in Hong Kong, the crew involved in moving the cargo were murdered and thrown overboard. The story told to their families was that they had contracted an illness and had to be buried at sea. But that wasn't true was it Mr. Tsang?" Benjamin did not acknowledge his question.

Jackson spoke. "How could you know all of this if all the men were murdered on the ship?"

"Very good question, Jackson. The answer is that everyone was not murdered. One escaped. An individual of amazing insight and a will to survive. This man jumped overboard and survived in the open sea for two days before being picked up by another passing ship. He was also smart enough not to say how he ended up out at sea. He returned to Hong Kong, gathered his family and moved out of the city so he could not be found."

"Who was this man? Where is he now?" Asked Jackson.

"I will share that with you in a moment. But first I have one more brief story to tell. On or about the early 1970's, a young and aggressive businessman by the name of Benjamin Tsang was hired by South Harbor Investments. Over the next 20 years he worked his way up through the ranks and eventually became Samuel Cho's right hand man. This was a key goal of the man seated here in front of us."

"Benjamin Tsang was the eldest son and had one younger sister. When he was a small child growing up in Hong Kong, his father, who previously worked on cargo ships, moved the family out of the city and took up farming. Mr. Jun Sing Tsang, died approximately two years ago, if I have my dates straight." Benjamin simply nodded an affirmative. "Well, on his deathbed, old man Tsang produced a document that had been written almost 70 years earlier. He gave it to Benjamin to read and it appeared to be a far fetched tale. Didn't it Benjamin?" Benjamin showed little reaction as Jake continued.

"Your father had suffered an ordeal that angered you greatly. Especially since the freight line that your father had worked for belonged to none other than South Harbor Investments, *your company*!"

"So the sole survivor and only individual that could provide the possible location of the artifacts was Benjamin's father?" Asked Jackson in true amazement.

"It would appear so," replied Jake. "Mr. Tsang apparently started to research the matter and I assume that he was angry at the injustices done to his father. For the past two years, he has most likely been trying to fill in the missing pieces to this 70-year-old mystery. Mr. Tsang probably utilized past company records and payments to eventually track down the construction company used to create the mystery room to store the artifacts. A little further digging probably uncovered that in 1930, Charles Wilford the founder of the hotel was suffering from the stock market crash of 1929 and at a time of desperation, sold 50% of the Wilford to South Harbor Investments, then under the leadership of Mr. Soon."

"Once Samuel Cho took over, however, he could not understand why the company needed such an investment and willingly sold his shares of ownership back to the Wilford family. To many at that time, it was never known that these transfers of ownership ever took place.

Mr. Cho obviously did not know the relevance of the hotel at that time. When Mr. Tsang tracked down the location of the hidden artifacts to the Wilford, it was imperative that he again obtain ownership. In turn, he made a pitch to Samuel Cho to re-purchase the now run down Wilford. Cho went along with it because of their long-time business relationship."

"Then Mr. Tsang recommended that the hotel undergo a complete renovation. My guess is this plan generated some concern with Samuel Cho since it made no sense to be spending money on an investment they were simply using as a front for their operation. In fact, this has probably been a key factor behind the tensions that have been growing between Mr. Tsang and Mr. Cho."

Jake shook his head in amazement as he looked toward Benjamin Tsang. "It must have been quite remarkable to find out that the company that you had worked with for almost 20 years turned out be led by a man that tried to kill your father. Time to get even, eh Mr. Tsang?"

"Your investigative skills truly amaze me Mr. Oliver, but getting back to the connections you are making to me and this Mr. Smythe still has me a little confused. Your stories are, just that, stories. You have nothing to support your accusations and certainly no connection between this Mr. Smythe to myself."

"Well actually that's where you are mistaken," replied Jake in a somewhat casual manner that concerned Benjamin Tsang. "You see, the FBI was working secretly with a woman by the name of Naomi Shu. Does this name sound familiar to either of you?"

The look of recognition on Jackson Chi's face suggested he had not known the name. Benjamin Tsang, on the other hand, gave Jake a cold and determined stare.

"Well, as I was saying, Ms. Shu was what you might call a "double agent." She was working for our friend Mr. Smythe but also cooperating with the FBI. Now the FBI didn't know this at first but learned of it a short time later. I will get to that in a minute."

Jake made sure both men were paying attention as he continued. "Now this is the part I think you both will find very interesting. Remember when I told you that one of the security personnel for Baroni Security noticed Mr. Smythe driving around my neighborhood? After a little research he appeared to be a typical government worker. But a good detective plays hunches and that was the case here as well. Baroni Security tailed Mr. Smythe to a house owned by you, Benjamin."

"An interesting coincidence", replied Benjamin Tsang. "You mentioned that when they rescued your wife, two of the abductors were captured, two women to be specific. But where was this Mr. Smythe?"

Now for the first time in the conversation, Jake did not have a good answer. "At the moment, Mr. Smythe's whereabouts are somewhat unaccounted for."

Benjamin Tsang smiled. "I see, well please continue."

Benjamin's sudden relaxed demeanor concerned Jake. "Yes, well, earlier I mentioned a woman by the name of Naomi Shu. She was a young and beautiful woman who had agreed to work with the FBI with the hope of getting away from *your* organization and the likes of Nelson Smythe. Now we can only assume that Mr. Smythe discovered what Naomi was up to and got a little too rough. In fact, gentlemen, she died later from her injuries." Jake paused to see if he was getting the desired reaction from these two men. "Nice employee you have, Mr. Tsang. He gets his kicks out of killing defenseless woman."

Jake starred intently at Benjamin Tsang as he continued. "So now, let's see what we have here. We have a suspect, a Mr. Nelson Smythe that is observed a few too many times in my neighborhood. We follow him to a remote house that just happens to be owned by you, Mr. Tsang! We then observe Mr. Smythe's activities and discover that he also happens to be the new mystery boyfriend of my Director of Human Resources and has been pumping her for information, perhaps in more ways than one!"

"At the murder scene, it turns out that your Mr. Smythe must have been careless because some finger prints were later found that matched the prints on file for Mr. Smythe, or whatever his real name is. So, Mr. Tsang, in answer to your initial question, what we have is Mr. Smythe connected to kidnapping and murder. We have Mr. Smythe connected to you through a house that you own that just so happened to have my wife in captivity. I am also confident, that Jackson here as well as our union buddy, Lou Walizak, will provide full cooperation, given that you have set them up to take the fall for this entire fiasco! So, one way or the other, your ass is mine, *sir*!"

"This conversation is over," said, Benjamin Tsang, still acting far to calm, given the circumstances and this worried Jake. "I do have a few questions for you, however. Where, again is this Nelson Smythe character?"

Jake was annoyed to have to repeat himself. "As I stated before, Mr. Smythe was not at the house at the time of the raid but I am sure that he will turn up shortly."

"Oh, I feel quite confident about that, Mr. Oliver." Replied Benjamin with, what could only be described as a sinister grin. Benjamin's response and sudden demonstration of confidence confused Jake. Then he heard a sound come from the doorway, a click. Jake turned and saw a man dressed in a business suit. He appeared to be about 6 feet tall, Caucasian with light brown curly hair. In fact, most women would clearly consider this individual quite handsome and Jake could understand why Laura Sanders, his Director of Human Resources, had fallen for him.

"Mr. Smythe, I presume?" Stated Jake.

"It's been a long day, so far, Mr. Oliver and you are trying both my patience as well as my employer." The accent was either British or Australian.

Jake's eyes then dropped to the gun in Smythe's hand. "I hear that someone stood you up today for lunch."

Smythe smiled. "I guess I have you to thank for that, don't I?"

"So, what's the plan now gentlemen." Jake said. "Smythe here has the gun. Who is he planning to shoot?"

CHAPTER FORTY

Jake quickly accessed his options. As Smythe directed him to follow, all proceeded out of the office toward the elevator. "Where are we going?"

"For a little drive. Now walk!" Smythe used his gun to push Jake into the outer office.

"Benjamin, this was not our plan! You have deceived me!" Shouted Jackson. His anger was genuine and he started to approach Benjamin when Smythe pointed the gun at him and he froze.

"Out the door, Mr. Chi," motioned Smythe with his gun.

"What do you mean," demanded Jackson. "I have no intention of going with you anywhere."

Benjamin now stood and addressed Jackson. "I am afraid you have no choice my friend. You see, you have become a liability that I cannot afford at this time."

"But Benjamin, you can't_____"

"Oh, but I can and I will." Benjamin then motioned to Smythe with his eyes. He then roughly shoved Jackson through the doorway. Jackson and Jake noticed that Ms. Chuen was not at her desk. Both men wondered if Smythe had done something to her but said nothing.

Benjamin Tsang looked around and then turned to Jackson. "Where is your assistant?"

Jackson shook his head. "I do not know. She should be here."

Smythe looked around quickly. "She was not at her desk when I got here. Could she have overheard your conversations before my arrival?"

"It is not likely," replied Benjamin. "But I had not intended on taking any chances. It is of no matter, however, let's get out of here. We can return and take care of her later."

Smythe motioned for all to proceed out of the office and into an available elevator across the hall. They descended to the lower level of the parking garage. When the doors opened, Benjamin walked ahead to a Lincoln Towne Car that he had rented at the airport. Smythe looked around nervously as he motioned them to proceed to the car. Surprisingly, the garage appeared void of anybody at that moment.

Jake was concerned. He knew that if he got in the car with these men, there was a strong likelihood that he would not survive. His mind was racing as he considered what his options were. He then felt the cold steal of a gun barrel against the back of his neck and Smythe stood directly behind him and whispered in his ear.

"Don't even think about it Oliver! You try to be a hero and your dead right here, right now! Is that understood?" Jake nodded slowly. "Say it! Say, I understand and will not cause any trouble."

Jake fought his temptations to take on this arrogant bastard but he knew that such an attempt would be foolish and quickly regained his composure. "I understand."

Smythe roughly pushed him forward and directed him to get in the back seat and for Jackson to get in the front passenger seat. Benjamin got behind the wheel in the driver's seat and started the car. Smythe made one more quick scan of the garage and started to get in the back seat when the sound of a vehicle or rather two vehicles could be heard approaching.

Jake turned and looked out the window. Two dark four door sedans rounded the corner and skidded to a stop roughly 50 feet away. Four men in suits jumped out and crouched behind their open car doors. Guns were drawn and pointed in their direction.

Benjamin Tsang spun around and Jake could tell his mind was racing with questions and indecision as to what he should do. "It's all over, Tsang," shouted Jake. "That's the FBI and they know everything." Jake then looked to where Smythe had been standing and for the first time realized that he was no where in sight. Jake looked back at Tsang. His hands were gripping the wheel of the car tightly and his jaw was tight. Jake suspected that he too had just noticed Smythe's absence. "Your buddy, Smythe, has deserted you. It's over Tsang."

The FBI agents approached the car and when they determine that the men in the car were unarmed, opened the doors and pulled Benjamin and Jackson from the car. Jake got out just as Agent Garrison approached. Benjamin and Jackson were handcuffed and taken away. Garrison looked around. "Where's Smythe?"

"I don't know. He was with us at the car and then just…he just vanished when you guys came around the corner."

Garrison turned and yelled to five of his men standing nearby. Seal off the building. We are still missing Smythe. Find him!" He then turned back to Jake. "You alright?"

"I am now! You guys sure know how to call it close."

"Sorry, when we heard they were taking you to the parking garage, we just figured it would be easier to confront them here."

"So you got all of our conversation?"

"You bet. The wire you had on came in loud and clear."

Both men turned when they heard Benjamin Tsang protest as an agent began to take him away. "Look, we had a deal. I supplied you with information!"

"You weak, coward," scowled Jackson. "What Oliver said was all true!"

Benjamin glared at Jackson. "If you had done what you were told all of this would not be happening!"

Garrison then interrupted. "Gentlemen, both of you will be given ample opportunity to share your perspectives on crime." He then nodded to his men and they led them off to one of the cars and drove away.

"So, I guess you got what you wanted," commented Jake.

"Not quite," replied Garrison. "Look, don't get me wrong, we appreciate your help but we still haven't implicated the big fish in your organization."

"Perhaps you have," explained Jake. "From what you just heard, it is quite apparent that Benjamin Tsang was the key player here. What else do you need?"

"But we don't have anything directly on Samuel Cho."

Jake shook his head. "Look, I agreed to help you uncover what was going on at my hotel and I have done that."

Garrison gave Jake a hard stare. "Yeah, you have done what we agreed to but I have a strong suspicion, Jake, that you are holding out on me."

Jake returned the stare for a few seconds before responding. "I have to go. Just like you, Agent Garrison, I still have some unsettled business to address." He began to leave and then turned back toward Garrison. "What about Smythe?"

"If he's still in the building, we'll find him." Jake simply nodded and then walked to his car.

The FBI agents searched the building for the next several hours but found no sign of Nelson Smythe. He had evaded them again and simply vanished.

CHAPTER FORTY ONE

Jake arrived at the Wilford and went directly to the Presidential Suite. He knocked on the door and Ed Lee greeted him at the door. “Come in Jake, we have been expecting you.”

Jake entered and found Samuel Cho seated on the plush couch that was part of the luxurious parlor area of the suite. He was sipping a brandy and motioned for Jake to have a seat. Jake noted that he appeared to have aged more from the last time they met less than a month earlier. Jake chose a wingback chair across from Mr. Cho and Ed Lee took another chair a short distance away.

Samuel Cho sipped his brandy and held up the glass and looked at the thick liquid in the glass. “Am I to assume that all went as planned?”

“Yes,” replied Jake. “Right now, Jackson Chi and Benjamin Tsang are with the FBI.”

“And the FBI, do they plan to come for me?”

“No. They have nothing to directly tie you to the illegal activities of South Harbor Investments.” Jake’s use of the word *illegal* appeared to have struck a nerve with the elderly man.

“And your wife. She is safe?”

“Yes she is. We raided the house just before my meeting with Tsang and Chi.”

Samuel Cho now put down his glass and looked directly at Jake. “So, Jake Oliver, you have had a busy day. And I must say, a job well done.”

Jake leaned forward in his chair, a somber expression on his face. "Well, I am glad you approve." He then reached inside his coat pocket and handed the elderly man an envelope with a single piece of paper inside.

Samuel Cho looked at Jake questioningly as he opened the envelope and pulled out the letter and read its contents. A frown appeared on his face. Ed Lee studied the face of his employer and recognized the trouble look.

Cho slowly folded the letter and placed it on the coffee table that sat between he and Jake. "I am confused by your letter Jake. I felt that we made our position quite clear during my last visit. Leaving South Harbor Investments is not an option. Now we certainly appreciate what you have done and how you have protected the organization. Or should I say, how you have protected me. But this changes nothing."

Jake leaned back in his chair and smiled. "Actually, it does." Jake pulled out another envelope. This one was larger and clearly contained more documents. He placed it on the coffee table. "In that envelope is a printed summary of detailed financial transactions that have taken place involving the illegal laundering of money from South Harbor Investments for the past year. You will note that most of these transactions took place before my arrival and with a little further homework, the authorization for these transactions can be traced directly back to the chairman of South Harbor Investments. To you sir!"

Samuel Cho grabbed the envelope and pulled out its contents. He put on a pair of reading glasses that were in his shirt pocket and Jake noticed that his hands were shaking slightly. For the next several minutes, the old man read in silence. When he was done he placed the documents on the coffee table, removed his glasses and leaned back on the couch. "This is very disturbing, Jake. Would you care to share with me how you obtained this information?"

"Yes, I agree that the information is very disturbing. And no, I will not share with you how I obtained it. But I think you will agree that it is accurate."

"What is the meaning of this?" Samuel Cho asked indignantly.

"I was gathering this information to give to the FBI in exchange for keeping my ass out of jail! I don't think that is too hard to figure out."

"But you clearly had someone helping you."

"Yes, that is correct."

Samuel Cho looked first at Ed who sat quietly and said nothing and then turned and looked out the window. It had turned into a sunny day in the City and the glare from the windows of the building across the street caused him to squint. "And do you intend to turn this information over to the authorities?"

"Not if I do not have to, since the information implicates both of us, as you so adroitly put it during our last meeting."

Samuel Cho looked directly at Jake. Ed Lee also stared in disbelief. For almost a full minute, no words were spoken and then Cho replied. "I…assume that you want something in return?"

Jake stood and walked up to the elderly man, whose stature and presence seemed much smaller at that moment than when Jake had first met him. "Actually, Mr. Cho I want absolutely nothing from you." Jake's eyes locked on him as he continued. "It is because of you that my wife was kidnapped, my children have been in danger, and you have had me jumping through hoops to keep both my ass and yours out of jail. In retrospect, I should be hanging you out to dry you son of bitch! But no, even after all of this, I want nothing from you or South Harbor. Consider, this information, my get out of jail free card!" Jake paused to allow Cho to absorb clearly what he was about to say. "Here's how it works, old man. A copy of these documents is in a sealed envelop and in the custody of an individual of unknown origin. In the event my family or I are injured or harmed in any way, this information will be given directly to FBI special agent John Garrison. And I am quite certain he will know what to do with them. So, Mr. Cho, consider this a stalemate where neither side wins but we both walk away."

Samuel Cho looked at Jake with a cold stare. His anger was apparent and he was clearly aggravated by the words and lack of respect that had just been shown to him. The arrogance he thought of this American to treat him in this manner was infuriating. Cho stood and began to speak when Ed Lee interrupted.

"Jake, perhaps you could allow Mr. Cho and I to have a few words in private?"

Jake continued to hold his stare on the old man as he replied. "I will be in the next room." Jake then turned and walked to the bedroom that connected to the parlor of the suite.

Once the door was closed, Samuel Cho turned to Ed and started speaking in rapid Cantonese. "I will not be treated in such a manner by this American cowboy!"

"I understand how you must feel but we have no alternative but to cooperate with his demands."

"But how? How did he obtain such detailed and confidential information? This was not common knowledge. He had to have had help from someone close inside my organization. Who?"

"I do not know," responded Ed solemnly. "But sir, we must proceed."

Samuel Cho began to resume control of his emotions and then waived for Ed to show Jake back into the room. Jake entered and took a seat. Samuel Cho, continued to remain standing and looked at Jake. "Jake Oliver, you are truly a worthy opponent and one that I clearly underestimated. I want to assure you that I may be old but I am not a man that should be taken lightly." He paused to gather his thoughts. "I will accept your resignation, sir, but I do want some assurances."

"Assurances," questioned Jake, "what kind of assurances?"

Samuel Cho waived his hand in a haphazard manner. "Your comment that if anything were to happen to you or your family. Such a statement is rather vague. What if you or your family are in a random car accident?"

Jake simply smiled. "For your sake, you better hope we drive safely. These are the terms, sir, and they are non-negotiable."

Samuel began to protest but Ed Lee signaled him not to press the matter. He regained his composure and then asked, "when would you be leaving?"

"Within the next two weeks. I have a few matters to put some closure on before my departure. I would also recommend that Jim Slazenger be assigned; at least, acting GM until you can find a replacement."

"Actually," replied Cho, "it will be my intent to sell this damn hotel as quickly as possible, given that your FBI now has it on their radar screen."

Jake nodded. "Yes, that would probably be the best course of action. "I would like to make another request." Jake then explained what this plan entailed and both men nodded their heads in agreement.

After Jake departed from the suite, Samuel Cho slowly sat back down on the couch and looked at his long time friend seated adjacent to him. "Truly a day of many surprises my friend."

"Yes, many surprises indeed."

"Who helped him?" Mumbled Samuel Cho to himself. *It has to be someone close and within my organization.*"

"It must be someone very close," replied Ed evenly.

Samuel sighed deeply. "Ah…but who, my friend?"

CHAPTER FORTY TWO

After a long awaited family reunion at the Oliver home the night before, Jake and Marilyn invited Andy Baroni and the Slazenger's over for dinner to thank them for the support they had given. Marilyn fixed an elegant dinner that had no equal to the finer restaurants in San Francisco and after Jim indulged himself in a third helping of the dessert she had prepared, he finally stated that he was whipped, which drew a little chuckle from the others at the table. During dinner Jake summarized his final meeting with Samuel Cho, leaving out some of the specific details.

Everyone moved to the living room for coffee and after dinner drinks. Jake took everyone's order from the bar and started toward the kitchen.

Jim sat down on one side of couch next to his wife and called to Jake. "What I am still not clear on, Jake, is how you were able to obtain such detailed information concerning the history of the Wilford, South Harbor's ownership of it back in the 30's, and all that stuff about Tsang's dad and the voyage to San Francisco."

Marilyn was quick to respond. "Actually, I can probably answer some of your questions." Jake smiled and continued to the fix everyone's drinks. "Shortly after we arrived in San Francisco, I did some research on the Internet concerning the Wilford. Obviously the hotel had a rich history and I thought it would be interesting. I reviewed old newspaper articles, stories written by past guests, tax records, you name it. Somewhere I came across an article written by a former worker of the hotel after he retired. The article was for a documentary that a local cable station was compiling on Charles Wilford. In that article it mentioned that there were rumors that, right after the stock market crash of 1929, Charles Wilford was in serious financial trouble and had sought assistance from overseas investors. I mentioned this to Jake one evening and I guess he just sort of stored it away in that amazing mind of his. Frankly, I am never quite sure if he hears half of what I am saying." This comment drew another chuckle from the group.

Jake then returned and passed out the drinks each had requested. "I heard that last remark. I will have you know that I am a good listener…sometimes."

After the laughing subsided, Andy spoke. "So Marilyn does the initial detective work. But I am with Jim. How did you find out all the rest of the information."

Jake continued. "Obviously, as the weeks went by, we all knew that things were not right in 'the city by the bay' and clearly the Wilford had some 'bats in the belfry'. So when I received information that Benjamin Tsang was the one that had specifically recommended that South Harbor purchase the Wilford, I used the Internet and looked for connections between Tsang, South Harbor and the hotel.

"When I researched Tsang's background I came across a web page that apparently Benjamin Tsang's sister had put together to commemorate her family. This web site included an Internet copy of a journal apparently written by her father, fortunately it had been translated into English. This journal chronicled the mysterious voyage to San Francisco in 1930 and placement of mysterious cargo in the basement of an unidentified building and then the unbelievable tale of his shipmates being killed and thrown overboard."

"At first, I felt it sounded like a fantasy story told by an old man to entertain his children. But then I remembered Marilyn telling me about the problems the hotel experienced during the depression, which occurred at about the same time as this old man's story. I read the rest of the story and the descriptions he gave of the building in which the unidentified cargo was placed. My gut feeling was that it *could* have been the Wilford."

"Next, I looked up information on major events that occurred in Hong Kong around the dates of old man Tsang's great voyage. Front page of the local newspaper told of a collection of ancient Chinese artifacts that had been stolen while on display at a museum and were never found. The coincidence seemed too amazing."

Jake looked at Jim as he sipped his drink and then continued. "Jim, you might recall that I mentioned to you that the 'as built' blueprints for the basement were not correct. In other words, the drawings did not match the current layout of the walls in the basement. I noticed this during a review of the plans in Ed Lee's office. When I started to uncover what Jackson Chi and Lou Walizak were up to, what bothered me most was why South Harbor was spending money to renovate the hotel. It just didn't make sense to call attention to it any more than necessary. In particular, why create a BART subway entrance and incur such costs when all they supposedly wanted the hotel for was to launder money."

Jake looked around the room at his dinner guests and all sat there mesmerized. He was embarrassed to be monopolizing the conversation for so long. "So, I just sort of put all of these pieces together and well…there you have it."

Jim shook his head. "Absolutely unbelievable!"

"You got that right, Jim," said Andy. "Jake, you can come work for me anytime with detective skills like that."

Jake smiled. "Well, let's not forget the fine detective work of Baroni Security. They're the reason, I have Marilyn back safe and sound." All raised their glasses in cheer.

"Oh, did you miss me honey?" Asked Marilyn coyly.

"Well, yes dear I did. We were running out of food from the grocery, none of us had any more clean clothes, the house was a mess and_____"

"You are positively awful!" Shouted Marilyn as everyone broke into laughter.

"Getting back to the original founder of South Harbor Investments, what was his name, Soon?" Asked Jim.

"Yeah, Chiang Moy Soon was the founder and chief operating officer of South Harbor Investments."

Linda Slazenger now spoke. "You said he disappeared on or about the same time as the artifacts. Is there a connection?"

"Not directly that I have been able to determine so far," replied Jake. "The articles I reviewed on the internet strongly suggested that

Mr. Soon may have been involved in the theft of the artifacts. Apparently the circumstances in which his security people mishandled the matter caused these suspicions. He actually disappeared a few days after the artifacts were taken while a preliminary investigation was underway by the local Hong Kong authorities."

"Sounds to me like the board of directors lost patience with their appointed leader and decided to make a change," stated Jim.

"Actually, Jim you may be more right than you know. That was clearly what was suspected when he disappeared. There was also some questions regarding the man that would replace Soon, a young and aggressive officer of the company by the name of Samuel Cho."

"Ah, so it is possible that good ol' Mr. Cho got tired of being second in command and decided to take charge." Said Linda.

"Again, another strong possibility. The newspaper articles I read, suggested that Cho may have arranged for Mr. Soon to lose face and then received direction from the board to make his move."

"Was any legal action ever taken against Mr. Cho?" Asked Linda.

"Not that I could find. Apparently without a body they had nothing to prosecute him on. There was also the possibility that Mr. Soon had simply fled the Country. Eventually the entire matter was dropped and I am sure that South Harbor Investments did all that it could to assure that the authorities let the matter fade away as quickly as possible."

Jim stood to stretch his legs. "So it is safe to assume that Mr. Soon never got a chance to enjoy his heist if, in fact, he was behind it"

"Why is that? Asked his wife, Linda.

"Because, if he was behind the caper in the first place, and he had simply gone in to hiding, he would have eventually turned up to claim his goods. But he never did. So my hunch is that he is buried in the foundation of some skyscraper South Harbor was building at the time. Kinda like the methods used by our Mafia to deal with those that fall from grace."

Linda shook her head. "You may be right but how do we know that Samuel Cho was not behind the heist as part of an elaborate plan to overthrow his boss and take charge of the company?"

Andy interrupted to respond. "Excuse me Jim, but I would like to answer this one. Linda, if that was the case, why hadn't Cho dug up whatever is in the Wilford basement after all of these years?"

"To be quite honest," interjected Jake, "I don't think Samuel Cho had a clue where the artifacts were hidden. Remember that if we make the assumption that Mr. Soon arranged the theft of the artifacts and then was immediately replaced by Samuel Cho. It is quite possible that Cho never new what Mr. Soon had done with the treasure. If he had, he certainly wouldn't of sold the hotel back to the Wilford family a few years later.

Marilyn then spoke. "What I find so ironic is that Benjamin Tsang's plan was to destroy Cho's reputation and take over the organization. Kind of history repeating itself, wasn't it? Obtaining the treasure in the basement must have simply been for Tsang's personal gain. In other words, besides being a vindictive bastard, he was greedy to boot!" This drew another chuckle from the group.

"You mentioned that two men got on the boat in San Francisco for the voyage back to Hong Kong and that they were the men that killed the workers to assure their silence. Any idea who they were?" Linda asked as she leaned forward as if enthralled in a high suspense movie.

"Actually, I was curious about that also," replied Marilyn. "After I returned home from my *vacation of captivity* in Marin County, I looked up the website Jake found that had been put together by Benjamin Tsang's sister. I read the journal entries from her father in detail. He noted overhearing a conversation between the two men. He stated that they always appeared to be cautious not use their names but on several occasions he overheard the older man referred to as Mr. Chen Ma. Given that there was a Mr. Ma that was noted on the documents involving the transfer of partial ownership of the Wilford back in 1930 to South Harbor Investments, I would assume that this was Mr. Soon's contact in the states that dealt with Charles Wilford."

The younger man on the boat was referred to as Wai Lin Lee. Since that is such a common Chinese name, however, I wouldn't know where to begin."

All nodded their head in agreement with the exception of Jake, who appeared momentarily lost in thought. Marilyn recognized this look. "Jake, you have something to add?"

Jake looked up. "No, it's nothing." Marilyn wasn't convinced but did not press the matter further in front of their dinner guests.

Andy then broke the moment of silence. "Well, I don't know about you guys but I have a busy day tomorrow and so do all of you. Jake, what time do you think you will have the wall opened up in the basement. I want to get there and sell popcorn."

Jake was still somewhat deep in thought. "A…oh the basement? Try being there around 2 p.m. It should be open by then."

Jim then lifted his glass. "Here's to buried treasure. May it bring the Wilford renewed luck and prosperity." All toasted their glasses and downed the rest of their drinks.

Marilyn and Jake walked their guests out to the street and waived bye as they drove away. Jake looked down the street and noticed a dark sedan parked on the street roughly two blocks away under the shadows of a tree. He could not tell if there was an occupant inside but he was not concerned. Agent Garrison had advised him that his men would be keeping a lookout, just in case the elusive Nelson Smythe decided to make a surprise appearance but the odds of that were unlikely. Most felt that Smythe was quite far away by this point in another hemisphere of the world plotting his next terrorist assignment.

Marilyn looked at her husband with profound respect. "Come on Sherlock, you have a busy day tomorrow."

CHAPTER FORTY THREE

There was a buzz of excitement throughout the Wilford. The staff had not been told specifically what was going on but the construction crews and trucks that arrived earlier that morning told them that something was about to occur. Initially, they thought it must be the start of the long awaited renovation of the hotel. The more senior and experienced members of the staff, however, were familiar with such activities and this was different they said. For one thing, no supplies or new furnishings had yet arrived. Such items would usually have been put in storage and the housekeeping staff would have known about such things. The engineering staff were particularly interested by the type of tools and equipment being brought to the basement. Jack hammers, stone cutting equipment, hydraulic lifts. These were tools used for heavy demolition.

Dan Kowalski had arrived early that morning and assisted the contractors in getting access to the areas they required. The rest of the engineering staff arrived a short time later and approached their boss. Jerry Simpson had worked with Dan for the past 10 years. When he saw the construction crews entering the hotel he was surprised that his long time friend had not mentioned this to him the evening before when they had gone out for drinks at a nearby bar he and the other guys frequented.

"Hey Dan, what gives?" Asked Jerry as he walked up and stood next to his boss.

"An exciting day, my friend. If things happen the way Mr. "O" says, we are all in for a great surprise."

"A surprise? I don't understand. I thought the renovation was not scheduled to begin for a few months.

"This has nothing to do with the renovation. It has to do with something that happened over 70 years ago."

Jerry took off his hat and scratched his head. "You're losing me Dan."

Dan just smiled. "Just sit tight and do me a favor. I will most likely be tied up with this most of the day. Can you get the men organized and assigned the tasks of the day. We have a full house upstairs and need to be on our toes."

"Sure, I'll take care of it but this better be good."

....

Jake arrived at the hotel and noticed Ed Lee getting out of his car. He approached the architect, whose hands were full of rolled up blueprints and a 35-mm camera slug over one shoulder. "Here, Ed, let me give you a hand with all of that."

Ed turned and saw Jake. "Thank you. I will probably not need any of these but I wanted to come prepared. My key concern is that this is a bearing wall that we are opening up. Structurally, we need to be careful."

Jake nodded. "I understand. How did they create the opening back then?"

The look of concern was visible by the hard lines that appeared on his forehead. "Well, one would hope that they took the necessary precautions such as constructing some additional vertical supports once the opening was created. My concern is that the workers that probably created the opening back then were most likely railroad workers who specialized in digging tunnels. The key difference here is that this was not simply a tunnel they had to dig. It involved breaking through a wall that was holding up a 12 story building."

Jake nodded, now understanding Ed's concern as he continued. "In addition, this building has experienced 70 years of earthquakes and ground shifts. This is not a simply matter of knocking down a wall with a sledgehammer."

"Well, Ed, with you directing the effort, I feel confident that all will go as planned."

"I am glad your confidence in my abilities is so high, especially after what has occurred …." Ed's last words drifted off.

They entered the building and proceeded to the northeast corner of the basement. Along the way several of the hotel staff asked Jake what was happening. He simply smiled and told them to be patient and let the men do their work.

When they arrived at the designated area, Dan Kowalski was coordinating the removal of banquet chairs and tables that needed to be moved to access the designated section of wall. Partitions were already in place to protect the hotel staff from debris and dust that would be created from the demolition activity. Since this was going to take a little time, Jake felt it was a good opportunity to speak with Ed.

"Ed, there is something that I need to discuss with you."

Ed looked at Jake as if he suspected what Jake was about to ask him. "Jake Oliver, you have proved to be a worthy and honorable individual throughout these past few months. It has been regrettable that I could not respond to you in a completely truthful manner at times." He then paused to gather his thoughts. "But I will respond to you truthfully at this time."

Jake had grown to like and respect Ed Lee. Although his choice of employer had clearly been a mistake, it was Jake's impression that Ed had managed these unfortunate circumstances to assure his ethics were not tested beyond their limitations. It was because of this acquired respect that Jake found the questions he was about to ask difficult.

"Ed, it is about your father." Ed looked on with a somber expression.

"Jake, you truly amaze me. What is it that you wish to know?" Jake hesitated uncertain how to proceed so Ed continued. "My father was a good man, Jake, but he made mistakes early in his life. Mistakes that he regretted and paid for everyday until his death." Jake nodded and Ed continued. "Yes, my father was on the *Golden Star* on its return trip to Hong Kong. That was your question was it not?"

Jake again nodded. "Ed, I am not here to judge. I just wanted to put some closure on this issue."

Ed walked over and sat down on a wooden crate that was a short distance away. "My father wanted to move to the United States from Hong Kong but he was very poor. My mother was already pregnant and they wanted to make sure I was born as a citizen of the United States. Jobs were scarce at that time for a common laborer such as my father. He ended up getting a job, however, with South Harbor Investments through a friend. This friend told my father that South Harbor was looking for individuals to go to the United States. So he applied for work."

"He was told that all he had to do was make sure that cargo that South Harbor was shipping to San Francisco arrived at its designated location and that the buyer paid the money that was due. It was not until later that my father found out what happened to individuals that did not agree to pay as expected. At first, all my father had to do was rough up the individuals that were late in paying up. You know, scare them into paying what was due. He did not like this but, as he later told me, he was desperate." Jake nodded in understanding,

"My father did as he was told and caught the eye of one of South Harbor's upper management, a Mr. Ma, who handled the affairs of the organization in San Francisco. Mr. Ma requested that my father be transferred to San Francisco and this was agreed to. My parents took the next South Harbor Freighter coming from Hong Kong and arrived in late November 1928. I was born three months later." Jake now took a seat next to Ed.

"Life seemed good for my parents to some extent. My father was paid exceptionally well even though he could never tell his friends what he did exactly. As time went by and I became older, my father later told me that he became cold and callused toward his job. Then one night, he was called by Mr. Ma who told him to be at a designated pier later that evening and advised him to plan on taking a trip for a few weeks. My father assumed that this was just another shipment arriving that South Harbor did not want to advertise which was the reason for its arrival so late at night."

Jake took the opportunity to speak when Ed paused momentarily. "Ed, you have known this all these years?"

"No," replied Ed. "My father never spoke of these events throughout my childhood. It was not until much later in my life that he shared with me what he had done for South Harbor. He did so to warn me about the individuals that I was going to apprentice with in Hong Kong. He only told me censured parts of his life, however, leaving out the true horrors of his actions. His goal was to deter me from making the same mistakes he had. But I was young and ambitious and determined to not let this organization steal my soul so to speak. I saw Mr. Samuel Cho as a key contact for me to make international inroads for my career in architecture."

"My bonus was meeting my wife, Kathy Cho, Samuel's daughter. Kathy was a young and beautiful girl who had clearly grown up completely unaware of the darker side of her father's career. And I guess, I was pretty oblivious as well. We became engaged and were married six months after my arrival in Hong Kong."

Ed was staring off as he completed this last sentence and then turned toward Jake who was listening with fascination. "Ah, I must be getting old. Here I have gone and drifted off the subject, my apologies."

"Samuel Cho took good care of my father and helped him get his own fish market set up shortly after his arrival. Although he was still required to perform duties for Mr. Ma, I later learned that my father's business provided an excellent front for South Harbor to smuggle merchandise into the states." Ed now paused and collected his thoughts.

"Now on the night the *Golden Star* was scheduled to arrive you will recall Mr. Ma advised my father to plan on taking a trip for several weeks. This concerned my father but he trusted Mr. Ma and agreed to be there at the designated time."

Ed now stood and walked over to observe the progress of the men in clearing the area in the basement. Jake signaled one of his bellmen and asked him to get them a black coffee and a hot tea from the restaurant upstairs. Ed then returned and again took a seat on the wooden crate.

"Jake, you asked me how I know all of this. My father died just six months ago. He had cancer and his death was long and drawn out. He always felt it was his penance for the sins he had performed earlier in his life. One evening, he just began to talk and told me everything while I sat next to him in his bed. He died two days later."

Jake nodded solemnly and then noticed the bellmen returning wi their drinks. Ed thanked him and then continued. "My fath described to me the arrival of the ship and the men used to unload large wooden crates. He asked Mr. Ma what was in the crates but Mr. Ma said that was highly confidential and he was not to talk about this event to anyone."

"My father described himself in those days as a rather cocky and outspoken individual. He stated that he was actually excited about the activities taking place, like it was a big game of some type."

Jake then responded. "And Mr. Ma was the older wiser partner. The voice of reason."

Ed nodded. "It would appear so. My father told me the cargo was loaded on two trucks, and a limited number of the crew went along to unload the cargo at its final destination. He described them parking in an alley behind a grand hotel and unloading the crates in the basement of the building. He then described taking the crew back to the ship and quickly departing for Hong Kong." Ed then paused. The stress of what he was about to talk about was clearly weighing on him.

"Ed, if you would prefer not to speak of this______"

"No," interrupted Ed. "I want to answer your question." Ed sipped his tea and then continued. "My father did not know what Mr. Ma had planned. He assumed that they were to scare the crew before returning to port to guarantee their silence. But when Mr. Ma pulled out a gun and killed the foreman the reality of what was about to happen closed in on my father. He said the crew was taken to the top deck and then one by one shot and thrown overboard. It was the darkest day in his life."

Jake listened intently not knowing how to respond. The man in front of him was sharing one of his families deepest and darkest secrets. "Ed, I am sorry to have asked about this."

"No, Jake, it is I that should be sorry. It was I that was foolish in researching what and where the artifacts were hidden. You see, I too, determined that the missing artifacts were most likely what my father was describing. I knew this. What I did not know, however, was what hotel my father had been referring to. My hope was to find the artifacts and return them to China to restore my family's heritage so to speak."

"But Benjamin Tsang beat you to the punch. His father, the sole survivor of that doomed crew pointed him here," stated Jake.

Ed simply nodded. “Tsang’s motivation was greed and power. Your intervention, Jake Oliver, has allowed me to complete my goal and restore my father’s heritage.”

Jake then smiled and looked toward the basement wall. “Well, Ed, what do you say we go digging for some treasure?” Ed smiled and they proceeded to the area that was cleared and ready for demolition.

Ed worked with the general contractor for the next hour identifying exactly where to break through the wall and how the opening would need to be supported. Then the work began.

The aged concrete proved to be a real challenge for the workers but was still no match for the modern demolition equipment they used. A key moment was when a small opening was made in the wall and it was determined that there was open space behind a wall that should have been dirt. Gradually, the opening was enlarged and within the next three hours, it was large enough to drive a small car through. Heavy iron I-beams were used to brace the opening on each side, with a third section across the top to support the structure of the hotel above.

Large floodlights were brought in and set up that illuminated the opening. By this time, many of the management staff had joined the employees on break and had gathered around to see what the excitement was all about. Jim Slazenger appeared with Andy Baroni in tow. Jake looked at them and Andy responded. “Hell, I just wanted to see what all the fuss was about!”

Ed and Jake walked up and looked into the opening. There was a space of approximately two feet that had been dug away from the wall of the basement and then there was a heavy steal door that appeared to be embedded into the heavy earth that surrounded it. Ed asked one of the workers for a hammer and entered the opening and stepped up to the steel door. He used the hammer and hit the door several times. The noise was deafening to Ed in this small enclosed space but muffled to the others that stood in the basement. He hit the door a final time and then exited the opening.

“From the sound, the space behind the door appears to be hollow. In other words, there is clearly a space or room behind this door!”

Jake looked at him. “You appear surprised.”

“Yes, I am to some degree. There was always the possibility that this room had collapsed over the years burying its contents. But the echo sound when I hit the steel door suggests that this had not yet happened."

Ed then directed the general contractor to have his men use a cutting torch and cut an opening in the center of the steel door. This process took another hour. When the last of the cuts were made, a pry bar was brought in and used to knock out the section that had been cut away. Again the floodlights were arranged and illuminated the area as best possible. Ed then looked at Jake and both approached the opening with a flashlight and peered into a room that had not seen the light of day for over 70 years.

By this time, a large crowd of managers, staff and construction workers were gathered around the opening in the basement. Marilyn Oliver arrived with Linda Slanzenger. Fred Plummer, the Food and Beverage Director had arranged for soft drinks and snacks to be set up a short distance down the hall. Always the host!

Laura Sanders was there with Mike Reynolds, the Director of Sales, who was videotaping the moment they entered the vault. Obviously, he was thinking of the positive publicity that such a find would generate for the hotel. In fact, he had even arranged for a writer and photographer from the San Francisco Chronicle to be present as well as a roving anchor from the NBC affiliate TV station. Both reporters were busy questioning the staff of the hotel.

Shannon Kincaid was standing next to Dan Kowalski and actually grabbed his arm as Ed and Jake entered the vault through the steel door opening. Olivia Fernanadez, the executive housekeeper, Kono Hisitaki, her houseman and Harry Walters, the hotel's bell captain all stood and stared in anticipation of what was happening at that moment.

Jake entered first with Ed right behind him. They used their flashlights to scan the room's contents. Wooden crates were stacked to the ceiling of a room that appeared to be 20 ft. by 30 ft. with a 10 ft. ceiling. All four walls and the floor of this room were concrete. Although there were stress cracks in the concrete, the room had held up exceptionally well.

Jake shined the flashlight around and something reflected back at him. He moved the beam of light across the room a little slower and both men froze as they saw the reflection of a pair of eyes staring at them from the back of the vault.

CHAPTER FORTY FOUR

Samuel Cho paced around nervously in his hotel suite 12 stories above at that same moment. He was clearly not happy with the turn of events and how cleverly Jake Oliver had manipulated him. He wanted to be downstairs when the vault was opened but had decided against it, given the cameras and press that would be present. As far as he was concerned, the sooner he left San Francisco, the better.

He had to admit, however, that the outcome had been reasonably positive. Things could have been far worse, Cho. He could have been in custody at that moment. A disgrace to his fellow business associates and to the world during the last few years of his long life. Cho stood and fixed himself a drink. It was early but, if the basement of the Wilford was truly the holder of a lost fortune of artifacts, he had to appear relaxed and assured when he spoke to the press.

....

"For a minute there, I thought we had some company in here." Jake said nervously.

Ed smiled. "You were not alone with that thought, my friend. But the eyes that are staring back at us are over 2000 years old and attached to a six foot golden dragon.

"You know, for a moment I thought we had found old man Chiang Moy Soon himself, down here with his precious artifacts."

Ed patted Jake on the back. "Now *that* would have been the ultimate find! But my hunch is that someone made sure Mr. Soon would never be found."

Both men looked up involuntarily thinking of Samuel Cho sitting upstairs in his suite and then smiled as they backed out of the underground vault. They had successfully confirmed that the missing Chinese artifacts of the Western Han Dynasty, that had been stolen from a museum in Hong Kong over 70 years ago, had now been found. Jake looked at the congregation that had formed and then said. "Ladies and gentlemen, we have just had a close encounter with a six foot golden dragon with ruby eyes that is over 2000 years old!" The entire basement erupted in applause and cheers.

....

An hour later, the archeological firm that Jake had contacted to extract the artifacts was on site and busy removing and cataloguing each piece.

At five o'clock, a press conference was called and held in the ballroom of the hotel. Jake started the conference by explaining to the press what had been discovered in the basement. When asked how such a find had come about, Jake responded as truthfully as he felt was necessary, indicating that extensive research on the history of the hotel had identified a business transaction between Charles Wilford and an overseas investor from Hong Kong. He further explained that apparently Charles Wilford agreed to store these artifacts for the Hong Kong investor. Then a pre-written press release was handed out with the answers to some of their other questions.

The press, however, had many further questions and wanted to know more specific details as to who the Hong Kong investor had been and how he had obtained the stolen artifacts. But these questions would have to go unanswered for the time being.

Jake then introduced the chairman of South Harbor Investments, the principal owner of the Wilford Plaza Hotel. Samuel Cho stepped up to the podium and addressed the audience in front of him. One reporter was exceptionally vocal and captured Mr. Cho attention.

"Mr. Cho, the value of these ancient artifacts is obviously priceless. What do you intend to do with them?"

The showman in Samuel Cho truly came out that day. He looked at the crowd that had gathered and then looked briefly at his notes and then again at the eyes that were now upon him. "Thank you all for coming today to this most historic occasion. The artifacts that are currently being unearthed below us are a very special part of Chinese history and I am glad to be a part of their retrieval."

Samuel then looked over at Jake and Ed standing off to the side of the stage before continuing. "I am pleased to inform you that it will be my intent to donate this most important archeological find back to the Chinese government, where it rightly belongs."

As a rash of questions erupted from the press, Ed Lee turned to Jake and extended his hand. "Jake, as I said earlier, you have restored by father's tainted heritage and your insistence that Samuel donate the artifacts to the Chinese government was not only the correct thing to do but a brilliantly strategic move to assure Samuel keeps his part of the bargain. You have brought the issues of South Harbor into the public eye and that was the last thing Samuel Cho ever wanted. Now he will be prompted more than ever to sell off all of his investments in the US and using a favorite American western term, 'get out of Dodge!'

Jake just smiled. "Well, it's not as good as seeing his ass in jail, but payback can certainly be hell in this case. Especially when the Hong Kong authorities reopen the investigation as to how the artifacts got here in the first place."

The following week, it would be announced that South Harbor Investments was selling the Wilford and was currently entertaining offers from local San Francisco investors.

CHAPTER FORTY FIVE

Jake was putting the last of his personal belongings in a box that sat on his desk. It was four o'clock on a cool and crisp December afternoon. Although he had been in this position less than three months, it felt like much more time had passed. He sat back down in his chair and turned toward his computer, which was downloading the last of his personal files when he heard a knock on the door. He turned and saw Jim Slazenger standing there with a big grin on his face.

"What are you grinning about?" Asked Jake. "Checking out *your* new office?"

"No, I thought I would be dignified enough to wait until you officially get your ass out of town!" Replied Jim.

"Have I lost complete control and respect around this place?" Jake responded with a sly grin.

"Not exactly, boss. It is time to for you to join the festivities downstairs. I was appointed the official messenger."

"Oh, I see. Well I guess we shouldn't keep everybody waiting. By the way, did I mention that I hate this type of stuff?"

Jim smiled. "You did and I don't give a shit."

"Nice talk from the hotel's General Manager." Jake and Jim walked downstairs to one of the hotels more elegant banquet rooms, the *Golden Gate*. This ornate room featured three crystal chandeliers that had been installed when the hotel was built in 1908. The walls of the room featured some of the hotel's most detailed and crafted crown molding and baseboards that accented a hand painted mural that depicted scenes of San Francisco. The most striking aspect of this wall mural was that the scenes being depicted continued all the way around the room from wall to wall. The room could seat roughly 80 persons for a formal sit down dinner. But for a going away reception, a few more people could be accommodated.

Jim dropped back as they entered the room allowing Jake to enter by himself. The management staff of the Wilford and a few other invited guests that filled the room broke into applause. Jake looked around at the faces that had become his new surrogate family both with admiration and sadness. Part of him felt as though he was deserting the fort, but another part of him recognized that his job was done here and it was time to move on and let the next man take command. And that next man in this case was Jim Slazenger.

For the next hour, Jake made his way around the room and said his good byes. A plaque was presented to him with the humorous yet truthful inscription, "for uncompromising dedication and outstanding service in the line of fire."

Jake shared a few words of thanks to everyone and the going away party subsided shortly after five o'clock. Marilyn walked in as the last of the hourly staff were leaving that had been dropping in throughout the event and approached her husband. "So, did you survive another going away bash?"

"You know. I honestly don't know which is more difficult. Coming or going from each hotel I manage."

"I know. But this one got under your skin. This is your type of hotel. Lot's of history, a rich heritage, and, of course, the usual list of problems."

Jake smiled. "Yeah, this one is kinda special. So what's the plan for this evening?"

"The managers have arranged a little get together at a small, out of the way restaurant down on Union Street. Are you all packed up and ready to go?"

Marilyn had dropped off Jake earlier that morning and used the Jaguar to run some last minute errands. Her car had already been picked up for shipment to their new home later that week. The girls were spending the night at a neighbor's house attending a slumber party of sorts. Jake and Marilyn loaded up the car and drove to the restaurant where the managers had agreed to meet. They had some difficulty parking but eventually found a parking space on a side street a few blocks away. The walk from the car was what Marilyn referred to as 'Invigorating.' Jake summed it up as 'just plain cold.'

The atmosphere in the restaurant was quiet and relaxing. The managers and their spouses had all gathered in a back room of the establishment and the drinks were flowing freely. Dinner consisted of a variety of heavy appetizers that were brought in and placed in the center of the table for all to share.

Fred Plummer, always critical of the food and beverage operation of any place other than his own was holding court at one of the long tables. He was questioning the young waitress about the menu, the number of covers they did each night, and who was the chef. Laura Sanders scolded him for giving the poor girl such a bad time. Her recommendation was to have another glass of wine, which he gladly agreed to do.

Laura was still hurt and angry by the events that had occurred. She was embarrassed that she had been used as a pawn by what she now knew to be a cold-blooded killer. But as Jake looked her way he noted that she was making eye contact with a man seated at the bar. This amused Jake as he assumed that Laura's ego and self esteem must not be that bruised!

Mike Reynolds had brought a date. A stunning young blonde that had caused all of the other male manager's heads to turn when they arrived late. All assumed that she must be a model or actress, given that Mike was noted for running in such crowds. As the Director of Sales, his mind was still racing with the opportunities that he had before him. The prospect of new owners for the Wilford, the positive publicity the hotel was now receiving and the thought of breaking in a new GM were the key issues on his agenda.

Olivia Fernandez and her husband were seated across the table from Jake and Marilyn. Marilyn and Olivia seemed to hit it off immediately and were deep in conversation most the evening. Unfortunately, Olivia's husband spoke very little English so conversation with this man was difficult. Jake was pleased to note, however, that Olivia had decided to promote Kono Histitaki to be a supervisor over the other housekeeping housemen. In turn, she had invited Kono and surprisingly, he and Olivia's husband had hit it off well.

Shannon Kincaid was seated next to Dan Kowalski and as the evening progressed, both individuals began to let their guard down confirming to all that clearly some type of relationship existed between the two managers. But from Jake's point of view, it was a relationship that still had a long way to go. Especially when Dan noticed Mike Reynold's date walk in. Shannon had grown angry with him over this issue and the two appeared to be in a heated discussion that Jake had no intention of interrupting.

Lastly, Jim and Linda Slazenger were seated next to Jake and Marilyn. In the short time that Jake had worked at the hotel, these two individuals had demonstrated how special they truly were. Their willingness to help and the support they provided established them as friends that the Oliver's felt would continue for many years to come.

At around ten o'clock, Jake stood and informed the group that he and his family had a big day ahead of them and would need to be leaving. He used this opportunity to personally thank his managers for the support and understanding each had demonstrated toward he and his family in the short time they had worked together. Handshakes and hugs were given and received from around the table and then Jake and Marilyn left the restaurant and walked to their car.

"What a wonderful night," stated Marilyn as she inhaled the cool moist foggy air. "This was a good staff, Jake. They seem so much more sincere than others that you have worked with at previous hotels."

"Yeah, I agree. They are a good team and work with each other well. All I hope is that the new owners of the hotel recognize this inner strength and retain them to maintain management consistency and effectiveness."

They rounded the corner and walked up *Webster Street*. Marilyn asked, "I am going to miss this city. Any thoughts about your new property?"

They arrived at the car and Jake first opened the passenger door for Marilyn and then walked around the front of the car to the driver's side door. Before getting in he spoke across the top of the car. "I'm afraid that, so far, I know very little about the resort. But from speaking with the owner, it appears that the challenges the hotel is currently facing are right up my alley!"

This drew a chuckle from Marilyn. "Always the problem solver. You know, just for once it would be nice if you got a hotel that was running smoothly and all you had to do was make a lot of money for the owners!"

Jake laughed. "Now honestly, Marilyn. What fun would that be."

They both got in the car and Jake inserted the key in the ignition. Just before starting the car he turned toward Marilyn when the cold hard steel of a gun barrel pressed up against his cheek. Marilyn turned and screamed when she saw what was happening.

"Well aren't we just the happy couple!" Said the man dressed in black who had apparently been hiding on the floor of the back seat. Marilyn immediately froze as she recognized the voice. No sound came from her mouth even though she wanted to scream at the top of her lungs.

Jake did not move but his eyes were rapidly searching Marilyn's face and the emotions that played across her it. The gun barrel was pressed hard against his right cheek and kept him from turning his head further to see the face of the man holding the gun. But seeing the man was not necessary.

"Mr. Smythe," Jake replied, "I am surprised to find you still hanging around town these days. I thought you were a smart guy."

"Oh, I am, Mr. Oliver. You can count on that. Let's just say that I had some unfinished business to take care of, mate." Smythe's Australian accent was more pronounced than Jake had remembered during the other times they had spoken, either on the phone or that afternoon in Jackson Chi's office.

At that moment, Marilyn's voice had finally returned and she inhaled deeply. "What do you want?" She was scared and her mind was racing as she quickly looked around the outside the car hoping someone might be passing by. But there was no one.

Smythe also looked around as he reached over and locked Marilyn's door. His hand brushed her shoulder, which caused her to lurch forward. "What I want, Mrs. Oliver, is your husband."

Jake attempted to turn his head further to look at Smythe but he held the gun tight and limited his movement. "O.K., you got me. Now let my wife go and we can leave." Marilyn shook her head and her eyes locked on Jake's indicating that such an idea was out of the question but did not speak.

"Sorry, mate, but that is not an option." Smythe looked around again and then pressed his gun harder against Jake's cheek. "We are all going to go for a little drive. Either of you jerk me around, as you yanks like to say, and I'll go after those two little girls of yours!"

Jake looked at Marilyn. He recognized the panic that was now building and he gave her a reassuring look and then spoke. "Alright, no problems. I am starting the car now." Jake's voice and his eyes were locked on Marilyn's and provided her the reassurance she needed and she began to get control of her emotions. Jake started the car and then continued to speak. "You know, Nelson. Can I call you Nelson? I am a little confused. You must know that your employer is in one the FBI's finest jail cells. Therefore, there is no way he will be able to pay for completing whatever you were hired to do."

"I appreciate your concern with my financial situation, Jake. And yes, I am quite aware of what has happened to Mr. Tsang. In fact, you have done an exceptional job of destroying some well thought out plans that has cost me considerable time and money. That is why I am here with you right now."

"So you plan to get your fees out of me?" Jake looked in the rear view mirror and half smiled. "If that's the case, I hate to disappoint you, but we have very little of value."

Nelson Smythe gave Jake a half smile and looked back at him in the rear view mirror and their eyes locked on each other. "I don't want your money, mate, I want you to die!"

The smile on Jake's face quickly vanished. His eyes dropped to the instrument panel in front of him and then, out of habit glanced at the outside driver's side mirror. At first Jake thought he saw some faint movement but then it vanished.

"Alright, folks. We are going to go for a little drive." Jake suddenly felt the gun that had been pressed against the back of his head for the past few minutes disappear. He looked away from the mirror and turned toward Marilyn as she gasped for breath. Nelson Smythe had shifted in the seat behind them and now had grabbed her by the hair and held his gun against the back of her head. Jake noticed that the barrel of the gun seemed exceptionally long in the darkness of the car. His mind quickly determined, however, that most likely the gun had a silencer of some type. “Try anything stupid, Jake, and Marilyn is going to sleep for a very long time.”

Jake looked at Marilyn. The fear in her eyes was apparent and Jake’s frustration and anger was equally apparent. He looked away and his eyes fell on the outside passenger side mirror. This time he realized that he was not mistaken. There *was* movement in the dark behind a trash container on the sidewalk roughly 30 feet behind their car.

Jake’s attention was suddenly distracted by Nelson Smythe’s voice. “Now we drive, Jake Oliver.”

Jake glanced again toward the mirror and then responded. “Alright, we drive, but if we are both going to be killed, why should I do anything you ask?”

Smythe smiled. “Very perceptive, Jake, but you were not listening carefully. I do not need to kill your wife. It is you that I want. Do as you are told and she will live.”

Jake glanced at the outside passenger mirror again. He hoped that from Smythe’s angle in the back seat, it appeared like he was looking at his wife with concern. “And I am to simply take your word on that?”

Smythe smiled. “Consider it professional courtesy.”

“Alright then,” replied Jake, “we have a deal. But you have the gun pointed at her and not at me.”

“You’re a smart man, Jake.” Smythe said sarcastically. “Obviously, I cannot shoot you while you are driving. It would place all of us in danger. Get the picture?”

“Yeah, I get it.”

Marilyn now spoke in anger. “No! We don’t have a deal with this mad man!” Smythe grabbed her hair and pulled harshly. She stopped talking abruptly.

“Listen to your husband, Mrs. Oliver, and don’t be stupid! Now drive!”

Jake had been looking at Marilyn with their eyes locked while he spoke. He then glanced at the outside passenger mirror. Marilyn was not initially sure what he was trying to tell her. He then broke eye contact with her and turned to face the front of the car. He reached for the shift control located on the console between the front bucket seats of the Jaguar. His eyes then darted toward the outside driver’s side mirror and he used his foot to lightly tap on the brake. The brake lights blinked several times and this prompted the individuals approaching the car from behind to stop and crouch low to the ground.

"Drive, or she dies!" Shouted Smythe.

"Alright, I am going," replied Jake. Jake shifted the car into reverse and backed up slowly. The Jaguar was parallel parked on the right hand side of a one way street. Another car that appeared to be late model Honda was parked behind them. Smythe started to look around at that moment. Jake again tapped his foot on the brake quickly and it had the desired effect. The man approaching again dove to the ground for cover. Smythe did not notice anything. Jake continued to back up and the car solidly hit the Honda. Jake then cursed. "Damn!"

"Cute, Jake, just get us out of here!"

"Alright, alright." Jake started to shift the car into drive. He again looked in the outside mirror. The individual crouched near the rear of the car pointed toward the passenger side. Jake then let his right hand drop to the buttons located on the center console that controlled the electric windows. He felt quickly in the dark and his fingers located the controls for the driver's side rear window. He pushed the button and that window suddenly started to lower.

Smythe turned toward the open window in an unconscious reaction. As he did, Jake pushed the button for the rear passenger side window. Smythe quickly turned his head toward that window and found himself staring down the barrel of 9mm semi automatic pistol that was less than one inch from his nose. Smythe's eyes grew wide in disbelief.

Marilyn suddenly heard another male voice that spoke in a harsh whisper. "Blink, you bastard, and I blow your head off!" Smythe froze and did not move. "Lower your gun or I blow your head off now!" Smythe stared at the gun. He could not see the face behind it. He quickly considered his options but decided he could not win this one. The hand holding the gun on him was too calm, too professional. He pulled his gun away from Marilyn's head and released his grip on her hair. Marilyn instinctively leaned forward.

Both rear doors opened and a pair of hands grabbed the gun out of Smythe's hand from the driver's side. Then another pair of hands yanked Smythe from the car and threw him to the ground. Marilyn turned and saw the familiar blond hair of Cliff Weber of Baroni Security. His knee was resting in the middle of Smythe's back who lay face down on the sidewalk with Andy Baroni holding a gun to his head. She then spun around and looked at Jake who gave her a sigh of relief.

Jake got out of the car and walked around and opened the door for Marilyn. She jumped into his arms and burst into tears. Jake comforted her as he looked up and saw Andy Baroni standing in front of him with a broad smile on his face. At that moment, the sound of a police car could be heard approaching. A few minutes later it screeched to a stop and the two of them handcuffed Nelson Smythe.

Marilyn released her grip on her husband and turned to face Andy and Cliff. "I don't understand. Where did you guys come from?" She then looked at Jake. "You knew?"

Jake shook his head to the negative. "No. They surprised the hell out of me!" He looked at the two men. "But I can tell you, that seeing you guys in the mirror was the best sight I could imagine." Jake stepped forward and shook Andy and Cliff's hand. "Andy, how did you know? Where did you two come from?"

Andy again smiled. "Actually, it was just a hunch. It bothered me that we never had any closure with this bastard. He had simply vanished. But then my gut feelings started kicking in and, well, I just figured that this guy must be pretty pissed at you for screwing up his job. So, I put a couple of my men on you to watch for him to possibly make a move. Since tonight was your last night in town, I decided to pull the shift with Cliff. I figured if Smythe was going to make his move, it had to be tonight." Andy turned toward Smythe who was being put in the back of the squad car. "And the dumb bastard didn't let me down!"

Jake and Marilyn both smiled in amazement. "Mr. Baroni, you are truly the best. Can you imagine what Garrison and the others with the FBI are going to say when they find out that you brought in this guy. They will want to pin a medal on you!"

"Oh, I don't know about that. The FBI is rather territorial. Most likely, they will be embarrassed. You see, John Garrison filled me in. They seem to think that the man we know as Nelson Smythe is really a renowned world terrorist by the name of Niles Swarthenson. A

Hong Kong national by birth with Australian parents giving him dual citizenship. He has evaded the international authorities for the past 10 years."

"You would think that a pro like that would not be suckered into simple revenge because of a botched job," said Jake.

"Yeah, you would. But his rap sheet indicated a real mean streak and track record for pulling such stunts. One of his few weaknesses. And well…"

Jake placed his hand on Andy's shoulder. "Thanks Andy. You don't know how much."

Andy simply looked down. "That's my job, sir. Now, go home folks. I believe you have a long trip tomorrow."

CHAPTER FORTY SIX

The Oliver's were just about finished loading the car for their early morning departure. The movers had finished packing and loading their furnishings the day before and Marilyn's car had been shipped to arrive the day after they got to their new destination. Therefore, Jake and Marilyn had spent one final night at the Wilford and then returned that morning to load the Jaguar with some of the more personal items that could not be entrusted to the moving company.

The discovery of the Chinese artifacts at the Wilford had generated a tremendous amount of positive publicity for the hotel and prompted local residents to relive the rich history of this grand hotel. Apparently, it had also peaked the interest of investors who were already in discussions with South Harbor concerning the purchase of the hotel.

Jim Slazenger had been appointed the new general manager by Samuel Cho and the staff was quickly accepting their new boss. Jim had initially expressed some concerns that such an appointment might be short lived if new owners took over the hotel. But Jake had reassured him that he should pursue the assignment aggressively and that good General Managers were always in demand.

Jake and Jim had formed a strong friendship in the short time they had worked together and both suspected that this friendship would last for many years to come. Little did they know that their paths would cross again and again both professionally and socially in the years to come.

Marilyn returned to the house to make one last check and make sure they had not forgotten anything. She also took the opportunity to call Linda before they took off. Sarah and Briana were saying goodbye to their friends from next door. Jake stood back to admire his masterful job of packing the car. He was pleased with himself because the trunk could actually close! It was then that he noticed a dark blue Ford sedan drive up and stop in front of their, soon to be, vacated home.

John Garrison and Sandra Kelly got out of the car and approached. Jake gave Sandra a warm smile. "Hi, Jake," she said, "thought you could sneak out of here without saying bye?"

Jake shrugged. "Well if it isn't special agents, Kelly and Garrison. I was wondering if I would get a chance to see you two before I left."

"That's nice. So you actually missed me?"

Jake smiled. "Sandra, for what it's worth, you made a damn good secretary. This could be your fall back position if working for Mr. Garrison gets to be too boring."

Garrison stamped out his cigarette and approached. "Nice to see you two sharing this special moment." This drew laughter from both Jake and Sandra. "Jake, we just wanted to say thanks for your help and all."

"How is our friend, Nelson Smythe?"

Sandra responded. "Well, I guess you know that his real name is Niles Swartheson and he is a real heavy weight in international terrorist circles."

"Yeah, Andy filled me in the night before. I hope catching him scores you guys some brownie points or something."

Garrison smiled. "Actually, he *was* more than we bargained for. As you know our main objective was to get your ex-boss, Mr. Cho." Jake just nodded. "It certainly was disappointing that you were able to help us take down almost everyone else but not your fearless leader."

The sarcasm in Garrison's voice clarified that he still felt slighted somehow. "I guess sometimes you just have to take what you can get." Jake replied evenly.

Both men stared at each other without saying a word for several moments. "Yeah, I guess so. It just surprised me that you were able to obtain some rather specific information on this Tsang fellow and his partner here in the states, Jackson Chi. In fact, you even uncovered the ties they had to Lou Walizak the last of a dying breed of Union thugs. At least we hope so. But you could not provide me with supporting documentation on the one target of this investigation." The tone and continual stare of Garrison suggested that he was not buying Jake's previous explanation of why Samuel Cho had not been involved.

Jake again shrugged his shoulders. "As I said, I guess those are the breaks. By the way, what will happen to our unhappy trio?"

Garrison broke eye contact and looked down at the ground. "Actually, Tsang, Jackson and Walizak are being rather predictable. Each is trying to blame the actions on the other two and, of course, they are innocent and there has been a great misunderstanding." Jake and Sandra laughed at Garrison's sarcasm. "Most likely all of them will have the opportunity to spend, at least a few years in jail."

Jake nodded. "And our terrorist friend?"

"He will be questioned for the next few weeks by us and then delivered to the British authorities who have been trying to track him down for many years. My guess is that he will be thrown in to a remote jail cell and spend the rest of his life behind bars."

"And Andy Baroni? I mean, he certainly played a key role in the success of this case."

Garrison fumbled and took several seconds to respond. "I have…I have to admit, Baroni Security did a good job uncovering Swartheson for us."

Sandra prompted him further. "John, tell Jake about Andy."

Garrison again hesitated. "Well, actually, I was quite impressed with Baroni and his organization. I also heard positive feedback from my men who worked with his men in the field. They told me that all of Andy's men performed flawlessly during their joint operation to rescue your wife." Jake nodded as he continued. "So I have since confirmed with Baroni that the FBI may need his assistance at times."

Jake again nodded his approval. "Good. Glad to see that you recognize a good organization and Andy may get some extra work out of the deal."

Garrison looked around one last time. "Well, Jake, that about sums up everything. "You and your family have a safe trip today and make sure we know where to find you if we need to follow up on any issues." The two men shook hands and Garrison walked to his car.

Sandra nodded indicating that she would follow in a few minutes. "So, Jake, what will you do now?"

Jake leaned against his car. "I have accepted a position as general manager of a historic resort and health spa in a little town north of San Diego. It's got the usual amounts of rich history and most likely its share of problems to overcome."

Sandra smiled. "Well, for what it was worth, I did enjoy working for you and hope there are no hard feelings for having to deceive you as I did."

"No hard feelings. You were just doing your job and you did it well."

"Actually, you taught me a few things. I learned that being the general manager of a hotel takes a lot of training, finesse, and the skills and insight to evaluate the human nature and reaction of the people around you. I observed how you methodically unraveled the mysteries and levels of deception that were present upon your arrival like a real pro. I can only hope that, over time in my profession, I acquire some of these skills."

Jake nodded. "Thank you for the kind words."

Sandra smiled, stepped forward and kissed him on the cheek. At that same moment, Marilyn walked out the front door and commented. "Jake, I leave you alone for just a few minutes and an attractive woman, from the FBI even, is giving you a kiss!"

Sandra backed away, her face turning several shades of red. Jake smiled and held up his arms in resignation. "Marilyn, its that charm and wit I keep telling you about."

Marilyn shook her head in disgust. "Really!" She then walked up to Sandra. "Sandra, thanks for coming by and thanks for keeping an eye on my husband these past few months."

Sandra was still embarrassed and looked around nervously. "Marilyn, I…don't want you to think that…"

"Oh, I don't." The two women looked at each other and Marilyn's gratitude was apparent. "Thank you for sticking your neck out to warn me when we had lunch that day. Given what has occurred, your efforts mean that much more to me now." The two women hugged.

"Best of success and be careful. You've chosen a dangerous profession so play it smart." Added Jake.

Sandra walked to the car and got in. Garrison looked across the seat with a stern look. "You got too close on this assignment." Sandra did not bother to respond to his comment as they drove away.

The Oliver's finished packing a short time later and departed on their eight hour drive down the coast. Their plan was to take the more scenic route of Highway 1 that followed the contours of the magnificent California coast. They quickly left the traffic of the city behind them and found themselves entering a thick fog bank that was rolling down the side of the hills that separated the inner peninsula from the coast. As they began their decent down Highway 1, the view of the ocean suddenly materialized as the car descended below the layer of fog and drove through the small community of Pacifica that was located at the water's edge. The view was breathtaking and no one in the car spoke. Perhaps all were thinking about leaving such a beautiful spot. Or perhaps some were thinking about the new friends they had met and were now leaving behind.

"Jake, something has still been bothering me." Said Marilyn

"What is that?"

"When you summarized at dinner the other night the key elements that helped you unravel the deceptions that were underfoot, I am still not clear on one point."

Jake glanced over at her briefly not wanting to take his eyes off the sharply curving road that followed the jagged coastline created by the pounding of the ocean's waves. "Which point is that?"

"Obviously, a key break in your investigation, if you want to call it that, was the mystery e-mail messages you received and the information this informant provided you."

Jake smiled. "You make this person sound like 'deep throat' from the Nixon Watergate scandal."

"Well, in a way, it is. Did you ever figure out who this person was?"

Jake nodded. "Actually, I figured it out a short time after I received the first message."

Marilyn looked at him in frustration. "Well, who was it? I mean, this person, had to have access to very confidential information that obviously Jackson Chi and Lou Walizak did not want exposed at any costs. And this person clearly took some major risks contacting you, given what was at stake."

Jake again nodded. "Yes, they certainly did."

Marilyn glared at her husband recognizing when his stubbornness was about to show. "And you are not going to tell me are you?" Marilyn turned in her seat and looked forward. It was at that moment that she noticed a small intricately carved statue sitting on the dashboard. It appeared to be that of a Chinese warrior of some type. The workmanship was outstanding and was carved from a piece of jade.

"Jake, where did this come from?" Marilyn asked pointing toward the statue.

"Oh, that was a gift." Jake replied casually. He then glanced at her and decided that he better explain further. "That is Kwan Koon, an ancient Chinese warrior, if I remember correctly. This artistic recreation of him is designed to ward off evil and protect."

Marilyn picked up the small statue and studied it carefully. "Well, I would agree with that. He looks pretty ferocious with that long sword he is wielding. But who gave it to you?"

Jake continued to smile. "The same individual that sent me the e-mails, my dear."

"'*The same individual that sent me the e-mail, my dear.*'" Marilyn repeated in mock anger. "Is that my hint?"

Jake continued to smile. "Let's just say that this was a woman that was greatly underestimated by her boss!" Marilyn now smiled in acknowledgement.

"Most women usually are," replied Marilyn, "but, in this case, obviously, Jackson Chi should have treated Ms. Chuen with more respect."

Jake laughed. "That's for sure!"

Printed in the United States
1518900001B/296